I0770210

RECLAIMING THE FROST

An Enchanted Tale

MALLORY WANLESS

Cover design by GetCovers

First edition

ISBN:

Paperback: 979-8-9888284-0-2

Ebook: 979-8-9855733-9-8

Also by Mallory Wanless

The *turmio* trilogy:
Storm and Flame: Enchanted I
Blood and Destiny: Enchanted II
Reign and Ruin: Enchanted III

Enchanted Standalones:
Reclaiming the Frost: Enchanted IV

Vexia Standalone Novellas:
Of Poison and Passion
The Royal Gambit
The Marked and The Menaced

** *** ** *

To those who love with their whole heart and refuse to give up.

** ** ** *

Content Warning

This book contains mild descriptions of child abuse, torture, rape (not seen on-page), moderately gruesome murder, and has an element of "why choose?"

If any of this makes you uncomfortable, please put this down and walk away. Not every book is for every reader and that is ok.

Chapter 1

W HEN ROSKA WALKED INTO the Great Hall on the eve of his eighteenth birthday, he found his brother and sister waiting for him. They might have been triplets, but their personalities couldn't have been any more different. Elena was clearly anxious, wringing her hands as she paced back and forth in front of her future throne—assuming King Niko ever got off his ass and proposed. Her brilliant blue lightning practically danced underneath her skin in her stressed state. Quinn, on the other hand, was considerably more laid back. Lounging on the King's throne, flames dancing in his hands, weaving in between his long fingers and casting strange shadows on the walls.

One solar cycle ago, Roska had been sitting around the table in the Great Hall with his brother, sister, mothers, father, three orphan sisters, and the new King of Waverly. They had been eating dozens of cakes to celebrate the birthdays Quinn and Roska hadn't acknowledged. Elena, being the kind-hearted woman that she was, had surprised them with a party to make up for all the birthdays they'd missed. It had been wonderful and magical and brought tears to Roska's eyes.

Roska shrugged out of his travel cloak and dropped his pack into an empty chair. Demoni, his clever little frost dragon familiar, slithered down his back and jumped off to join his siblings' familiars. Agon—Elena's electric weasel—and Lyra—Quinn's sarcastic firefox—where they were curled up on several large pillows before the low fire smoldering in the Great Hall's large stone hearth.

"Oh, thank the gods! You're back!!" Elena rushed across the room and threw her arms around Roska's neck. He stumbled back, surprised by her outpouring of affection, instinctively wrapping his arms around her.

"Of course I'm back. Why wouldn't I be?" Roska leaned back, trying to get a better look at his sister. Despite having been born only minutes apart, Elena fretted over both him and Q as though she were their mother, or at least their much older sister. In fact, according to Beatrice—their actual mother—Elena was only three minutes older than Roska and a full two minutes *younger* than Q. A point Quinn often liked to bring up when she was fussing over him.

"I was so worried." Elena released her hold on him, slightly, moving her hands to his shoulders as she tried to turn him this way and that to examine him for obvious signs of injury. "We hadn't gotten word from you in a while. I feared the worst."

"She always fears the worst," Quinn said, his eye-roll practically audible.

Roska placed his hands over Elena's, squeezing gently. "I'm sorry, El. I didn't send word because there was nothing to say. I should have sent a missive to inform you that I was coming home." *Home*. It was such a foreign concept, but that truly was what the castle had become. Roska hadn't spent as much time in Riverayn as Elena, but the rooms he shared with Quinn in their suite at the capital had quickly become his safe space.

"No news then?" Q asked. He extinguished his fire and stood from Niko's throne, crossing the room to join them. "I'm sorry, Ros. No one in Nexton knows where she's gone?"

Roska shook his head, trying to hide his heartbreak. "No. It seems like Brigit just disappeared. I spoke with the tavern owner where she was working when we met, but he didn't know anything. Couldn't even tell me about her family or where she was from. I thought maybe she'd gone back home, but no one seems to know that might be."

Elena's eyes glittered with unshed tears. "I'm so sorry, Roska. I can talk to Niko, if you'd like? See if he can send some inquirers out to search for her?"

Roska shook his head. "Thanks, El, but no. If she wanted to be found, she wouldn't make it this hard. She's moved on, and so should I."

Roska didn't miss the sad look his siblings exchanged, but he didn't want to discuss Brigit anymore. He'd been looking for her for a full solar cycle now. She clearly didn't miss him. He needed to let her go.

"Besides," he continued, "I've got work to do. The Brotherhood has its minions everywhere. I should be focusing on tearing them down, not searching for a girl I haven't spoken to in moons and likely doesn't even remember me."

"Ros, I don't think—" Elena began, but Roska cut her off with a firm, but not unkind, smile.

"It's ok, El. Really. It just wasn't meant to be."

❄ ❄ ❄ ❄ ❄ ❄

Roska spent every waking moment of that planting season interviewing every single employee at the castle. He'd driven himself to the point of exhaustion when Elena and Quinn cornered him in an empty hallway on the way back to his room. Roska planned on taking a quick nap—no more than an hour—before meeting up with Commander Jamieson to discuss their next steps.

"Roska, can we talk to you for a moment?" The hesitation in Elena's voice caught Roska's attention more than her actual words. Something was wrong.

"What happened? Who's hurt? Mother? Belladonna? Gods, did Father finally test his 'unkillable theory' too well and actually kill himself?" Their demi-god father, Aiden, had been pushing his supposed immortality more and more these days. Roska was starting to worry the man had a death wish.

"Nah, Ros. It's nothing like that. We just need to talk." Quinn threw an arm around Roska's neck and half guided, half dragged him into an empty library. Unceremoniously dumping Roska in an empty chair, Quinn flopped back into the chair to his right while Elena perched on the very edge of the chair across from him.

Roska looked at them both, eyebrows raised in confusion and mild annoyance. He had things he needed to do. The Brotherhood's influence still filtered through the castle, and he had to stop them. It was his only purpose in this godsdamned world anymore.

Bit dramatic, don't you think? That can't be all we're good for anymore.

Roska ignored Demoni's chilled words, focusing on his sister instead. Demoni huffed an annoyed, icy breath, then climbed down from his shoulder, jumping off the chair and joining Agon on the windowsill looking out over the crystal blue lake in the courtyard below.

Frustration radiated off of him as Roska tried to keep his emotions—and powers—in check. "If no one is hurt or dying, then what's going on? I've got things I need to be doing."

"That's actually what we wanted to talk about," Elena began, her nervous gaze flitting from Roska's to Quinn's and back again.

"It's just that... well, I don't really know how to say this without sounding harsh..."

"You're obsessed, Ros. And you're going to push yourself into an early grave if you keep going on like this." Quinn's blunt words were like ice in Roska's veins.

No. Ice would have been familiar, comforting even. This was more like his siblings were calling his efforts a waste of time. Belittling his work and making him question everything.

Demoni hissed at him from across the room. "Stop that shyt. You know that's not what they meant."

"What? What does he think we're saying?" Quinn sat up in his chair, instantly alert and mildly defensive.

"He thinks you think he's wasting his time hunting down the Brotherhood," Demoni answered before Roska could even voice his protestations.

Traitor, he thought bitterly.

You're being a fool. I'm not going to ignore that. You're dictating my life too, you know. She flicked her tongue out at him. From the outside, it might have just looked like a dragon merely tasting the air, but Roska knew what *that* tongue flick meant. It meant if she had fingers, she'd be giving him one finger in particular.

"You're hyper-fixated on this, Ros." Elena leaned forward, breaking Roska's staring contest with his dragon. "I agree with you; we need to root out all of the Brotherhood's dark influence, but you can't keep going nonstop like this. You need a break."

"A break?" Roska let loose a derisive laugh. "Do you think the Brotherhood is taking a break? I can't rest until they're done. Don't you get that?"

Gods, Roska was so muxing tired of trying to explain this to everyone. The Brotherhood was the root of all evil in their world. He *had* to stop them.

Elena raised her hands defensively. "Roska, please listen."

"No. I can't stop until they're destroyed. They've caused so much pain and suffering. More than you could possibly know." Roska shoved up from his chair, roughly brushing his white-blond hair from his brow. "They're insidious. They've snuck into every level of this muxing government and are trying to puppet the entire thing!"

"With all due respect," came a strong, confident voice from behind him. "No one is puppet-mastering my kingdom and you really shouldn't talk to your sister like that."

King Niko strode into the room like he owned the place. Which Roska supposed he did, but at that particular moment, Roska couldn't have given two shyts if the man was the god of all creation.

"With all due respect, *Your Majesty*." Pure, unadulterated sarcasm dripped from Roska's tone. "You wouldn't know if you were being manipulated. That's how the Brothers operate." Roska wiped a hand over his tired face. "But you're right, I shouldn't have snapped like that. I'm sorry, Elena." Gods, he just wanted to go to bed.

"You can root out evil *and* take care of yourself, Roska." Elena's voice was gentle and full of concern.

"Keeping that in mind, I'm going to say something you aren't going to like." Niko sat on the arm of Elena's chair, facing Roska as he absentmindedly toyed with a lock of her hair. A strong wave of jealousy washed over Roska as he watched the unconscious act of affection. Moons ago, he'd thought he would have Brigit by his side, helping him create a balance between fighting the vile nature of the Brotherhood and finding joy in everyday life. Instead, he was alone and drowning.

"Ros, did you hear that?" Quinn nudged Roska gently with his shoulder.

When had Quinn gotten up? Roska hadn't even noticed him cross the room. He was so lost in his thoughts.

Roska blinked, trying to wipe thoughts of Brigit from his mind. "Sorry, what?"

"You're banished," Niko said with all the grace and authority provided to him by his position as King of Waverly.

* * * * * * *

Roska's jaw nearly fell to the floor. What the mux? Banished?

Disbelief and impotent rage flooded his system, icy mist pouring unbidden from his palms and rapidly dropping the temperature of the room.

"Whoa, hang on there, Frosty." Quinn stepped forward, positioning himself between Roska and Niko, breaking Roska's fixed glare. "Bro, you're gonna freeze us all if you don't reel that shyt in a bit." Tossing a quick glance over his shoulder, Quinn spoke on a rushed breath. "Niko, you better elaborate quickly. I'm not sure I can counter the shyt that's flooding out of him."

Niko rose, hands lifted in surrender. "Roska, I know you've got important work to do here. You and Jamieson have already taken down so many sects of traitors just in the last three moons, but you need a break. Banishment seemed like the only way to *make* you stop and take care of yourself for a change."

Rage still flowed freely through Roska's veins, but the truth of Niko's words slowly began to melt the ice wall around his mind.

Banished.

Where the hells would he even go? He didn't have any other home. He supposed he could go back to Harbor Ridge and stay with Mother for a while. Or maybe Belladonna would let him stay in her cottage in the Dark Woods for a time?

"I've already planned it all out with Amelia." Quinn interrupted Roska's thoughts. "She's really excited to finally meet you."

At the mention of this magical woman, both Q and Elena's faces spread into warm smiles. Amelia was a very special woman to them both, but Roska had never had the nerve to actually travel to Andover and meet her. Even during his cycle of searching fruitlessly for Brigit, he hadn't wanted to risk meeting her. What if she didn't like him? What if she saw how damaged and utterly broken he was and decided he wasn't worth her time? She'd been so kind to Q and Elena. If Amelia didn't accept him, Roska worried that would mean he was truly a wreck of a person. Undeserving of love, just like the Brothers had always told him.

Quinn clasped Roska's shoulder triumphantly. "It's gonna be great, Ros. You're gonna love her."

Elena stepped up and gingerly took hold of Roska's frosted left hand. "She's going to love you too, don't worry. Amelia is the best person I've ever met."

Mother Goddess, please don't let me disappoint this woman.

❋❋ ❋❋❋ ❋❋

Quinn accompanied Roska, insisting on doing a "proper introduction" and visiting with his surrogate mother, as he hadn't seen her in moons.

The woman was a saint. Or a goddess. Or both, Roska couldn't be sure. The second they'd walked into her inn, Amelia had dropped everything—literally, it was a bit of a mess—and rushed over to embrace Quinn.

"Praise the Mother!" the plump woman cried out with a huge smile that caused her eyes to practically disappear. "I haven't seen you in ages, boy. Where the hells have you been?" She swatted Quinn good-naturedly on his arm as he blushed from her attention.

"Sorry, Mom, I've been a bit busy. You know, helping save the world and all that." Quinn's words were sarcastic, but his tone was filled with a love that Roska had rarely seen his brother express. Roska was a little surprised that Q had referred to Amelia as "mom" since he only ever referred to their biological mom as "Mother." Quinn, seeming to notice Roska's reaction, draped an arm around Amelia's shoulders and turned to face Roska. "Mom, I'd like you to officially meet my brother, Roska, and his frosty little dragon, Demoni. Ros, this is Amelia. The only mom I ever needed."

"I'm honored to meet you, darlin'." Amelia held out her hand, offering a formal shake rather than the warm embrace she'd given Q. Roska appreciated the space she was giving him, allowing him to make the first physical contact. While he was jealous of the hug she'd given his brother, Roska wasn't sure he would have been comfortable hugging this woman just yet. He knew she was a kind, thoughtful person, based on the stories his siblings told, but Roska always preferred to reserve final judgment for himself.

Roska clasped her warm, rough hand firmly in his slightly chilled one. "The pleasure is all mine. I've heard so many good things about you, I thought it was finally time to meet you for myself."

"And Niko kicked him out," Lyra added with a foxy smirk.

Before Quinn could respond, Amelia tutted Lyra's remark, giving her a chastising look. No words, and yet Lyra seemed to feel guilt at her nonverbal admonishment. It was very impressive. Roska had never seen anyone correct Lyra's behavior so effectively.

"Well, then let's get you settled, darlin'. You're welcome to stay here as long as you like." Amelia slipped her hand through the crook of Roska's arm and led him through the inn's dining hall, into the kitchens, and up a winding staircase to the second floor of the cozy building.

She set them up in Quinn's old room and told them to come down for some lunch whenever they were ready. Lyra followed Amelia out the door, obviously intent on stealing scraps of food from the kitchen.

Roska looked around the room. It was bigger than he'd expected, although not as big as the bedroom he had in the capital. A single bed sat against the wall under the only window in the room. A desk with a single wooden chair sat in the far corner. A wardrobe took up a decent amount of wall space, leaving just enough room for a fireplace directly across from the bed. Based on its placement, Roska suspected its chimney met up with the massive stone hearth in the kitchen, driving all the smoke from the cooking fires up and out of the inn.

"What do you think?" Quinn asked, pride beaming from his face, and then flicked a burning ember from his hand onto the dry logs that sat carefully stacked in the hearth.

Roska surveyed the space, picturing a young Q playing in this room, tossing knives at the side of the wardrobe—based on the massive collection of small nicks and cuts the thick wooden cabinet bore—and sleeping in the bed looking out at the stars. "It's really nice, Quinn. I never thought I'd see your childhood room, but this seems like a wonderful place to grow up."

"It was," Quinn said with a soft smile. "But that's not what I meant. I meant, what do you think of Amelia?"

Roska didn't bother suppressing the grin that tugged at his lips. "She is everything you said she was and more."

Quinn clapped his hands in triumph and flopped back onto the bed. "I told you! She's the muxing best."

Roska hung his pack on the nail that had obviously served as Young Quinn's coat hook and took a seat in the chair by the desk. "So... how is this going to work? There's only one bed, and I'm not sleeping with you again. You kick like a mule in your sleep."

"I do not!" Quinn argued, but the twinkle in his eyes belied the truth. He knew he was a terrible bedmate. "Besides, I'm not sleeping here. I just came to drop you off. Lyra and I are going to spend the growing season hunting and staying in our hut by the river."

Roska froze at the thought of being left alone in a strange new place. He hadn't been properly alone since he met his siblings.

Quinn seemed to notice Roska's sudden anxiety—or maybe he just noticed the temperature dropping in the room. He jumped up from the bed and crossed the room in three steps, kneeling before Roska and placing his warm hands on Roska's chilled shoulders.

"Hey, it's all right. I wouldn't leave you if I thought something would go wrong. Amelia is the absolute best human on this muxing planet, and I know she'll take the best care of you. Just give it a shot, ok? If you feel uncomfortable or don't want to stay after a couple days, join me at the hut. You remember where it is, right?"

Roska nodded dumbly. He'd been to the hut a few times, he could find it again easily enough. It was directly upstream from the bridge that led into Andover from the Dark Woods.

"It's gonna be great, Ros. I promise."

Chapter 2

R OSKA AND QUINN JOINED Amelia for lunch in the tavern, but at
sunset, Quinn bid them both farewell, giving Roska one last
reassuring hug, and disappeared out the door.

"I'm not sure what your plan is, darlin'," Amelia began as she
putted around the dining hall, collecting empty plates and heading
into the kitchens, indicating that Roska should follow her. "But
you're more than welcome to stay here as long as you'd like. Q
mentioned before that you like gardening? I could really use some
help out there. It's gotten a bit overwhelming for these old bones
of mine."

Roska watched the woman unload fifteen soiled plates from a
tray and pump water into a large kitchen sink before turning the
massive pig that was roasting on a spit in the center of the kitchen.
If this was her "old bones" being overwhelmed, he couldn't imagine how impressive and capable she'd been twenty cycles ago.

I think she's just being kind, Demoni put in. *Trying to make us
feel needed so you don't spiral out about being a burden.*

Roska didn't say a word as he accepted Demoni's interpretation
of the events. She was probably right, after all. Instead, he walked
over to the sink beside Amelia and took up a drying towel. If he
was going to be banished here indefinitely, he'd be as useful as
possible.

"I do like gardening," he said as they finished the last of the dishes. "It was the only place I felt peace when I was living in the Brotherhood's compound."

Amelia's eyes widened ever-so-slightly at the mention of the Brotherhood. Roska had assumed Q had told her about his upbringing, but based on the shock she tried to hide in her eyes, he hadn't.

"I'm sorry," Roska added quickly. "I didn't mean to upset you. I thought you knew."

Amelia dried her hands and rested one firmly on Roska's forearm. "You didn't upset me, love. Well, I guess you did, but not because of something you did or said. I'm upset that you had to go through that experience. You should have had a loving home, and instead, you were stuck with those muxing bastards." She squeezed his arm gently, compassion glistening in her eyes.

Roska got it now. He understood the incomparable love and affection Quinn and Elena felt for this woman. She was the kind of mother he'd always dreamed about when he was lying awake on his dirt floor bedroom, crying from his "reeducation sessions" at the hands of the Brothers.

"Come on, dear. Let me show you the garden."

* * * * * * *

Amelia took him in and cared for him as if he were her own, and it had shocked him to his very core. Their own mother hadn't been so welcoming when he'd first been dumped back at her feet by her investigators, and she was still rather stand-offish at times, but Mother was a decent woman and took care of them when they really needed it.

Over the course of the next few weeks, they'd gotten into a very comfortable rhythm, with him handling the dishes and the bulk of the heavy lifting in the garden, and her cooking far too much food for him at every meal. Elena had once mentioned that food was Amelia's love language. Roska hadn't known what that had meant at the time, but he fully understood it now. She was the best type of caretaker a person could imagine. Roska hadn't gone into much detail about his upbringing with the Brotherhood, but Amelia knew enough about the group to know his childhood had not been a happy one. She'd taken it upon herself to rectify that as much as she possibly could. Which meant that she fed him more than he could reasonably eat at every single meal, taught him all the spells she could think of, and helped him in the garden, sharing her tips and listening intently to his. Most importantly, though, was that she didn't judge him when he'd wake screaming in the night. No matter how much time or distance he put between himself and the Brotherhood, memories of his life there still plagued his dreams.

Some nights, after he'd woken screaming, she would sit quietly at the foot of his bed until his breathing returned to normal and he drifted off to sleep again, never saying a word. Other nights, when the dreams were especially vivid, she would wrap her arms around him and rock him, gently rubbing her hand up and down the length of his spine, soothing him as best she could. She never asked him about any of it. She simply waited until he was ready to talk. Roska truly appreciated her patience with him.

Elena and Quinn had always been kind and considerate of his troubled past, but the concern that had been etched on their faces every time they heard him cry out in his sleep had been devastating. It was clear that they wanted to ask, although they never pressed him about it. Amelia was simply there. No emotions or worry marred her face as she comforted him.

That was probably what made it so easy to open up to her after just over one lunar cycle.

The dreams had been especially cruel that night. Replaying the night the Brothers had removed Demoni's wings. Roska woke screaming, the scars on his back seeming to burn as though they were brand new. Amelia appeared before him like magic—and in hindsight, Roska realized that it very well could have been magic that allowed her to appear suddenly. She didn't say a word as she sat beside him at the top of the bed, offering him a comforting hug, which he'd lunged into with clumsy speed. He was desperate for the kind touch of another. Something to block out the ugly memories of their past. Demoni had coiled herself around his arm, stroking her head back and forth across the crook of his elbow, trying to calm his racing pulse.

Amelia stayed quiet. She sat with him, holding him for as long as he needed. Roska hadn't even noticed the tears falling from his eyes until he pulled back and saw the wet stain on her blouse.

"Gods, I'm sorry," he muttered, embarrassed, casting his eyes to his lap.

"Hush, love. You've nothing to be sorry for." She brushed the sweat-damp hair from his brow.

They sat in silence for a moment longer before she moved to get up and leave. Roska's mouth started moving before his mind realized the secrets he was spilling. "They cut off her wings," he whispered gruffly. "As punishment when we tried to escape."

Amelia sat back down, taking his hand in hers, stroking her thumb across the back of his hand. Still, she said nothing.

Her continued silence was the permission he needed to unleash the memories he'd kept so carefully locked away. "It was the only time we ever tried to run away. I was probably nine or ten cycles old. Late one night, after a particularly savage beating. My back was still bleeding from the lashing, but I knew we had to escape or they'd end up killing us. I'd swiped an empty grain sack from the pantry and stuffed a few dry rolls into it. We had just made it through the gate that led to the main road when the Brothers caught us." Roska choked on his words for a moment, taking several deep breaths before he continued. "They grabbed Demoni from the sky, catching her by her beautiful wings and squeezing until we both cried out in agony. It felt like they were crushing the bones of my spine as they squeezed her wings tighter. One of the Brothers grabbed me by the hair and another punched me in the stomach several times. I must have blacked out because the next thing I remember, we were in Grand Maester Auron's chambers. I was tied to a chair and Demoni was trapped in the Grand Maester's grip. They had waited until I was awake, aware of what they were doing, and then they brought out a wickedly sharp scythe. He stretched her wings out—one at a time—and Grand Maester Auron severed them from her back with that damned scythe. It felt as though they'd flayed my own skin off. I didn't think it could get worse until Grand Maester Auron took a poker from the fire and used it to cauterize the gaping wounds on Demoni's back." Demoni's grip on his arm had reached a painful tightness as he spoke, but Roska hadn't moved to lessen her hold on him. It was a harrowing memory. The pain in her grasp was the only real tether he had to the present. The only thing keeping him from being truly engulfed by the memories.

Amelia still didn't utter a word, but her grip on his hands had tightened ever-so-slightly. She was not unaffected by his words, she was just trying to keep her emotions in check for him.

They sat in silence for ages. The weight of Roska's words was a smothering presence sucking all the air from the room.

The sky outside his window had shifted into a blushing pink when Amelia finally spoke.

"Darlin'." She paused until Roska looked up to see the fire in her eyes. "I cannot imagine how strong you must be to have endured such hells with those wretched men. You are an amazing person with an amazing soul." She nodded to Demoni at that. "I am so blessed to know you, and I hope you see that you are worthy of all the wonderful things this world has to offer." She tightened her hold on his hands, holding him in her steady gaze. "Those bastards deserve every misery you rain down on them. I will help you bring an end to them in any way that I can."

✳✳ ✳✳ ✳✳

Roska's time with Amelia had taught him a lot. Gardening techniques, new recipes and spells, but more importantly, he'd learned to process much of his trauma. He'd always known that what the Brothers had done to him wasn't his fault, but that hadn't stopped the guilt from weighing him down on a daily basis. Amelia helped him to understand why he felt that way and showed him how to let it go.

Granted, he couldn't—or wouldn't—let go of the rage he felt every time he thought of those men and the agony they inflicted on those they viewed as different. He no longer felt the heavy burden of guilt that had been slowly dragging him down since he'd released the *turmio*. He accepted his role in what happened, but now he also understood that he had been manipulated into those actions. He'd truly believed he was doing what was right, but Roska understood that those feelings and beliefs weren't his own. They'd been literally beaten into him his entire life.

He still felt responsible for his actions, and he worked daily to make amends for the trauma he'd inflicted on the world while under the Brotherhood's mental reins, but he refused to let them ruin the rest of his life.

When Niko ended Roska's banishment and he returned to the castle nearly a full cycle later, he was determined to find a balance between his work—removing all influence of the Brotherhood's blind hatred from Waverly—and his own health and wellness.

He hadn't perfected the system, but he wasn't running himself into the ground as often, and that felt like progress.

※ ※　※ ※　※ ※

"Here. This is the last portion of visitors we haven't cleared." Roska pointed to the list of traveling merchants from Maehelm. "We need to speak with these people. They're the last ones."

They were so close to removing the Brotherhood's influence from the capital. Roska hadn't slept nearly as much as he needed this week, but they were *so* close.

Commander Calum Jamieson wiped a rough hand over his tired eyes, sighing loudly and leaning back in his chair. "I realize, as the King's beloved's brother and honored guest, *you* might not have obligations in the morning, but I've got field tests to run at dawn." Calum's smirk took the sting from his words as he kicked Roska out of his office that evening, after pointing out that it was well past midnight. "I need to get some sleep. We can keep working tomorrow."

Roska tried to put together a coherent argument for why they should keep pushing, but his brain and his mouth couldn't seem to put more than two words together.

"Looks like you could use some rest too, my friend." Calum waved a soldier into his office and suggested—more like commanded—Roska head to bed before he collapsed on the Commander's floor.

He didn't recall the trek back to his rooms, but as Roska strode into his suite, he could see the sky pitch black outside his balcony. He'd spent too long in the Commander's office again. Calum had been vital in helping Roska accomplish his mission.

Roska had refused to acknowledge how tired he was—he felt like they were *so close* to finally rooting out the last of the Brotherhood's influence in the capital—but as he shuffled to the armchair beside the hearth, he finally allowed himself to feel the sheer exhaustion threatening to engulf him. He leaned his head back, intending to rest for a moment, then bathe before moving to his bed.

His body had other plans.

Chapter 3

THE TRIPLETS' TWENTIETH BIRTHDAY was a huge celebration. Niko had originally intended to make it a national holiday, but Elena had talked him out of it. Instead, the young King, with the help of far too many event planners, orchestrated the most outrageous festival Waverly had ever seen. Diplomats visited from faraway countries, celebrating the King's beloved—and her brothers—and attempting to politic themselves into the King's good graces. Niko was either oblivious or truly an excellent actor because he never offended anyone and yet never committed to anything either. It was honestly very impressive.

Mother and Belladonna—with their familiar and moonbird, respectively—came from Harbor Ridge, along with some of their most talented enchantresses to put on a spectacular show of awe-inspiring magic. Castor, Zied, and Aleerah—once Aiden arrived—spent much of the day seeing just how frightening they could be until Mother finally put a stop to their antics. Roska thought it was amusing to see them all getting along so well. Belladonna's moonbird, Castor, and Aiden's direwolf, Aleerah, had always been close. Zied, Mother's snowy lion familiar, and Castor shared a love rivaling that of Mother and Belladonna themselves, but Zied and Aleerah hadn't gotten along very well. Not unlike Mother and Aiden.

It seemed the cycles had finally changed that. It was exciting—if a bit off-putting—to see the three magical creatures as thick as thieves.

"Roska, dear, can you help me with this?" Amelia's voice shook Roska out of his reverie, as she struggled under the weight of a large wicker basket.

Roska rushed to catch the basket before it went end over end, carefully taking the cumbersome item from her. Grunting, he repositioned his grip on the basket. "Gods," he muttered as he tried to find a better way to carry the awkward item. "What's in here?"

Amelia beamed up at him. "Just some things the children made for you and your siblings."

The children. The four little hellions currently serving as Amelia's fosters. She'd taken them in last frost season when a pox had torn through Andover, taking their parents from them.

"And where are those lovely little monsters?" Quinn asked, striding across the room and pulling Amelia into a tight embrace.

She returned his embrace, then pulled back and swatted his arm, seeming to have just caught his words. "They aren't monsters," she chided. "No more so than you were when you came to me."

Quinn smiled devilishly. "So they're pure terror then?" He winked and stepped just out of reach as she attempted to swat him again.

"Hush, you." Amelia fought a grin but failed to keep the amusement from her face. "The *children* were playing in the courtyard with Marty and Castor. That moonbird likes to pretend he hates children, but he goes out of his way to tease them."

Roska was still a little surprised to hear that Marty, Amelia's large orange tabby familiar, got along with the witch's moonbird, but in the grand scheme of crazy things in his life, that one didn't even make the top ten.

Quinn tucked Amelia's hand into the crook of his arm and began leading her—and Roska, who was still struggling under the weight of the wicker basket—to the guest suite they'd set aside for Amelia and her fosters. "How is Marty doing? I know he's not a fan of travel."

"Or Mother," Roska added quietly.

"It's true, Marty, Beatrice, Zied, and I haven't always seen eye-to-eye," Amelia began, reaching her empty hand back to hook around Roska's arm as well. "But we've had very surprisingly civil conversations over the last few cycles. Ever since she learned about my relationship with you, Q. And then with Elena and now Roska." Amelia smiled up at them both. "Your mother understands that she didn't handle things well before when I left Harbor Ridge to live out my life in Andover with Herb. But she's seen the error of her ways."

Quinn scoffed, and Roska felt his eyebrows shoot up behind his shaggy white hair.

"Don't give me that. Either of you." Amelia squeezed both their arms gently. "Those were her words. She muxed up. She knows that. Hells, she even thanked me for taking care of you three when she failed to."

Roska tilted his head at that, trying to imagine their mother apologizing to anyone, over anything. He couldn't picture it. Mother wasn't a bad person, but she was *incredibly* prideful and rarely admitted fault in anything.

"Believe it or not, she and I have made amends. Belladonna seems to have had quite the grounding effect on your mother."

"You should have seen her at their mating." Elena's voice caught them all by surprise as she turned the corner and joined them in the hall outside Amelia's designated suite. "I've never seen Mother cry. It was beautiful, if a bit terrifying."

Amelia released the boys long enough to pull Elena into a warm hug, placing gentle kisses on each of her cheeks before pulling back and studying her for a moment.

"My, you've grown so much. You're absolutely beautiful." Amelia beamed at Elena, tears brimming her eyes as she spoke.

"I couldn't agree more." Niko joined them in the hall, wrapping an arm around Elena's waist while placing a kiss on her temple.

Roska looked away. He was happy for his sister, naturally, but seeing them so close and casually affectionate still hurt. Roska couldn't fight the feeling that he would never find that. He'd thought for a moment, cycles ago, that he might find that with Brigit, but now he knew she likely never felt the same for him. She'd vanished without so much as a note indicating she was even still interested in him.

"Your Majesty." Amelia moved to a low curtsy, but Niko quickly released Elena long enough to place his hands on Amelia's shoulders and halt her movement.

"Please, Madam. You never need to bow to me. If not for your kindness, this magical creature"—he coiled his arms around Elena again—"wouldn't be here. I would likely have never met her, and my life would be utterly shallow and meaningless." He turned back, locking eyes with Amelia. "I should be bowing to you. If you ever need anything, and I mean *anything*, don't hesitate to ask."

Elena's eyes glimmered with unspent emotion as she looked up at the face of the man she loved.

Gods, Roska had prayed nightly to find Brigit, in the hopes that she might one day look at him like that. He was such a heartsick fool.

Lyra popped her head out of the door to Amelia's rooms. "If you lot are done being blubbering messes, we have a surprise in here."

Inside the room, Demoni, Agon, and Lyra had decorated Amelia's suite. Well, decorated as well as a dragon, weasel, and fox were capable. There was a roaring fire in the hearth, staving off the last of the frost season's lingering chill. Pillows were fluffed and inviting, spread out over the three couches that framed the fireplace. A tea tray was set up, steam still rising from the kettle that sat steeping between six porcelain teacups. A charcuterie board of cheeses, crackers, and meats practically covered the low table that sat between the couches and the fireplace.

Amelia clasped a hand to her mouth, clearly fighting back overwhelming emotion. Quinn let a low whistle loose at the impressive display.

"How did you manage this all by yourselves? Without a thumb between you?" Niko asked with an impressed smile on his face.

"They might have had a little help," came a soft but familiar voice.

Miguel stepped out from behind the door, holding it open for them as they all entered the warm, delicious-smelling space.

An unexpected warmth spread through Roska at the sight of Miguel. His dark eyes locked on Roska's for just a moment before he quickly offered a bow to the King and moved to exit the room.

"Where are you going?" Agon demanded.

"Uh, well, I thought I'd let you all catch up." Miguel looked a little flushed. He glanced quickly between them all and took another step toward the door.

"You can't leave." Lyra positioned herself between Miguel and his escape. "As our smartass King just pointed out, we don't have thumbs. Who will pour the tea?"

"Lyra." There was a hint of disapproval in Amelia's tone that seemed to make every living creature in the room stand a little straighter. No one wanted to disappoint her or be on the receiving end of her disapproval.

"Lyra's right," Quinn jumped in. Amelia's glare turned to him and he seemed to instantly regret his word choice. "Not about Miguel serving us," he added quickly. "But you should stay." He addressed Miguel directly, smiling warmly and almost trying to impart some sort of telepathic message to the man.

Miguel glanced at Roska, seeming to ask his permission or approval.

"Yes, please stay." The words left his mouth before Roska had a chance to fully register a thought.

Miguel took a step closer to him, speaking quietly enough that only Roska could hear. "Are you sure? I don't want to intrude."

Ever since he'd first laid eyes on the man, when they'd been searching for witnesses to bring charges against the disgraced Queen for treason and murder, Roska had felt a draw toward Miguel. The man had been working in the kitchens at the time, flour in his dark curls and jam on his apron. Something in Roska had clicked into the place at the sight of him, knowing that Miguel would be important to him, although he'd tried not to look too closely at that for several moons. They'd only recently begun to spend time together, typically in the gardens where they worked the land, traded tips, and shared stories from their lives.

Seeing Miguel now, deferring to Roska's comfort level, that warmth was back, creating a welcome tingle in Roska's chest. "I'm sure. I would love for you to get to know this woman. And I would enjoy having you here."

He hadn't really expected to be so open and honest, but the second the words left his lips, Roska knew they were the absolute truth.

* * * * * *

They spent hours visiting, telling embarrassing stories, and reminiscing about their respective times at Amelia's. By the time the tea was gone and all that remained of the snacks were crumbs and hard bits of cheese, Amelia's fosters came bounding into the room demanding her attention.

Roska and his siblings left Amelia to attempt to put the younger two down for a nap. Quinn offered to take the older kids to play by the lake while Elena and Niko went off to handle some political issue.

Miguel and Roska walked silently through the halls, slowly ambling back to Roska's suite. He was tired and could probably do with a nap himself, but he wasn't quite ready to say goodbye to Miguel. Having him there, spending time with the people he loved, had felt like the most natural thing in the world to Roska. He wasn't ready for that to end just yet.

So invite him into our room.

You don't think that would be too forward? I don't want to make him uncomfortable.

Look at how he's fidgeting. He doesn't want to leave any more than you want him to go. Just ask, or I will.

Roska chanced a quick look at Miguel's hands to see him picking at imaginary lint on his tunic. He looked... nervous?

Oh, Goddess. He looks so uncomfortable already. I can't ask him to stay. He clearly wants to be anywhere but—

"Miguel, would you like to join us for one last cup of tea before we have to head down for the evening's festivities?" Demoni's voice was soft, but Roska felt like she'd screamed the words. Heat immediately flushed up his neck and ears. He was certain his ears were a brilliant shade of red. More than anything, Roska wished he could disappear.

"I would love to," Miguel said with a wide smile. "I mean, if that's all right with you?" He directed the question at Roska, curiosity in his eyes as his words came out in a cloud of mist.

Shyt.

Roska looked at his hands to see icy water vapors pouring from his clenched fists and flowing across the stone floors. The temperature of the hall had decreased dramatically.

Get control of yourself. Demoni's hissed command shocked Roska back into the moment. She rarely raised her voice. He could count on one hand the number of times she'd snapped at him.

Shyt shyt shyt. I'm sorry. "I'm so sorry." Roska was wringing his frosted hands, willing his power to go back into the lockbox in his chest. "Yes, please. Join us for tea. Or perhaps coffee, if you'd rather? I just received a new shipment from Father. He's been traveling around in Maehelm and brought back some of their blends for me to try. Or the wine he brought in from Rolam? If that's more to your liking?"

He was rambling, he knew it, but Roska couldn't seem to shut his mouth.

Demoni slithered down his arm, launched herself from him, and grabbed hold of the latch on the door, using the weight of her body to fling it wide open. Dismounting from the door, she slunk behind Miguel and climbed up his clothing until she was resting proudly on his shoulder.

"Shall we?"

Roska gaped at his frost dragon, firmly wrapped around another man's body. She'd *never* been comfortable touching others and she'd never been so bold as to initiate such contact herself.

Miguel, seeming not to notice the look of pure shock on Roska's face, turned and strode purposefully into the suite, leaving Roska to stare unseeingly after them.

What the hells was that?

Chapter 4

"**S**O THIS IS WHERE the brother of the future Queen sleeps, huh?" Miguel appraised Roska's suite with a seemingly critical eye. "I've often wondered what this space would be like."

He wondered about my bedroom...?

Of course he did. He's interested *in you.* Roska could practically hear Demoni's eyes roll as she chided him from her perch atop Miguel's shoulders. *Now get in here and offer the man a drink.*

He hadn't even realized he was still standing in the open doorway of the suite he shared with his brother.

"Um, yes," Roska said, stepping into the room and letting the door close quietly behind him. "Well, I share this suite with Q, but since he's gone most of the time, it's really more my space than his. The books are mine, and the bedroom to the right. The mess"—he nodded to the pile of miscellaneous clothing and damaged tools that Q claimed to be fixing in the corner of the room—"belongs to my brother."

Why was he saying that? Why did he want to ensure that Miguel knew this was *his* private space, but that Miguel was truly a welcome guest? And why did he want Miguel's approval so badly?

Miguel turned his critical eye to Roska, a smile pulling at his soft lips. "I figured. You don't seem like the type of man to leave his dirty laundry lying about."

A low heat tinged Roska's face as he looked away from Miguel's burning eyes.

"Would you like a drink? Coffee? Wine?" Distraction. He needed to move and focus on something other than the heat currently pooling in his chest as he looked at the man across the room from him. Gods, Miguel was beautiful. Roska had been trying to ignore that fact for weeks, but now, alone in his suite with the man, it was undeniable.

"I'd love to try some of that coffee your father brought, if it's not too much trouble." Miguel moved to sit on the couch across from the fire, stretching his arms out across the back of the couch and Roska couldn't seem to tear his eyes from him as he attempted to retrieve the coffee from a small tin on a table near one of the floor-to-ceiling bookshelves.

Roska hadn't spent much alone time with Miguel since settling in the castle a few solar cycles ago. He'd seen the man around the castle, of course, and they often worked in the gardens together—Roska's preferred form of meditation—but they'd never been alone together. Not like this. It was unnerving how calm and confident Miguel was in Roska's space. It would have been presumptuous, bordering on disrespectful, if it were anyone else, but something about the way Miguel settled into his space—whether it was the warm smile that seemed to have permanently taken up residence on his beautiful face or the soothing way his voice calmed ever frayed nerve in Roska's mind—made Roska feel as though this moment had been inevitable. They were always leading in this direction, even if he hadn't noticed it until now.

Silence filled the room as Roska finally pulled his gaze from Miguel's calmly commanding presence. He filled the cast iron kettle and hung it on the hook over the fireplace, stoking the fire and waiting for the water to boil.

Roska was pleased to realize that the silence that hung in the room was palpable and yet utterly serene. He'd been so anxious upon enclosing himself with Miguel, but now that they were there—Roska in an armchair beside the fireplace and Miguel still confidently sprawled on the long couch—it felt like the most natural thing in the world.

The water boiled, and Roska moved to pull the whistling kettle from the fire, but Miguel jumped up and beat him to it. In his haste to retrieve the singing iron, Miguel took hold of the kettle with his bare hand.

"Mux!" He nearly dropped the heated kettle directly into the fire, pulling his hand back quickly and blowing on the singed flesh.

Roska rushed to his side, kneeling and gingerly taking the man's injured hand and immediately blowing onto the inflamed skin, easing a hint of his frost into his breath to soothe the burn more efficiently.

"My gods," Miguel whispered on an exhale. "You're astounding."

Roska froze in place, ice leaking from his fingertips and creating a small buffer between where their skin connected. He hadn't even realized he'd closed the distance between them until he glanced up and saw the flecks of gold in Miguel's eyes.

Mother Goddess. He was so close. All Roska had to do was lean forward a breath and his lips would make contact with Miguel's warm, bronze skin. Roska felt himself lean, nearly closing the distance entirely. Miguel's eyes glowed at the prospect. His interest shocked Roska even more than the pull that seemed to draw him incrementally closer and closer.

A log in the fire popped, collapsing in on itself and startling Roska. He immediately dropped Miguel's hand and rose from the floor.

"We should get you to a healer. You'll need a salve for that burn."

Miguel blinked a few times, staring at his hand before he rose and dusted off his knees. "It's nothing; I'm fine."

He didn't seem fine though. There was a hint of something that looked very much like *hurt* on the man's face.

But that couldn't be. Roska must have been seeing things. Miguel wasn't hurt that Roska had pulled away. They barely knew each other. The hurt on his face was clearly a reaction to the angry red mark that lined his palm.

Gods, you are stubborn and willfully ignorant.

Where the hells did you go? You left me alone with him and look what happened!

Demoni nosed open the bedroom door and slipped back into the shared living space. *I was trying to give you some privacy. You obviously can't be trusted on your own.*

Roska ignored Demoni's commentary and turned on his heel, crossing the room and opening the suite door. "I insist. I refuse to be the reason your hand is permanently maimed."

Miguel looked prepared to argue further when a servant appeared in the open doorway.

"Apologies for the interruption, sir," the servant said with a swift bow. "The King requests your presence on the Great Hall balcony. The festivities are about to begin."

Roska glanced out the window. Shyt, when had the sun gone down? Roska hadn't even realized they'd been alone for so long.

Miguel crossed the room, his face a mask devoid of emotion. "Thank you for the coffee." He offered Roska a subtle bow of his head. "I'm sorry we didn't get to enjoy it." And then he slipped past the servant and down the hall on swift, near-silent feet.

Roska stood rooted in the doorway, his mind traveling back to just moments before. Miguel's deep, delicious chocolate eyes staring up at him. Sparks of gold and heat shone through those enchanting eyes. He desperately wanted to know what Miguel had been thinking. Had he felt the same magnetic pull that Roska had? Would he have welcomed more of Roska's touch? Or would he have pulled away and shamed him for such behavior?

The servant shuffled their feet, subtly clearing their throat and shocking Roska out of his reverie.

"Right, yes. Lead the way."

❆ ❆ ❆ ❆ ❆ ❆

Roska's siblings, their parents, and King Niko were waiting just inside the Great Hall. He joined them, pulling their mothers into a warm embrace, clasping hands in greeting with their father. Belladonna fussed over his unruly hair for a moment before Mother took her hand and gave Roska a mildly apologetic smile.

"So glad you could join us," Niko teased as he shook Roska's hand. "Happy birthday, brother. I hope you had a pleasant afternoon."

Roska blanched at the hint of innuendo in Niko's words. Elena swatted Niko's arm, silently chastising his implications.

Did they all suspect his attraction to Miguel? Roska hadn't even acknowledged it himself until they were on the floor together moments ago.

Not everyone is as willfully blind as you. Demoni wasn't pulling her punches today, and Roska wasn't sure he liked that. She was usually more gentle with her criticisms.

I've run out of patience for your stubbornness. I'm not going to "handle with care" when you keep intentionally sabotaging our happiness.

Shyt, you could at least try *to find a more diplomatic way of bringing things up.*

I could, but that hasn't been working. Now, I'm following Lyra's advice and speaking my truth.

Of course Lyra was behind this. That damned firefox was incapable of tact, and now she was rubbing off on his frost dragon.

Niko threw open the balcony doors, effectively putting an end to Roska and Demoni's telepathic argument as cheers from the citizens below in the courtyard drowned out all thoughts of their disagreement.

The sun had fully set, cueing the enchantresses to begin their magical display. Fireworks—explosive displays of power and beauty—lit up the night sky, encouraged by the "oohs" and "ahhs" of the guests who filled the courtyard. It was an extraordinary show, and Roska was impressed that their mother had orchestrated the whole thing.

Beatrice hadn't been a good mother for many cycles, but since she and Belladonna had reconnected and mated, Beatrice seemed to be putting in a great deal of effort to make up for her previous cycles of failure. Their mating was something to be admired and emulated. They fought more often than not, but they challenged each other to do better, be more, and gods help anyone who stood in their way. Roska prayed to the Mother Goddess that he would find a love like that one day. He'd once hoped he'd have such a partnership with Brigit, but he'd accepted moons ago that they just weren't meant to be.

Niko and Elena stood hand in hand on the balcony overlooking the courtyard, the citizens of Riverayn waiting below. It was time for his annual speech. It was a tradition he'd started the first cycle they'd celebrated the triplets' birthday in the capital. As the enchantresses amplified his voice, he turned to face Elena, smiling down at her as she beamed at him with all the happiness in the world glowing through her eyes.

"Elena, my beloved Firefly," he began, his voice echoing throughout the capital. He took both of her hands in his, knelt before her, and asked, "Will you be my Queen?"

Tears flooded her eyes in seconds. Unable to speak, she nodded vigorously, pulling him to stand and throwing her arms around his neck.

Cheers reverberated off the castle walls, growing louder with each passing moment. Roska and Quinn clapped the loudest, calling on their magics to shower them in warm—but utterly harmless—embers and snowflakes. Beatrice and Belladonna held each other tight, tears reflecting in their own eyes. Aiden laughed heartily.

Roska was thrilled for his sister and Niko. They'd been through so much together. They deserved every happiness in the world.

Still, he couldn't shake the dark feeling in the back of his mind. Jealousy.

More than anything, as he watched his sister place yet another tearful kiss on her new fiance's lips, and his mothers' embrace with love radiating off of them, he desperately wished he could find someone to love him that way.

Chapter 5

Roska woke with a start to the sound of the door closing. He jumped to his feet, ice daggers forming in his palms as he turned defensively to see who had entered his private space.

"Oh, gods! I'm sorry. I didn't mean to scare you. I didn't realize you were even in here." Elena raised her hands in surrender.

Roska dropped his hands immediately, absorbing the ice back into his skin and dissolving the daggers. "Shyt, sorry, El."

Roska had spent the last few weeks disappearing into his work with Commander Jamieson, trying to come up with a plan to infiltrate the Brotherhood's compound and shut them down once and for all. He hadn't been sleeping much, preferring to work himself to the point of exhaustion rather than deal with dreams of lost loves and the horrors of his childhood.

"You're a bit jumpy. What are you even doing in here? I thought you were helping Miguel in the kitchen gardens today." Elena quick-stepped across the room, making a beeline for the bookcase to the left of the fireplace.

"Mother of all... was that today? I can't believe I forgot!" Roska brushed a hand roughly through his hair. "I don't know where my head's at these days."

"You've been a bit busy lately," Elena mused, her back to him as she studied the bookshelves before her. "What with rooting out all the evil traitors in the country and plotting to take down the Brotherhood. It's not like you've been distracted or anything."

He knew she was teasing him, trying to draw a laugh. Still, Roska couldn't help but feel like he wasn't doing enough. The Brotherhood had been thoroughly excised from Riverayn, but they still lurked in the shadows, waiting to find a way back in.

Shaking his head, Roska focused his attention on his sister. "What are you looking for? Can I help?"

"Ros." Elena turned, hands on her hips, brown curls bouncing around her shoulders. "You can't help me because you're supposed to be helping *Miguel.*" She chuckled, turning back to the shelves and grabbing a thick black book with faint gold lettering on the spine. "Besides, I found what I was looking for." She tucked the book under her arm and faced him. "Ros, I know you've got a lot going on, but the whole reason you agreed to help Miguel was to take a break from all the Brotherhood shyt and get back to something you truly enjoy with someone I thought you cared for."

Her words lifted at the end, almost a question. Roska had been spending more time with Miguel lately—taste-testing new wines and coffees Aiden sent him, reading, and enjoying the peaceful silence that seemed to settle between them so easily—but he didn't want to go so far as to admit he cared for the man. They were friends, of course, but he didn't even know if Miguel felt that way about men.

He might not feel that way about all men, but it's pretty obvious to anyone with eyes that he's interested in more than a friendship with you. Demoni's blunt observations cut through Roska's self-doubt. She breathed an icy sigh of frustration from her thick pillow bed before the hearth. It was warm outside, the growing season in full force, but the maids were kind enough to keep a fire burning in his rooms all cycle-round. Demoni took full advantage of the flames whenever they were in their rooms, abandoning her regular perch around his neck to bask in the warmth of the fire.

He's my friend. We've never had a friend who wasn't also re-lated to us. Maybe that's just how friends are, Roska countered, but even as he thought the words, he knew it wasn't true. Friends didn't offer lingering glances or unnecessary touches. Friends didn't stay up all night talking about everything and nothing until the sun broke over the horizon, only to come back the next night and do it all over again.

It had been exhilarating. And exhausting. They hadn't slept for two days, not wanting to miss a single moment or conversation. On the third night, they'd sat together on the couch in his living space and fallen asleep within moments. Roska had woken first the next day, embarrassed to find his head resting on Miguel's chest, the man's arm around his shoulders. They'd never spoken about it, and he'd quickly moved before Miguel woke, but it was one of the most peaceful nights of sleep Roska had ever experienced.

Elena stood in front of the bookshelves, eyes flicking between Roska and Demoni. She could tell something was going on between them, even if she couldn't hear the thoughts they shared. "Whatever she's saying, I agree with Demoni." Elena took a seat in the armchair closest to the shelves. "You might not see it—although I don't know how that's possible unless you're truly blind—but that man is *interested* in you. More than just friendship. And I think you feel the same way." She studied him for a moment, looking for something, although Roska couldn't guess as to what. "If I'm wrong, then please forgive me for pushing, but I don't think that I am." Roska took a seat in the chair beside her as she reached out for his hand. Grasping hold of him, she squeezed and added quietly, "You deserve to be happy, Ros. You deserve to find love, with whomever you feel drawn to."

Roska returned her squeeze and settled back into the chair. "I'm not worried about the fact that he's a man, if that's what you're thinking." Elena's scarlet blush confirmed his suspicions. "The Brotherhood might be a group of bigoted mass murderers, but they were also very open when it came to this sort of thing. They pressed the idea of relations with women in order to procreate and carry on their non-magical lineages, but they also accepted that men could find comfort with other men. It was a compound filled entirely with men, after all."

The red faded from her skin as Elena contemplated his words. "I suppose that's really not that different from Mother and the enchantresses at Harbor Ridge. The women are *strongly* encouraged to have children, but equally discouraged from investing in long-term relationships with men. However, sapphic relationships are really common."

"I noticed that when we were living there before. My being hesitant with Miguel has nothing to do with him being a man." He didn't elaborate any further.

Elena sat quietly for several long moments, probably waiting for him to continue. When it was clear he had no intention of divulging any more information, she raised a curious eyebrow and asked gently, "Is it because of that girl? Brigit? Would you like to try finding her again? I'm sure Niko would be more than willing to send some of our best inquirers to look for her. Maybe she's come back to that inn in Nexton by now."

Roska laid his head back against the chair, eyes closed in defeated frustration. He didn't respond to Elena's offer, but he knew she wouldn't be offended or upset. He was tired. Tired of searching. Tired of hunting. Tired of fighting these seemingly unending battles. He was just so muxing tired.

Elena rose from her chair, tucking the book back under her arm and resting a hand on his shoulder. "The offer stands, Ros. Just say the word. We have the best inquirers on the continent. They'll find her, if that's what you want. Until then though"—she sent a small bolt of her electricity through her fingers into his shoulder, jolting his eyes open as he glared up at her—"you promised to help Miguel." She smiled as she skillfully dodged the snowball he tossed at her. "You don't have to act on the feelings you clearly have for him, but you promised to help, and I will not let you turn yourself into a liar because you're nervous. Besides, getting out into the gardens will be good for you. Get back to your roots." She smirked at her own bad pun, ducked a second snowball, and dashed out the door. She didn't bother closing the door as she called back to him, "Get moving or I'm going to send the girls to reorganize your books."

Roska sat up quickly at her threat. The girls. The former chambermaids turned Personal Tour Guides for the future Queen. Delilah, Ivy, and Lilly were sweet and much more confident after three cycles under Elena's loving hand but damned if they weren't small terrors when it came to books. Delilah, now nearly fourteen cycles old, was a voracious reader, but not terribly considerate of the books. She'd leave them in unstable stacks on the ground, promising to put them back where she got them "after this chapter." She read four or five books at a time—a feat Roska couldn't comprehend because how could she keep all the storylines separate? Ivy, who just celebrated her twelfth cycle last moon, was not interested in reading—much to Elena and Delilah's dismay. She was, however, very interested in rearranging his shelves based on the color of the books. Which drove him absolutely insane. He hadn't memorized the color of his book covers. Lilly, only nine cycles old, was more interested in drawing in the margins of his books than reading them.

Roska had spent weeks perfecting his system of book organization: first by genre, then theme, then alphabetized by author's last name. There was no way in hells he was letting those girls touch a damn thing in his room.

No. Muxing. Way.

Grunting, he forced himself to his feet, strode over to the fireplace to scoop up Demoni—who was giggling maniacally as though she thought Elena's threats were the most entertaining thing she'd heard all day—and headed out to the gardens.

* * * * * *

Miguel was waiting for him, hands on hips, dirt on his brow, when Roska crossed through the garden gate.

"I'm so sorry," Roska said, slightly out of breath after racing down multiple winding staircases. "I fell asleep. It was rude and inconsiderate of me."

Miguel raised an incredulous eyebrow. "Sleeping is rude?"

"When I promised to help you out here? Yes. I made a commitment. I should have prioritized that, not sleeping in the middle of the day." Roska brushed his silver blonde hair from his face in annoyance.

Concern filled Miguel's gaze as he studied Roska's face. "Roska," he said gently, lowering his hands and taking a few steps closer. "You have been working nonstop to root out the Brotherhood's informants and influence. If I know you at all—and I like to think that I do"—he offered a small smile—"you haven't had a decent night's sleep in weeks." Roska dropped his eyes, face warm with nervousness. Miguel closed the distance between them, placing a cautious hand on Roska's shoulder, right beside Demoni's head. "I know you're tired and overworked. That's why I asked you to help me out here." He gestured to the luscious green plants all around them. "You once told me that working in the garden at the Brotherhood's compound was the only happy memories you have from your childhood. I wanted you to enjoy a few moments here, take a break, and let your mind relax. You can't save the world all by yourself, and you sure as hells can't do it on little-to-no sleep. You need to pace yourself, Ros."

His grip on Roska's shoulder tightened, drawing Roska's gaze up to meet his. His soft brown eyes were pools of calm and comfort that Roska would happily have drowned in, if he didn't have an evil cabal to dismantle.

"I'm worried about you," Miguel said quietly, his voice a warm breath on Roska's cheek. As Miguel lowered his eyes, Roska was mesmerized by the thickness of his black eyelashes against his tan skin. Demoni's weight shifted, breaking Roska's enthrallment.

"I know." Roska lifted a hand to rest on Miguel's shoulders, thumb brushing the sun-heated skin at the collar of his tunic. "I appreciate your concern."

Of its own volition, Roska's thumb began gently stroking back and forth, softly caressing the tan skin at the edge of Miguel's collar. The simple action soothed his anxiety while fueling another fire within him.

Miguel leaned into Roska's touch, closing his eyes and seeming to bask in the feel of Roska's fingers on his skin.

"Apologies, my lord." A startled voice shocked them both out of the moment. "I didn't realize anyone was out here." The servant ducked her head, and quickly turned tail, and fled the garden.

"I think we surprised her." Miguel chuckled. He offered Roska one final squeeze on his shoulder before releasing him and turning away. "We have work to do anyway. I've got fresh seedlings to plant: tomatoes, bell peppers in every color, and a few apple trees I'm hoping will thrive out here. And then we have to harvest the carrots and I'd like to try growing potatoes from the scraps I saved from last week's feast. They're starting to sprout already, so we need to get them buried today."

Roska was only half listening. He was still staring at the garden gate, where the young girl had fled at the sight of them.

"Ros?" Miguel moved to stand in front of him. "Everything ok?"

Roska shook his head, trying to shake the image of the girl's shocked face from his mind. "Nothing. It's nothing." *Was she offended by seeing two men in an intimate moment?*

More likely, she was just embarrassed to have walked in on the future Queen's brother with a servant. That sort of dynamic isn't exactly the norm, Demoni offered.

Roska wondered at that for a moment. Perhaps she was right. It's not as though the previous King had kept his "relationships" strictly heterosexual. Although he had plenty of dalliances with servants.

Yes, but they weren't consensual.

How can you be so sure? Roska pressed. *It's entirely possible that some of his partners genuinely wanted to be in his bed.*

It is plausible, but when one is the King, it is nearly impossible for a potential partner to decline. I would be willing to bet that none of the bodies who warmed that man's bed did so without a shadow of doubt or hesitation.

"Are you going to help me or just stand there daydreaming all day?" Miguel's teasing tone brought an end to Demoni and Roska's debate. Regardless of what the girl thought, Roska was here to help, as promised.

Kneeling down in the gravel walkway between garden beds, Roska began pulling weeds, aerating the soil, and planting seedlings. Working in the garden was meditative, and the next several hours passed quickly and peacefully. The sun was beginning to set as they finished planting the last of the apple saplings. Wiping his hands on his breeches, Roska stood and surveyed the garden. It looked beautiful before, but with all the fresh plants and new growth, it was serene.

"Thank you," he said quietly.

Miguel came to stand beside him, admiring their handiwork. "Thank *you* for helping. This would have taken me days to accomplish on my own."

Roska leaned into Miguel's shoulder, wanting to touch him but unsure if it would be a welcome gesture. Miguel instantly wrapped an arm around Roska's shoulders and led him through the garden gate to the water pump. They washed the dirt and mulch from their hands, then splashed the cool water on their sweaty faces.

"I really needed this," Roska admitted as he used the bottom of his tunic to dry his face. "I haven't felt this at peace in ages."

"I could tell. You can't carry the weight of the world on your shoulders all alone, Roska." Miguel dried his hands on a towel that hung by the pump. "You have to let someone help you. At the very least, you need someone to unload on and vent to. Someone to listen to your problems without trying to solve them for you."

A smile tugged at Roska's lips. Miguel was referring to Quinn. Q was the oldest of the triplets, and over the last few cycles, he'd taken it upon himself to try and fix everyone else's problems. It was sweet but exhausting. Especially when many of his solutions involved violent confrontations with pompous royals and courtiers. Violence was *not* the answer to everything, despite Quinn's assertions to the contrary.

"I appreciate that." Roska turned his smile on Miguel. "I'm starving. What's for dinner, Chef?"

"Ha! I'm no chef. I just make the breads and jams. And I have no idea what the rest of the kitchen staff is making tonight. I've been bumped from kitchen duty and relegated to garden caretaker for the season." Miguel tossed the towel back over the pump handle and led the way back toward the kitchens.

"Are you in trouble?" Roska immediately felt guilty. He'd been taking up too much of Miguel's time. He hated to think that in spending time together, Miguel had neglected his kitchen duties to the point of being demoted and kicked out of the kitchens he loved so much.

Miguel seemed to sense the path Roska's mind had traveled down. "Roska, stop what you're thinking. I *enjoy* working in the gardens. I was only teasing. It was a bad joke."

Roska studied Miguel's face, trying to determine if he was lying then or lying now. When it seemed clear that Miguel was, in fact, just teasing about getting kicked out of the kitchens as punishment, Roska relaxed. He couldn't stand the idea of anyone suffering simply because of their association with him, but he also knew that this was a feeling he'd have to battle for the rest of his life.

Feeling like a burden. An inconvenience. A problem that needed to be solved. It was all a direct result of his upbringing with the Brotherhood and yet another thing he wanted to destroy them for.

No one should be forced to grow up the way he had. No one should have to deal with the mental hurdles he was forced to address every waking moment.

The only way to fix himself was to rid the world of the Brotherhood and all of their influence. And he was the only one who could do it.

Chapter 6

"Forgive the interruption, my lord, but the King has requested your presence in the war room."

Roska was certain he would never get used to being referred to as "my lord," but Niko had insisted on giving both him and Quinn titles when Elena had accepted his proposal. It had been a few moons and Roska still caught himself looking over his shoulder to see who the servant might have been addressing before realizing they were talking to him.

He offered them a curt nod and headed off to find the King. The "war room" was a large study with tables covered in books on strategy and history, along with maps marking all the places they'd successfully excised the Brotherhood from, as well as the towns and cities they had yet to free from the Brotherhood's hateful influence. Over the last few moon cycles, the yellow sun-shaped pieces—denoting King Niko's influence—had been taking over Waverly, replacing the black pieces that marked the Brotherhood's influence with comforting consistency.

The room was quiet when he entered. Niko wasn't there yet, so Roska wandered around the tables, checking the updates the King had made to their intel. Seeing the maps now, Roska fixated on the cluster of black markers surrounding the area Mother had pinpointed as the location of the Brotherhood's compound. They hadn't been able to get eyes inside the compound itself. Castor had tried getting an aerial perspective in his moonbird form, but the Brotherhood quickly recognized the oversized raven as a witch's familiar and opened fire on him. It was informative, despite Castor's complaints to the contrary. Prior to that encounter, they hadn't even known that the Brotherhood was armed. During Roska's time there, growing up in the oppressive and abusive compound, the Brothers had never possessed weapons. Clearly, they'd made some adjustments since he left.

Once he'd gotten over the initial attack, Castor had been willing to try infiltrating the compound a second time. He'd shifted into a dormouse and attempted to creep into the walls, but he'd been unable to cross their borders. To hear Castor describe it, the Brotherhood of the Healing Light had used magic to ward and protect themselves from invasion. Roska didn't doubt the shifter's word, but he had a hard time reconciling the idea that the Brotherhood—those hells-bent on removing "the scourge of magic" from the world—would resort to casting spells of any kind, even in self-preservation.

It's not that hard to believe, Demoni chimed in. *After all, they had no problem using us to cast the spell and release the* turmio *all those cycles ago.*

"Oh, good! You're here." Niko strode into the room, letting the door close loudly behind him. "I have some good news!"

"You and Elena finally picked a date for the wedding?" Roska sat in one of the over-stuffed chairs beside the war room fireplace.

Niko glared at him. "Don't even get me started on that shyt." He collapsed irritably into the only other chair. "Between your mother's schedule, my kingly duties, your demi-god—and possibly schizophrenic—father, and your witchy mum's celestial calculations, we may *never* get married. Belladonna insists on finding the perfect day with all the right symbolism and magical shyt. Beatrice is always hosting visiting royals and negotiating peace on behalf of the witches so that they might return to their homelands—if they choose. And Aiden... well, Aiden is insane."

The King ran his hands roughly through the tight black curls that draped over his furrowed brow.

"You know, Elena will marry you tomorrow. She doesn't care about all the pomp and circumstance." Roska offered the tired King a warm smile, hoping to impart a bit of comfort or relief.

"I know, you're right. But I'm the King. Pomp and circumstance is sort of a requirement." Exhaling roughly, Niko closed his eyes and laid his head against the deep red cushion of the chair. "It's just so overwhelming sometimes, you know?"

Roska agreed quietly, staring off into the fire. They sat in companionable silence for several long moments, each stewing in their respectively overwhelming burdens. Roska wasn't a king, but he was carrying the weight of all magical beings on his shoulders as he fought to dismantle the Brotherhood and their hate-filled mission.

"Wait, I called you here for a reason." Niko practically jumped out of his chair and headed over to the map table. Roska followed.

Niko pointed to the spot they'd identified as the center of the compound. "We've managed to get a man inside. We have successfully planted a mole in the compound and set up communications with him."

Roska was stunned. They'd been trying to get an "inside man" for the last two solar cycles. They would *finally* be able to get a clear vision of what was going on behind those thick walls and learn what other defenses the Brotherhood had at their disposal.

"Thank the Mother," Roska exhaled. Turning to face Niko, he added, "What do we do now? What does he know? When can we invade and finally finish those bastards off?"

Icy mist poured from Roska's hands. He couldn't see his eyes, but he could tell by Niko's raised eyebrows that they were likely glowing a bright teal. Over the last few solar cycles, Roska had gotten a good handle on his powers. He rarely iced over anything accidentally, but when it came to the Brotherhood, Roska's powers seemed to have a mind of their own.

❄❄ ❄❄ ❄❄

"Hey, uh, Ros?" Niko stepped into his field of view. "Roska, it's getting a tad chilly in here. Mind letting up a bit?" The King's breath puffed from his mouth in a white cloud of mist.

Roska hadn't realized how much time had passed. His mind had been thoroughly engulfed in vivid images of the fall of the Brotherhood and the brutal and overly violent death of Grand Maester Auron. Blinking several times to clear his mind, Roska looked around the room. A layer of ice covered everything, freezing the yellow and black markers in their respective spots on the massive map of Waverly. The fire—which had been roaring in the hearth just moments ago—had dwindled down to sad embers, struggling to stay alive and utterly incapable of staving off Roska's cold.

Shyt. It happened again.

You were doing so well. It's all right. No one got hurt. We can undo this. Demoni's comforting voice did little to balance out the snide, cruel voice of the Grand Maester as his memory flared in Roska's mind.

"You are a devil, child. You and those powers of yours are pure evil and you don't deserve the scraps of food we waste on you."

Such words were usually accompanied by a few swift kicks to Roska's gaunt midsection. It was a wonder any time one of those kicks didn't crack a rib. Although, there were numerous kicks that did cause serious damage over the years. Roska was certain that, at this point, his ribs were nearly unbreakable, after having been broken and healed so many times over.

Niko gently grasped Roska by the shoulders. Roska flinched so violently that he nearly impaled the young King with a shard of ice.

"Mux!" Roska tried to pull away, to save the King from his uncontrollable violent outburst, but Niko held fast.

"You are safe here. No one can hurt you." Niko's voice was calm. He didn't even seem to notice the sharp blade of ice that was a mere hands-breath from puncturing his lungs. He didn't loosen his grip and he positioned himself more fully into Roska's field of view. "Ros, I know you went through hells with those bastards, but we've got them now. We can stop them for good. I just need you to pull back your magic a bit so we can take a look at this map and make a plan."

Roska couldn't believe how calm the King was. If he moved his hand slightly to the right, Roska could easily slice through Niko's doublet and impale him with an icy dagger. Instead, Niko was holding steady, forcing Roska's gaze to meet his and being absurdly calm.

He has spent a lot of time with your rather volatile sister. Maybe he's grown overly confident. Demoni studied them both from the table. *Or maybe he just trusts you to not hurt him.*

Well, that's stupid. Roska didn't trust himself; why in the name of the Mother would Niko have such faith in him?

Still, Roska took a few steadying breaths and began to rein in his powers. The temperature in the room rose quickly as the fire roared back to life.

Seems his faith was well placed, Demoni observed pointedly.

Roska ignored her, nodding almost imperceptibly to Niko in apology for nearly killing him and thanks for helping calm him down. Niko was a wonder in his own right. The man had been raised by two selfish narcissists and he'd still grown to be the most level-headed, selfless person Roska had ever known.

Niko studied him for a moment longer, probably making sure Roska wasn't going to lose control again, before giving his shoulders a quick squeeze and releasing him, turning back to the thawed—although now slightly damp—map of Waverly.

"According to my spy, the Brotherhood has been stockpiling weapons, both magical and non-magical, since the fall of the *turmio*. It seems they're expecting us." Niko motioned to the small farming hamlets near the Brotherhood's compound. "The townsfolk here are none too happy with the Brotherhood, but they are too frightened of their power to want to fight against them. I'd love to send our army in and demolish that place once and for all."

"You intend to take an army?" Roska was a little surprised by the boldness of Niko's plan. He was King, after all, so the army was his to command, but Roska had been picturing a much different tactic.

"I'd *love* to, but I can't. Muxing politics and bullshyt. To the other countries on the continent, the Brotherhood just looks like an ignorant collection of tottering old fools. Sending in my army would look like I'm declaring war on grandpas. The rest of the continent—who already have issues with me for various reasons—could take advantage and declare war on us."

Roska didn't know much about the world of politics, and he preferred it that way.

"If your spy is correct, showing up with an army is exactly what the Brotherhood is expecting, anyway. We need a subtler approach. One they won't see coming."

Smiling, Niko gestured to the map. "What did you have in mind?"

They spent the rest of the day planning a covert invasion of the Brotherhood's compound. Roska knew his way around the stone fortress. He knew secret passageways that the Brothers had long since forgotten about. None of them allowed for ingress or egress, but once the royal spy got him inside, Roska would be able to sneak about the compound unnoticed.

"You can't do this alone," Niko stated flatly. It wasn't an observation or a request. He was asserting his kingly authority. "Your sister will never forgive me if I send you on this mission alone and you don't come back in the *exact* same physical condition as when you left."

"I'm not taking your army," Roska argued. "And I'm not taking Elena or Quinn. This is *my* fight. I have to be the one to finish it." He couldn't really explain why he felt that way, but Roska *knew* he needed to do this without them.

Much to his surprise, Niko nodded. "I understand. But I still can't let you go alone. Talk with Jamieson. Take a handful of his best Shadowcloaks. An archer. A paladin or two. An assassin. What? Oh, don't look at me like that. Every royal family has a team of assassins, even if it's just to have their perspective when planning personal defense. I've never employed them to actually assassinate anyone." Roska raised a doubtful eyebrow at the King. "I *haven't*," he insisted. "I only consult with them to improve our defenses to keep *your sister* safe, as well as the rest of your outrageous family."

Roska chuckled despite himself. Niko had probably had to consult with the assassins often in the beginning. Roska's entire family hadn't been great at making friends or navigating the world of royals and courtiers when Niko first took over the kingdom. Hells, Quinn nearly got in a duel with some courtier's spouse when he complimented the woman on her dress. Her husband had thought Q was hitting on the woman. Niko had walked in to find the husband's sword drawn and Q looking incredibly amused with his hands aflame and Lyra circling the husband, teeth bared and tail on fire.

Niko had definitely had his hands full in those first few moons.

"Talk to Jamieson," Niko ordered, firmly but kindly. "I will allow you to go, but only if you agree to take a few of my most skilled people with you."

Roska knew this wasn't an argument he would win. And likely, bringing the King's Shadowcloaks with him would only improve his chances of success.

"Yes, Your Majesty," Roska teased. He held out his hand, and they clasped forearms.

Now the real work would begin.

Chapter 7

ROSKA LOOKED OUT ACROSS the training field, practically blinded by the sun reflecting off the shields and helmets of the soldiers running through various training and formation drills. The orders shouted by captains were nearly drowned out by the rattling clash of steel on steel as the soldiers sparred. From his vantage point on the wall surrounding the field, Roska could see hundreds of soldiers in various acts of violence. Honing their skills with pikes, swords, daggers, and bows.

Commander Jamieson strode purposefully across the wall, a team of guards following in his wake. "My lord," he said with a quick bow. "The King informed me that you need a select team of Shadowcloaks to aid in your mission. I've a list of my top suggestions ready for you, sir."

Roska held in the exasperated sigh that threatened. He'd been telling Calum for moons to stop calling him "lord". The Commander was as stubborn as ever. "Thank you, Commander," he replied with a hint of mock annoyance in his words.

Calum Jamieson had been the first man to welcome Roska to Riverayn after they'd ousted the Queen and he'd decided to take up permanent residence in the castle. Calum had even given him a tour of the entire capital and offered him a private guard of his own. Roska had quickly declined the offer, not feeling important enough to warrant such an extravagance. Not to mention, he was quite capable of defending himself if needed.

Jamieson gestured for Roska to follow him. Crossing the wall, they entered a watchtower and went down the spiral stairs that lined the wall. Roska trailed behind the Commander as he led the way through several rooms within the military complex until they reached his office. Calum's guards took position outside the door, leaving Roska alone with the Commander.

"Calum, you really have to stop calling me lord." Roska couldn't hold it back anymore. He took a seat across the desk from the Commander as Demoni slid from his shoulder to investigate the room. Ever since learning the disgraced Queen Rosalina was a witch and could control animals—as well as create violent tornadoes—Demoni had taken to doing what she called "security sweeps" any time they entered a new room or were about to discuss sensitive information.

She nodded the "all clear" and returned to Roska's chair, coiling herself into a ball in his lap.

"Respectfully, that's never gonna happen." Calum smiled widely. "At least not in front of my soldiers. Whether you like it or not, the King granted you a title and rank. You *are* a lord."

It was the same argument they'd been having for moons. It would never end. Roska didn't think he'd ever feel comfortable with a title, but he couldn't exactly expect others to dispense with formalities just because it made him uncomfortable. Instead, he opted for avoidance and changed the subject. "Tell me about your recommendations."

The Commander's amused grin changed to one of pride as he sat behind his desk and pulled out a literal list from a drawer.

"Isn't that a bit unsafe?" Demoni asked. "Keeping a list of names just sitting there in your desk drawer like that?"

"My desk is safely secured in my locked office, in the center of the military compound deep within the castle walls of Riverayn. One might argue that this is the safest place in Waverly," Calum remarked confidently. "But you're right. It would be foolish to keep a list of Shadowcloak names in my desk." He held up the paper for them to see. It was nonsense. A random collection of letters and numbers that didn't make any coherent words.

Roska leaned forward and took the paper when Calum offered it to him. "What the hells is this? It's gibberish."

Calum took the note back, seeming almost offended by Roska's claim. "It's not gibberish," he argued. "It's coded. The names of the Shadowcloaks is a closely guarded secret. The King and I are the only ones who know the names of every member. They work in groups of three or four and rarely know any of the others. If a member dies on a mission, the remaining members debate, discuss, and vote for a replacement. They bring their choice to me, and the King and I make the final decisions. These"—he held up the sheet of gibberish—"are my top choice operatives for this mission. You will need a sharpshooter, a poison and plant expert, an explosives specialist, and a beast."

"I'm sorry, a beast?"

"Unofficial military term." That proud grin was back on Calum's face. "A beast is what we call those soldiers who can take a hit and keep on coming. They don't slow down or surrender. They fight until they can't move or the enemy is dead."

Roska shuddered at that description. He wouldn't want to face a beast, but having one on his side would definitely be helpful.

"Who did you have in mind?"

* * * * * *

As it turned out, Calum had a team already lined up, he'd just been waiting for Roska to admit he'd need help.

Calum led Roska to a small study that served as a mission briefing room. It had a round table in the center of the room, around which sat the Commander's recruits.

"This is Balor," Calum began, pointing to a mountain of a man.

Balor stood at the mention of his name, his massive frame instantly dwarfing the room as he ducked to avoid hitting the candelabra that hung from the ceiling. His bald head was marred with a myriad of scars, none of which were as unsettling as the one that crossed from the center of his brow, down and through what remained of his left eye. His eyelid had been sewn closed, but Roska could tell by the concave nature of the socket that an eyeball no longer inhabited the cavity.

"He will serve as the beast of this crew," Calum stated the obvious with a sly grin. "He's an expert with all weapons, but is particularly adept with his battle axe."

At this, Balor retrieved his axe from where it hung at his side. Roska stared openly at the wickedly sharp blade that curved protectively over the beast's hand as he showed off his magnificent weapon. The edge of the blade was sharp enough to shave with, but the part that held Roska's attention were the engravings on the flat of the blade. Three interlocking, swirling lines seemed to draw him in. The lines were deep, dug firmly into the thick blade of the weapon. Roska thought the grooves seemed a bit tarnished until he realized with a shock that the reddish-brown staining wasn't a result of age. It was dried blood.

"That is an impressive weapon," Roska said quietly, suddenly a bit nervous around the man towering over him.

Balor offered him a cocky smirk. "Aye, the axe is fine too." He tossed a wink over his shoulder to the others at the table. Quiet chuckles echoed in the small room at Balor's innuendo.

Heat flooded Roska's face, and he was eternally grateful for the poor lighting in the room.

Jamieson rolled his eyes at Balor but moved on as though the beast hadn't said anything. "Up next, I'd like to introduce the best sharpshooter in all of Waverly: Zara Fletcher. Aptly named for her skill with the bow as well as the crossbow, daggers, and any other weapon that can be used as a projectile."

Zara didn't rise from her seat, which Roska decided he preferred. She didn't bow to him or make any remarks about his status. She offered him a curt nod before flicking her shrewd lavender eyes back to the dagger she'd been sharpening. Her dark hair was nearly the color of the midnight sky. Black, with just a hint of blue, and short enough that it barely covered the tips of her ears. Which were... pointed?

Fae? Demoni asked, echoing the thoughts in his mind.

Looks like it. I didn't think there were any Fae left in Waverly.

Maybe we don't mention Aiden until we know how this Fae feels about him and his history with her people.

Good idea.

Aiden had a complicated history with the Fae. Some days, he claimed the Fae cursed him with the ability to see the future. Other days, when he'd had a little too much wine, he'd say that he stole the gift of prophecy from them. Roska had no way of knowing what story was true, or if the truth lay somewhere in between. Regardless, it was safest to leave Father out of this for as long as possible.

"Asha will be serving as your bomb expert for this mission."

Asha waved kindly from her seat at the table. She wore a sleeve-less black tunic, with her burnt orange hair coiled into a tight ball at the nape of her neck. Her freckled skin wrinkled softly around her clear blue eyes as she smiled up at him. Roska couldn't help but notice the numerous small scars covering her hands and exposed arms.

"Lastly," Calum continued, "we have the poisoner and healer for the mission. I think you'll recognize him."

Roska followed the Commander's gaze to a mop of messy black hair half covering a pair of honey-brown eyes. Eyes that had seen right into his soul just hours before.

"Miguel?"

Chapter 8

"M IGUEL? *YOU'RE* ONE OF the King's Shadowcloaks?" Roska couldn't comprehend the truth, even as it stared him in the face.

"Yes." Miguel didn't even look ashamed at having lied to him for *cycles*. Hells, Miguel had been lying to Roska since they *met*. And yet, he stood there, calmly holding Roska's confused stare with a passivity that grated almost as much as the realization that everything between them had been a lie.

"How could you keep this from me?" Roska's mind was spinning. He recalled every moment they'd shared, dissecting each touch, every comment, every godsdamned word.

Commander Jamieson looked between Roska and Miguel before muttering quickly, "I think we'll give you two a few minutes," and exited the room, taking the rest of the crew with him.

"I was under orders," Miguel spoke softly as the door closed behind them. "I'm one of the King's poisoners. I've spent my life building up an immunity to all plant-based poisons. I work in the kitchens as part of my cover to ensure that the King's food remains safely poison-free. I taste-test everything before it even touches his plate. Or your sister's, now. I ensure the safety and purity of their food."

Roska stared open-mouthed at the man he thought he knew.

"I know this all comes as a shock, but I'm the same guy, Ros. Just with a little more backstory than you knew." Miguel offered him a sheepish smile, still refusing to apologize for the cycles they'd spent together in which he'd kept life-altering information from Roska.

"You lied to me. For *cycles*. I don't know what's true and what's fiction. I can't trust a word you say." Frosted mist poured from Roska's hands as he paced back and forth. He left icy footprints in his wake as he wore a path across the small room.

"I was following orders."

Roska turned angrily on Miguel. "That's bullshyt, and you know it." Rage radiated off Roska in frozen waves, rapidly dropping the temperature in the room. "Following orders is an excuse to do cruel things without taking responsibility for your actions."

Miguel balked at Roska's accusation. "I was *never* cruel to you."

"You think it was kind of you to hide the truth from me? Spend cycles getting to know me? Watching me fall apart on numerous occasions? Getting close to my family? Letting me think we were creating some kind of unique bond?"

"I care for you, Roska. That was never a part of my mission, but it is the truth." Miguel took a few tentative steps toward Roska, forcing their eyes to meet. "I care for you." He reached out to touch Roska's shoulder, to offer some form of comfort or consolation, but Roska pulled away.

"What was your mission then?" His words came out in a mist of frozen air. Roska didn't mean to snap as harshly as he did, but the feeling of betrayal shook him to his core. Anger fueled his powers, creating a layer of ice on everything, despite the bright growing season sun shining through the small window across the room.

"I was assigned to keep you safe, that's all. You stubbornly re-fused the Commander's private guards, so he sent me to make sure nothing and no one hurt you." Miguel spoke with such firmness that Roska wanted to believe him. But how could he? The man he'd come to know and trust had been lying all along. Roska couldn't believe a word out of his mouth now. No matter how pretty the words—or the lips that spoke them.

"For how long? How long have you been spying on me and lying to me? Since my birthday? I thought that moment with us—with the kettle—had been genuine, but honestly, Miguel, has anything between us ever been genuine?" Roska turned away, walking to the window and attempting to focus his energy to rein in his powers before he froze them both to death.

"Ros, please." Miguel sounded truly apologetic. "I'm sorry. I never meant to upset you. I just wanted to keep you safe. That has *always* been my sole purpose and my mission." He took a few cautious steps closer as Roska continued to stare out the window. He spoke softly, as though he was afraid he would spook Roska into fleeing the room entirely. "Honestly, I would have made that my personal mission even without the Commander's orders."

Taking a deep, steadying breath, Roska turned to face the man he thought he knew—the man he thought he could love. "I can't do this with you."

With that, he left the room, a thick layer of ice covered the windowsill he'd been clinging to, and a feeling of shattered dreams hung in the air.

❋ ❋ ❋ ❋ ❋ ❋

Roska avoided Miguel for the next few days. He threw himself into plans for the mission, studying the maps and memorizing the layout of the Brotherhood's compound. The structure hadn't changed much since he'd left them, but it had been over four cycles. Some improvements had been made to their defenses, including new warding that the King's spy had mapped out as best he could, considering he was magept and didn't really see or feel the magical boundaries the Brothers had erected around their facility.

He wasn't ready to address everything with Miguel. Thankfully, Miguel seemed just as willing to throw himself into work. They didn't see much of each other as they prepared. When they did, they were both cordial and polite, but nothing more. No more fleeting touches or prolonged glances.

Asha was quickly becoming Roska's favorite crew member. Quick to laugh, easy to talk to, and clever. So muxing clever. Every time someone brought up a flaw in their plan—mostly Zara, who seemed quite adept at pointing out all the problems without bothering to offer a single solution—Asha was there with a clever workaround or an alternative that nullified Zara's "concern."

Balor proved to be a man of few words. More often than not, the words he did speak were heavy with double entendres and not-so-subtle winks at Asha, who couldn't help but giggle at every one of his comments.

Roska probably would have found it all entertaining if it weren't for the weightiness of their mission.

He finally snapped one evening. "Can you two be serious for a moment?" They'd been working well into the night, eating a rushed dinner around the table of the mission room. They spent days—and many late nights—studying maps and poking holes in their own plans so that they might find solutions for potential issues now, in the safety of the castle walls, rather than flying by the seat of their pants in the field.

Asha, to her credit, didn't balk at his snipe. Instead, she offered him a wide smile, winked at Balor, and directed their focus to a potential entry point. "See this wall here?" She pointed to an exterior wall with a carrot she'd been munching on. "If I set a bomb at the base of it, it will create a rather beautiful distraction that will allow Zara to sneak in through the sewer grate over here."

Zara grunted in annoyance. She'd stopped arguing the point, but she'd made it abundantly clear that she did *not* appreciate any of the plans that required her to traverse through sewers. She would be willing to do it—she'd clarified—but only if there was no other option.

"The wall you're talking about blowing up connects to the kitchens. I don't want any unnecessary injuries or casualties." Roska spoke without thinking. He knew the Brothers were abusive, heartless, single-minded men who had never bothered to be concerned with his well-being. He couldn't explain or understand why he still felt compelled to protect them.

Miguel caught his eye but didn't say anything. Instead, he turned to study the map with Asha. "If we do it in the middle of the night, no one should be in the kitchens. Even the bakers wouldn't be up to start the day's bread until closer to dawn."

Roska offered Miguel a small smile of appreciation. It was Miguel's attempt at a peace offering. He knew Roska didn't want to hurt anyone—except Grand Maester Auron—if they could avoid it, so he was trying to create options that would allow for minimal bloodshed. They wanted to put a stop to the Brotherhood's single-minded hatred and destruction, not validate their fears of magical creatures and their allies.

"Aye, fine. But I will get to cut some bastards before this is done, right?" Balor drew his large axe from the hook on his belt, brandishing it in the most dramatic—and likely impractical—way as he showed off for Asha. Asha, however, was now thoroughly engulfed in planning and devising just the right explosives to damage the wall and call attention away from the sewer drain, without demolishing the kitchens or blowing a crater in the compound.

"Why aren't we just blastin' our way in, anyway? These guys are the worst. Can't we just blow them to hells and be done with it?" Balor put his axe away when it was clear Asha wasn't paying attention to him anymore. "Would be a lot simpler," he added with a shrug when Miguel pinned him with an irritated glare.

"This is a *stealth* mission, Balor." Zara rolled her eyes dramatically. "Means we aren't making a show of ourselves. Ideally, they won't even know that we're there until we cut off the head of that wretched snake."

"I understand stealth," he practically growled at her. "What I don't get is why. Why are we being stealthy when they've been attacking and manipulating the entire country from the shadows for cycles?"

"*Because* they've been in the shadows." Zara's contrite tone implied that she thought this answer was simple enough.

Balor's confused expression proved her wrong.

"Bal, gorgeous, we can't attack them outright because it would make the King and the royal army look like the aggressors to the rest of the continent." Asha didn't look up from her figures as she worked out the math and ratios for her distraction bomb along the edge of one of the maps. "The King can't send his army or blow the Brotherhood's compound to hells because the rest of the continent will see it as him declaring war on those who disagree with him."

"The Brotherhood has been manipulating things for cycles, you're right," Roska continued for her. "But because they've been in the shadows this whole time, the rest of the continent doesn't see them for the threat that they are. If King Niko sent us to blow them away, our neighbors in Rolam—who are already unhappy with the King's open-door policy for witches—and Slyvestris—who hated the last King and still hold hostilities towards King Niko—will see it as an opportunity to rally their armies and declare war on Waverly."

"Muxing politics," Balor grumbled, grabbing a roll and flopping petulantly into a couch by the fire. Roska flinched as the chair gave an ominous crack but surprisingly didn't break under the weight of the beast.

Roska couldn't help but agree. It would be simpler to destroy the Brotherhood and everything they represent, but he couldn't. He told himself it was all political. That he would happily erase all evidence of the Brotherhood from the planet, but deep down, he knew that wasn't the truth.

He'd spent the majority of his life within those walls. As miserable as that life had been, there were still some small memories that he didn't want to give up. Time in the gardens with Brother Liam. Sneaking books of fables from the library. Learning about his family and studying their magical history. It wasn't something he'd readily admit, but he had some fond memories of his time there and he wasn't ready to burn it all to the ground.

Except Grand Maester Auron, Demoni cut in.

Yes. That man deserves all the fires and torment Hells has to offer.

Chapter 9

"Roska?" Elena called out as she walked into his suite.

"In here!" Roska answered.

She turned the corner into his study to find him nearly buried under a pile of books and maps.

"Ros? I need to talk to you." The hesitation in her voice made the hairs on the back of Roska's neck stand on end.

He practically jumped out from behind the desk, placing his hands on her shoulders, and studied her face. "What's wrong?" he asked quickly. Had something happened with Niko? Was there another assassination attempt?

"Niko got word from the spy inside the Brotherhood's compound." Elena's eyes flicked around the room. She seemed to be trying to look everywhere but at him.

"El, what's going on?"

Roska guided her over to the couch beside a bookcase by the window. She looked like she was about to faint.

"It's—oh gods, Roska, I'm so sorry." A sob escaped her lips as tears began to flow freely down her cheeks.

"Elena, talk to me. What did the spy say?" A sense of imposing dread filtered into the room. The air itself felt like it weighed a ton.

"They—they took her," Elena spoke between broken sobs. "The Brotherhood kidnapped Brigit."

The world crashed around him.

Brigit? His Brigit? But how?

"According to the spy," she continued, swiping at the seemingly endless river of tears on her cheeks, "they took her cycles ago. He's been infiltrating the ranks and was finally let into the inner sanctum. The spy said they'd been following you and watching you since you left them." Elena studied his face now, trying to read his emotions. "Apparently, they didn't trust that they'd brain-washed you completely, so they sent spies to keep an eye on you. When they saw that you were helping us to stop the *turmio*, they knew that we would win and they'd lose. They took her as punishment or collateral. To protect themselves for when we inevitably turned our attention to them."

He couldn't believe what she was saying. He *couldn't* be the reason Brigit had been left to suffer at the hands of those abusive, bigoted, self-righteous Brothers.

As cruel as it sounds, it makes sense. Demoni interrupted his rage-filled spiral with her quiet observations. *They have always had contingency plans and backups for their backups. Of course they've been watching us since we left. We were foolish to think they'd just let us go.*

Her bitterness seeped in, mixing with his own until he couldn't tell where her resentment ended and his began.

They should have known better. *He* should have known better.

And now Brigit was paying the price.

"How long has she been there? Is she all right?" He knew the answer to the second question, but couldn't help voicing it.

"The Brothers bragged that they'd had her since before the *turmio* fell."

Gods. That was three and a half solar cycles ago.

"How do we get her out?" It was the only acceptable course of action.

Likely, she would hate him for this. She would probably never forgive him for getting her roped into all this, and then leaving her to suffer for cycles.

You didn't leave her. You didn't know she was there. We looked for her as soon as we could. We had no way of knowing she'd been taken.

"Roska, this is not your fault." Elena's words echoed Demoni's thoughts. "You couldn't have known they were following you. You had no reason to think they would do anything to her. This is *not* your fault."

"Respectfully, you're wrong." Roska rose from the couch and began angrily pacing the room. "I should have known. I should have expected this kind of shyt from them. I should have protected her. She's only in that hells because of me. Because she was kind to *me*. If I'd left her alone, none of this would have happened. She's been suffering unimaginable pain and torment for *cycles* because I liked her."

"Roska," Elena began, rising from the couch and stepping into his path. "You didn't hurt her. You didn't do anything to her. The Brothers are heartless, evil monsters. You are not responsible for their actions."

Roska was about to argue further when Agon nosed open the suite door and bounded into the room. Roska hadn't even noticed the electric weasel wasn't with Elena.

"Niko is meeting with your Shadowcloak team in the war room," Agon said to Roska. "They're reviewing the missive from the spy, as well as the maps to try and pinpoint where she's being kept within the compound."

Roska turned on his heel, scooped Demoni up from the pile of maps she'd turned into a nest on his desk, and practically ran from the room.

Their attack plan was now a rescue mission.

* * * * * * *

The next few days passed in a blur of maps, plans, missives from Niko's spy, and consultations with various "experts" in their respective "fields"—which just meant that Balor went out drinking with his fellow beast-type friends when he was supposed to be helping with the plans—until it was *finally* time to pack and leave.

Niko had attempted to convince the crew that he should accompany them on this mission, if for no other reason than that they could take one of his blood magic ships and get there in half the time. Elena put a halt to those plans with one lightning-filled glare. Instead, they took the King's fastest horses, packed as light as possible, and prepared to leave at dawn.

Roska was pacing in his room as the sun set out his window when a gentle knock came at his door. Assuming it was a guard with one last message from the spy, or Miguel hoping to smooth things over with him before they left, Roska called for their entry, not bothering to stall his pacing or even turn to greet whoever it was.

"That's how you greet your favorite sister?" Elena teased as she entered the room. She was carrying a large bundle of fabric. Agon slipped passed her, bounding across the room quickly, and stretched out along the windowsill as though it belonged to him. Demoni flicked her tongue at him in greeting but didn't move from her pillow by the fireplace.

"I didn't think you'd be coming by tonight." Roska moved to take the bundle of fabric from her and motioned for her to take a seat. "What's all this?" He began to unroll the bundle until he recognized it for what it truly was. "Your cloak?" The enchanted cloak that Amelia had given Elena all those cycles ago, before the *turmio*, before she even knew she had brothers.

"I thought you could use it. It's just been hanging in my wardrobe for moons. You need it more than I do these days. It will make the journey a little easier." She brushed an errant curl behind her ear. She looked... nervous? But that was absurd. Why would she be nervous? He was the one going on the mission. Elena would be safe in Riverayn.

She's nervous for you, *you dolt*, Demoni said.

Roska sat the cloak down on the side table, sat next to Elena on the couch, and offered her his hands. She grasped them quickly and tightly.

"Everything is going to be fine," he said, desperately trying to infuse his words with a confidence he didn't altogether feel. "We've got the best crew in the kingdom and an excellent plan. Plus, about a hundred contingency plans, should the original plan fail."

He gave her a weak smile, hoping to hide his own nerves behind a wall of manufactured courage.

Tears lined Elena's lashes as she studied his face. Roska looked away, knowing if she looked too closely, she'd see through his facade.

"I just want you to be safe." Her voice was strained from unspoken emotions. "I know how important this is, and I can't wait to meet Brigit when you bring her home. I just wish I could go with you."

Roska slid one hand from her grip and cupped her cheek, wiping away the tears that had begun to fall. "I will be ok. We'll be back before you know it." He didn't mention his own fears: that Brigit might want nothing to do with him, after cycles of captivity simply because she knew him. He couldn't think about that now. He needed to focus on freeing her first. He'd worry about their potential future once she was safe and recovering from the ordeal.

"I'm just glad Q's not here," Roska added, changing the subject to a lighter, less emotionally charged topic. "He would be shyt at a covert mission." He chuckled to himself trying to imagine their fiery brother sneaking into the Brotherhood's compound.

Quinn was a skilled hunter, but he wasn't the best at containing his rage. Roska knew Q would not have been able to keep his cool as they snuck into the compound to rescue Brigit.

"I don't know. Those Infernals of his would be quite handy." Her laugh was watery as she tried to embrace his lighter topic.

"True, but giant flaming soldiers aren't exactly stealthy."

They both chuckled, trying to picture Q on a covert mission against an enemy he truly—and justly—hated. Their FlameBorn brother was the epitome of hot-headedness. Having him on this particular mission would only spell disaster. Fiery, deadly disaster.

With the mood officially lightened, Roska rose and offered Elena his arm. "Shall we head down to dinner? I heard the King is having a feast for no apparent reason this evening with a random selection of soldiers."

It was a lie, of course. Niko had asked the kitchens to make a special meal for their crew, a sort of farewell dinner. But, being a covert mission, they couldn't really announce the reasoning behind the feast. Instead, Niko had announced it as part of his new initiative to get to know his soldiers better, on a more personal level. Elena had confided in Roska that she worried Niko might actually make this a regular event: hosting a random selection of soldiers for a fancy weekly feast. The soon-to-be Queen wasn't all that comfortable in crowds. In fact, she dreaded all things related to her future royal position.

Roska felt for her. It was hard to put one's self out there for the benefit of others. But El was doing an excellent job of embracing her new life. Roska imagined Niko would keep up this tradition, at least for a while. If for no other reason than to endear himself more to the soldiers who served him. Niko was a well-liked King, but there was never any harm in ensuring that those who fought and protected him truly cared for him and felt seen by their King.

Roska also suspected that Niko was still trying to undo the impact left by his cruel father and conniving mother. The servants and soldiers had suffered a great deal under his parents' rule. Over three cycles later, Niko was still fighting to prove that he was nothing like his parents.

Roska pulled Elena into a one-armed hug. He was going to miss her while he was gone, but he knew she would be in good hands.

❋ ❋ ❋ ❋ ❋ ❋

The dinner was delicious. The banquet table overflowed with meats, breads, cheeses, wines, ciders, and seemingly endless desserts. By the time they finished their meal, Roska wasn't sure he'd have the energy to climb the stairs back to his room.

The crew would be leaving at dawn. After giving Elena one last hug, he planted a kiss on the crown of her head, shook Niko's hand, and slowly made the trek back to his bed.

His mind raced with endless possibilities and fears of how things could go wrong. As he crossed the threshold into his suite,

Roska wasn't sure how he'd ever quiet his mind enough to get any sleep at all. Still, he toed his boots off by the door and shuffled mindlessly to his bed.

Thankfully—and likely due in no small part to his full belly—Roska was asleep the instant his head hit the pillow.

Chapter 10

ROSKA'S DREAMS WERE PLAGUED with memories of his time at the compound. Flashes of the abuses he'd been subjected to for cycles. The endless barrage of insults, the beatings, the days and nights without food as "penance" for the sin of his magical existence.

He bolted upright in his bed, throwing the sheets from his body as a sheen of sweat coated his clammy skin. Demoni crawled into his lap, exhaling icy breath on his bare chest to try and cool him, bringing him back to reality.

He was safe. He was no longer a child in the hands of those monsters. He was free.

Brigit wasn't free, though. She wasn't safe.

Roska wasn't convinced that the Brothers would treat her as harshly—*you mean violently and heartlessly?* Demoni interjected—as they treated him, but he knew they hadn't been kind to her either. Hells, they'd been holding her hostage for cycles simply because she'd been nice to him. She was suffering because he'd shown an interest in her. Roska couldn't sit still any longer.

Lifting Demoni from his lap, he placed her gently on the bed and dressed quickly. Grabbing Elena's cloak and shoving his feet into his boots, he scooped Demoni back up and was out the door, heading to the kitchens as the sun began to rise in the distance.

Balor eyed him curiously as Roska began filling a pocket with an entire roasted chicken, wrapped in wax paper and thick linen. "What in the name of the Mother are you doing?"

"Packing food," Roska said, matter-of-factly. "What does it look like?"

"It looks like you've lost your senses, boy. How the hells do you think that will—" His words trailed off as he watched the chicken disappear into the pocket, along with two more waterskins, half a dozen rolls, and a carafe of coffee.

"There's no way you can put all that in there without making a mess and ruining all that food." Zara studied him incredulously.

"I don't know how it works," Roska said with a shrug. "It just does. Here, watch." He took the cloak off his shoulders, grasped the collar with one hand, and twirled it over his head. He felt ridiculous and knew he probably looked utterly insane, but when he handed the cloak over to Zara to inspect, he felt an entirely unjustified sense of pride at her astonishment.

She pulled out the carafe first, still warm without a single drop of coffee spilled. Then the rolls, fluffy and seemingly untouched, the sealed waterskins, and lastly, the roasted chicken. Everything looked exactly the same as it had when he'd put them into the enchanted pockets.

"That doesn't make any sense," Zara muttered to herself, thoroughly inspecting the pockets and then the food again. "It has to be some sort of trick."

"It's magic," Miguel said, stating the obvious. "It doesn't have to make sense, but it's definitely not a trick." He took the cloak back from her and refilled the pockets before handing it back to Roska. "As much as I would love to sit here and study the magic holding this beautiful thing together, we have a prisoner to rescue and a collection of vile bigots to put down. We should get moving."

At that, they all seemed to remember themselves, collecting their supplies and heading out to the stables where a team of five horses awaited them. Asha was already loading her saddle bag with various soon-to-be explosives when they stepped onto the straw floor of the stables.

"I've stashed a few things in each of your bags," she said by way of greeting. "Nothing volatile on their own, but if I store them all together in my bags... well, let's just say things could get a bit heated if certain things touch before I'm ready." She tossed a confident smirk over her shoulder as she stuffed a couple of small parcels into the last saddle bag.

Chapter 11

HOPE WAS A WASTE of time and energy. She learned that after the fifth straight moon with naught but angry men and stale bread to keep her company. Initially, she'd had no idea why they'd taken her or how long they'd kept her. She only knew that hoping to be rescued was a waste of what little energy she had. After her first visit with the Grand Maester and his inquisitor, she knew they were after Roska, the boy from the tavern in Nexton, although she had no clue why.

Turned out, when a person is left to survive on dense bread, dirty water, and the occasional scrap of meat or the odd moldy vegetable, they are quickly drained of all energy and their mental capacities are limited to convincing their body to stay alive. Critical thinking went out the iron-barred window.

At least, that's what happened in her experience.

So when the stranger dressed as an initiate offered her a thick slice of warm, soft bread, and a chunk of roasted venison, she'd been convinced she was hallucinating.

The next day, when he brought her a flagon of cold, clean water, she'd nearly cried.

She had no idea who he was, but after the third day of his coming to visit her in the night, bringing fresh food and grime-free water, she started to have hope.

Just a faint spark of hope in a hurricane of mental torment and anguish, but it was something. The first time she'd felt anything other than misery in ages.

She had no idea how long she'd been in that hells. She'd stop tracking the moon after her first solar cycle in captivity. Her mind wandered from time to time, attempting to bring her relief from the hells that she spent her days—and often nights—trying to survive. Images of her sisters. How were they? Did they miss her? Were they worried about her? Did they think she'd forgotten about them and that's why she'd stopped sending money?

Roska. That sweet boy from Nexton. He'd been so shy and cute with his white hair constantly falling in his eyes. Their first interaction had been a bit strained, but once they got over the initial awkwardness, he'd been the highlight of her day. She wondered how he was. Did he come back to find her like he said he would? Or did he move on with his life? She hoped he'd moved on. He deserved to be happy.

The monks had stopped torturing her when it had become clear that she didn't know anything. They'd interrogated her for moons; asking strange questions about Roska and his family. His cocky brother, Quinn, and their father. Aiden had seemed nice enough, but not nearly as clever as the Brothers seemed to believe. She'd thought he was a bit scatterbrained, honestly.

Her nails had finally grown back, after having been violently ripped from her fingers, but they were brittle and misshapen. Her legs, where the monks had burned her with red-hot pokers, had long since healed, although the scars were gruesome. At least she still had proper use of the limbs. Unfortunately, she couldn't say the same for her left hand. The inquisitor—an exceptionally monstrous man called Brother Jeremy—had lost his temper during their last encounter and smashed the hand to rubbish.

Thankfully, that had been his last visit.

She studied her hand in the faint moonlight. Her fingers hung at slightly odd angles, and thick scarring ran over the back of her hand where her bones had broken through the skin. She couldn't grip anything with that now-useless appendage. She thanked the Mother that at least it wasn't her dominant hand. Not that it mattered, really, if she was going to die here like she often imagined she would.

For reasons she had yet to figure out, the monks had sent healers to tend to her many wounds over the moons, treating any fevers and pus that resulted from her interrogations. They'd healed her hand as best they could, but it would never be the same again. She couldn't comprehend why they'd put so much effort into keeping her alive. When it had been made clear that she didn't have the answers they were looking for, why in the name of the Mother didn't they just kill her and let it be done?

It wasn't until the initiate spoke to her, after nearly a full week of midnight visits, that she began to understand there was something bigger at play.

"What is your name, *cherie*?"

Sitting on the floor of her cellar prison, she'd looked up at the small window along the ceiling of her cell. It was barred with iron, making it useless for escape, but it did provide her with light during the day, and a glimpse of the sky as the seasons changed. She'd been surprised by his odd accent. Working in the tavern, she'd met many strange folks from even stranger lands, but she couldn't recall hearing an accent such as that.

"Brigit." Her voice sounded wrong. Strained. Raw. She'd spent moons screaming in agony and crying out to the Mother to release her from this hells. She wondered now if she might have caused permanent damage to her vocal cords.

"Pleasure to meet you, Brigit," he'd said, offering her a dramatic bow that seemed entirely ridiculous considering they were whispering through the barred window where he knelt to peer down at her. "My name is Pierre Louis Thibodeaux Beauchamps. I'm here to facilitate your escape. Assuming you'd like to leave these lovely accommodations?"

She couldn't see his face properly in the dark, but she could hear the sarcasm in his voice. Then his words hit her. Escape? Was that even possible? It had been so long since she'd even thought the word. She'd been convinced that she would die there in that drafty, ever-damp cell.

She stared, open-mouthed at the silhouette of the stranger in her window.

Escape.

"Gods, yes please."

Chapter 12

"WE'RE SUPPOSED TO MEET our friend in the tavern," Miguel said over his shoulder, addressing the group as they slowly trekked alongside their mounts in the slick mud of the road. "Our friend" obviously meant the King's spy, but they'd agreed to refer to the man as such to avoid suspicion should their conversations be overheard upon entering populated areas.

It had taken longer than Roska liked to reach the small farming hamlet just west of the Brotherhood's compound. Ideally, they would have taken Niko's blood magic ships and arrived in a matter of days. However, since Niko couldn't join them without causing an international incident and the boats didn't work without Niko's blood on board, they'd been forced to take the long route. Weeks, instead of days. Roska's nerves were fried. He hadn't slept properly since he'd learned Brigit was being held by the Brothers. The planting season's rains had slowed them down as well, making the trip drag on for days longer than it should have. Not to mention, they were all soaked through and irritable.

The sun was sinking below the horizon when they finally made it into town. They headed straight for the inn, dropping their horses at the stable and shuffling in, tired and muddy, unloading their packs and taking over the largest table in the far back corner of the inn's tavern. The tavern would serve as their base while they updated their intel from the spy and made any adjustments to the plan.

"When is he going to get here?" Roska asked, failing to keep the impatience from his voice.

"We're supposed to send him a signal once we've arrived, then he'll meet us at midnight." Miguel waved the waitress over and ordered a pot of coffee for the table, as well as a cauldron of whatever soup was freshest and a loaf of bread.

Roska shifted uncomfortably in his chair. He'd never ridden a horse before. It had taken him days to gain the confidence to ride without having someone else hold his horse's reins. He wouldn't classify himself as a skilled rider after this excursion, but he felt competent now. His legs, however, fluctuated between feeling like jelly and feeling as though they might snap in two.

"It gets easier," Asha said, noting his discomfort. "It takes a little while to get your riding legs."

Balor's guffaw echoed through the small tavern. "Riding legs? What the mux are riding legs?"

Asha tsked, taking a sip of her coffee before replying, "I think it's pretty self-explanatory."

"I've never heard it called that before," Balor continued.

"What do you call it then?" Asha asked, putting her mug down and tearing off a piece of bread to dip into her soup.

"I don't think there's a name for legs that are used to being wrapped around a horse." Balor looked thoughtful for a moment, then a devious sparkle glinted in his eyes and he opened his mouth to add something, but Zara cut him off.

"Don't." She held his gaze, eyes narrowed, brow furrowed. "Whatever crass comment you're about to make, keep it to yourself." Zara's eyes dipped to Balor's crotch, then back to his face.

"Nothing you're about to say is going to be remotely amusing to anyone but you, and it's likely to be a lie."

Now it was Asha's turn to cackle in amusement.

Balor's face went blank for a moment, then he joined Asha in raucous laughter. He slapped a hand on the table, splashing broth from their bowls as he cheered Zara's insult. It took an embarrassingly long time for him to calm down, but when he did, he turned to Zara, wiping the tears of laughter from his eyes. "That was excellent."

Roska often wondered what the history was between this crew. The way they talked and teased, he couldn't decide if they were lifelong friends, or complete strangers who didn't give a shyt what the others thought.

Trying to get them back on task, Roska turned to Miguel. "What's the signal?"

"For our friend? I sent it off as soon as we got into town before we even left the horses at the stable. He'll be here tonight."

Tension coiled in Roska's shoulders. What if Brigit was dead? They hadn't heard any new information from the spy since they left Riverayn nearly three weeks ago. A lot could happen in three weeks.

She's ok. Demoni's thoughts were a cool salve on the inflamed nerves of his mind.

How can you be so sure?

I trust that the Mother Goddess wouldn't have brought her into our lives just to have her die at the hands of those bigots when we're so close to saving her.

Roska wasn't sure where Demoni's blind faith came from, but he desperately wanted to share her beliefs. He wanted to believe that he was meant to meet Brigit, meant to rescue her, meant to keep her safe for the rest of their days. He wanted to trust that the Mother was guiding him to her and they would get a happy ending. The one he had let himself dream about in those early days, after the *turmio*, when he was settling into life with his family and searching for Brigit in and around Nexton.

He desperately wanted to believe.

But he couldn't shake the feeling that things were going to get a lot worse before they got to any happy ending.

* * * * * *

"Pierre Louis Thibodeaux Beauchamps, at your service." The man removed the ratty, threadbare beret from his head and dropped into a dramatic bow. When he righted himself, he wore a crafty, Cheshire grin showcasing a chipped front tooth. "Most just call me Lou." He offered them a sly wink and Roska was quickly reminded of a trickster fox from one of the fables Brother Liam would read to him as a child when none of the other Brothers were around.

This was Niko's spy. This was not a man to be trusted. So, naturally, Roska knew they would end up relying on him heavily. They weren't thieves, but they'd need to be to pull this off. Lou seemed like the man for the job.

Miguel had suggested the others get some rest while he and Roska took the meeting with the spy. He said it was because they were all tired and wouldn't get much sleep once things really got moving. They'd have to leave town quickly and likely ride through the night a few times just to put enough distance between them and the Brotherhood's compound when all was said and done. Roska suspected that it was more about giving him privacy—in case their informant had bad news for them—than it was about getting a decent night's sleep.

Roska studied the spy for a moment longer while Miguel went to the bar to get them a bottle of wine and three glasses. They would need alcohol for this.

Once he'd returned with the wine, Miguel sat at the table beside Roska—and across from their shady new partner—offering the man a glass.

"Thank you kindly, *cher*." He raised his glass subtly in salute and took a long swig of the blood-red liquid. "I have some good news and some less-than-ideal news."

"Is she still alive?" Roska asked roughly.

"Oh, yes!" Lou offered him a large grin, revealing that chipped tooth again. "She's very much alive. She's not... unharmed," he hedged, "but she's alive and eager to leave."

Roska felt some of the tension leave his body. "Does she know we're here?"

"Not yet." Lou took another sip of his wine. "I didn't want to get her hopes too high just yet." He shared a knowing look with Miguel before he continued.

Miguel placed a glass of wine before Roska, but he ignored it. He didn't have time for wine. He needed answers from Lou and he needed to get inside that damned compound and save Brigit from their violence. He was terrified to see what state she was in when they finally got to her.

"What's the news?" Miguel asked.

Lou's face lost any hint of amusement as he leaned over the table, dropping his voice to a whisper. "She's alive, that's true enough, but she's in rough shape and won't be able to ride un-aided."

Ice flooded Roska's veins at Lou's words. Cool mist flowed from his fingers where they gripped the table. Miguel, not taking his eyes off Lou, slid a hand from the table to rest firmly on Roska's thigh. He squeezed gently, offering support and strength as he questioned the spy.

"What do you mean?" Miguel's voice was pitched low as well. He used his free hand to take a sip of wine, trying to maintain the appearance of three friends catching up in a tavern, rather than reveal the truth of their endeavor to prying eyes and ears.

"She's been through it, *cher*." Lou addressed Miguel's question but held Roska's gaze, speaking to the FrostBorn as though he already knew the connection Roska shared with Brigit. "Her legs are scarred. Looks like burns. She can walk, though, so that's good. My biggest concern is her hand. The left one. It's been smashed to bits. I'm not sure it'll ever be useable again."

Roska watched Lou's lips as they continued to move, but he couldn't understand the man's words any longer. All sound was drowned out by the pounding of his heart.

Maimed.

Those muxing bastards had maimed her, simply because she'd been nice to him.

He was going to end them all.

❋ ❋ ❋ ❋ ❋ ❋

Roska was sitting, glaring into the flames of their hearth, when Miguel walked into the room. For several long moments, neither of them said a word. Miguel took careful steps, joining Roska on the small bed closest to the fire. The inn didn't have many rooms, so their crew had split into two rooms, each room containing two beds. Balor had volunteered to sleep in the room with Asha and Zara. After some poor attempts at innuendo, Balor had agreed to sleep on the floor and leave the beds to the girls. Leaving Miguel and Roska to share the other room.

Sitting side-by-side, their knees brushing against each other, guilt nearly overwhelmed Roska. Here he was, enjoying the warmth of the fire, safe and comfortable with a man he truly cared for, while Brigit was enduring unimaginable pain, alone in a prison cell. All because of him.

"None of this is your fault." Miguel seemed to have developed a knack for reading Roska's mind and feelings.

"You know that's not true."

"You can't blame yourself for the actions of bigots. You had no way of knowing they were watching you. Or that they would take her." Miguel nudged his knee, drawing Roska's attention from the fire to the man's soulful brown eyes. "You are not responsible for this. The second you learned she was being held, you sprung into action." He held out a hand in a "here we are" gesture. "We are all here for her. For *you*. We will get her out and get her home safely."

Roska wanted to believe Miguel was right. That they'd be heading back to the safety of Riverayn with Brigit by the next dawn, but he was too much of a realist to trust things would work out the way he intended.

A realist or a pessimist? Demoni interjected.

The two are often one and the same, he countered.

"Get some sleep. We'll finalize the plans tomorrow, and do the last bit of recon at dusk. We will get her out of there tomorrow night. I swear to the Mother." The heat and vehemence in Miguel's vow brought tears to Roska's eyes.

Brushing them away roughly, he offered Miguel a quick nod. Miguel gave his leg a reassuring squeeze before rising from Roska's bed and retiring to his own.

Roska laid back in his bed, arms crossed under his head as he stared blankly at the ceiling. He had no idea how he was going to get any sleep.

Demoni curled herself into a cool, teal ball in the middle of his chest. Closing her eyes, she thought to him, *It will all work out. I can feel the Mother with us. She will protect us and ensure the safety of our mission.*

Roska didn't bother responding. He didn't share Demoni's faith, but there was no point in arguing. She believed in the Mother Goddess and Her divine will. Roska was less sure of a higher power. If the Mother truly loved and cared for all of Her children, why the hells did She put him through such a torturous childhood? Why did any child have to suffer at the hands of evil men? If the Mother was truly as great and loving as believers claimed, why didn't She intervene?

Roska's eyes drifted closed as his mind wandered through the religious lies he'd been force-fed his whole childhood. His dreams were filled with images of doting mothers turning their backs on their children as they were taken away by faceless men dressed in the Brotherhood's garb to be punished for sins they had yet to commit.

✳✳ ✳✳✳ ✳✳

The morning came quickly with the angry caw of several roosters, rousing Roska suddenly from a restless sleep. The sun was just beginning to rise, a faint pink chasing away the deep purple of the night sky.

Shifting in his bed, Roska stretched his arms and tried to work the kinks out of his neck. Demoni uncoiled herself, flicking her tail from side to side and yawning so widely that Roska could count every single one of her tiny, knife-like teeth.

"Oh, good! You're up." Balor stormed into their room, entirely uninvited, with a pot of coffee in one hand and three mugs in the other. "The ladies kicked me out just before dawn. Apparently, they didn't want an audience while getting ready for the day." His smirk belied the disappointment in his words.

As much as Balor liked to pretend he was a "ladies' man"—his words—Roska was beginning to see that the giant of a man was actually a true gentleman. Roska was willing to bet that Asha and Zara hadn't sent him away at all. As women in the King's army, they were used to sharing barracks and showers with other soldiers, regardless of gender. Roska had seen both women relieve themselves on the side of the road over the course of their journey. It seemed far more likely that Balor had simply left their room, by choice, to give the women privacy.

Balor pulled a chair into the middle of their room, placing himself between the two beds, filled a mug, and handed it to Roska, who accepted it gratefully. He inhaled the steam and scent of coffee, allowing the alluring warmth to shake the last of the night's bad dreams from his mind.

"Goddess bless you," Miguel groaned, taking a mug for himself and wrapping his hands around the warm ceramic.

Balor chuckled at Miguel's dramatic moan as he took a long sip of the coffee, waggling his eyebrows at Roska. "You two have a good night?"

Blood rushed to Roska's face at the implication of Balor's comment, but Miguel just waved him off. "We met with the spy last night. The girl hasn't been moved, but his assessment leaves me to think that we need to acquire another horse."

Balor took a swig of his coffee. "Where do you suppose we get a new horse? Not like this town is crawling with extra... well, extra anything. I doubt anyone here would be willing to part with their workhorse."

Roska hadn't considered that. They were in a small farming hamlet. The only horses they were likely to find here would be workhorses. Built for strength, not speed. Even if they could find someone willing to sell, the horse wouldn't be very effective in their escape.

Miguel seemed to be coming to the same realization he had. "Mux. Ok. I guess one of us will have to double up."

"It will be me," Roska stated flatly. They were all putting their lives on the line to save Brigit. He wouldn't let them get slowed down and risk capture as well. "My horse is the strongest," he added. It was true. Niko had loaned Roska his own personal mount. The mare was built for strength *and* speed. She would easily be able to carry both him and Brigit, and then he could ensure her safety.

Balor and Miguel shared a look before Miguel nodded in agreement. Roska wasn't sure what the look meant, but he didn't have time to worry about that now.

"Let's go see if the ladies are ready. I'm hungry." Balor rose from his chair, swallowing the last of his coffee.

Roska finished his drink and followed Balor out the door, Miguel on his heels.

Zara and Asha were waiting for them in the dining area downstairs. Biscuits, bacon, eggs, and another large pot of coffee were spread out on the table before them.

"Food!" Balor cheered, pulling a chair out and piling obscene amounts of food onto a plate.

"Gods," Zara swore, eyes wide in mock horror. "You'd think he hadn't eaten in weeks by the way he acts."

Asha laughed, stealing a biscuit from Balor's overflowing plate. "Save some for the rest of us."

Roska and Miguel joined them at the table and they made quick work of the meal while Miguel filled the ladies in on their latest information.

"So we go tonight," Zara said, using a biscuit to soak up the last of the creamy white gravy from her plate.

"I'll get my devices set up as safely as I can here, then put in the final pieces to create an explosive diversion once we get to their walls." Asha's grin at the prospect of blowing things up made Roska a little anxious. He'd yet to see her in action and he wasn't sure what to expect.

The final plan was for Balor to accompany Asha, in case she ran into any Brothers while setting her charges. Zara would sneak in through the sewers and meet Lou along the edge of the courtyard on the far west side of the compound, and he would take her to Brigit. Miguel and Roska would be waiting by the side garden gate—their intended escape route—with the horses. Balor and Asha would set the charges and disappear into the nearby woods. They would all meet up at a fork in the river at dawn.

Unfortunately, things never quite go according to plan.

Chapter 13

A SHA'S "SMALL, BUT DRAMATIC" explosion shook the ground and startled the horses where Roska and Miguel lay in wait on the far side of the compound. He didn't want to think about the amount of damage she'd just inflicted on the centuries-old fortress. Right on cue, he heard shouts of alarm and racing footsteps as the Brothers rushed to defend themselves.

"Zara should be breaching the sewers now," Miguel whispered from his crouched position beside Roska.

Roska tried to picture the scene in his head. He imagined standing in the courtyard, facing the large fountain in the center of the space. This time of year, the fountain would be filled with crystal clear water, cascading down a highly polished marble waterfall, babbling peacefully in the quiet of the night. The fountain would be surrounded by stone benches at the cardinal points and lush greenery encircling it all. There were cobblestone paths leading to the benches and around the fountain. It was honestly one of the few places Roska had truly enjoyed during his time with the Brotherhood.

Zara would be pushing aside the drainage grate that had been dug into the ground behind the western bench. From there, she'd creep through the greenery until she found Lou. Together, they would sneak through the halls until they reached the room where the Brothers were keeping Brigit. Based on the description and location Lou had given them, Roska knew the Brothers were keeping her in his old room. His cell. They probably thought it was poetic. Roska thought it was cruel and heartless, but those words could easily be used to describe all of the Brotherhood's actions since their conception.

Roska watched the clouds slowly drift across the night sky. The smoke from Asha's bomb faded away and the shouting died down to quick commands and hurried footsteps.

"Something's wrong," Roska thought aloud.

✳✻ ✳✻ ✳✻

Something was definitely wrong. From her cell, Brigit could hear the shouts of warning and heavy footsteps as the Brothers raced around overhead. Something had exploded. The impact of it had roused her from yet another nightmare. Standing on her toes, she strained to see what was going on outside the tiny window of her room. Unsurprisingly, she saw nothing.

"*Cherie*," came a harsh whisper from beyond the thick door that trapped her in this godsforsaken prison.

"Pierre?"

"Who the mux is Pierre?" A female voice sounded suspicious and annoyed through the door.

"Aye, *cherie*, it's me. We've come to take you home."

Her heart lept in her chest. *Home.* She was finally going to leave this hells.

"Stand back," the harsh female voice said. "I'm going to set some charges along the hinges and blow the door open."

Brigit nodded, then realized the woman couldn't see her. She stepped against the far wall and shouted as loudly as she dared, "I'm clear."

A small spark, followed by a moderately loud pop preceded the door being forcefully shoved open. Standing in the doorway, Brigit realized that the woman wasn't a woman at all, but a female Fae.

There was a hint of pointed ears peeking out under the hood of her cloak, shielding most of her face from view. Her sharp eyes seemed to assess Brigit as she breached the room.

"Can you walk?" she asked bluntly.

"Yes."

"Can you ride?"

Brigit hesitated. "I... well, I ne'er have before. And wit this"—she held up her ruined hand—"I'm no sure I'd be able to hold on."

"Not to worry, *cherie*." Pierre's kind voice drifted into the room from where he stood in the hall. "We have a shortage of horses, as it were, so you'll be riding with someone regardless."

"We need to get moving." The Fae peeked out the cell window—Brigit noted irritably that the female was at least a head and a half taller than her and could see out the small window without issue. "They'll be onto us soon enough."

Brigit followed them out the busted door. She didn't have shoes or a cloak. The Brothers had stripped her down to her chemise when she'd first arrived. She had no idea what had become of her clothing. Still, she followed after her rescuers, bare feet padding silently over the cold stone floors.

Just as they reached a small, wooden door along the western side of the compound, Brigit heard him. The voice of her tormentor. The voice that haunted her dreams.

"And where do you think you're going?" Grand Maester Auron spoke calmly as he grabbed a fistful of her matted red locks.

The female drew a dagger and hurled it at the Grand Maester without hesitation. It speared the man in the meat of his forearm, forcing him to release his hold on Brigit.

Pierre pulled Brigit behind him, blocking her view as the Grand Maester growled, ripping the blade from his skin. Blood immediately began to flow from the wound, but the Fae didn't stop there. She pulled three more daggers from within the folds of her cloak, throwing them rapidly and with deadly accuracy, striking the Grand Maester in both thighs and his other arm.

"Get her out of here," she hissed. "She is the mission. I'll handle this and meet up with you when I'm done."

Pierre seemed uncertain, but one last—rather vicious—look from the Fae and he grasped Brigit's arm, leading her through the door and freedom.

* * * * * *

Shouts of rage echoed through the stone walls as the small door was thrust open and Roska got his first glimpse of Brigit.

She was gaunt and pale, although he couldn't be sure if that was because she was backlit by the torchlight pouring through the open door, or perhaps the light of the full moon washed out her skin tone. Her hair had faded from a vibrant red with bouncing curls, to a dull orange, matted and flat. She seemed to be walking with a limp, but that could have been because Lou was practically dragging her along behind him. Everything in Roska screamed at him to run to her, wrap her in his arms, and carry her to safety. But he couldn't do that. For all he knew, she didn't even remember him. He refused to overwhelm her and invade her space. Especially since she would never have been taken and tortured if it weren't for him.

"Where's Zara?" Miguel whispered harshly.

Lou waved him off. "She'll be along shortly. Tying up a loose end."

"You left her behind?" Roska's voice was harsher than he intended. Seeing the state of abuse Brigit was in had broken something inside him. Rage flowed through his veins and he struggled to contain his power. She'd been through so much; she didn't need to see him lose control, too.

Amusement sparkled in Lou's eyes. "Have *you* ever tried to tell that female no?"

Miguel chuckled as he collected the horses from their hiding spot deeper in the trees. "Good point. Don't worry, Ros. Zara goes on plenty of solo missions. She'll catch up. We should get going." He handed Roska the reins to his mare. "Lou, will you be joining us?"

The sly man shook his head. "Not this time. My mission isn't complete. I'll meet up with you when I can."

With a quick nod, Lou disappeared into the night, leaving the three of them alone. Roska watched Brigit, studying her every movement.

What if she doesn't remember me? he thought nervously to Demoni.

Now really isn't the time... We need to get her to safety, then we can worry about her feelings for you.

Knowing she was right, Roska spoke quickly, avoiding any pleasantries as he offered to help Brigit onto his horse. "If it's all right with you, I'll lift you up."

Brigit studied him shrewdly for a moment, then offered a silent nod. Roska placed his hands firmly—but as gently as possible—on her hips and moved to lift her onto the mare's saddle. She placed her hands on his shoulders to steady herself, and that's when he saw it. Her left hand was a crumpled mess of battered flesh and bone. He tried to quell the rising rage as he hoisted her onto the mare. Brigit shifted awkwardly for a moment, her dress forced scandalously high up her thighs as she sat astride the horse. Roska pointedly looked away, trying to offer her as much privacy as he could in this moment.

He mounted the mare behind her, grabbing the reins with both hands. "If this is uncomfortable, please let me know. I don't want you to fall from the horse, but I want to respect your space as well."

The woman had endured unimaginable torture for Goddess only knew how long. He didn't want to push her boundaries. He just wanted her to be safe.

"This is fine," she said quietly. Her arms brushed against his own and he noticed just how cold her skin felt. Pulling the enchanted cloak tighter around them both, he turned to face Miguel, who waited in the shadows atop his own horse.

They turned from the compound and rode off into the woods, just as the sounds of thundering footsteps and angry shouts echoed out from the small door left open in the compound's wall.

✳✳ ✳✳ ✳✳ ✳

He'd come for her. Brigit was still in shock at having been rescued by the only man she'd ever felt a real connection with. His body was practically flush against her as they rode through the woods, fleeing the hells that she'd been trapped in for gods-only-knew how long. Brigit basked in the warmth of his thighs pressed against hers, his arms wrapped around her waist, holding him to her as though he never wanted to let her go again.

Realistically, Brigit knew he was only holding onto her so tightly because he feared she'd fall from the mare. She'd seen the look on his face when she'd touched him with her ruined hand. He was disgusted by it.

How could he not be? Brigit had never been a prize to begin with. Now, thanks to those sons of bitches, she was nothing but damaged goods. She would be a burden to any man.

Still, she couldn't help but curl into him just a bit more, pressing her back into his chest and soaking up the heat he provided.

Granted, his body wasn't much warmer than hers, which concerned her a bit. But his arms tightened at her waist—*purely a reflex*, she told herself—and leaned her head back on his shoulder.

Gods, she was so tired.

Chapter 14

T HEY RODE IN SILENCE as the sun rose in the sky. Brigit hadn't spoken a word, which was understandable, but Roska's mind wouldn't stop racing.

Lou had warned him that Brigit had been tortured and permanently injured, but knowing something and *seeing* it were two very different things. It had taken all of his self-control to rein in his frost so he wouldn't freeze her as he'd lifted Brigit onto the mare. Those muxing Brothers had destroyed her hand. Scars marred the previously soft skin of her left hand. Vicious ropes of thick, raised tissue, the clear result of her hand having been smashed and the bones puncturing the skin in several places. Her nails seemed warped and jagged, and her fingers looked to be permanently stuck in a half-clenched position. Roska wondered if she'd be able to use that hand at all.

The healers in Riverayn will be able to help her. You have to stop fixating on it, though. You know better than most, the scars don't define a person unless you let *them.* Demoni's cool words soothed his frayed nerves some. She was right. Brigit was more than the marks on her flesh. She was a muxing goddess, and she was far braver than he'd ever been.

In the back of his mind, he wondered about the rest of their crew. Was Zara all right? Did she make it out of the compound?

Where were Balor and Asha? What other mission did Lou have to complete in the Brotherhood's compound? No matter how hard he tried, though, his mind kept turning back to Brigit and his concerns for her mental and physical state.

Getting her out of the Brotherhood's grasp was the easy part. Now they needed to help her heal. Physically and mentally. The wounds that marred her body would heal far quicker than the ones that scarred her soul. Roska wondered if she would ever be that carefree, quick-to-smile girl he'd met back in Nexton again.

She's been through an ordeal, that's true. But she's here. Alive. That shows just how strong she is. She will recover. She might not be the same girl she was before, but you would be a fool to expect that. Demoni adjusted her position on his shoulder, nudging his cheek with her chilly, scaled nose. *But you aren't a fool. You'll give her the space she needs and be there to talk if and when she's ready.*

Roska wanted to reach up and scratch under his tiny dragon's chin, but he didn't quite trust his skills as a horseman to drop the reins, and the way Brigit was leaning into him, he suspected she might have drifted off to sleep. Instead, Roska pressed the side of his face into her scales and rubbed her side with his cheek in thanks.

Roska knew it would probably be a while before Brigit was ready to open up about all that she'd endured in the compound, but he would be waiting. Now that she was safe, he had all the time in the world.

❋ ❋ ❋ ❋ ❋ ❋

They were supposed to regroup at the bend in the river northwest of the Brotherhood's compound at dusk. The sun had well and

120

truly set and the others still hadn't made it to the meeting spot. Roska was worried.

"Where are they?" he asked for what felt like the millionth time.

"They'll be here," Miguel reassured him, stoking their fire and turning over the leaf wraps.

Roska, Miguel, and Brigit had arrived at the river hours before dusk and had set up camp. Demoni fished dinner for them all, Miguel built the fire, Brigit wrapped the fish in large leaves from the trees along the riverside, and Roska paced nervously along the treeline. He wasn't the most adept at hunting and camping—that was more Quinn's purview—and he felt useless. He kept watch, though, constantly looking through the trees and praying to the Mother for a sign of their crewmates.

"Have some tea." Brigit came to join him as he studied the shadows in the trees. "Worryin' won't make 'em appear any faster."

Roska silently chided himself. Brigit had just spent solar cycles in his old cell with the Brothers. The scars on her legs and her ruined hand could only hint at the hells she'd endured. And yet, here she was comforting *him*.

"Thank you," he said, taking the steaming mug and smiling down at her gratefully. Thankful for the tea, but more so for her physical presence. The tangibility of her was soothing, calming his anxiety and putting things into sharp perspective.

Her lips turned up into the barest hint of a smile before she turned away and went back to tending the fire. Roska watched her walk through the tall grass looking ethereal in her thin, flowing white gown, bare feet disappearing in the lush green of the planting season. The wind blew along the river, causing the leaves to rustle in the trees and the fire to flicker and dance.

Brigit rubbed her arm with her good hand, and Roska instantly felt like an idiot.

"Are you cold?" he asked, stepping up and taking the enchanted cloak off his back. Without waiting for a response, he wrapped the thick wool around her shoulders, closing the clasp under her chin. His fingers gently brushed her collarbone as he positioned the cloak properly. Her skin was chilled, much like his own, but that was normal for him.

As the prophesized FrostBorn, his body naturally functioned at a cooler temperature than most. Brigit, on the other hand, was a perfectly normal human, and as such, she should not have felt cold to the touch. She was likely freezing. *Why hadn't she said anything?*

"Thank ye." She blushed, grasping the edge of the cloak and wrapping it tightly around her bad arm. "I swear, I had more clothes when they took me." Humor twinkled in her eyes as she looked up at him.

Miguel chuckled at her dark joke. Brigit's eyes flicked to the back of his dark, curly head, a hint of a smile tugging at her lips once more.

She astounded him. While Roska didn't know the details of her experience with the Brothers, the scars that marred her body told a very violent story. How she could find humor in this was beyond him. Roska had been completely closed off and disconnected for many moons after he'd left the Brothers.

But she wasn't let go. She was rescued. Maybe that makes a difference? Demoni canted her head, watching Brigit fiddle with the cloak's clasp. His frost dragon was just as baffled by the woman's resilience as he was.

Whatever it was that enabled Brigit to joke about her abduction and subsequent torture and abuse, Roska admired dearly. He was about to voice that feeling when they heard a shuffle in the woods behind them.

Spinning quickly on his heels, Roska positioned himself between Brigit and the source of the noise, drawing on his power to form a pair of wicked ice daggers in his palms. He would not let them take her again. In a heartbeat, Miguel was by his side, guarding Brigit as well, with his own blades at the ready.

They studied the trees in the growing darkness, flinching at the slightest sound, for several tense seconds. Quinn had warned Roska about fire blindness, and Roska was kicking himself now. His eyes had grown accustomed to the light provided by the flames, and now he was struggling to see anything in the shadows of the trees.

"Stay with her." Roska's voice was barely a whisper as he stepped farther into the woods.

Demoni slipped from his shoulders and crept ahead of him. If they were lucky, they'd be able to catch their stalkers by surprise.

Roska heard voices a few paces ahead, so he crouched low behind a thick fir tree, gripping his daggers tightly as he prepared to attack.

"Gods, you reek." A familiar male voice broke the silence of the woods.

"Well, you would too if your horse had gotten spooked and tossed you into a pile of wolf shyt."

The answering guffaw startled Roska at first. But he quickly recognized that carefree laugh.

Balor.

Roska stepped out from behind the tree, directly into the path of the beast of a man and his considerably smaller female companion.

Balor drew his axe in an instant, leveling the blade at Roska's throat before quickly lowering it when he realized who stood in their way.

"Ros! I nearly cut your head off. What the mux, man?" Balor chided, but the giant grin plastered across his face took the bite from his words.

"I don't know if I should be impressed that you snuck up on us or ashamed that you caught us both unprepared," Asha chuckled and clapped Roska on the back in greeting.

"Gods, you truly smell terrible," Roska said, crinkling his nose in disgust. "Where are your horses? What the hells happened to you two?"

"It's a long story," Balor answered. "Got any food? I'm starving."

Asha rolled her eyes. "When are you not?"

Roska led them back to camp, sending Demoni ahead to let Miguel and Brigit know all was well.

Miguel whispered something to Brigit as Roska led Balor and Asha into the clearing. Nodding, she turned from where she'd been half-hidden behind him and knelt by the fire. She began unwrapping the fish from the leaves they'd been baking in and laying them out on fresh leaves that would serve as their plates for the evening.

Roska introduced Brigit to Asha and Balor. Brigit was quiet, but kind, giving them both a small nod and a smile. She offered them each a fish bundle as they took a seat on some large rocks around the campfire. In the light of the fire, Roska could see that not only was Asha covered in shyt, but both of them were bleeding. Balor from his axe arm, his shirtsleeve torn by what looked like claws. Asha had a cut above her right eye, some shallow scratches on her cheek, and a deep gash in her thigh. Roska was surprised she hadn't been limping.

"So, you want to explain how you lost two of the King's horses?" Miguel asked as he settled onto his own stone chair and pulled a waterskin from his pack.

"It's not that simple," Balor started, but Asha waved him off with a dismissive gesture.

"We were ambushed." She took the water Miguel offered, swallowing several long pulls before handing it to Balor and continuing. "Muxing wolves. They were hunting our horses as soon as we mounted them."

Balor choked on his fish, laughing at her word choice.

"Oh, shut up and eat. You're such a child." Asha's cheeks darkened as she chided Balor.

"And then...?" Miguel prompted, getting Asha back on point.

"Right. So we're fleeing the explosion, being hunted by muxing wolves, when this massive wolf comes out of nowhere! I didn't think wolves hunted like that, but somehow, they'd split up and this big muxing bastard jumped out in front of my horse, spooking her and sending me flying."

"Right into a fresh pile of wolf shyt!" Balor cut in, cackling as he remembered the moment.

Asha's glare would have melted a lesser man. Balor, however, was entirely unfazed as he continued to laugh while shoving fish into his mouth. "It was muxing glorious," he added around a mouthful of food.

"Oh, yes, being thrown from a terrified horse while surrounded by wolves is great entertainment. I can't wait to do it again," Asha deadpanned, glaring daggers at Balor.

"So, anyway, I jumped from my horse to kill the big daddy wolf while Asha here pulled herself out of the shyt. My horse took off, chased by the rest of the pack." Balor finished the story with a casual shrug.

"Would ye like me to tend to those cuts?" Brigit spoke softly and kept her eyes down.

Roska was grateful to see that Balor seemed to pick up on Brigit's anxiety and visibly tried to make himself as small and non-threatening as he could before he answered her. "I'm all right, darlin', but it's kind of you to offer."

Asha was about to speak—most likely to decline as well—when Miguel spoke up. "That gash on Asha's leg looks like it needs to be cleaned and stitched. How are you with a needle, Brigit?"

"I'm decent." She looked up and smiled at him.

"Boil some water, and I'll get my herbs to help speed along her healing. Can't have that leg getting infected. We need to get back to the capital as quickly as possible." He looked pointedly at Asha as he spoke. Daring her to argue. Instead, she merely grunted, muttering something about not needing any damn stitches, but she didn't fight him.

Brigit grabbed their water bucket and headed toward the stream. It was only a few paces away, but Roska didn't want her out of his sight. Not yet, anyway. He rose and followed after her.

"Thank you for helping take care of them," he said once they were out of earshot. "I know Asha is too proud to say anything, but that wound looks bad. She'll be grateful for your care, even if she doesn't say it."

"O' course." She beamed up at him from where she knelt by the riverside. "I'm happy to be of use. 'specially since neither of 'em would be here if it weren't for me."

Roska debated responding at first but decided honesty would be best. "Actually, we've been planning to take down the Brotherhood for moons. We moved up our timeline and shifted the mission objective when we learned they had you, but I fully intend to tear that compound to the ground."

Brigit watched him, seeming to study him and weigh his words. Rising with the now full bucket in her hands, she locked eyes with him. "I canna fathom the hells ye went through wit those monsters. I haird 'em complainin' about how ye betrayed 'em. That damned Grand Maester raged about it several times. Goin' on about how they'd taken ye in an' raised ye."

Roska looked away. He didn't want her to see the shame in his eyes. He hated the Grand Maester, and yet hearing that the man was disappointed in him still hurt far more than he wanted to admit.

Cold fingers gently touched his cheeks. Brigit placed both hands ever-so-lightly on his skin. Not forcing him to look at her, but encouraging it. Roska tried to blink away his tears before letting his eyes find hers again.

"I dinna give a flyin' shyt what that vile bastard says about ye." Her fingers tightened slightly as she said the next words slowly and deliberately. "Ye saved me. Ye risked everythin' to rescue me. Nothin' that man says about ye is true. Ye are a godsdamned hero, Roska."

The outpouring of adoration that glowed in her eyes shook him to his core.

He did not deserve this woman.

Chapter 15

The next morning, over a breakfast of biscuits, jam, and coffee, they began discussing next steps. Brigit only half listened, knowing she was just along for the ride regardless.

"The King is going to have your ear for losing not one, but two, of his best horses." Miguel chuckled as he spoke, but Brigit was taken aback by his words. The King was going to take an ear from them because they were attacked by a pack of wild animals? Gods, he really was as cruel as folks in the village had always said.

Her disgust must've shown on her face because Roska nudged her knee with his own. "Everything all right?" he asked gently.

"Oh, aye." She nodded. It wouldn't do any good for her to express her dislike of the King. She'd never actually met the man. All of her opinions of him were based on secondhand stories of his insatiable lust, disregard for consent, and overall greedy behavior. Like as not, their King would simply instruct them to steal—sorry, *commandeer*—a few horses in the next town to replenish what was lost.

"You sure about that, dear?" Asha asked. "Your face seems to be telling a different story." Her smile wasn't unkind, but it did seem guarded. Although that could have just been Brigit projecting her own self-preservation instincts.

"It's none o' my business." Brigit hoped that would be answer enough. She should have known better.

"Speak your mind, darlin'. No one's judging here." Balor offered her a fresh biscuit and a warm smile.

Brigit worried her lower lip, debating her options. She trusted Roska—from what little time she'd spent with him, he'd seemed like a kind man. If he trusted this crew, then she ought to as well, she reasoned. Not to mention, they'd all just risked their lives to save her.

She stared at the food in her lap, tearing her biscuit into tiny pieces as she spoke. "Well, it's just that I dinna kin how four such honorable souls, such as yerselves, can be so willingly tethered to such an arrogant, self-righteous tyrant." She hadn't meant to blurt it out so bluntly, but she'd never been very good at biting her tongue.

No one said a word. Nervously, Brigit looked up from her destroyed biscuit to see four pairs of eyes, wide and baffled, staring openly at her.

"I'm sorry. It wasna my place to—" she began, but Roska cut her off, placing a cool hand on her fidgeting fingers.

"It's ok. You don't have to apologize. Everyone is entitled to their opinion." His reassuring words and kind touch brought her eyes back up to study his face. "But I think perhaps you have the wrong King in mind. The King you described is dead. King Niko rules the country now. He's about as different from his father as humanly possible. And," he added with a proud smile, "he's engaged to marry my sister."

Niko. The prince? People had rarely spoken of him, except to admire his beauty.

"Engaged?" Brigit's mind couldn't wrap around the idea of the popular—and often described as promiscuous—Prince had become King *and* settled down? "Wait, ye have a sister? I thought it was just ye an' yer brother." Brigit remembered the blond boy from the inn back in Nexton. He'd been kind and sweet, if a bit full of himself.

"Yes." Roska sat back, his smile turning inward. "I have a brother, Quinn, whom you met before. But we also have a sister. We are triplets. Our mother is the headmistress at the school for enchantresses, Harbor Ridge. You already met our father as well. Do you remember Aiden? He's a demi-god."

Brigit's emotions must have been written all over her face again because Roska's inward smile quickly turned into a bright red blush. His eyes dropped to his lap, suddenly very interested in the hem of his tunic.

"My life is a bit more... complicated than I let on before." He looked up at her from beneath his near-white eyelashes.

Complicated seemed like a massive understatement.

Deity father. Triplets. Magical mother.

"Anythin' else I should know?" she teased, desperately trying to take everything in stride.

"Um..." he hedged, but sighed, seeming to accept something. "There's this." He held up his hand, cool mist pouring from his open palm. Then, without warning, a snowball appeared in his hand. Then it shifted, turning harder and taking the shape of a dagger that appeared to be made entirely of ice. "I'm Frost-Born. The first one in over a hundred solar cycles, according to my father. Elena is StormBorn and has lightning running through her veins. Quinn is FlameBorn. He can control and manipulate fire. You might have noticed his fox. She has fire powers very similar to Q's. Demoni here," he lifted a small dragon from around his neck, settling her in his lap, "is my familiar. She has frost powers as well."

Brigit stared, unblinking, at the dagger in his hand. It looked familiar. "Ye made these last night, did ye no'? I thought I saw weapons in yer hands, just before they showed up. They dinna look like typical daggers, but I dinna realize..." Her voice trailed off as she stared at the magical weapons in his hands.

"Gods," she whispered. "Yer amazing."

*　*　*　*　*　*　*

Heat flushed his face as Roska looked away from her awe-filled gaze.

Roska was relieved beyond words by Brigit's reaction to his powers. He hadn't been sure how to tell her about everything; he'd been so tightlipped about his family and their origins when he'd last seen her. Back then, he hadn't really expected to see her again, so he hadn't seen the point. Now, though, seeing her so fixated on—and amazed by—his powers was more than he could have ever hoped for.

He quickly recalled his powers, causing the daggers to vanish. Brigit gasped, but that heart-warming smile never left her face.

Roska was at a loss for words. He'd never expected her to be so welcoming and accepting of his magic and the secrets he'd kept from her. Especially since those secrets were the reason she'd been taken in the first place. He had no idea what to say or do next.

Thankfully, Miguel seemed to pick up on his uncertainty and announced that it was time to get moving. Roska—begrudgingly—gave up his seat on the mare behind Brigit to Asha. Asha couldn't walk with her newly sewn leg and it would be a while before Brigit could regain enough strength to be able to keep up with the pace Miguel set.

The day passed quickly, with Balor disappearing once or twice to backtrack and see if he could find any sign of Zara as well as covering their tracks to ensure the Brothers wouldn't be able to follow them. Miguel kept reassuring Roska that Zara would be fine. Half-fae that she was, she was more comfortable in the woods than any level of civilization. Not to mention, apparently, she was a favored assassin and was used to working alone. According to Miguel, this was one of only a handful of missions Zara had been assigned that included a team. She'd be fine, he promised. Roska tried to relax and trust Miguel's judgment. This was clearly his world, even if it all seemed stressful and foreign to Roska.

They ate a light lunch without stopping, trying to put as much distance between themselves and the compound as possible.

❄ ❄ ❄ ❄ ❄ ❄

At dusk, Miguel announced it was time to make camp, picking a spot along the river as they all fell into their now routine nightly chores. Roska pulled three tents out of the enchanted cloak's pockets, and with Balor's help, they had a decent, cozy campsite set up. Brigit, despite her objections, looked completely exhausted. Miguel sent her to bed with Asha, disregarding the latter's protests that she was fine.

Miguel pulled Asha aside and whispered something in her ear. Roska couldn't hear exactly what he said, but he caught Brigit's name in the hushed exchange and determined—based on Asha's quick change in attitude and sudden willingness to stay in the tent—that Miguel had assigned her to be Brigit's personal guard, should the Brothers come looking for her.

Roska took first watch. He was too wired to sleep, anyway. Plus, Balor looked drained, and Miguel hadn't slept for more than an hour at a time since the night they'd stayed in the inn of that small farming hamlet. Once the other men were settled in their respective tents, Roska positioned himself on the forest floor, leaning against a tree stump with his back to their dwindling fire. He would keep the embers burning, but he refused to risk any more fire blindness. Demoni curled up on the stump behind him, keeping watch across the glowing embers and into the woods beyond.

You're spiraling. I can hear your thoughts racing. It's giving me a headache.

Roska huffed a quiet laugh. *You've been spending too much time with Lyra. Her snark is rubbing off on you.*

Is it snark? Or is it just blunt honesty? Demoni flicked her tail into the back of his ear.

Probably a bit of both, although complaining that my *thoughts are giving* you *a headache seems more like a you problem than honesty.*

And now you sound like you've been spending too much time with Elena.

Roska laughed again, less quietly. Clamping one hand over his mouth to avoid waking anyone, he used the other to flick a small snowball over his shoulder, nailing Demoni in the middle of her back. She hissed at him but didn't retaliate.

They sat in companionable silence for the next few hours, looking out for any sign of threats within the shadows of the trees that surrounded them. Roska knew his thoughts were still spiraling, and he was sure Demoni had plenty more to say on the topic, but they didn't discuss it again.

They both knew that nothing she'd say would make a differ-ence. He had too much trauma to deal with—being told since birth that he was worthless and a plague on the earth had a pretty damning effect on his self-worth. One late-night conversation with Demoni wouldn't fix that. Even the love and affection from his family wouldn't fix him. Nothing external could fix his internal struggles. He had demons in his mind that only he could fight. Demoni would be a great help in his internal battle, but she had her own monsters to slay. They might share a soul—and a *highly* traumatic childhood—but they were separate beings and would have to deal with their problems as such.

Eventually. But not now. Now, they needed to focus on getting Brigit back to the safety of Riverayn and get her started on her journey to recovery.

That sounds like avoidance to me, Demoni chimed in.

Sounds like self-preservation to me.

Chapter 16

A FTER HER OPEN KINDNESS, Roska had shut down and avoided being alone with Brigit—in an effort to protect himself, he'd told Demoni, but she'd called him out for it. Accusing him of cowardice. He refused to admit it, but he knew she was partially right. Roska couldn't risk getting attached to Brigit. He knew she'd want to go back to Nexton and her safe life in the inn as soon as she was able. No point in getting attached to someone who would leave the first chance they got.

They'd spent two days slowly trekking along the riverside, trying not to jostle Asha's leg too much and regularly changing her bandages. Miguel was an impressive healer, but Asha was a miserable patient. She never wanted to sit still long enough for Miguel to properly wrap her leg. After the third attempt, in which Asha ripped the linen bandage when Miguel was only halfway through wrapping it, Miguel snapped.

"I swear to the Mother, if you don't muxing sit still, I'm going to have Balor hold you down. Nothing should be *this* hard, Asha." Miguel pinned her with a vicious glare while Balor tried to cover his laughter. Asha finally relented long enough for Miguel to get her bandages straight, and then she and Brigit mounted Roska's mare once more as they slowly continued along the riverside back toward the capital. Balor, Roska, and Miguel stayed on foot.

Miguel's horse had been re-designated as their pack horse, loading it down with all of their supplies so that Roska's mare could focus on carrying two riders.

It was incredibly slow going, which was why Roska hadn't been at all surprised when Zara rode up to join them by midmorning on the third day.

"I thought you'd be halfway to the capital by now," she said, slowing her horse to meet the strides of theirs.

"Yeah, no shyt," Balor grumbled. He'd been complaining about their pace since they left.

"Well, we would be moving quicker, but *some* of us lost our mounts before ever leaving the compound," Miguel teased, but there was no real bite to his words. Everyone knew the loss of the horses—while unfortunate—was a result of things beyond their control and therefore no one's fault.

"What happened to you?" Roska asked, taking in Zara's blood-soaked tunic and her torn cloak. The hood seemed to have been ripped clean off.

"Turns out, the Brothers dislike Fae even more than they dislike enchantresses." She spoke flatly, but Roska thought he heard a hint of rage boiling just below the surface. Zara turned her head, giving him a glimpse of her left ear. Blood matted her hair, and it looked as though her ear was only partially attached. "I was running out of throwing knives, but I had that damn Grand Maester trapped in a corner when a couple of big muxers came out of nowhere and pinned me in. That damned leader of theirs was so smug. He pulled one of my own daggers from his arm and..." She gestured to her bloody ear.

"Gods, they tried to cut your ear off?" Roska felt sick. He knew the Brothers were cruel, but this sort of racist violence seemed over the top, even for them.

Zara nodded slowly, gingerly touching her torn ear and wincing at the contact. "I think they wanted to keep them as trophies. One of the sick bastards was shouting about getting a jar to put them in."

"Those muxing monsters," Asha swore, pivoting in her seat to get a better look at Zara. "Gimme five minutes and I'll have the perfect present for them." There was rage in her voice as well. "They won't know what hit them."

"That's too good for them." Brigit's voice was soft, nearly drowned out by the babbling of the river and the rustle of the leaves overhead, but the strength in her words floored him.

Roska didn't know how to respond, but Miguel did.

"Don't worry. They'll get exactly what's coming to them. We'll make sure of it."

Miguel pulled a large linen wrap from his pack along with some clean cloths and a bottle of pure alcohol. Zara dismounted long enough for him to clean her wound and wrap her entire head to keep the ear clean and attached. "That's the best I can do for now. We'll get the healers to patch you up properly when we get home."

❄ ❄ ❄ ❄ ❄ ❄

That evening, as they made camp along the riverside, Brigit watched Roska and Miguel move with practiced efficiency as they set up their tent and began to unpack the cookware while Balor went off in search of fish and Zara and Asha collected firewood.

Brigit was still nervous, but she was finally starting to breathe easier, knowing that this troupe of skilled fighters was protecting her. They had her back, and she could trust that they would keep her safe. Brigit pulled Roska's cloak tighter around her shoulders, taking her first proper deep breath in cycles. She strolled slowly over to stand by the soon-to-be fire circle and stared unseeingly into the woods.

"I'm sorry I didn't think to bring you clothes," Roska said as he came to stand beside her. He looked as though he was considering wrapping his arms around her again, but he stopped himself.

Brigit couldn't blame him. Roska was a beautiful, powerful man. He could have anyone he wanted. He didn't need to shackle himself to a broken bar wench out of some misplaced sense of responsibility.

"Ach, no. This is more than enough, thank ye." She rubbed her hands up and down her arms, creating a bit of friction within the cloak. She was chilled, sure enough, but more than that, she felt terribly exposed. Her mother would have berated her for her lack of attire, despite the fact that she'd been tortured and imprisoned. Her mother, narrow-minded woman that she was, would have had quite a few comments on Brigit's current predicament.

Miguel came to stand at Brigit's other side, glancing quickly between the two of them before offering her a waterskin and a warm smile.

Brigit accepted the drink with a smile of her own and took a long swig.

Miguel nodded and knelt before them, clearing the last of the woodland debris and creating a firebreak with stones to encircle their fire. "I have a spare tunic, if you'd like," he offered without looking up. "It's not much, but it would be an added layer, if you're chilled."

"I'm fine, I swear," she began, but was quickly cut off by a stern look from the curly-haired man kneeling before her.

"Respectfully, your lips are blue. On him"—Miguel nodded to Roska—"that's normal. On you, it's unsettling."

Brigit balked for a moment, but then Miguel smiled widely at her over his shoulder. He was teasing. Gods, Brigit had forgotten what it felt like to just relax and enjoy a moment with someone.

"Aye, if ye insist, Captain." Brigit grinned, using the title she'd heard Balor throw at Miguel once or twice, typically with a hint of mockery in his tone.

Roska chuckled to her left as Miguel rose and stepped toward her. In someone else, the move might have seemed threatening, but with Miguel, it seemed more playful. He stood before her, locking eyes with her for a breath, then grabbed the hem of his tunic and pulled it over his head. Standing before her in all his tanned and toned glory, Brigit forgot to breathe for a moment. Her eyes instantly flew to the hard planes of his chest and abdomen, but her view was suddenly obstructed when a weight of warm cloth landed on her head.

Reaching up, she removed his shirt from her face to see a huge grin splitting the cocky man's face.

Without a word, he strode to his mare and pulled a fresh tunic from his saddle bags. He pulled it on and turned back to face her, still grinning like a fool.

"You might want to put that on quick. It won't hold my warmth forever." With that, the smug arsehole turned on his heel and ventured into the woods.

Brigit blinked, frozen in place and completely oblivious to the world around her.

"Well, that was entertaining." Roska's voice shocked Brigit back to reality.

She quickly turned to face him, worried that she'd upset or offended him somehow, but was surprised to see a flush in Roska's cheeks that she was sure matched her own. Roska locked eyes with her, and for a split second, she thought he might touch her.

His hand seemed to twitch at his side before he tightened his fingers into a firm clench.

"Would you..." he began, then swallowed and tried again. "What I mean is, um, if you need some... help with that, I can, uh, I can help you get dressed." He said the last few words on a rapid breath, as though he was scared if he didn't say it quickly, he wouldn't be able to get the words out at all.

Handsome as ever and still so shy.

"Aye, I'd appreciate that." Brigit reached up to undo the clasp on the cloak, only to fumble it with her ruined hand. The flush on her cheeks instantly curdled as she felt a wave of embarrassment wash over her.

Roska, either oblivious to her botched attempt at undoing the cloak or—more likely—too kind to react to it, stepped up and unhooked the clasp with ease. Brigit shrugged out of the warm cloak, laying it atop the nearest tent for a moment while Roska took the tunic and gently looped it over her head. He pulled the cloth down her body, his fingertips brushing her thighs as he straightened the bottom of the long tunic. Brigit's skin tingled where his cool fingers made contact, but she tried desperately to contain her reaction.

Roska reached behind her, reclaiming the cloak from where she'd laid it, and wrapped it around her once more.

He beamed down at her, warmth in his gaze, and—impossibly—a hint of teal light seemed to glow in his eyes as he closed the clasp. His fingers traced her skin, ever-so-lightly, where the cloak ended and her oversensitive flesh lay exposed to his touch.

Brigit's heart skipped a beat as she closed her eyes and leaned into the feel of him. Memories flooded her mind of the last time they'd been together. He'd come to say goodbye at the inn in Nexton. Brigit had known Roska, Quinn, and their father wouldn't stay at the inn forever, but it had still hurt when they'd left. She'd had to fight back the urge to throw her arms around him and ask him to stay—not to mention more than a few tears—as she bid him farewell.

Now, he stood before her, fingers sending flares of heat and tingles through her body. She opened her eyes again to find him staring down at her so intently she thought she might collapse under the weight of his gaze. In the back of her mind, she knew if she did fall, he would catch her.

The sound of footsteps and conversation shattered the moment, both of them quickly taking a step back as though they were about to be caught in a compromising position.

They had been, Brigit realized. She had been seconds away from throwing caution to the wind and kissing that beautiful man.

Gods, she needed to get a handle on herself. Even if Roska had felt the same magnetic pull that she had, he couldn't be with her. He was the son of a god and the most powerful enchantress in the country. He was the product of prophecy. He was the muxing brother-in-law to the muxing *King*.

And she was just a broken, maimed bar wench.

He deserved better than she could ever be.

❄ ❄ ❄ ❄ ❄ ❄ ❄

Dinner could have been delicious or cold as raw fish in the middle of the frost season for all Roska knew. His mind was still entirely wrapped up in the almost-moment he'd had with Brigit. What would have happened if the others hadn't returned then?

He'd desperately wanted to kiss her, but after everything she'd been through as a result of her connection to him, Roska couldn't expect her to want anything to do with him.

He needed to give her space. He needed to let her process everything that had happened to her. He couldn't dump his emotional nonsense on this girl who had already been through hells on his account.

Gods, he needed to get a grip on himself.

Without a word, he crawled into the tent he shared with Miguel and Balor, closed his eyes, and willed himself to not want her anymore.

Or at least to have the self-control to not make his desire for her *her* problem.

* * * * * * *

After nearly two weeks of trekking through the woods, the walls of Riverayn were in sight. Brigit had never seen such a place. The walls practically glowed through the trees with the sun setting behind them.

"We should make it to the castle gates by midday tomorrow." Miguel turned to Zara. "Can you send a message ahead so they can have a healer waiting for us?"

As if on cue, an orange and white ball of fur leapt out from some bushes a few paces ahead.

Brigit squealed and jumped, but to her surprise, the mare didn't seem bothered by the creature at all. The horse sidestepped around the fox—that was what the furball turned out to be—and kept walking as though nothing had happened.

"No worries, love," Asha soothed, placing a gentle hand on Brigit's shoulder. "That's just Lyra."

Lyra... why does that name sound familiar?

Before her mind could connect the dots in her faded memories, a tall man stepped out from behind the trees, joining them along the riverbank. His hair was shorter and darker, but she recognized him right away. Quinn. Roska's brother. She'd spent a few days with them both when they'd been staying at the inn in Nexton. Quinn was clever and troublesome. Not quite a prankster, but definitely someone who liked to tease. He was rougher now, his face carpeted in a dark brown beard, but his deep green eyes were just as bright as ever.

He strode up to Roska, looking as comfortable and confident as ever, clasped his brother's hand, and pulled him into a one-armed hug, clapping him firmly on the back.

"Thank the Gods," he exclaimed, pulling back and putting his hands on Roska's shoulders as if inspecting him for wounds. "Elena has been going nuts worrying about you. Apparently, you're late."

Roska chuckled and shook Quinn off. "Yeah, sorry about that. Things took an unexpected turn." He nodded over to Asha's clearly bandaged leg and the linen wrapped around Zara's head. "But we're all good now. Can I assume she'll have my ear upon our return?"

Quinn's guffaw spooked a mother bird in a nest overhead. "Oh, yeah. She's been pacing the eastern wall since breakfast yesterday. I'm sure she's got a whole speech prepared by now."

"Have my ear." That's what they said about the King an' the horses. It meant yellin'? Why the hells would they word it in such a confusin' an' ridiculous way?

"Brigit!" Quinn looked up at her on the horse in front of Asha. "It's so good to finally see you again. You know, our boy here has been looking for you for—what's it been Ros, like three cycles now?"

Roska's face turned a brilliant shade of red. Brigit wasn't sure she'd ever seen that color on anything other than fresh strawberries. Maybe an overripe apple.

"Aye, it's good to see ye again, sir." Brigit attempted an awkward bow from where she sat on the horse.

"Sir?" Quinn clicked his tongue. "Please, just call me Quinn. Or Q."

"Or shythead," Balor chimed in. "That's what we call him on the training fields."

Q locked eyes with Balor, then slowly raised his fist. Brigit blinked and suddenly the man's hand was on fire. On *fire*!

The fox—Lyra—jumped in between Balor and Quinn, snarling, baring her teeth and her muxing tail was on fire too!

A massive ball of snow fell from the sky, smothering Quinn and Lyra's flames and soaking Balor's clothes.

"What the hells, Ros?" Quinn groaned, shaking the snow from his hair and dusting off his shoulders.

"You're scaring our guest." Roska looked pointedly from his brother to her. Brigit realized a moment too late that she had a death grip on the reins. She forced herself to loosen her hold on the leather and looked away from the brothers.

"Shyt," Quinn muttered. "I'm sorry, Brigit. I didn't mean to scare you. We were just muxing around. Right, Balor?"

Balor shook his head like a dog, flinging snow from his hair, smiling widely and clearly trying to contain his laughter. "Yeah, we're just teasin'. Didn't mean to scare you, darlin'."

Lyra leapt out of the snow pile she'd been buried under and snapped her vicious teeth at Balor as she shook snow from her fur. "Speak for yourself," she grumbled.

"Ye... ye talk?" Brigit didn't think she could handle any more dramatic reveals.

"Mux." Roska and Quinn swore at the same time.

"Of course I talk," Lyra said matter-of-factly. "Most of the time, I'm the only one saying anything intelligent or worth listening to."

A soft hiss came from behind Roska. "I disagree."

Muxing hells. The little dragon talked too? Brigit was fairly certain her brain would implode any second.

"Why don't we give you two a moment?" Quinn offered. Asha slid off the horse and wrapped an arm around Zara's shoulder, and the rest of the crew wandered into the woods muttering about finding dinner and a place to set up camp.

Brigit watched them go, stunned to her core and thoroughly shaken.

"I'm sorry." Roska's eyes were downcast and he seemed to be trying to make himself as small as possible. "I should have explained everything from the beginning. I just didn't want to overwhelm you."

"Too late fer that, love."

He toed a fallen branch with his boot, hands clasped behind his back. Carefully, Brigit maneuvered herself off the back of the mare—no small feat—and moved to stand before him.

"Is there anythin' else I need to know?"

Roska looked up from his boots, although he was still looking down at her. She was fairly certain she'd never get over how tall he was. Hells, the top of her head barely reached his chin. He studied her, seeming to appraise her. Several moments passed. Brigit worried that he was going to shut her out again. These last few days, when he'd barely spoken to her, had been unbearable. She couldn't go back to that.

"I'm stronger than ye think. I can handle it. I jus' need ye to be honest wit me."

She held his gaze, willing him to see past her injuries into the strength that had sustained her over the last few cycles. It must have worked because he sighed and spoke.

"You're right. I should have told you everything from the start. Can we sit?" He led her over to a large rock sticking out of the river and gestured for her to have a seat. Roska sat beside her for a moment, then stood again and began pacing.

When his footsteps began to wear a path in the grass, she said, "Pacin' must run in yer family."

Mentioning his family and bringing back the comment Quinn had made about their sister seemed to shake Roska out of his reverie. He chuckled and raked his fingers through his snow-white hair. "Yeah, I guess it does."

"Why do ye say "have yer ear"? It's a confusin' phrase an' sounds so brutal compared to the reality of a lecture." Brigit really wanted to ask him a million questions about his family, their magic, the talking animals, and so much more, but she thought starting somewhere more neutral might help him open up.

Roska exhaled a quick laugh. "Honestly, it's something that Amelia used to threaten Q with when he was a kid. He was a... challenging child. Wild and willful. Amelia used to threaten to have his ear if he didn't start listening to her." He smiled fondly at the mention of this woman. Brigit had no idea who Amelia was, but it was clear she was very important to Roska. "She never meant it literally, of course. Mostly, it just meant she was running out of patience and he was going to end up scrubbing pots in the kitchen if he didn't stop whatever trouble he'd been starting."

"She sounds..." Brigit searched for the right word, and Roska watched her intently. Amelia was important to him. If she said the wrong thing, she might drive him away. "Impressive."

Roska's smile turned inward. "She is. Closest thing to a mother Q ever had, and a damn fine woman. She took him in when he was barely ten cycles old. Raised him. Took Elena in when she'd gotten kicked out of Harbor Ridge by our mother. She even found a room for me when I was—" He snapped his mouth shut, that vibrant red creeping up his neck again.

"When ye were what?" she prompted.

Raking his fingers through his hair again, Roska's gaze fixated on her hand. He'd been doing that a lot when he thought she wasn't looking. He blamed himself, she realized. He felt responsible for her injuries. She raised her good hand to him, offering it and pulling him down to sit beside her.

"This," she said, raising her smashed hand, "is *no* yer fault. The only person who deserves the blame for this is the man who did it. Ye dinna hurt me, and ye dinna order the Brothers to hurt me."

Ever-so-gently, he took her damaged hand in his, tears brimming his eyes. "But if you didn't know me, if you weren't important to me—"

She cut him off, placing her uninjured hand on top of his. "*Ye dinna hurt me.* Did ye know the Brothers were watchin' ye?"

"No."

"Did ye order 'em to kidnap an' torture me?"

"What? No! Of course not." He blanched.

"Then this isna yer fault."

"That's what I've been trying to tell him." The voice was raspy, feminine, and a bit gravelly. Brigit jumped as the dragon uncoiled itself from Roska's forearm. "I'm Demoni. It's a pleasure to officially meet you."

The creature flicked its tongue at her. Its onyx eyes sparkled in the fading light.

Brigit fought her instincts to pull her hands away and instead lowered her face to get a better look at the creature. She was stunning. And she was definitely female. Brigit wasn't sure how she knew that, but something about the creature exuded feminine energy. Demoni—as she'd called herself—had the most beautiful teal scales covering her whole body. Small, spiked horns adorned her long, skinny face. Her feet held fast to Roska's sleeve, tiny claws digging into the fabric to keep her in place. Her tail, which was still wrapped firmly around Roska's forearm, seemed to be as long as her whole body. But what caught Brigit's attention most was the pair of scars that ran on either side of her spine, from her forelegs to the middle of her back.

"What happened to ye?" Brigit asked quietly, studying the raised scars that marred the otherwise flawless teal scales.

"The Brotherhood." When Demoni didn't elaborate, Roska continued for her.

"When we were about ten cycles old, we tried to escape. Demoni used to have wings. Thick, leathery wings. The Brothers caught us and Grand Maester Auron took her wings as punishment."

His voice was flat, emotionless, but Brigit could see the pain simmering in his eyes.

"They cut them off and sealed my wounds with a fire poker." Demoni's voice was equally devoid of emotion.

"Gods, I'm so sorry ye went through that." Brigit didn't know what else to say. There was nothing she could say to make the abuse the little dragon had suffered any better or lessen the pain they'd been forced to endure.

"It's ok." Roska shrugged awkwardly. "It was over ten cycles ago. We've healed and are fine now."

"What do ye mean 'we've healed'? I thought it was Demoni who was hurt?"

"We are tied to each other. He feels what I feel and vice versa." Demoni's statement didn't actually explain anything.

Roska, seeming to understand that Demoni's comment left much unclear, offered a more thorough explanation. "We share a soul. Demoni and I can communicate without speaking, and we feel everything the other feels. If one of us gets hurt, we both feel it." He released his hold on her hands, turned his back, and raised his tunic to reveal two massive, raised scars along his own spine. "They cut and burned her, so I was cut and burned as well."

Tentatively, Brigit reached out and brushed her fingertips over one of the thick scars. Roska shivered at her touch but didn't pull away.

"They're monsters," Brigit whispered in disgusted awe.

"You'll get no argument from me," Roska said, dropping his tunic and turning back to face her. "Demoni is my familiar. We are tethered together for life. If one of us dies, the other will quickly follow. Quinn and Lyra"—he nodded in the direction the others had headed—"are tethered the same. I'm FrostBorn, as I said before. Quinn is FlameBorn. Elena is StormBorn, and her familiar, Agon, is an electric weasel known as a *raju*."

Brigit took Roska's hand again and rested their clasped hands in her lap. "Do all magical beings have talking, magical animals too?"

Roska shook his head. "According to Father, familiars with their own magic seems to be something unique to the three of us. All enchantresses have talking familiars, but the animals don't have powers of their own. And witches have familiars, but theirs are all the same animal, called a moonbird. It looks like a massive raven. But moonbirds are shapeshifters and can turn into any creature—including humans—as long as they've seen them in person."

"I dinna realize witches were still around. I thought they'd all been killed off an age ago."

"That's what we thought, too. Turns out, witches are just better at hiding in plain sight. Niko has been changing the laws to make Waverly a safe haven for witches since he took power."

Niko. King Niko. Brigit wasn't sure she could trust anyone with that much power and authority, but it did seem promising that he was using his crown to make things better for the marginalized and persecuted.

"Ye really like him, huh?"

"Niko? Absolutely." Roska squeezed her hand. "He's a good man. A good king. You'll see when you meet him."

Brigit wasn't sure any royal could live up to that level of praise, but she guessed she'd be able to form her own opinion when she met the King on the morrow. Whether she was ready or not.

honed our powers, sure, but I also wanted to use that time to teach El and Ros some more practical skills. Hunting with a bow is a lot stealthier and more effective than bolts of lightning or ice swords."

Roska had heard this argument a hundred times, so he tuned Quinn out. He'd learned to shoot a bow, but he'd also learned to fire ice darts with such precision that he no longer bothered with a weapon. He could kill a deer with a single dart to the heart at a hundred paces. Once he'd showcased that skill to Q, his brother had stopped pestering him to practice with a bow. Instead, they went on regular hunting excursions during the harvest season. It was one of Roska's favorite things about the changing seasons and the only real bonus about the colder weather, as far as he was concerned.

Roska thrived in the growing season, whereas Q—with his fiery magic—was in his best form during the frost season. They were polar opposites in that regard and in many other ways. Honestly, looking at them from the outside, it probably didn't make sense that they got along so well. And yet, Roska couldn't imagine his life with his brother by his side. Mocking him. Teasing him. Teaching him. Roska gave as good as he got.

The conversation continued on around him, but Roska's mind had wandered off into thoughts of the morning. Returning to the castle triumphant—minus a couple of horses—and finally introducing Elena to Brigit.

"Hey." Miguel's quiet voice drew Roska out of his reverie. He took a seat on the log beside Roska, bumping his knee with his own. "Where's your head at?"

Roska glanced around, but if the others had noticed Miguel's movements and query, they were hiding it well. Quinn was animatedly telling the story about when they'd been attacked by a pack of wolves in the Dark Woods. He had everyone's attention.

"I'm good," Roska said, truthfully. "I mean, everything that's happened in the last few weeks, it could have gone a hells of a lot worse."

"Yeah, but it could've gone better," Miguel countered. Roska watched as Miguel ripped a long strand of grass from the ground and began tying it into knots. One knot on top of another, perfectly stacked. It was impressive.

Roska nodded to the grass in Miguel's hands and asked, "What are you doing?"

Miguel blinked and looked at his hands. He chuckled, "Sorry. Nervous habit."

"What do you have to be nervous about?"

He tossed the grass away and turned back to face Roska. He chewed on his bottom lip before he spoke. Weighing his words, maybe? "I'm worried about you," he said quietly. "She's a lot worse off than we'd expected, and I know you blame yourself."

Roska tried to look away, but Miguel placed a hand on his knee, squeezing gently and holding Roska's gaze.

"None of this is your fault. No—" He held up a hand to cut Roska off before he could argue. "You didn't do this to her, and you didn't know they would go after her. You looked for her for *cycles*. You did everything you could." He moved his hand from Roska's knee to grasp his hand, tightening his grip to emphasize his words. "What happened to her was *not your fault*." He squeezed their combined hands with each word to make sure his message got through.

"That's what I've been tryin' to tell him. Stubborn man keeps takin' the blame for shyt he dinna do."

Roska's eyes shot up to see that Quinn's reenactment had stopped and the others were all watching his interaction with Miguel and now Brigit.

Heat flushed his face as he tried to pull his hand from Miguel's. He wasn't ashamed of his feelings for Miguel, but he hadn't been entirely open with Brigit about his relationship with the man either. How would she react? Miguel held fast, though, and Brigit took Roska's free hand with her undamaged one.

"He's always been like that," Quinn added. "He's got a big heart, and it makes him take responsibility for anything and everything that goes wrong in the lives of the people he loves."

Roska's eyes narrowed as he turned a heated glare on his brother. For calling him out for his "unreasonable" behavior—as Q and Elena had often called it—and for his use of the word "love." Roska had no idea how to describe his feelings for Brigit, or Miguel for that matter, but he didn't like Q throwing the word love around so freely. Roska could count on one hand the number of people he trusted enough to allow himself to love. He wasn't sure he was ready to expand onto a second hand just yet.

Chicken.

You really need to stop spending so much time with Lyra, Roska replied, looking over at his familiar where she lay curled up against Lyra's fiery tail.

Demoni's tongue flicked out at him.

"I think I heard something beyond the trees," Asha announced, entirely unconvincingly. "Z, Balor, let's go take a look. Don't want the Brotherhood sneaking up on us, and all that." Awkwardly, Asha managed to stand before Zara joined her and hoisted Asha's arm over her shoulder, helping her wander off into the woods.

Balor looked at Roska, Quinn, Brigit, and Miguel—like he didn't want to leave and miss the drama unfolding before him.

"*Now*, Balor," Zara demanded.

Grumbling, the beast rose and followed the women into the woods.

"What I mean is," Q said, trying to recover, "you take the blame for shyt you had nothing to do with or no control over. Like everything with the *turmio*."

Roska huffed an indignant laugh. "Nothing to do with? Seriously, Q. The damned thing wouldn't have been released at all if it wasn't for me. That one was entirely my fault, along with all the death that followed."

It had taken Roska a full solar cycle before he could look out at the cemetery at Harbor Ridge and not feel crushed under the weight of those senseless deaths. Those children would still be alive if it hadn't been for his stupid actions.

"You were *brainwashed*, Ros. You can't be held responsible for your actions when you were being so thoroughly manipulated." Quinn had said these same words to him over and over again since that damned tower their mother had locked them in. It didn't mean that Roska truly believed it.

He'd never wanted to hurt anyone, of course, but he'd been raised—*You mean abused,* Demoni corrected—to believe that magic was a scourge and the root of all the problems in Waverly. He'd believed that releasing the *turmio* would make the world a better place. The Brothers had explained the way the *turmio* would work, like a virus attacking and killing magic. Roska had foolishly thought that it wouldn't kill anyone, especially not children. He hadn't understood that by killing the magic in a person, it killed their familiar and ultimately the person as well. A familiar was a magical being's soul given physical form. Looking back, it was obvious that the *turmio* would kill, because it was impossible for one to live once their soul had died. So many children had passed unto the Fade as a result of his ignorant actions. It didn't matter what Q—or anyone—said, it *was* his fault.

"See, you're doing it again, right now!" Quinn pointed at him accusingly. "You're taking the blame for shyt when it's not your burden to bear. The Brotherhood abused, tortured, and manipulated you. You were a means to an end for them. A weapon that they honed and fine-tuned until they were ready to aim and fire, sending you off to do their dirty work and die for their muxed up cause."

Roska knew he should be embarrassed by Q's words and how openly he talked about Roska's trauma, but he couldn't bring himself to feel anything. Locking his emotions down and freezing them out had kept him alive throughout his time with the Brothers. It was easy to crawl back into the safety that numbness provided.

Brigit and Miguel, however, didn't seem as willing to let him lock his feelings away.

"Stop that right now," Brigit snapped, tightening her grip on his hand. "Ye dinna get to hide away like that. Ye keep thinkin' yer responsible for all the shyt in the world? Fine. Then I'll spend the rest o' my days convincin' ye otherwise." There was a fire in her eyes, a passion that wouldn't be denied.

Miguel squeezed his other hand. "As will I. You don't get to take the blame for the actions of others. Especially your muxing abusers. I'll tear them down and remove them from this planet before I let you take responsibility for them."

Roska tore his gaze from Brigit's fiery eyes to Miguel's. The vehemence in his words was matched by the rage boiling just below the surface of his molten brown eyes.

Roska looked down, blinking quickly as he studied their joined hands. They were here for him. Supporting him when he clearly didn't deserve it. He didn't deserve anything they had to offer. It would be selfish of him to let his feelings for them grow. Gods, he desperately wanted to be selfish.

Hot embers landed on his thigh, just above his knee. It quickly burned through his trousers and he glared up at Q. "What the mux?"

Q raised his hands in innocence. "It wasn't me!"

Lyra smirked her foxy grin at him. "Stop being an idiot and let these fools love you already." She lowered her tail again, laying it over Demoni's body. "Gods, you're right," she spoke to the frost dragon. "He's *exhausting*."

Chapter 18

ROSKA WOKE TO THE faint sounds of conversation and the heavenly scent of freshly brewed coffee. He had slept hard, not even waking when it was supposed to be his turn for night watch. He had a sneaking suspicion that no one bothered trying to wake him. Truthfully, he hadn't slept that well in ages. Possibly ever.

He'd spent the night in a tent between Brigit and Miguel. They'd insisted on sharing the tent, pointing out that the crew only had two tents, so sharing was inevitable. Q and Lyra had taken first watch. Balor, Zara, and Asha had shared the other tent. As they were getting settled that night, Roska had wondered briefly if he should be embarrassed or uncomfortable bedding down with the two of them, but sleep had taken him so quickly, he hadn't had much time to think about it.

Now, in the first blush of morning, he searched his feelings. He was pleasantly surprised to find that he only felt peace as he lay between the two of them. It might have been unorthodox, but it felt entirely right to him. Looking down at their sleeping faces, Roska had a sense that Brigit and Miguel shared his unexpected sense of serenity at being together as they were. He hoped that was truly the case and not simply him projecting his feelings and desires on them.

He had no idea how a relationship between the three of them would work in the long run, but Roska was undeniably relieved to be with the two people he cared for so deeply. He scooped up Demoni, wrapping her around his neck, and ducked out of his tent to see hints of the sun rising over the horizon, barely visible through the trees that surrounded them.

"Good morning, sleepy head!" Quinn tossed him a fresh biscuit, but Roska—not being fully awake yet—missed it. Thankfully, Demoni caught it with her vicious teeth before it could fly past his head. Roska took the warm bread from his frost dragon, scratched her under her chin, and sat beside Q on a log before the fire.

"You're chipper," Roska observed as he took the mug of coffee Zara offered him.

"He's been like this all morning. He's almost as exhausting as you." Lyra's voice rose from the far side of the fire. Roska hadn't even seen her lying there. Looking closely, though, he noticed her tail was resting in the middle of the fire.

"Shut it. I'm allowed to be happy," Q snapped, but there was no bite in his words.

"Why is your tail in the flames?" Demoni asked Lyra, ignoring Quinn entirely.

"The wood was too wet to light, and Mr. Way-Too-Happy wanted to have breakfast ready and waiting when you all woke up. I'm your stove this morning." Lyra shot an annoyed look toward Quinn. "You're welcome," she deadpanned.

"Well, I could have done it myself, but it was getting a bit too complicated trying to keep a fire burning nonstop while also cooking. I sacrificed a few biscuits to the breakfast gods before Lyra consented to help."

"Who are the breakfast gods?" Brigit asked curiously, brushing her wild curls from her face as she stepped out of their tent with Miguel right behind her.

Lyra laughed. "They're gods he made up to justify burning three biscuits before admitting he needed help."

"I didn't make them up!" Quinn countered. All eyes turned to Q, patiently awaiting this revelation of new, mealtime-specific deities. After several long, awkward moments, he finally grunted. "Mux all of you." He turned back to the bacon he had cooking in a cast iron skillet over the fire. "You're welcome for breakfast. Ungrateful heathens," he muttered to the food.

Everyone laughed, although it was Balor's loud guffaw that spooked the birds overhead.

"Thank ye for cookin'. It smells amazin'." Brigit came to sit beside Roska, reaching out and gingerly swiping a slice of bacon from the plate Q had set on a stump serving as their table. Her first bite of breakfast elicited a moan so full of pleasure that it bordered on obscene. Brigit's skin turned a beautiful, bright red as she clamped a hand over her mouth as though to catch the sound and shove it back inside.

"That good, huh?" Miguel asked, nudging Brigit with his shoulder as he knelt down and grabbed a piece of bacon for himself. Taking a generous bite, he mimicked Brigit's exclamation of pleasure. "Damn, Q, that's really muxing good!"

The laughter that erupted around the fire spooked any animal within a hundred paces. Miguel confidently stole Roska's coffee mug and took a deep swig before offering it and a second piece of bacon to Brigit.

Roska watched her anxiously, worried that Miguel's actions might upset or offend her. To his relief, she smiled widely at him, taking the proffered food and drink.

"I canna remember the last time I had bacon. Or coffee." She took another generous bite of the meat, her eyes rolling back in her head in pleasure. "Gods, I've missed this."

Roska smiled down at Brigit where she sat on the forest floor, leaning against his leg. Zara refilled their empty—and apparently shared—mug of coffee. Roska took a sip of the dark, aromatic liquid and let his mind wander.

How had he been so lucky to find such wonderful people? Not just find, but adopt into his life. This little crew was quickly becoming as much a part of his family as his blood relations.

Pouring the last of the coffee into his own mug, Quinn beamed at Brigit. "I think it's time our lovely Brigit met the King and future Queen of Waverly."

* * * * * *

After breakfast, they cleaned up, broke down the tents, and loaded the horses back up. Quinn had said it would be about a half day's trek to the castle from their campsite, which meant they should arrive just after midday. Brigit had never been to the capital before. As soon as the brilliant white walls were visible just beyond the trees, she gasped.

Roska was leading her horse—Asha had insisted on walking. She refused to show weakness before the King. Balor and Miguel had argued that she was being stubborn and foolish, but when she threatened to hide bombs in their chamberpots, they'd both shut up. Brigit rode alone, with Roska walking along beside her. He pulled the horse to an abrupt stop when he heard her breath catch.

"Is everything all right? Are you hurt? Do you need a break?" His eyes flew over her body, searching for obvious signs of injury.

"I've ne'er seen anythin' like it." She exhaled the words in an awe-filled breath.

The walls surrounding the castle were pristine, unmarred white stone. It almost looked as though the entire thing was made of one large, seamless block of basalt. From her vantage point, Brigit could just make out the bright red tiles that served as roofing on the various towers spaced evenly along the wall.

Roska followed her line of sight, and warmth crept into his voice. "Oh, yes. It is beautiful, isn't it?"

"Did you know that the original wall was built by the children of Lugh?" Miguel stopped beside them, standing up with a look of pure admiration on his face. "Around one thousand cycles ago. They built it as a fortress to protect the citizens during the Second War of Kings. Lugh and his many children took pity on the innocents being slaughtered by the soldiers simply because they didn't have anywhere to hide or keep them safe. They built the entire wall in under a week. At least, that's what the legend says."

Brigit looked away from the near-blinding white wall just in time to see a subtle look pass between Roska and Demoni. She was about to ask about it when Quinn joined them. "Lugh? Hey, Ros, wasn't that the guy that Aiden said..." His voice trailed off, leaving his question hanging unfinished.

"I'm not sure," Roska replied. He looked uncharacteristically stoic. "We'll have to ask him next time we see him. Where is he these days, anyway? Have you heard from him?"

"Last I heard, he was spending too much time in the kitchens at Harbor Ridge, and Mother was about to have him banished from the entire school." Quinn laughed and kept walking. "Seems he's been trying to steal all the honey butter bread and the head chef is ready to slaughter him and turn *him* into a meal."

"I can't imagine he'd taste very good," Roska replied, smiling up at Brigit before pulling the reins and leading onward the horse.

"I don't know. Supposedly wine tastes better with age. Maybe demi-gods do, too," Lyra commented, hopping out from the brush along the riverside.

Roska visibly shivered. "I have no desire to find out."

Chapter 19

Quinn had told Brigit that the view she was getting wasn't the most impressive entry into the castle walls. They were entering through a smaller side gate along the river primarily used by local merchants and traders. Supposedly, she wasn't getting the full picture of the beauty that encompassed Riverayn.

Brigit wasn't sure her mind could have comprehended a prettier view. They exited the woods and stepped onto a small, cobblestone road that led to the side entrance. Roska informed her that if they followed the road away from the capital, it would lead to some of the smaller trading villages nearby. Villages that thrived due almost entirely to their proximity to the capital and their willingness to do the hard labor that the wealthy refused to do. The leather worker, blacksmith, and cotton farmers, for example, lived in the closest trade village.

According to Roska, Niko had passed a few labor edicts in the first few moons of his tenure as King, making the lives of those citizens considerably more comfortable. "Including, but not limited to, a trade agreement amongst the merchants that set a fair market value for all the wares, in an effort to keep the traders all well and fairly paid for their labors."

It all sounded grand, in theory, but Brigit wasn't ready to take Roska's word that the traders were all thrilled with this agreement.

She imagined some had thrived on the competition and under-cutting their rivals. She thought back to market days in Nexton: bakers competing for her coin by trying to offer her the lowest price. The market was particularly vicious when the foreign traders came through on their way to or from the Dragon's Teeth pass.

She kept those observations to herself for now, though. Brigit was a guest in the King's house. She needed to respect his laws and practices. If they were still in Nexton, she might have felt comfortable expressing her thoughts openly, but this close to the fire, she thought it was safest to keep her mouth shut, lest she get burned.

Small stands and carts of vendors set up along the road into the city. Brigit stared openly at all the amazing wares that were so readily available. Miguel nudged her leg, pointing out some of his favorite suppliers and offering to give her a more in-depth tour of the village once they got settled. The look of pride and excitement in his eyes was enough to make her want to go anywhere with him. Miguel had an energy about him that made everything seem new and exhilarating.

"There are a few gardens just inside the walls here that I would love to show you, when you're feeling up for it," Roska added. "There's an entire garden devoted to fragrant, seasonal flowers. It's designed in a circle, sort of like a floral clock. Each quarter of the circle is devoted to a specific season, and only one season blooms at a time. It's one of the most beautiful places in the whole castle."

Brigit couldn't even imagine such a magical garden. It sounded amazing. "I'd love to see that. I've ne'er been much of a gardener myself, but I'm always impressed with the people who manage to keep plants alive."

Miguel shared a knowing smile with Roska over the horse's neck. She was missing something. Some inside joke or something they shared, just the two of them. Brigit paused, searching her feelings to find any sense of jealousy or exclusion at their connection. Instead, all she felt was a growing warmth surrounding her heart. These men wanted to show her their world. They wanted to bring her into every part of their life, and she couldn't wait to immerse herself in them entirely.

❄ ❄ ❄ ❄ ❄ ❄

If this was the "less impressive" side gate, Brigit couldn't even begin to imagine what the formal entry to Riverayn looked like. The gate itself was made of thick iron bars and was wide enough for two horse-drawn carriages to pass, side by side, with room for pedestrians to move between them. Two guards stood on either side of the open gate, white tunics blazing in the bright sunlight. Brigit couldn't take her eyes off them as they followed the line of traders entering the side gate.

From her vantage point atop the horse, she had a clear view of the guards as they approached. The men wore stoic faces, almost as though they were impersonating statues, but she could tell they were hyper-aware of their surroundings. Their bodies were still as stone, but their eyes never settled on one thing for more than a few heartbeats. They both had a fist resting firmly on the hilt of their short swords, prepared to draw at a moment's notice if need be. And yet, none of the merchants or traders in line ahead of them seemed wary or concerned by the presence of the armed guards. If anything, the merchants seemed friendly with the guards. Many of the younger women batted their lashes blatantly at the guards, *trying* to catch their attention. It was bizarre.

Finally, it was their turn to pass through the gate. Quinn and Balor led their little troupe, smiling at the guards. Balor even punched one of the men in the shoulder. Much to Brigit's surprise, the guard didn't react. No, that wasn't accurate. He reacted by breaking into a large grin and punching Balor right back. As though they were actually friends. The entire scene was disturbing and thoroughly disorienting. The guards who came to Nexton from the capital had been cruel, spiteful, and vindictive men. They certainly weren't friendly, or *playful*.

A sudden cold shock wrapped around Brigit's leg, slithering up her thigh and sending a shiver up her spine.

"It's ok," came a soft hiss. Looking down, Brigit saw that Demoni had made her way across Roska's shoulder and settled in her lap. "The guards look intimidating, but they are good men. Niko's Commander, a man named Jamieson, culled all the rot from their military ranks two cycles ago. All that's left are the strong, kind, and honorable ones."

Brigit didn't know how to respond, so she simply nodded. She understood that the frost dragon was trying to comfort her, but truthfully, having a talking dragon in her lap didn't really ease her anxiety. Her entire world was topsy-turvy, and Brigit wasn't sure it would ever right itself again.

❋ ❋ ❋ ❋ ❋ ❋ ❋

Roska appreciated Demoni's attempts to put Brigit at ease. He hadn't asked her to do it, and he'd been thoroughly shocked when she left her perch on his shoulder to climb onto the horse with Brigit. Still, the look of anxiety—bordering on terror—didn't fade from Brigit's face as they crossed through the gate and entered the city proper.

Quinn and Lyra ran ahead to let Elena know they were coming so she'd be ready and waiting in the Great Hall. Balor, Zara, and Asha split off to head to their barracks and get cleaned up before the welcome home reception Elena had planned for them in the evening. Roska felt it was a bit over the top, but Elena always insisted on a welcome-home meal whenever a crew returned to the capital after a mission.

Niko had let slip once that they didn't have a reception after *every* mission because some were so covert that even Elena wasn't allowed to know about them until moons after they'd been completed. Roska knew she'd be unhappy to find that her future husband was keeping such information from her, but he also knew Niko wasn't doing it as an act of cruelty or because he distrusted her. He was simply protecting her from the darker side of his role as King. Some missions were deadly and didn't end well. Those missions would weigh heavily on Elena if she knew of them, so Niko deliberately kept her shielded from them.

Roska had been immediately conflicted by this revelation. He knew Elena would hate being intentionally sheltered, but he also understood Niko's desire to protect her from the uglier side of ruling. Truthfully, he would have preferred Niko *not* confide in him. Knowing everything as he now did, Roska felt like he was an accomplice to Niko's lies.

Well, maybe not *lies*, but definitely deceptions and omissions. Which were just as bad as outright lies more often than not.

Your mind is everywhere. If you are this uncomfortable keeping Niko's confidence, then you need to tell him. Demoni still sat wrapped around the horn of the saddle with Brigit as they slowly made their way to the castle.

I can't. He needs someone he can talk to who isn't going to judge his every action or try and sway him to their own desires. The statement was true enough, but it wasn't the only reason Roska didn't tell Niko to be honest with Elena. Roska hated conflict. He and Elena were much alike in that regard. He avoided causing strife as much as humanly possible.

Before their argument could continue, Brigit gasped again. Following her line of sight, Roska looked down the road. They'd just turned a corner, and the castle was in full view now. The windows sparkled in the sunlight like glittering jewels against the pristine white of the basalt bricks that made up the castle. Roska wondered about his ancestors, the ones who supposedly built the castle and the walls protecting it. He'd been surprised when Miguel had told that story. A story as heroic and kind as that seemed like something their father would have bragged about endlessly.

Maybe he wasn't a part of it, Demoni suggested.

It was a valid theory. There was a long period of time in which Aiden's mind had been a wreck. When he'd been cursed—as punishment—with the gift of prophecy by the Fae, his mind had been reduced to flashes of visions from across time. Roska planned to ask him about it, nonetheless, whenever he saw their father again. Aiden didn't come to the capital much. Too many people, he said. It messed with his head, seeing all those faces and getting flashes of their potential futures. Aiden promised to come to Elena's wedding, but he didn't want to spend too much time surrounded by so many people.

"You'll have to dismount here." Miguel's words to Brigit disrupted Roska's thoughts, bringing him back to the present. They were standing at the edge of the courtyard that led to the grand entrance of the castle. Roska hadn't even noticed they'd made it that far into the city. "Can't ride into the Great Hall," he added with a grin.

Roska reached up and offered Brigit his assistance. When she gave him a quick nod of consent, Roska carefully placed his hands on her waist and lowered her safely to the ground. He tried to ignore the shock of power that rushed through him as his fingers made contact with the warmth of her body. Demoni hopped from the saddle to land smoothly on Roska's shoulders.

"Thank ye," Brigit said softly, her eyes meeting his for a moment before quickly looking away as a light flush bloomed across her cheeks.

Miguel, seeming to have noticed their interaction, chuckled to himself, took the horse's reins, and turned to walk away.

"Wait, are ye no comin' wit us?" Brigit seemed on edge again. Roska wasn't sure if he should be offended that she was so quick to want Miguel with them, but he also understood the impulse. Miguel had a very grounding personality. His presence always helped Roska feel more comfortable. He couldn't fault Brigit for feeling the same.

"Do you want me to?" Miguel seemed a bit out of sorts. Like he didn't know if he should stay with them or give them space.

Roska decided to settle the matter once and for all. "I know I'd feel more relaxed if you were there. If anything, you make an excellent buffer." His lips quirked up at the ends, a small smile to show he was kidding but also reinforcing his desire to keep Miguel close.

"Aye, it would be nice to know more than one person in the room." Brigit's face beamed at them both.

Whatever this relationship was, it was quickly becoming apparent that they were all happier together.

"Well, in that case, let me pass this girl off to the stable hand and we'll head in." He turned to lead the mare to the stable but not before Roska caught a glimpse of the wide grin that had split across the man's beautifully tan face.

"Thank ye for encouragin' him to stay," Brigit said once Miguel was out of earshot. "I'm sure yer sister and the King will be kind, but I dinna kin if I can answer all their questions. Havin' the two of ye by my side..." She trailed off, seeming unsure how to finish the sentence.

Roska reached out and took her hands in his, being careful not to jostle her ruined hand. "I don't normally speak for Miguel, but I think it's safe for me to say that you will have both of us beside you for as long as you'd like."

It was a bold pronouncement, and one he might not have had the full authority to make—Miguel had his own thoughts and opinions, of course—but Roska felt confident that, on this, he and Miguel were of one mind.

Miguel returned and they crossed the large stone courtyard, currently in the process of being redecorated with fresh flowers and banners to honor the upcoming festivities. The walkway leading up the Great Hall was lined intermittently with alternating trellises of jasmine and roses. The heady scent of the flowers was intoxicating.

The doors to the Great Hall stood open, letting the warm breeze drift into the expansive room, bringing with it the scent of flower blossoms. Once inside the hall, the scent of the blooming jasmine and roses warred with the mouthwatering scents of fresh-baked pies and smoking meats. Elena was definitely planning an elaborate feast, and it smelled *delicious*.

** ** ** ** ** **

Roska led them through the Great Hall, watching the awe and amazement pass over Brigit's face as she took in all the beauty the castle had to offer. He'd been living in the castle for so long, he'd lost his ability to be impressed by its intricately designed stained glass windows. Elena had been slowly replacing all the windows depicting the savage treatment of witches in Waverly with images honoring the magical women of old. Seeing Brigit experience it all for the first time reminded Roska of how he'd felt when he and his siblings had first arrived in the castle.

A door behind the thrones on a dais across the long hall opened, and Elena strode into the room. Roska smiled at her, but she didn't look up. She had her nose buried in a book as she deftly maneuvered around the thrones and side tables to reach the dining table that was in the process of being decorated for their welcome home feast.

Brigit subtly positioned herself behind Roska. He knew it was simply because she was nervous—Brigit had mentioned she didn't have any good experiences with royals. He also knew that Elena would quickly help Brigit see that not all royals are the same. Roska imagined they'd become fast friends.

He hoped they would, anyway.

Roska loudly cleared his throat, dragging Elena's attention from her book.

"Thank the Mother!" His sister tossed the book carelessly onto the table and rushed toward Roska, pulling him into a near-strangling hug as she welcomed him home. "You were gone for ages. I was worried something had gone wrong."

Roska smiled down at her, pulling back from her hug to get a better look at her. "I'm sorry, El. It took longer to get back than we had planned."

"Yes, I heard you fed some of my best horses to a pack of wolves?" Niko strode into the room, an eyebrow raised incredulously, but there was no bite in his words.

"They just looked so hungry, Your Majesty," Miguel replied with a carefree shrug.

Elena released Roska and turned to face Brigit. "And who might this lovely lady be?"

Roska beamed at Brigit, holding his arm out to her. She grabbed hold of his hand as though it were the only solid thing in the room. "This is Brigit."

❋ ❋ ❋ ❋ ❋ ❋ ❋

"It's a pleasure to meet ye, milady." Brigit made to curtsy, but her legs were sore from traveling—not to mention moons of torture—and she nearly fell over from the effort.

"Oh, goodness!" Elena rushed forward and caught Brigit by the shoulders before she could make a right fool of herself.

Heat flushed her cheeks as Brigit kept her eyes downcast. Yes, technically, Elena wasn't Queen yet, but she was betrothed to the King. Brigit didn't want to start her relationship with a royal off badly. As it was, she'd already revealed herself to be a clumsy idiot.

"Are you all right?" Elena asked, her voice soft and gentle. Brigit's eyes flicked up of their own accord, studying the woman's face for a moment before she remembered her place and quickly looked back down at the floor.

"Aye, yes, milady. I'm sorry for my disrespectful appearance. I should have cleaned myself up before meeting ye. Beggin' yer forgiveness, milady." Brigit attempted a curtsy again, but Elena's grip on her shoulders made it nearly impossible for her to accomplish the task.

"Brigit, please. You don't have to be formal with us. I'm Elena, Roska's favorite sister, and you are absolutely perfect." Elena's warm smile brightened a hole deep in Brigit's heart, burning away some of the darkness that had taken hold when she'd first been kidnapped. She released her hold on Brigit's shoulders just as Roska stepped closer and wrapped an arm protectively around her waist.

Elena's bright eyes shifted to Roska, scrunching her nose dramatically. "*You* smell atrocious."

"Gee, thanks, El," Roska teased. "I did just come home from a very successful covert mission. I haven't had a chance to get cleaned up yet." He released Brigit and grabbed hold of Elena, pulling her into a tight hug and rubbing his face against her head.

"Oh, gods!" Elena shoved uselessly against him. "Let go of me! You're filthy."

Roska laughed but released her.

"Go take a bath. For an hour." Elena pushed him away. "But first, take Miss Brigit here to one of the guest suites and get her settled. I'll send Delilah up to help you in the bath, if you'd like," she added to Brigit, subtly glancing at Brigit's damaged hand.

Brigit covered the hand protectively, trying to portray a confidence she didn't feel as she said, "Thank ye for the offer, milady, but I'll be all right on my own."

"Great! Be back here in a few hours for a delicious feast." Niko clapped his hands enthusiastically. "Miguel, hang back for a minute. I want a recap of what happened while it's all still fresh in your mind."

Miguel looked to Brigit, almost as though he was asking her permission to stay and speak with the King. It was odd but also sweet. He knew she wasn't comfortable in the castle and he wanted to take care of her. Brigit gave him the most confident smile she could muster while curling into Roska's warm embrace a bit more. Trying to convey that she understood what he was doing and she appreciated it, but she was ok. Roska would keep her safe as well. Miguel gave her a warm smile, then turned back to the King. Roska took Brigit's hand once more, leading her out of the Great Hall and down a long hallway filled with lush carpets and elaborately detailed tapestries.

Brigit didn't bother hiding her amazement at the luxury of the castle. It was the finest place she'd ever been, by far. It was absolutely stunning, but it also raised a lot of questions about the opulence of wealth and the overindulgence of royals to brag about their exploits. The tapestries depicted tales of conquering kings, showing off their abilities to massacre soldiers to achieve their own ends. The artwork was incredible, but the stories behind them were terrible.

She stopped suddenly before an image of a battle. Well, not quite a battle. There were dozens of individuals, each with a bright white or yellow aura, encircling bloody and broken people. The people were cowering and hiding their faces. At first, Brigit thought the glowing creatures were attacking the broken people, but looking closer, she saw angry men with bloody swords and spears pressing in on the glowing creatures.

Roska stepped closer, studying the image with her. "Gods, I think this shows the creation of this castle." His words were a warm breath on her cheek as he leaned over her shoulder to get a closer look a the scene. "Those people with the bright lights all around them. I think those are the children of Lugh that Miguel spoke of."

Brigit reached out a hand and gently brushed her fingertips around the circle protecting the clearly injured people. "I think yer right. Look how they're keepin' these folks safe from those angry soldiers. Sounds like the story he told."

"I'll have to ask Father about it next time he's here."

Brigit wasn't sure if Roska meant for her to hear him, as he spoke rather quietly, but with his mouth that close to her ear, it would have been nearly impossible for her *not* to hear him.

Turning her head slightly, her lips nearly brushed his cheek as her eyes flew to his.

Roska seemed to realize a moment too late just how close he'd gotten to her. Muttering a quick apology, Roska took several steps back and gestured for her to follow him to the guest suite.

Brigit couldn't help but feel something missing at the sudden distance he put between them. She tried not to flinch from the clear discomfort he'd felt at being so close to her. Following in step behind him, Brigit massaged her maimed hand, wondering if she'd misinterpreted all his kind actions. Perhaps he wasn't interested in her at all. Perhaps it was simply that he felt responsible for her and was trying to rectify that.

Gods, she had been such a fool. Thinking someone as powerful and handsome as him would be interested in anything from a stupid, broken tavern wench. He deserved so much more than she could ever offer him.

Chapter 20

HE'D NEARLY KISSED HER. Mux him, but Roska had nearly leaned in and kissed Brigit right then and there. The rest of the walk to her room had been utterly silent and tense. He'd practically run from her room the second her door had closed, choosing to flee to the safety of his own suite before attempting to process what the hells had just happened.

He sank into the steaming water in his copper tub, letting the heat wash over him. What the hells was wrong with him? He shouldn't have been crowding her like that, and he sure as shyt shouldn't have nearly kissed the woman they *just* rescued from being held and tortured for cycles.

She seemed fine with your closeness to me, Demoni interrupted his thoughts. *If anything, she seemed hurt or disappointed after you stepped away.*

You can't be serious. Roska knew Demoni liked to spare his feelings, but that was an outlandish claim. Brigit wasn't hurt by—

You didn't see the look on her face. Confusion, then rejection. She cradled her hand the rest of the walk to her suite.

Shyt. You don't think she *thinks I'm put off by her injuries, do you?* Roska hated to think he'd inadvertently caused Brigit further pain in his efforts to respect her space. Demoni couldn't be right. He'd crossed a line with Brigit, and he shouldn't have invaded her personal space after everything she'd been through. Roska remembered how raw and exposed he'd felt when he finally started processing the trauma of his time with the Brotherhood. He'd needed space and flinched at the slightest touch. It had been so hard to see the look of hurt on his siblings' faces when he pulled away from them, but their closeness made him physically sick. Roska couldn't stand the idea of making Brigit as uncomfortable as he had felt. Yet, he also hated to think that Demoni might be right, and by pulling away he'd hurt Brigit more.

I think you should talk to her *about this. Not me.* With that, Demoni slunk from the bathroom, leaving him to stew in his feelings while he scrubbed away the dirt and grime of their mission.

✳✳ ✳✳✳ ✳✳

The feast Elena had planned was just as outrageous as he'd expected, and Roska couldn't wait for it to be over so he could talk with Brigit. He needed to explain his actions and try to repair any damage he'd caused.

Balor, Zara, and Asha had been invited to join in the feast, as well as Jamieson and about fifty other soldiers—to hide the fact that they were celebrating a successful covert mission. Three tables ran the length of the Great Hall, laden with seemingly endless platters of meats, breads, cheeses, fruits, and every dessert imaginable. Servants were weaving between the tables, offering various wines and whiskies to the guests.

Roska was seated between Miguel and Brigit, across from Quinn and Elena with King Niko at the head of their table. He'd tried leaning over to whisper his apology privately to Brigit, but she either hadn't been able to hear him or hadn't wanted to. He couldn't blame her. He was the one who'd violated her space. He was the one who crossed a line.

Gods, he really needed to fix this shyt.

King Niko tapped his knife to his wine glass, standing and drawing the attention of the dining hall. "I just wanted to take a moment to thank you all for being here and welcome back those who've just returned from missions far and wide. Our country wouldn't be the thriving, prosperous place that it is without the time and dedication of you all. Thank you for your service. Eat, drink, and let's have a great night!"

Cheers erupted around the room as the soldiers toasted their king, each other, and themselves. The sounds of celebration quickly picked up again, making it virtually impossible for Roska to have a private conversation with Brigit.

The dinner dragged on for hours. Normally, Roska might have enjoyed the festivities—although he generally avoided large crowds because the noise and sheer energy of interacting with so many people was exhausting. Tonight, though, it was nearly unbearable. He wanted to take Brigit's arm and escort her to an empty hallway to ensure he hadn't hurt her feelings and try to repair their fragile relationship. Demoni pointed out that that course of action would be rather extreme and likely not end with the results he desired. Namely, a second opportunity to kiss his fiery goddess.

That was what he'd decided he wanted, after all. He strongly cared for Miguel, but he wanted Brigit too. He would likely have to choose at some point, but for now, he just wanted to hold her and make her feel safe and loved.

Loved? Demoni asked curiously.

Yes, I think that's what this feeling is. Do you disagree?

Demoni was across the hall, curled up with Agon and Lyra on the dais as though they were the rulers of this kingdom and not the humans before them. She flicked her tongue out and seemed to be discussing something with the other familiars before responding to him.

Lyra says you've loved Brigit since we met her in Nexton. I think that might be a bit of a stretch, although Agon did point out that you seem much more relaxed and confident when she's around. If it's not love yet, it soon will be.

Roska glared past Miguel at the animals lounging on the dais. *Can you three please stop talking about me? It's weird. Besides, I thought you didn't like gossip.*

Oh, this isn't gossip, she countered. *It's discussing changes in our home. It affects us all, so we like to keep each other abreast of any changes in our situations.*

Gods, familiars really were the worst sometimes.

✳✳ ✳✳ ✳✳ ✳

Eventually, people began to slowly trickle out of the dining hall, some being practically carried by their comrades after overindulging in the King's wine collection. Brigit watched them leave, hiding her mirth behind her still mostly full wine glass.

Typically, she preferred whisky, but since this was a royal affair and her first time dining with the King—and a large collection of his soldiers—she wanted to keep her wits about her. Roska had assured her that King Niko was nothing like his father, but that didn't mean she was ready to drop her guard just yet.

Miguel leaned forward, looking at her past Roska. "If you're ready to get some rest, I'd be happy to escort you to your room."

Her heart fell a little at his offer. She was ready to go to bed, and she definitely would need an escort—the castle was huge and she was sure she'd get lost for days if she tried to make her way back alone—but she'd hoped Roska would be the one to take her. She had some words she needed to say to him.

Namely, that if he was so uncomfortable with her body, he could burn in hells. She didn't need his approval. Then she'd head back to Nexton in the morning. It had been a few cycles, but she felt confident that she could get her job back at the inn. She really needed the money. She couldn't rely on the King's good graces forever.

Roska seemed taken aback by Miguel's offer as well, but he tried to cover it by saying, "We could both take you." A small smile graced his lips, tugging at her emotions and breaking her heart just a little.

"Aye, that would be kind of ye." She bid goodnight to the King, Elena, and Quinn, pushed up from her chair, and took Miguel's proffered arm.

"Right this way, milady," he teased, waving his hand dramatically before them as he led the way out of the Great Hall.

They walked in companionable silence for a while, taking turns seemingly at random until they reached the door to the guest suite she'd bathed in earlier that evening.

Miguel dropped her hand and bowed. "Your rooms, Mistress." The smile on his face seemed to glow, his eyes sparkling in the torches that lined the hall.

"Why thank ye, good sir," Brigit replied, mimicking his tone and returning his bow with a curtsy.

Roska shifted uncomfortably beside them both. Brigit got the suspicion that he wanted to say something but held back.

Mux him. If he wasn't interested in her now that she was damaged then he didn't deserve her in the first place. When she'd met him in the inn, she'd thought he was the sweetest, most kind-hearted boy she'd ever met. Clearly, she'd misjudged him. Maybe all this time living in the castle with his fancy ass family had driven him to believe he was better than her. Or maybe he just couldn't stand the feel of her now that she was maimed. Either way, he could go straight to the deepest circle of hells, and she'd happily tell him that herself.

She turned on him to give him a piece of her mind when he suddenly blurted out, "I'm so sorry. I was an idiot and a fool. I shouldn't have tried to kiss you. After everything you've been through, you don't need another man trying to take what you didn't give freely. I didn't mean to hurt you or upset you. I was a muxing idiot and I'm so sorry."

Mouth hanging open in astonishment, Brigit stared at him as her brain tried to catch up with the words that had just fallen from his lips.

"You tried to kiss her?" Miguel's eyes flicked between the two of them. "When?"

Brigit had honestly forgotten Miguel was still there, and based on the bright red hue covering Roska's face, he had too. "Um, earlier. When I brought her to her room."

"Gods, you really are an idiot. We *just* brought her home from a muxing torture dungeon, and you think she wants any sort of physical contact?" Miguel swatted the back of Roska's head, lightly but enough to muss his hair in the most adorable way.

"Can ye both shut it for a moment? This doesna feel like a conversation we should have in the hall." Brigit opened the door to her room and beckoned them both to follow her in. Once she closed the door behind them, she rounded on them both. "First of all, I'll decide if an' when I'm ready to kiss, an' with whom I share my time. Those muxing Brothers took a great deal from me, but I willna let them take the rest o' my life." She turned her fiery gaze on Roska. "I did want to kiss ye earlier until you pulled away an' showed your disgust for my injuries." She raised her broken hand to emphasize her point. "Aye, I'm damaged now, but I'm no incapable or undesirable. If ye canna see past my injuries then ye can get the hells outta my life right muxing now. And ye," she said, her eyes narrowing at Miguel, "I dinna need ye tellin' him how to handle me. I'm damn well capable of settin' my own muxin' boundaries. Do ye understand?" She raised an eyebrow, daring him to argue, but all he did was nod in agreement, a ghost of a smile dancing on his lips.

"Good," she said with a final nod. "Now get the hells out o' my rooms. I canna stand the sight o' ye."

Brigit turned to open her bedroom door but froze at the soft female laugh that seemed to tinkle in the air. Turning back slowly, she found the source of the light laughter. The frost dragon had come with them. She hadn't even noticed her around Roska's neck.

"Gods, I knew I liked you," Demoni said. "You are absolutely fantastic. I don't think I've ever heard anyone put these two in their places like that. Except maybe Elena."

The dragon climbed down Roska's shoulder, wrapping around his back and leg until she reached the ground, then quickly closed the distance between them. Brigit knelt down to meet her, unsure why, but it felt like the polite thing to do. Demoni climbed into Brigit's lap, locking eyes with her and sharing a bit of her cool magic to soothe Brigit's—justified—rage.

"I know these guys are idiots a lot of the time," the little dragon began. A huff of indignation earned the guys a glare from her beady black eyes. Once she seemed sure there would be no more interruptions, Demoni turned back to Brigit. "They are dumb, but their hearts are in the right place. I hope you will forgive them and choose to stay here at the castle, at least until we get this shyt with the Brotherhood settled. Maybe you can teach them how to behave around a pretty girl. Neither of them have much experience."

Brigit couldn't contain the laugh that bubbled out of her throat at that. Miguel and Roska looked both embarrassed and amused by the interaction unfolding before them. Brigit stayed on the floor a moment longer, Demoni in her lap as she studied the men standing there. A hint of a smile on Roska's face as amusement sparkled in Miguel's eyes. More than that, though, they both seemed to be impatiently awaiting her answer.

Warmth tugged at the corners of her lips. Giving in, she nodded. "Aye, all right. I'll stay for a bit, but the two of ye have to stop decidin' what's best for me, ye hear? I can take care of myself." She scooped the dragon into her arms, her scales surprisingly soft and smooth against her scarred and bruised flesh. Brigit stepped up to Roska, placing Demoni back on his shoulder and cupping his face. "An' I will decide who I want to kiss, an' when."

She brought her face closer to his, her lips just out of reach from his. "Do ye accept my conditions?" she asked quietly, her words a warm breath on his lips.

He nodded dumbly, his eyes flicking from hers to her lips.

Brigit then leaned in, pressing a gentle kiss to his cool, soft lips. Roska seemed utterly floored by her boldness, as she stepped back to see his eyes flared wide.

Is he holdin' his breath? Sweet boy. I wonder if tha was his first kiss.

Miguel broke the silence, slapping a hand on Roska's back and saying, "Come on, lover boy. Let's let this fine lady get some much-needed rest."

Roska blinked slowly, his gaze never leaving hers as a slow smile spread across his face.

Aye, he is a sweet one, she thought as Miguel led Roska from her room and she wandered to her bed. Collapsing in a heap of tired muscles and racing thoughts, Brigit drifted off to sleep imagining all the things those cool lips could do.

Chapter 21

"Pardon the interruption, milord." A nervous guard stepped just inside the door to Roska's suite. Pulling his eyes from the book in his hands, Roska saw a look bordering on terror cross the guard's face for just a moment before he cleared his throat, pushed his shoulders back, and offered Roska a small bow.

"Everything all right?" Roska asked, suddenly feeling a bit nervous.

"Yes, sir. You have a, um, a visitor." The guard's voice pitched up slightly at the end of his pronouncement. A question, almost.

"Is he in there?" An angry female voice called out from behind the guard.

Wait, Roska recognized that voice.

Is that Aleerah? Demoni asked, raising her head from the back of the couch she'd been lounging on.

Sounds like it. What the hells is she doing here? Did we know she and Aiden were coming for a visit?

To the guard, Roska said, "It's fine, Copperfeld. She's family. Send her in."

Copperfeld seemed to relax at Roska's words, bowing and quickly departing as Aleerah shoved the door wide open. Roska wasn't sure he'd ever get used to the massive size of Aleerah. The only remaining dire wolf in the entire world, she was easily twice the size of Mother's snowy lion familiar, Zied. Aleerah's hackles were raised, her beautiful coppery fur standing on end as she stood in the doorway.

"Come on in, Aleerah. What's going on? Where's Aiden?" Roska tried to see past her massive form, assuming his father was simply standing in the hall waiting to come into the room.

"He's not here," she said bluntly. "We have to go. He needs to talk to you. Now. Follow me." With that, she turned tail and bounded down the hall, not bothering to look behind her and see if he was coming.

Roska swore under his breath, and he quickly shoved his feet back in the muddy boots that he'd dropped at the door. Demoni leapt off the couch and ran up his back as he was getting the final boot situated, then they bolted out the door, chasing their father's familiar through the castle halls, out into the city, through the eastern gate, and into the woods beyond.

*＊ ＊＊ ＊＊ ＊

Roska was sweaty and panting from having chased after Aleerah. His hair clung to his forehead as he tried to wipe the sweat from his brow. He was out of breath from the unexpected physical exertion, but he was the picture of health and stability compared to his father.

"You have to go back there." Aiden's hair stuck out at odd angles, as though he'd been repeatedly running his hands through it. He seemed frantic, pacing in the woods before Roska. "You have to go back now."

"Go back? Go back where?" Roska hadn't seen Aiden in moons. Watching their demi-god father wearing a path in the forest undergrowth, he was torn between confusion and worry for their father's mental health.

"To the Brotherhood! Gods, haven't you been listening?!" He pounded angrily at his head. Roska got the impression that his father was hearing things that no one else could.

"Um, Father, that was the first thing you said since I got out here." Roska knew their father was a little scatterbrained, but he seemed considerably worse than normal. "Are you all right, Father? Maybe we should go inside and see if there's a healer available to take a look at you."

Aiden was even more disheveled than his typical laissez-faire attire. He hadn't shaved in weeks and his clothes were more dirt and stains than clean cloth.

"What the mux are you talking about, boy?" Aiden pulled at his hair in frustration—or distress? He waved Roska off as he was about to answer. "It doesn't matter. You have to go back. You missed something. I can't see it. I can't tell, but something is there. Something needs you. Something *you* need."

"Father, please slow down. You're not making any sense."

"I can't slow down! It has to be now! You must go. NOW."

Aleerah stepped into the clearing, glancing over her shoulder as though she feared she'd been followed. "He's been having a constant flow of visions. It's been weeks. I can't make heads or tails of it, but he's convinced that the only way to stop the Brotherhood for good is if you and Demoni go back there. Alone. You have to find whatever it is that Grand Maester Auron has and take it back."

Cold fear gripped Roska's heart in its tight fist. "What are you talking about? What does he have?"

"I don't know!" Aiden wailed.

"He can't see it, only that it is the root of all evil. Or the root of their power? Or maybe it's both. He's been annoyingly unclear on that." Roska should have been put off by Aleerah's dry tone, but it actually soothed him some. If she could be so glib, then maybe things weren't as dire as Aiden believed.

Or maybe she's just trying to stay calm because he's clearly not.

Good point.

As his familiar, the dire wolf had always been Aiden's calming force. It was entirely possible that she was just as scared as he was and she simply didn't show it.

"Why me?" Roska asked. He didn't want to go back there. He'd been prepared to invade their compound when it had meant saving Brigit. But now he was supposed to return to the site of his worst nightmares for some unknown reason? Without any sort of backup or assistance?

Aiden held his gaze, giving him a look of sadness and regret. "It has to be you. It all started with you. It has to end with you."

＊＊ ＊＊＊＊＊

Aiden's insistence that Roska return to the Brotherhood's compound was unsettling, but Roska couldn't ignore it. He'd known, when they were standing outside the compound waiting for Zara and Lou to bring Brigit out, that something was in there, waiting for him. There had been a sinking, icy feeling in the pit of his stomach as he'd waited in those godsforsaken woods. At the time, Roska had convinced himself that it was just nerves, due to the overly stressful nature of the mission they were on, but now he realized it was something else entirely. Something within that compound was calling out to him, trying to draw him back in, and he'd missed it.

He had to go back.

Unfortunately, Roska knew he wouldn't be able to properly explain this feeling or why he needed to go alone to anyone—especially not Q—so he planned to sneak out after everyone else had gone to sleep. He'd borrow a horse from the stables and be long gone before anyone woke. It wasn't a flawless plan, by any means, but it was the best he could come up with. If he could get far enough away before anyone noticed he was missing, he might be able to keep them all safe and retrieve whatever item Aiden *sensed* in the compound.

The problem was, after Aiden calmed down and became coherent, he'd forgotten—or lost track of?—the item within the compound that Roska needed to get. Or steal. Or reclaim.

It was all very confusing. Aiden kept talking in circles and Aleerah couldn't make any more sense of his words than Roska could. The only thing they'd been able to determine was that Roska and Demoni had to be the ones who retrieved it, and they had to go alone. According to Aiden's choppy—and headache-inducing—explanation of the potential future paths, if they took anyone else with them, the mission would fail and they—along with whoever they brought with them—would almost certainly die.

It was easily one of the most frustrating things about Aiden. He had the gift of prophecy, but he'd been cursed with it and wasn't able to control or manipulate it. Hells, most of the time, he couldn't even understand what he *saw* until it was playing out before his eyes in real time and it was too late to change anything.

Truthfully, the fact that he was trying so hard to alter the future scared Roska. Their father hadn't even fought to change things when Elena had been destined to get sucked into a hells dimension to save the world from the *turmio*. This level of interference from their father was unheard of and terrifying.

How bad would things get if Roska didn't accomplish this mission within the Brotherhood's walls?

* * * * * *

Roska couldn't remember much about dinner that night. He was there in body, but his mind was elsewhere. Food kept appearing on his plate, and conversations droned on around him, but he was lost in his own thoughts—making plans and backup plans—to pay any attention to the world around him.

At some point, food stopped coming, dinner ended, and Roska rose from the table, heading for his rooms to pack and prepare to leave as soon as silence settled on the castle.

He was halfway up the stairs to his suite when someone shouted his name.

No, not someone. Some*ones*.

Miguel and Brigit were quick on his heels, racing to catch up to him. Roska debated rushing ahead and locking himself in his room, but Demoni's sharp claws dug into his shoulder, reminding him that he wasn't the only one in this relationship. And running away never solved anything.

"Are ye all right?" Brigit asked, slightly out of breath from having practically chased him from the dining hall.

"Yes, of course," Roska lied, looking anywhere but their eyes.

"Liar." Miguel never did pull any punches. "What's going on? You've been weird since Aiden arrived."

Roska was stunned. He thought he'd been more subtle than that. "How did you know Aiden had come?"

Miguel raised an incredulous eyebrow. "You really think a dire wolf racing through the castle would go unnoticed?"

You've been so wrapped up in your own thoughts that you haven't noticed that they've been watching you all night, Demoni added.

Mux everything. I can't tell them what's going on! Aiden said if anyone came with us, they'd die. Roska couldn't let anything happen to them. Brigit had already been through enough because of him. He refused to put either of them in harm's way ever again.

You might not have another choice, Demoni countered.

"If you two are done arguing about whether or not you should let us in on whatever is on your mind," Miguel interrupted, looking pointedly from Demoni to Roska, "we're not going anywhere, so you might as well just tell us."

Brigit crossed her arms across her chest, nodding solemnly. "We're here for ye, Roska. Whether ye like it or no. Fess up."

Roska glanced nervously over their shoulders. Q or Elena might be coming down the hallway at any moment. If Brigit and Miguel picked up on his anxiety, then it was very likely that his siblings had as well.

"Fine," he conceded. "But not out here. I don't want anyone to overhear."

He led them up the stairs and straight to his room without another word. It wasn't until they were secure in his rooms, with the doors firmly closed and locked, that he faced them. Roska didn't know what to say, but he knew he wouldn't lie to them. He couldn't. They clearly saw right through his weak attempts at falsehoods anyway.

The awkward silence dragged on for what felt like ages but was likely only a few minutes. Miguel and Brigit gave him some leeway. They simply took seats on the couch across the room and waited quietly for him to reveal his truths.

Finally, he couldn't take it anymore and blurted out. "I have to go back to the Brotherhood's compound. Alone."

Brigit's eyes widened as Miguel's mouth dropped.

"Why?" she whispered, her voice barely audible and soaked in fear. Brigit had put on a brave face as they'd been fleeing the compound, but it had quickly become clear that she had a great deal of trauma from her time with the Brothers. Hells, she'd been having night terrors and panic attacks since they'd reached the castle.

Roska quickly moved from pacing before the fire to kneeling in front of her, taking her hands gently in his while Miguel scooted closer to her on the couch and wrapped an arm around her shoulder. For several moments, Roska focused on his breathing, taking large, dramatic inhalations and slowly blowing out the breaths just as dramatically. Brigit, her eyes locked on his lips, began breathing along with him. Miguel was stroking her arm, breathing slowly with her as well. These were techniques Elena had helped Brigit adopt over the last few days to help maintain control during a panic attack and limit their intensity. It wasn't a flawless system, but it seemed to make Brigit feel more at ease, knowing there were things she could do to help calm her racing heart in the midst of an attack.

When the panic faded from her eyes, Roska moved from kneeling before her to sitting beside her on the couch, still firmly holding her hands.

"Aiden had a vision." He ran his thumbs slowly back and forth over the backs of her hands, soothing himself as much as it soothed her. "The Brothers have something. Some sort of magical item that is giving them more power. The *turmio* was meant to wipe out all magic in one go, but when we stopped that from happening three cycles ago—according to Aiden's visions—they started removing magical creatures on their own. The Brothers never intended to get their hands dirty in their efforts to erase magic, but clearly, they aren't opposed to it. His vision was unclear as to what, exactly, this item is, but he said that Demoni and I have to be the ones to find it and stop them."

"Alone?" Miguel asked, his hand still absentmindedly rubbing Brigit's arm.

"Yes."

"Why?" Brigit asked again.

"I'm not sure, honestly, but he was very clear that if anyone came with us, the mission would fail and anyone I brought with us would almost certainly die."

Miguel's brow furrowed. "That's why you've been so distant. You're trying to keep us safe by pushing us away?"

"I can't risk losing either of you." Roska's voice cracked as tears pooled along his lashes.

It was Brigit's turn to comfort him now, using her good hand to tightly grasp his and drawing his eyes to hers. "We aren't going anywhere. If ye need us to stay put to keep yer mind focused on the mission, so be it." She looked over her shoulder at Miguel. Miguel wasn't happy about her words, but he nodded after a moment, effectively consenting to let Roska go alone. Roska knew he'd hate it, but it was for Miguel's safety that they both stay in Riverayn.

"What about yer siblin's? And yer father?"

"If you're up to it, I could use your help, actually," Roska said. "Both of you."

Chapter 22

IT WASN'T FAIR OF Roska to ask them to lie for him, he knew that, but he couldn't think of another way. If Elena or Quinn found out what he was planning to do, they'd try to stop him, and he couldn't let that happen.

Roska trusted Aiden's visions, even if they didn't initially make sense. They always did in the end. He hadn't even been back long enough to fully unpack, so he threw the cloak back on and slipped out the door of his suite. Brigit would be reaching Elena now, seeking out his sister under the guise of getting to know her better—which wasn't even a lie, really, because Brigit had admitted she wanted to bond more with his family. Miguel was in the kitchens, packing food for him, and then he'd meet Roska in the stables.

Demoni had gone ahead, to ensure that Quinn and Lyra were nowhere nearby. She'd slunk into their rooms to find them both peacefully asleep on their couch. Quinn and Lyra had spent most of the night drinking and "bonding" with the Shadow-cloaks. He'd likely be hungover all day. It was a lucky break, likely one of the few Roska and Demoni would be granted.

His steps were silent and quick as he crept down the stairs, into the servants' halls, and out to the gardens that led to the stables.

"I don't like this," Miguel muttered as Roska entered the shadowy expanse. Most of the horses were bedded down and sleeping—or nearly asleep—save one. A young stallion, black as night with a thirst for adventure in his dark eyes.

"I know." There wasn't much else to say. Both Miguel and Brigit had made their objections very clear, but they were also supportive and respected his choice. With caveats.

"If you aren't back in two weeks, we're coming to get you. With the full force of the King's army in tow." Miguel tightened the straps of the saddle on the horse.

"Miguel," Roska said, placating. "I agreed you could bring the army if I don't return. But I need a few weeks. I'm not sure how long it will take me to get back or what condition I'll be in upon my return. We can't start an international incident because I was late for breakfast."

"Three weeks. That's the longest I'm willing to wait. This is a stupid, dangerous mission. I'm not just going to sit around on my hands when I know I could be helping you."

"You won't be sitting on your hands, Miguel. I need you here to keep her safe. She's been through so much, more than either of us will ever know. I can only do this if I know you're here, protecting her. Helping *her*." Roska knew he was begging, but he spoke the truth. Miguel was the only other person in the world who cared for Brigit almost as much as he did. "She suffered because of me. No, stop." Roska raised a hand to silence Miguel's protests. "I know it wasn't directly my fault, but I also know that none of this would have happened to her if she hadn't known me. I'm going to fix this. I will get whatever it is that Aiden *saw* and I will come back to you." He cupped Miguel's face, stroking the man's warm, tan cheeks with his cool thumbs. "I will come home to you. Both of you. Have faith in that, if nothing else. The Mother Goddess can't keep me from the two of you for long."

Miguel closed his eyes, leaning into Roska's hands, and exhaled a shuddering breath. He slowly lifted his lids, eyes locking on Roska's mouth for a moment. His own tongue slipped out and moistened his lips as his gaze heated. "I can't lose you." His voice was barely a whisper, his eyes shifting to meet Roska's.

"I swear to the Mother, I will come home as quickly as I possibly can."

Miguel leaned in, closing the small distance between them, resting his forehead against Roska's and closing his eyes. Their breath mingled as they stood together in the darkened stable. Roska tilted Miguel's head up, their noses brushing before their lips gently grazed each other. It felt as though lightning passed through them. Not entirely unlike the shocks of Elena's familiar, Agon, when he was expressing annoyance. Miguel's sharp inhale caused Roska to freeze. He nearly pulled back when he felt Miguel's hand firmly grasp the sides of his neck and draw him in tightly. Their lips crashed into each other in a blaze of passion and heat, unlike anything Roska had ever known. All the air rushed from the room, and the world disappeared around them as Roska's body honed in on the only thing that mattered: the feel of Miguel's warm skin pressed firmly against Roska's ever-cooled flesh. His hands slipped into Miguel's curly locks, fingers tangling in the coils at the base of his neck as he shifted his head and deepened their kiss.

Carefully, he parted his lips, letting his tongue slip through and tease Miguel's lips, seeking entry and permission. Miguel's responding groan was answer enough. Roska stepped forward, pressing himself entirely against the length of Miguel's body as he wrapped a hand around the man's waist while keeping the other firmly entangled in his dark mane. Miguel's arms tightened around Roska's waist as their tongues dueled for dominance.

Backing Miguel up farther, Roska shifted his grip to free one hand and ensure that he didn't push Miguel into any nails hanging on the wall. Pressing him up against the wall, Roska broke their kiss, only to trail his lips along Miguel's strong jaw, nipping and kissing along the way. Miguel gasped and Roska's lips found that sweet spot just below his ear, biting just enough to draw a moan from Miguel's throat before kissing the pain away.

The sound of footsteps, marching in their direction, broke the spell around them.

"It's the guards. Making their rounds, no doubt," Miguel said, slightly breathless. His half-lidded eyes seemed blurry and unfocused. Miguel's hair was a tousled mess, thanks entirely to Roska's attentions, but he couldn't bring himself to feel any guilt about it. Miguel looked absolutely Goddess-sent with his cheeks flushed, eyes heated, and hair a mess. Roska couldn't help but imagine how the man would look after a night together.

"Stop looking at me like that." Miguel smiled sheepishly.

Roska blinked quickly, brushing the hair from his brow. "Like what?"

"Like I'm a dessert you've been waiting your whole life to devour."

Roska bit his lower lip. Miguel's description was far too accurate to ignore. Stepping in again, he pressed a gentle kiss on the man's beautiful lips. Roska desperately wanted to continue this, but he knew if he didn't leave now, he'd never go.

"We'll pick this back up when I return." Roska placed one last kiss on Miguel's slightly swollen lips, heavy with the implications of what was to come, then he stepped away. He ran his fingers through his hair, his body suddenly coursing with unspent energy.

We'll be back as soon as we're done. Demoni's thoughts surprised him. Roska turned around quickly to see her waiting patiently coiled around the saddle horn, pointedly looking away from them.

"I'll be waiting, impatient and frustrated." Miguel's playful grin carried the meaning of his words, made all the more clear as he adjusted his trousers and attempted to tame his hair.

Roska took a few confident steps toward the stallion, offering the horse his hand in greeting. He'd never met this horse before and wasn't feeling the confidence he projected as he stepped toward the beast. He knew that the quickest way to befriend an animal was to offer it snacks. While the horse nuzzled his open palm, Roska reached into one of the cloak's pockets and pulled out a fresh carrot. He gave it to the horse before patting his thick neck and mounting onto the saddle.

Looking down at Miguel from this new height, Roska briefly worried that this would be the last time he ever got to look upon that beautiful face.

Don't think like that, Demoni chastised. *We'll be back soon, once we've reclaimed whatever Aiden foresaw and finally put an end to those bastards.*

Roska gave Miguel one last look, picked up the reins, and rode out into the night.

Chapter 23

"**W**HAT DO YOU MEAN he *left*? When? Where did he go?" The panic in Elena's voice made Brigit feel guilty for the part she'd played last night: distracting the future Queen so that Roska could sneak off without anyone noticing.

"Apologies, Milady." Brigit offered the deepest bow she could muster with her body still bruised from her time in captivity. "He was very clear that he had to go alone. He asked us to cover for him so ye wouldna worry."

Brigit realized that had been a fruitless endeavor, but they'd tried their best. Roska hadn't even been gone twelve hours.

"Clearly that worked flawlessly." King Niko's glare scared her almost as much as his dry tone. Roska had assured her that he was a good man, and she would be safe in Riverayn, but Brigit couldn't help wondering if Roska had misjudged him.

"He's on a mission for your father," Miguel chimed in, addressing Elena and ignoring King Niko entirely. He seemed utterly unfazed by the King's ire. His hand firmly gripped Brigit's arm, gently forcing her out of the bow she'd been maintaining. He hooked her hand in the crook of his arm. Giving her a reassuring smile, he turned back to the King. "Aiden had some sort of vision and told Roska he had to go back to the compound. Alone." He flicked his eyes to Elena at the last word. Trying to impress upon the King and his fiancée the importance of Roska's *solo* mission without outright telling royalty how to act.

Brigit admired his confidence. He was so self-assured as he addressed the King. He spoke plainly, without fear of reprisal. Brigit, on the other hand, could barely meet Elena's eyes and steadfastly refused to look King Niko in the face. Guilt and a hint of regret drove her to keep her eyes downcast, as was proper. At least, that was proper with the last king. Perhaps King Niko truly was different from his father. He hadn't had anyone flogged or executed since she'd arrived. Granted she'd only been in Riverayn for almost a week, but the previous king had been known for daily—very public—brutal punishments and executions. At the very least, King Niko was more private about his acts of violence.

Elena's knuckles turned white as she gripped the arms of her chair. They were seated at the dining table in the Great Hall. The future Queen had insisted on another family meal, but Quinn hadn't arrived yet. Elena had immediately questioned them about Roska's whereabouts before they'd even made it to the table. Brigit hadn't had it in her to lie to royalty. Roska hadn't been clear as to how long he'd be gone, or how long he'd expected them to cover for him. Perhaps she should have let Miguel handle all the questions.

Miguel led Brigit to the long table laid out with biscuits, cinnamon butter, fresh fruit, bacon, and sausage, dropping her hand to pull out a chair for her before taking the seat to her right. Brigit kept her eyes fixed on the plate before her. She liked Elena. She seemed kind and open and over the moon to meet Brigit, but that didn't mean that she would tolerate lies or deceit. Brigit was still a commoner in the royal house.

"Brigit," Elena's voice was softer than the silk sheets that covered her bed in the guest suite Roska had set her up in.

Looking up slowly through her lashes in an effort to keep her eyes as downcast as possible while still responding, she answered, "Yes, milady?"

"Please." Elena reached across the table, placing her hand palm up before her. "I'm sorry. I didn't mean to upset you. I'm just worried about my brother." Tears lined the woman's eyes as Brigit studied her features.

She really was beautiful. The soft lines of her lips curled up slightly at the ends, a perpetual smile on her face. Her smart brown eyes missed nothing but glowed with a hint of blue that Brigit thought she might have imagined. Loose brown curls framed her kind face.

"Please, forgive me." Elena leaned forward a bit more, stretching her hand out to Brigit, trying to close the distance between them.

"Of course, milady." Brigit couldn't bring herself to touch the proffered hand. Elena's hand was smooth, flawless, and unmarred by the world. Brigit's calloused and broken hand would have disgusted the young woman, and she didn't think she could handle the look of discomfort that would flash across Elena's face once their skin touched.

An awkward silence hung over the table for a moment, but Elena quickly took her hand back and added, "You really can just call me Elena. All of this 'milady' nonsense is silly. I'm just a person, Brigit. I promise."

King Niko's guffaw startled Brigit so much that she nearly knocked over the glass of orange juice she was reaching for.

"Shyt, sorry," he said as Elena smacked him playfully on the arm. "I just think it's funny that you're out here telling anyone you're a normal person, Firefly. Aside from being my betrothed, you're also an amazingly powerful enchantress. Not to mention clever, stunning, and a muxing demi-god, for the Goddess's sake. You are far from normal, my love." The smile that broke across his face was pure love.

Maybe he wasn't so bad after all.

"I just meant she doesn't need to walk around on eggshells around us. Gods, Niko, you're impossible." Elena's face was a warm shade of pink as she tried to hide her smile.

Brigit understood now why Roska loved being in the city so much. Seeing this kind of love every day would make anyone hopeful for a brighter future.

"Would you like some berries?" Miguel offered her a bowl of deep red berries.

Brigit stared. "Gods," she whispered reverently, "are those... garnet emberberries?" Carefully, as though she thought they might vanish the instant she touched them, Brigit took a single oblong berry from the bowl. With the same care that one might give a newborn babe, Brigit cradled the berry in the palm of her hand. She couldn't remember the last time she'd had a garnet ember-berry.

"Aye," King Niko said, tearing his eyes from his beloved. He watched Brigit with a hint of amusement sparkling in his eyes. "One of the merchants from Sylvestris brought them in earlier this week. The first batch of the season, he claimed, so we should be getting more over the coming weeks."

Brigit stared at the berry, confused for a moment as to why it was getting blurry, only to blink and realize that tears had started forming in her eyes. Gods, this was embarrassing. Crying over food at the King's table? Her mother would... well, her mother wouldn't do anything anymore, would she?

"Are you all right?" Miguel leaned closer, placing the bowl of berries on the table and wrapping an arm around her shoulders.

"Aye, gods. I'm a fool." Brigit roughly wiped the tears from her cheeks and eyes, trying to will a convincing smile onto her face. "I jus' havna had these in ages. My mum used to make the most delicious pie wit 'em to celebrate the start of the season." Try as she might, the tears wouldn't stop falling. She hadn't thought fondly of her mother in ages. Why would something as simple as a berry cause such an outrageous onslaught of emotions?

Elena rose from her seat across from Brigit and quickly rounded the table, wrapping her in the warmest hug she'd had since her mother's passing. Miguel shifted his hand from her shoulders to stroking her back, not quite ready to let her go. These simple acts of kindness broke her. The dam she'd been maintaining for cycles—the one that held back all of her heavy emotions and enabled her to keep that cheery smile on her face all the time—shattered to a million tiny pieces as the tears flowed freely down her face.

She hadn't let herself miss her mother. The woman had been firm and impossible, but strong and loving. She'd raised Brigit and her sisters on her own after their father left. He'd been gone—lost in his cups—for moons before her mum had finally kicked him out. He never even tried to come back. They'd managed for a few cycles, their mother making coin as a seamstress, along with selling their excess crops—when the seasons were good. She'd been tough on her girls, raising them to be independent in a world that thoroughly frowned upon such behavior. When the sickness came, the frost season Brigit had turned fifteen, their mother had faded quickly. Within the first moon of the season, she'd been confined to her bed. By the time the moon had cycled again, she was gone. Brigit had tried to care for her sisters as best she could, but she'd only been a child herself. Eventually, she'd taken her younger sisters to live with the town's baker and her family. The woman had always been kind to them, giving them day-old loaves for free. Brigit trusted that she'd take good care of her sisters, and left to find work. That was how she'd ended up in Nexton in the first place. Working in the inn and sending nearly all of her coin back to the baker to help care for her sisters.

It had been three solar cycles since she'd sent word or coin to them. Gods, she had no idea if they were even still living with the baker. Evalyn would be nearly eighteen now. That would make Aileen sixteen. Gods, could that be right? How could she have missed so much time with them? She missed them and worried about them constantly. Would they even remember her?

❇ ❇ ❇ ❇ ❇ ❇

It felt like hours had passed before the tears finally ceased and Brigit pulled back from Elena's strong embrace. Swiping at the last of the tears that slid down her raw cheeks, Brigit tried to hide her embarrassment, but there was no point.

"Oh, Gods," she exclaimed. "Yer beautiful dress. I've ruined it with my foolishness." Brigit used her napkin to try and blot out the tears that soaked Elena's shoulder.

"Hush now," Elena cooed, taking the napkin from Brigit's hand and placing it aside. "It's just a dress. I'm not worried about that. I'm worried about you. Do you want to talk about her?" Her eyes were just as warm and welcoming as her tone. Elena ran her hands up and down Brigit's arms. The slow, repetitive motion was far more soothing than Brigit would have imagined.

"There's no much to say, really. My mum was a lovely woman. She passed many cycles back. I hadna thought much about her," Brigit looked away, ashamed. She'd been deliberately not allowing herself to think of her mother. Strong as she'd been, Brigit knew her mother wouldn't have approved of how Brigit had been living her life in Nexton. She wasn't a prudish woman, but she firmly believed that physical acts of love should be confined to the bedroom, exclusively between a man and a woman after they'd been formally mated. Brigit's flirtatious behavior and "loose morals" would have enraged her mother, but it was the best way to make tips while working at the tavern.

Brigit couldn't help but think that her mother would have blamed her for the actions the Brotherhood had taken against her. She would have claimed that it was Brigit's lifestyle that had led her to be kidnapped and tortured in the first place. She might have even gone so far as to say she deserved what had been done to her.

Brigit knew that wasn't true, but she could still hear her mother's harsh voice in her head, telling her if she'd just been a good, modest girl, none of this would have happened.

"We all have complicated relationships with our mothers." Elena paused, looking at King Niko across the table. "If you ever decide you want to talk, I would be more than happy to listen." The smile she gave was small but genuine.

Brigit didn't know much about Elena's mother, Roska had mentioned she was the Headmistress of Harbor Ridge, but they hadn't spoken about her much. Brigit got the feeling that the woman was a bit distant and hard to connect with. She could relate to that. As much as she loved and admired her mother, Brigit couldn't help but feel slighted that the woman who'd raised her had been so narrow-minded about some things.

She returned Elena's smile, whispered a watery thanks, and that was the end of it. Elena squeezed her shoulders one last time, then rose and returned to her seat as if nothing had happened.

Brigit appreciated that. She didn't think she would have been able to keep a handle on her emotions if they'd pressed her about her mother.

Miguel's hand shifted from its position rubbing her back, to resting gently on her knee. He caught her eye as Elena and King Niko filled their plates. He cocked an eyebrow as if to say "Are you ok?", to which she gave him a subtle nod.

She wasn't entirely all right, and she might never be, but she was alive. She'd survived hells that, at the time, she'd thought would surely kill her.

She was so much stronger than she'd ever thought she could be.

Miguel kept his hand on her knee throughout the meal, skillfully serving himself and her one-handedly. Brigit ate slowly, savoring the garnet emberberries along with the buttermilk biscuits, bacon, and scrambled eggs.

Quinn strode in as she was finishing off the last bite of her gravy-soaked biscuit.

"You started without me?" He clutched his chest in mock offense. "How could you?"

"You were over an hour late." The voice surprised her. Elena's blue-black weasel was stretched out along the back of her chair. He flicked sparks at Quinn as Elena threw a biscuit at him.

Brigit wasn't sure she'd ever get used to these talking animals.

Lyra dashed in and leapt into the air, skillfully catching the biscuit.

"Rude." Quinn glared at the firefox. "That was mine."

Lyra gave Quinn a look that Brigit could only classify as a smirk. She hadn't even known foxes were capable of smirking.

Quinn pulled out a chair beside Elena and began filling a plate with bacon and biscuits.

"You really need some fruit, too." Elena had a very maternal air about her as she pressed a bowl of honeyed strawberries into her brother's hands.

"Gods, you're worse than Amelia," Quinn sighed but accepted the strawberries. He began shoveling food gracelessly into his mouth as though he hadn't eaten in days. "Where's Ros?" he asked around a mouthful of bacon.

"He left," King Niko said flatly.

"Oh, yeah? Where to?"

King Niko's glare was fixed on Miguel, prompting him to supply an explanation.

"Your father came to him yesterday and informed him that he'd had a vision," Miguel began.

"Oh, Gods. This isn't going to go well." Lyra hopped into the empty chair beside Q, stealing a strip of bacon from his plate.

Miguel's hand tensed on Brigit's knee for a second before he took a deep breath and continued. "According to Aiden, there's something in the compound that only Roska can retrieve. Honestly, it was all really confusing and unclear, but Aiden insisted that Roska had to go and he had to do it alone."

"So he snuck out in the middle of the night like a child, stole a horse, and took off without so much as a goodbye," Elena finished for him.

"I don't know if it's really stealing if he's a member of the King's court," Lyra observed pensively. "I think they just call that 'borrowing.'"

Brigit tried not to laugh at Lyra's comments, but truthfully, the fox had a way of putting things into perspective that was both succinct and mildly condescending. It was a trait Brigit envied.

"Regardless," King Niko cut in before someone got into an argument with the fox about definitions and threw the entire conversation off. "He's gone. He's insisting on doing this alone, which I find to be incredibly irritating, but I also understand it. Which, in truth, makes it all the more infuriating."

"So we're just supposed to let him go and hope for the best?" Quinn raised an incredulous eyebrow.

"Of course not," Miguel stated matter-of-factly. "We made an agreement with him." He nudged Brigit with his shoulder to identify her as part of that "we" he spoke of. "He has exactly three weeks to get back here before we"—he nodded to Brigit again—"go looking for him."

"Aye," she agreed, finally finding her voice again. "We agreed to abide by yer father's vision, for now. Roska was scared tha somethin' would befall anyone who went wit him. But we canna let him go too long. We canna lose him. We willna lose him." She said that last part with such ferocity that Q and Elena both stared at her for a moment.

Brigit thought they might laugh at her for her aggressive need to keep Roska around, but she was relieved to see the fire in their eyes burned just as brightly as the fire she felt in her heart.

They might not know each other well, but it was clear they all had an undeniable love for Roska.

If he didn't come home safe and soon, they would all be going after him.

Despite his dire warnings to the contrary.

Chapter 24

ROSKA AND DEMONI RODE through the night for as long as they could before he started drifting off to sleep atop the horse. The second time Demoni had to bite his ear—although he still wasn't convinced she *had* to do that—to wake him before he fell off, they decided to stop and make camp for the night.

Nights in the planting season were warm enough that he didn't bother taking the time to make a fire. He tethered the horse to a low limb, giving the stallion plenty of room to wander or graze, then wrapped himself and Demoni in a thick, woolen blanket, lay down in the soft grass, and passed out.

They woke a few short hours later—only slightly less tired—to the sound of birds chirping overhead in the early morning light. He quickly packed the blanket away in the saddle bag, led the horse to the river for some fresh water, and stretched his spine until it cracked a few times, working out the last kinks of their arduous journey.

Roska wondered how Brigit was adjusting. He'd only spent a few nights with her at the castle. Not *with* her, in that she had her own rooms, but she'd only been in Riverayn for a few days. He knew how overwhelming the city could be, especially after having been held captive by the Brothers for so long. Roska wished he'd been able to stay with her longer and help her get acclimated to the new environment before leaving her alone again.

She's not alone, Demoni reminded him. *She's with your sister, brother, Niko, and Miguel. She'll be well taken care of.*

You're right, he exhaled harshly, splashing cool river water on his face to wash the sleep from his eyes. *I just wish we could have stayed with her. I know they'll all keep her safe. I just wanted to be there. I* really *don't want to go back to the compound.*

Neither do I, but we both felt something there. Calling to us. Maybe that's the thing that Aiden wants us to retrieve. Regardless, those bastards have had enough time on this planet to get themselves right, and they continue to choose violence and bigotry. It's time we put an end to them.

Demoni's words were harsh, leaving a bitterness in his mind, but he couldn't disagree. The Brothers had had cycles to see the error in their ways and correct their behavior. They'd willfully chosen to maintain a lifestyle of hatred and abuse. Roska didn't like to think anyone was beyond redemption, but people like Grand Maester Auron made him doubt the goodness of humanity as a whole. That man was a poison that infected everyone around him.

They mounted the horse again and continued onward. If they could maintain this pace, they'd make it to the compound in five days. Assuming the weather stayed fair and the rains didn't come back with a vengeance. He knew it wasn't likely that he'd make it home in the timeline Miguel had insisted upon, but he hoped Miguel would see that too. Miguel was worried, understandably, but he should be more thoughtful and cautious. As one of Niko's Shadowcloaks, he should understand the need for stealth and *hopefully* not come racing after Roska, risking both their lives in the process.

Roska snacked along the way but rarely came to full stops for more than a few minutes. The horse needed breaks, of course, so he'd dismount and walk alongside the beast for stretches at a time, but for the most part, it was a quiet journey. Roska's mind was left to wander, causing him to become far more introspective than he ever liked.

In the evening, as the sun was setting on the third day, his mind had ventured into a dark place, reliving some of the worst tortures the Brothers had inflicted on him in an effort to "purify him" from the evilness of his magic.

Can you make anything other than snowballs or daggers? Demoni's odd question jolted him out of his reverie.

What?

I was thinking, since Quinn can make those flaming giants—his Infernals—can you make something else? We've never really tried.

It was an interesting question. Quinn had stumbled upon his ability to form giant warriors from the combination of his flame and Lyra's. They'd come in quite handy in defeating the Queen a few cycles back. Roska hadn't considered that he might have a similar power.

He dismounted from the horse, removing the saddle, bags, and blanket from the stallion, and allowing him to wander and graze while Roska set up camp for the night. Niko had banished metal bits from the stables shortly after he'd taken power, finding that the horses were just as eager—sometimes more so—to follow orders and directions without the uncomfortable metal in their mouths. Roska didn't bother removing the bridle from the stallion, knowing that the horse was quite capable of munching on grass without a metal bit hindering his ability to snack.

I've never tried, Roska replied, getting back to Demoni's curious thought, *but it would be helpful if I could form my own army before venturing into the compound.*

Demoni leapt off into the woods, slowly bringing back mouthfuls of dry sticks and twigs to start their fire for the night. Roska set about clearing a space for the flames, surrounding it with rocks he found along the river's edge, and creating a sort of ramp for the dry logs to slowly roll down so that the fire might continue to feed itself throughout the night. Another trick he'd learned during his annual hunting trips with Quinn. While his brother was never really bothered by the cold, Roska and Demoni had a harder time regulating their body heat. Aiden explained once that it had to do with their powers and the toll their respective magics took on their bodies. Magic required balance. Roska's temperature was always a bit colder than everyone else's, and he struggled to stay warm without an external heat source in the frost season. Quinn, on the other hand, was always hot, and dreaded the heat of the growing season, complaining that he could never truly stay cool.

After dinner—dried meat, an apple, fresh water from the river, and a travel biscuit—Roska and Demoni sat in the glow of the fire, and he let his mind wander again.

Holding his hand, palm up, in his lap, Roska called on his power, drawing the frost to his hand until it began to take shape. A ball. It was the first thing he'd learned he could do and it was the easiest. Staring at the ball, he imagined it growing, taking the shape of a humanoid creature—not unlike the flaming giants Q had created. But nothing happened.

Perhaps you need my power, too? That's how it works for Quinn and Lyra. Demoni climbed into his lap, making her way to his arm and coiling herself around it until her head rested at the base of his wrist. Roska felt the coolness of her scales against his flesh, but still, nothing changed.

Maybe we aren't doing it correctly, Roska wondered. It would have been nice to have Q with them, explaining how his powers worked so that they might emulate that.

In the shadow of the branches above them, Roska heard the hoot of an owl. He tried to find the source of the sound, but the creature was too far beyond the light from their fire.

Look! Demoni shouted in his mind.

Roska tore his gaze from the woods to see that the snowball in his hand had vanished. In its place sat a small bird made entirely of ice. Roska hadn't known he could make such beautifully detailed statues with his ice. Hells, he hadn't even meant to change the snowball to ice in the first place. He lifted his hand, bringing it closer to his face to admire the fine detailing of the bird's wing, when the ice bird moved. It cocked its head, as though it was studying him as well.

Roska nearly threw the ice creature.

He'd created a *living* bird out of his ice. Entirely on accident.

What the hells...

The little bird hopped from the palm of his hand to the tip of his fingers, then launched itself into the air. It flew in small, tight circles overhead. Roska's mouth hung open in utter confusion as he tracked the bird's flight.

How did you do that? Demoni asked, her head following the movement of the bird as well.

I have no idea.

It was the most unsettling truth he'd spoken in a while. He had no clue how he'd taken their powers and formed a living creature with their combined magics.

He leaned back against a nearby tree trunk, watching the bird's graceful movements. Roska closed his eyes, trying to recall exactly what he'd been thinking when he'd formed the bird, only to get an entirely new shock. A moment after his vision went black, a blue haze filled his mind's eye, and then he was looking down at himself. He sat on the forest floor, resting against the thick trunk of a tall balsam fir tree, Demoni still wrapped around his hand. The frost dragon's eyes were tracking his movements.

No, wait. Not *his* movements. She was watching the ice bird. He was seeing through the eyes of the ice bird!

Gods, how was that even possible?

Roska's eyes flew open as he bolted upright.

What the hells is wrong with you? Demoni tightened her grip on his arm, her tiny, sharp claws digging into his flesh as he jostled her with his sudden movements.

You didn't see that? Roska looked up again, searching out the bird in the air above them. It was starting to melt, losing its shape and ability to fly.

See what?

I closed my eyes and I saw what the bird was seeing. I saw us down here from its vantage point up there.

Roska raised a hand and the ice bird quickly—and with very little grace—landed in his outstretched palm.

You could see through its eyes? Demoni's gaze fixated on the melting bird. Her tongue flicked out, smelling and tasting the creature. *How is that possible?*

I have no idea. The bird was gone, only a small puddle remained as Roska wiped his hand on his trousers.

I wonder what else we can do.

Chapter 25

I T TURNED OUT ROSKA could make quite a few things with his ice.

Over the next two days, Roska and Demoni toyed with their combined powers while continuing their journey to the Brotherhood's compound.

They formed mice, squirrels, butterflies, an owl, a few different types of snakes, and even a horse, although that one startled their stallion and melted rather quickly. Roska determined that riding a horse made of ice wouldn't be practical anyway, and it would be useless in covert missions since it was a brilliant light blue color and stood out starkly against the greens and browns of the forest.

The smaller creatures—the rodents, birds, and bugs—would make excellent spies, though. In fact, their creations and the skill he was gaining while practicing with them triggered the beginnings of a plan in his mind. Roska hadn't had a plan to gain entry into the compound when they'd initially left Riverayn, but he was quickly formulating one as he spied on the world through the eyes of the ice-robin that flew ahead of them. He knew his creations would be more effective in the cooler seasons, as the planting season sun was melting them away with frustrating efficiency, but they would work well enough for what he had in mind.

From his vantage point through the ice-robin's eyes, he could see the edge of the forest and the walls of the Brotherhood's compound in the distance. They'd reach it by nightfall.

Do you think it's wise to approach tonight? Demoni's question was valid, but Roska got the sense that it was driven more by her anxiety about returning to that hells than any concerns about stealth.

I don't think anything we're doing right now is wise, Roska answered bluntly, *but it is our destiny, apparently, so we might as well get on with it.*

Roska typically took a more cautious approach to these things, especially when it came to confrontation, but if his plan worked as well as he hoped it would, there wouldn't be much by way of confrontation. They get in, retrieve whatever it was that was calling out to them, and get back to Brigit and Miguel as quickly as possible. As much as he wanted to take down the Brotherhood, he'd accepted that it wasn't a task he could do on his own. He'd get what Aiden's vision had sent them to reclaim, and then they'd head home and—with Calum and the Shadowcloaks' help—make a plan to finally excise the Brotherhood from Waverly.

The sun had well and truly set when they reached the edge of the forest. Roska loosely tethered the horse to a low tree branch, allowing the animal plenty of room to graze and reach the river for fresh water, then he and Demoni slunk to the very edge of the trees. Demoni moved from her position across his shoulders to coil around his forearm, breathing her ice into his hand as he called forth his own power. They mixed their magics to form a pair of small field mice.

Roska knelt down in the tall grass and let the mice loose in the field. As they raced across the open plain, Roska closed his eyes and focused on the first mouse. It was in the lead, bounding through the grass that now felt as tall as mountains. He took a deep breath and inhaled the scents of wet dirt and sweetgrass. The mouse reached the stone wall surrounding the compound in moments. Without warning, it shattered into a million tiny pieces, forcefully thrusting Roska back into his own mind.

What the hells? Roska glared at the walls surrounding the fortress of the compound.

Demoni blinked back into her body, her mouse having been demolished by some unseen force as well.

Roska was about to form a second pair of mice when he saw a figure shuffling on the other side of the windows in the compound wall. Slinking farther into the woods, Roska and Demoni pooled their magic and formed a fly, sending it buzzing across the field to peer into the windows of the compound. If they couldn't get inside, they could at least see what was going on through the windows.

Following the figure, Roska tried to get the fly ahead of the man, hoping to identify him or at least learn where he was going in the middle of the night. He was shocked when he caught sight of the man's face.

Lou?

※ ※　※ ※　※ ※

Roska lost his focus, and the fly flew into the compound wall, shattering the ice and leaving Roska staring, confused and disoriented, in the woods with Demoni still coiled around his forearm.

He searched the windows, trying to find the old spy, but he'd lost sight of him.

What the hells is Lou still doing in there? We left him weeks ago, he wondered silently.

Demoni shifted on his arm, climbing farther up his body to settle on his shoulders. *He did say he had another mission to complete here.*

Shyt. Someone's coming.

The side gate they'd used to rescue Brigit swung open and a hooded figure slipped out of the compound, closing the gate soundlessly behind them. Roska watched the figure creep quickly and quietly from the compound, heading straight for them.

We should move, Demoni said as the figure crossed the field with unexpected speed.

Ducking beneath some low tree branches, Roska and Demoni hid in the shadows of a cluster of saplings, keeping an eye on the hooded figure.

Just as the figure was about to breach the woods and be upon them, it vanished into the shadows.

What the mux? Where did they go?

Demoni shifted on his shoulder, angling her body to see around the bush, trying to get a better vantage point.

They couldn't have just disappeared. That's impossible. Roska felt a sudden chill in the air, the hairs on the back of his neck standing at attention.

"Well, hello, *cher*. I didn't expect to see you two so soon." Lou was standing directly behind them, a cocky grin split across his face, showing off that chipped tooth again.

"Muxing hells," Roska swore, nearly falling on his ass as he jumped at Lou's voice.

"How did you do that?" Demoni asked, her question more of an accusation than an actual query.

Lou winked. "I can't give away all my little tricks, now can I? Where's the fun in that?" He turned and started walking back toward their campsite.

How did he even know we were here?

Roska shrugged in answer to Demoni's question, but he quickly rose and followed the Shadowcloak to their smothered fire and tethered horse.

Roska set up fresh, dry wood and restarted their fire, all the while watching Lou move about the campsite as though he'd known they were here all along.

Once he got the fire going and Lou was settled across from him, Roska decided it was time for answers. "What are you doing here? How did you disappear like that? How did you know we were here?"

Lou chuckled, pulling a bundle of something from within the folds of his cloak, and began slowly unwrapping it. "Skippin' the pleasantries then? All right, *cher*. Let me first say that I knew you were here because you aren't as stealthy as you think. Hells, boy, you were sitting out in the open on the edge of the woods just staring at me. That hair of yours practically glows in the moonlight. What in the name of the Mother were *you* doing out there?"

Heat spread up Roska's neck at the admonishment. He thought they'd been better hidden than that. "I've been sent back here to retrieve something. That's not important right now," Roska snapped, trying to hide his embarrassment behind a facade of annoyance. "Why were you sneaking around in the compound in the middle of the night? And what is that thing?"

Lou had finished unwrapping the bundle, pulling out a jagged, violet crystal and holding it up to inspect in the firelight. "Magic doesn't work in the compound," he said, turning the crystal back and forth in his hands.

Roska stared at the man, confused by the non sequitur as well as the startlingly pretty item in his hands.

Magic doesn't work in the compound, Demoni repeated firmly in his mind. *That's why our ice animals exploded.*

Roska shook his head, mentally chastising himself for forgetting such vital information. Niko had told him that from the start. He should have known better than to try and infiltrate the compound with creatures made entirely of magic.

"What does that have to do with why you're here?" Roska tried to get the conversation back on point.

"I was sent here to infiltrate the Brotherhood, *cher*. Infiltrate and then do anything I can to bring them down from the inside." He tossed the crystal over the fire to Roska. The second it touched his skin, Roska knew it was no ordinary stone. There was a warmth radiating off the gemstone, and a low thrum of power resonated within. Roska turned the stone over in his hands, studying it as Lou continued. "From what I've gleaned, that stone is powering their anti-magic barrier. Once I destroy it, magic will be able to enter the compound again." He looked pointedly at Roska. "This isn't the only magical artifact their Grand Maester has in his arsenal. It's not even the only one I've seen him use. Based on what I've seen, this stone blocks magic from coming in, but doesn't stop magic from being used within the compound walls."

"What are you saying?" Demoni asked, slithering down Roska's arm to rest on top of a stone near the fire.

"I'm saying, *mon petit dragon*, that the Grand Maester can and does use magic within the compound."

"No," Roska spoke without thinking. "That's impossible. The man abhors magic." Even as the words left his mouth, though, he knew it wasn't true. He'd felt the barrier shatter his ice creatures. Castor had already informed them of the shield's existence. It was obvious that Grand Maester Auron didn't object to using magic when it benefitted him.

"*Cher*." Lou's voice held a tone of compassion and sadness that pulled at Roska. "I know this is hard to accept, but it's undeniable. The man is a hypocrite. It's that simple. Now, let's destroy this thing so I can go home. I'm sure my beloved is getting restless. I've been gone longer than I'd like."

Roska was intrigued by Lou's mention of a significant other, but he didn't ask. If Lou wanted to talk about them more, there would be plenty of time once the magical barrier was removed from the compound.

Roska attempted to freeze the stone and smash it with a rock, but his powers didn't seem to work on it. Hells, the stone simply absorbed his ice the instant it made contact with the shiny purple surface. He turned to Lou, eyebrows furrowed in annoyance. "Any other ideas?"

Lou reached into his cloak once more, pulling out a pickaxe with a sly smile. "How about this?"

"How the hells did you fit that in there?" Roska stared at the man in confusion. There was definitely more to Lou than he knew.

Lou didn't answer. Instead, he took the stone from Roska's hand and laid it on a flat rock beside the fire. He looked over his shoulder at Roska. "Might want to step back a bit, *cher*. I'm not really sure how this will work."

Roska scooped Demoni up and moved behind a thick tree, peeking around the trunk to watch.

Lou raised the pickaxe above his head, shifted his weight, and brought the tip of the axe down with exacting precision. A loud crack echoed through the forest, but the stone didn't break. Lou lifted the axe again, took aim, and swung with all his might. The sound of the stone shattering was akin to lightning striking directly in front of him. The air split with an explosive crack, the deafening roar of raw power unleashed around them, knocking both men to the ground and terrifying the horse. Roska was nearly trampled by the beast's attempts to flee. Thankfully, the tether kept the horse from escaping, but it took several minutes to calm the stallion.

"WHAT THE MUX WAS THAT?!" Roska yelled over the ringing in his ears, glaring at Lou, who was still lying on the forest floor, laughing like a crazed fool.

Stop shouting, Demoni scolded. *The Brothers could come looking for what caused that explosion. Your yelling will lead them straight to us.*

She was right, of course, but Roska was struggled to control his volume. He couldn't hear a damned thing. He only knew Lou was laughing based on the look of pure glee on his face and the way his body shook with unbridled amusement.

He might actually be insane, Roska observed, watching the man try to slow his breathing and control his laughter.

Roska shuffled away from Lou, offering the horse a few apples to soothe its frayed nerves. The sky was beginning to fade to a pale shade of lavender when his ears finally popped and Roska was able to hear properly again. Thankfully, the Brotherhood didn't come to investigate the explosion. They would have been sitting ducks—as Quinn would have said—unable to hear the Brotherhood's approach until it was too late.

Roska said a quick prayer of thanks for their fortune. He just hoped their luck would hold.

❋ ❋ ❋ ❋ ❋ ❋

They spent the daylight hours resting and talking. Lou had been embedded with the Brothers for moons. He was able to give Roska the most up-to-date information on the layout of the compound. Grand Maester Auron's office was the same, although from how

Lou described it, it had become considerably more crowded with storage and shelving. Roska wasn't sure why the Grand Maester would use his office for storage, but he supposed it didn't much matter. Since Roska didn't know exactly what he was looking for, Lou suggested starting there.

Roska hadn't wanted to return to the Grand Maester's office ever again, but he'd do what he must to destroy that vile man's hold on the country. He would do whatever was necessary to ensure that no one else ever suffered at the hands of that bigoted, self-righteous monster.

Night had fallen when Lou announced it was time for him to go. He grabbed his pickaxe and the remaining shards of the crystal, tucking them into his voluminous cloak. Then he offered Roska and Demoni a nod, bid them good luck, and slipped soundlessly off into the woods.

Roska slipped Elena's enchanted cloak on, pulling the hood tight over his head and testing the magic in it to ensure that they were truly camouflaged this time. Then he and Demoni crept back to the edge of the forest, pooled their magic, and formed two more field mice.

Turning the mice loose in the tall grass, Roska let his mind wander, taking control of the little mouse and racing across the field until it reached the compound's wall. The mouse turned and began following the wall until it found a hole in the stone large enough for it to squeeze through. Roska held his breath, feeling the tightness of the space as the ice-mouse forced its way through the tiny opening. When it burst through the other side, Roska was able to take a deep breath again.

Silently, Roska cheered Lou's success in destroying the magic barrier.

Through the mouse's eyes, Roska could see the torches that lined the hallway, leading off to the left and right. He paused for a moment, reviewing his mental map of the compound, then turned his head to the right. The ice-mouse turned to the right and tore off down the hall.

Demoni flexed her claws on his wrist, shifting her weight as she directed the other ice-mouse down the hall to the left. In the back of his mind, Roska couldn't wait to brag about this newfound skill to his brother and sister. Not only could he create animals from ice, but both he and Demoni could see through the creature's eyes and perceive the world through their senses. It was exhilarating.

Lyra is going to be so jealous, Demoni's smug voice echoed in his mind. Roska felt the rumble of his own chuckle, but he could barely hear it. His senses were focused on the ice-mouse he was leading through the compound's maze of hallways.

Roska had hoped that he'd be able to feel the pull of whatever was calling them through the bond he'd created with the ice-mouse, but it wasn't as strong as he'd expected. Either the item had been relocated, or it was calling to him directly and wouldn't reach out to an ice-creature.

Before he could reach the heart of the compound, the mouse melted into nothing, forcing Roska's mind back into his body. He blinked several times before his vision refocused on the world before him. Demoni's mouse lasted a few moments longer, but she was quickly returned to her body as well.

Well, that didn't work as we'd hoped. Roska slipped farther into the woods, checking on the horse before fishing some biscuits and dried meat from the enchanted cloak's pockets.

Perhaps, if we get closer, the pull will be stronger and we'll be able to send in more mice and find the source without having to venture inside.

Roska shared Demoni's apprehension about reentering the place where they'd been held captive and tortured for the majority of their lives. He didn't relish the idea of wandering those halls again either.

He brushed a nervous hand through his near-white hair. *Perhaps we should try a bird. Or maybe a moth. It would go unnoticed and be able to slip in through any open windows.*

They were stalling. They would have to venture within the walls to get whatever it was Aiden had sent them to retrieve, regardless.

Heaving a great sigh, Roska ruffled the horse's mane and offered him an apple from one of the saddle bags.

Roska knew he'd never feel "ready" to confront the Brothers, but he couldn't put it off any longer. Whatever Grand Maester Auron had, it was putting the magical world at risk. Roska was the only one who could stop it—although, Gods only knew why it *had* to be him.

We'll go in late tonight, he decided. *Once the bells call for two past midnight. The majority of the brothers will be asleep by then. It will be the best chance we have to get in, find whatever we're looking for, and get out unnoticed.*

Roska sat on the forest floor, resting against the rough trunk of a tree. Crossing his arms and ankles, Roska tried to relax his mind. He needed to get some sleep before venturing into the halls of that hells.

Demoni stretched out across his legs, keeping watch while he attempted to sleep.

Roska hadn't expected to drift off at all, but dreams quickly overtook him, drawing him into a hells-scape that was all too familiar.

✳✳ ✳✳✳ ✳✳

Grand Maester Auron stood over him, glaring down at him with a look of utter disgust and hatred. He held Demoni in a tight grip as he stoked the fire with an iron poker. Roska could feel the bindings digging into his wrists and ankles as he fought to get free from the chair he'd been roughly shackled to. Demoni hissed and snapped with her vicious teeth, to no avail. Grand Maester Auron chuckled, cruel and indifferent to their weak attempts to fight back.

"You can't stop this, boy," he said calmly. "This is for your own good. Perhaps now you will accept your place in the world. Your place in society."

He waved over two other, faceless Brothers. One wrapped a thick leather band around Demoni's maw, rendering her teeth impotent. The Grand Maester handed her to them, and the Brothers laid her out on the chipped wooden table before the fireplace.

Grand Maester Auron positioned himself across the table from Roska, ensuring that he had Roska's full attention and that Roska could see exactly what he was doing. The Brothers held Demoni down as Grand Maester Auron pulled out a wicked scythe from somewhere within his dark robes.

"This is your fault, boy. If you didn't insist on fighting me at every turn, I wouldn't have to punish you. Perhaps now you'll understand."

In one swift motion, Grand Maester Auron lifted one of Demoni's stunning, leathery wings, raised his scythe, and sliced the wing from her flesh.

Roska cried out in unimaginable agony. His own back felt as though it had been sliced open, and blood soaked his tunic as he screamed until his throat was raw. He watched in terror as the Grand Maester pulled the poker from the fire and pressed it against Demoni's gaping wound, cauterizing it and sealing it closed. Roska felt the blinding heat searing his back. He screwed his eyes tight against the pain, begging for the Mother to come and take them unto the Fade. Free them from this hells.

She never came.

Instead, Grand Maester Auron waited until Roska's screams subsided and he could open his eyes again. Roska sagged against his bonds, heaving sobbing breaths and fighting back an overwhelming wave of nausea.

"Have you learned anything from this, boy?" Grand Maester asked, his voice calm and unaffected by the violence his hands had wrought.

Roska, unable to speak, nodded sloppily, hoping that that would be sufficient. Forcing his eyes open, Roska sought Demoni's gaze. Her eyes were open but unfocused. Roska thought she might have died, but—from what little he knew about his connection with her—he didn't think it was possible for her to die and him to live on.

"I need to ensure that you fully grasp this lesson, boy."

Roska's eyes flew back to the Grand Maester just in time to see the man lift his blade once more, tearing through Demoni's other wing.

The agony overwhelmed him this time.

Blackness filled his vision, and Roska's mind quickly faded into blessed oblivion.

* * * * * *

It's time to go. Demoni's voice, coupled with the feel of her icy breath on his cheek, roused Roska from his restless slumber.

Shaking the nightmarish memories from his mind, Roska rose and stretched, hearing the delicious cracks of his spine. Sleeping upright against a tree trunk wasn't ideal, but the spinal adjustment thereafter was heavenly.

The bells just rang twice. There should only be a handful of Brothers awake now. Demoni turned her icy breath on their fire, putting it out in a matter of seconds and smothering it with snow to diminish the smoke it would create. *Do you want to try the mice again?*

No. As much as he wanted to delay their entry into the compound, the mice wouldn't work any better a second time. Ice could only stay hardened and mobile for so long on a warm planting season night. *Let's try moths instead. At the very least, it will give us an aerial view and hopefully, we'll be able to spy any sentries out and about.*

Roska scooped Demoni up from her perch on a stone by their snow-covered fire, placed her on his shoulder, and ventured back to the edge of the forest.

The compound was dark. A few torches brightened every third window along the hall that Roska knew was just beyond the wall. Just enough light to see if one needed to use the outhouse in the middle of the night.

Demoni slid from his shoulder to wrap around his forearm once more, mingling her magics with his until two small moths rested in the palm of his hand. Closing his eyes, Roska willed his moth into the air, flapping its tiny wings with a speed he hadn't known them capable of as it soared across the field, over the outer wall, and into the garden that made up the center of the compound. Turning his head left and right, Roska used the moth's eyes to identify any potential threats within the garden.

The planting season air was too warm and humid to sustain the icy moths, and both creatures quickly melted away, but not before Roska saw Grand Maester Auron striding purposefully into the building that contained his office.

The moth vanished, and Roska was thrust back into his body. He couldn't decide if the ice filling his veins was a result of his powers or seeing the Grand Maester again. He told himself it was because the dream had brought such a violent memory back to the forefront of his mind, but he knew that was a lie. Grand Maester Auron was the only thing in the world that could still scare Roska. Hells, he'd faced down demons, fought against the corruption of the Brotherhood's influence, and even battled the fury of a scorned witch. Yet, that old man still had a death grip on Roska's soul. The mere sight of him brought up feelings of terror and helplessness.

You're right. He is *an old man. And we aren't the scared young ones that we used to be.* Demoni flexed her claws on his sleeve anew, tearing tiny holes in the fabric. *He cannot hurt us anymore. We are strong and powerful. We came here to stop him, and we will.*

Chapter 26

R OSKA RETURNED TO THE horse long enough to unburden himself with anything but the necessities. He kept Elena's cloak with him. Aside from the never-ending pockets, the cloak was enchanted to enable the wearer to meld perfectly with their surroundings, making them nearly invisible. He also grabbed the pair of iron daggers Quinn had gifted him last Frost Solstice, just in case his ice daggers failed him within the compound's walls. Lou had successfully destroyed the magic barrier, but Roska didn't know what other tricks Grand Maester Auron had up his sleeves.

He thought his powers would likely be fine since his ice creatures had survived within the walls until they melted, but he didn't see the harm in bringing extra, nonmagical weapons. Just in case.

With Demoni coiled around his neck, hidden beneath the hood of the cloak, Roska crept across the field. The moon was hidden behind a blanket of clouds tonight, allowing shadows to rule, even in the open, grassy field. Roska made quick work of the distance, flattening himself against the stone wall and keeping low to the ground. He hadn't seen any guards or sentries patrolling along the top of the wall, but that didn't mean they weren't there. Moths weren't known for their keen eyesight, after all.

Next time, we should try a hawk or a falcon.

I don't intend for there to be a next time, Roska stated. *Once we get what we came for and destroy that man, we'll never have to return.*

Flush against the wall, Roska could feel the pull stronger than ever. Something was calling out to them, desperate for their attention. He followed along the wall until they reached a gate. Quinn had taught Roska to pick locks last frost season when they were snowed in at Amelia's inn. She hadn't appreciated the scratches Roska had left on her locks, but by the time the snow had melted enough for them to venture outside again, Roska had gotten pretty decent.

Pulling the cloak tighter around him so only his hands were visible, he worked the lock picks Quinn had given him until he heard the faint click of the tumblers falling into place. Thank the Goddess, the hinges were well-oiled and didn't make a sound as he opened the gate and slipped inside. They stood in the shadow of the entryway, looking out into the garden. Grand Maester Auron had ventured into his office several minutes ago. For all Roska knew, the Grand Maester was already back in the garden, making his way to his bed chamber.

When they saw and heard no movement, Roska crept out into the greenery. He took slow, deliberate steps, allowing the pull deep in his chest to lead him, seeking out the source. Much to his dismay, it seemed to be leading him directly to the Grand Maester's office.

Are you sure this is right? Apprehension filled Demoni's voice.

Roska simply nodded, hiding in the shadow of a lemon tree that had grown so low it was practically a lemon bush. He was careful of the large thorns that protected the fruit from hungry animals. It wouldn't do well for them if one of those thorns snagged the cloak, revealing them to the guards who had to be nearby.

The Brotherhood wasn't usually one for excessive security, but Roska had to assume that after they'd broken in to rescue Brigit, Grand Maester Auron had taken steps to ensure such an infiltration wouldn't happen twice.

Still, they hadn't seen any guards or security of any kind. It was a bit unsettling.

From his vantage point in the lemon bush, Roska could just make out the shape of Grand Maester Auron behind the desk in his office through the warped glass window.

Calling on his powers, Roska formed two wickedly sharp ice daggers in the palms of his hands. He stepped out of the shadows and forced himself to approach the office door. Whatever was calling to him, it was in that damned room, and he was going to get it. Avoiding a direct confrontation with the Grand Maester was clearly not in the Fates' plan for him.

Despite his certainty that this was what he'd been sent to do, Roska froze outside the door. He had experienced the most painful and devastating of his punishments and abuse in that room with that godsdamned man. He'd thought he could push all that aside and do what he came here to do, but now, faced with the reality of his situation, Roska couldn't move.

Nervously, he flexed his grip on the frozen daggers in his hand.

This is what we came for. Demoni adjusted herself at his neck. *Whatever is in there, it belongs with us, not that vile man. We are stronger than him.*

Roska nodded once, recalled his power some so that the dagger in his right hand disappeared, and reached for the doorknob.

* * * * * *

"It took you long enough, boy. I thought I'd have to sit here all night waiting for you to show up." Grand Maester Auron didn't bother looking up as he chastised Roska's tardiness.

Roska stepped into the room, firmly closing the door behind him.

He didn't say a word as he studied the walls around him. The room was far more crowded than he remembered. Smaller. With shelves filled with strange objects. Jars of liquid with what appeared to be various body parts floating in them. He took a step closer and noticed the jars were neatly labeled. They weren't just body parts, they were parts from magical creatures. Claws of a *cait sith*. Pixie wings. Fins of a newborn mermaid. Vampire teeth. Elfish ears. The eyes of a witch.

Roska felt a wave of nausea roll through him when he saw the hands of a young enchantress floating in two jars.

"Admiring my collection, eh, boy?" Grand Maester Auron watched him closely, a look of smug pride plastered across his wrinkled face.

"This is sick," Roska hissed as he turned to face the man from his nightmares. "*You* are sick."

"No, stupid boy. I'm not the sick one. These creatures," he spat the word as though it left a foul taste in his mouth, "are abominations. They do not belong in this world. I'm doing what needs to be done to purify this world of those wretched monsters."

He rose slowly from his chair, hunched slightly forward as he rounded the desk between them and came to stand before Roska.

"You, foolish child, failed me."

Roska felt the sting across his face before he even registered that the man had struck him. Grand Maester Auron might have aged, but it clearly didn't slow him down when he was enraged. He raised his hand again, poised to deliver a second strike, but Roska caught the old man's wrist this time.

"No." Roska glared into the eyes of his abuser. "You failed *me*. You were supposed to care for me. I was a muxing child!" He shouted the last word as he tightened his grip on the man's wrist. "You were supposed to protect me. Instead, you abused and tormented me. You tried to turn me into a monster. Just like you." He threw the man's arm away before he did something he'd regret. Like stabbing the bastard in the throat with the ice dagger held firmly in his other hand.

"I was trying to protect the world from you. You and all the vile creatures like you." He spat—literally spat—at Roska as he stumbled to regain his footing. "You are a perfect example of all that is wrong with the world. I should have killed you when you first showed up on our doorstep. It was my own hubris that I believed I could save you from your wicked nature."

Grand Maester Auron reached for something behind his desk. Roska jumped back just in time as the cat o' nine tails whipped out at him. Throwing his dagger hand up, the ice blade sliced cleanly through the knotted throngs that had been skillfully aimed at his face. One hit from that weapon and Roska would have been unconscious and bloody on the floor. Instead, he stood straight, eyes glowing a vibrant teal as he called on his powers, plunging the room into near-freezing temperatures as he raised his hands. His daggers quickly morphed into a pair of long, curved swords. Widening his stance, Roska faced the Grand Maester, a cruel, vengeful smile cracking across Roska's face.

"You are the monster, and it is my job to rid this world of monsters. You taught me that, Grand Maester."

The old man paled as he stepped backward until he forced himself into a corner. Shaking his head, his voice wavered as he spoke. "No. No, I'm trying to save the world. You... you don't belong here."

"That's where you're wrong. I have always belonged. It's mindless bigots like you that shouldn't be here." Roska thrust his blades at the man, spearing through the sleeves of the Grand Maester's robes and pinning him to the stone wall behind him. Roska stepped into the man's space, his face mere inches from that of his former tormentor. "Be grateful that I am a kinder man than you. I will not kill you, although by all rights I should. That's not why I'm here."

Roska stepped away, suddenly feeling free, as though a heavy weight had melted from his shoulders. Sparing the Grand Maester one last look, he turned from the man and sought out the pull within himself again. Walking slowly around the room, he followed the feeling to a locked cabinet against the far wall.

"What's in here?" he wondered aloud.

"Stay away from there!" the Grand Maester demanded as he pulled against the blades.

Roska grabbed the padlock, instantly freezing it in his palm. Then he grabbed one of the iron daggers from his belt and smashed the handle into the lock, shattering it to pieces.

Grand Maester Auron's shouts faded to the background as Roska threw open the cabinet doors and finally saw what had been calling out to them.

Chapter 27

*A*RE THOSE...?

Yes, Roska answered.

He pulled out a wooden box with a glass lid. Inside the box, pinned like one might when displaying a prized butterfly, were wings. Brilliant, stunning, teal, scale-and-leather wings.

Demoni's wings.

Roska carefully placed the shadowbox on the desk, staring in disbelief at the beautiful wings. They looked as though time hadn't touched them at all.

The Grand Maester was still yelling, but Roska couldn't understand him over the blood pounding in his ears.

"How is this possible?" Demoni's wings hadn't decomposed.

To Roska's great surprise—which, at this point, was really saying something—the wings began flapping and pulling against the pins that held them in place.

Demoni leapt from Roska's shoulder onto the table, then smashed her tiny clawed hands into the glass, shattering the box and liberating her wings. Once free of their bindings, the wings soared into the air, circling overhead a couple of times before homing in on their target and diving at Demoni.

Roska ducked as the wings flew where his head had been a heartbeat ago. A searing pain in his back caused him to cry out, but it faded an instant later, leaving him feeling more whole than he'd felt in ages.

Silence fell upon the room like the first snowfall of the frost season.

Roska straightened and looked at the desk.

There, in the middle of the desk, hovering over the scattered remains of the shadowbox, was Demoni. The wings had somehow reattached themselves to her spine. Pride swelled in their shared connection as Roska wiped unexpected tears from his eyes.

The wind from her wings blew papers from the Grand Maester's desk as he struggled with renewed fervor to free himself from the blades still pinning him to the wall. Roska turned on the old man, teal glowing so brightly in his eyes it was as if he'd turned all the light in the room a bright shade of blue-green.

"You." The word was a vicious accusation. "You took these from her, from *us*, and kept them as a trophy?" It was an outrageous thought, but an even more disgusting truth.

The Grand Maester had the good sense to cower under Roska's rage-filled glare. "I was trying to save you, my boy." His voice was weak and pathetic. Roska towered over him, ice daggers forming in his hands, unbidden but wholly welcomed.

He raised one of the blades and leveled it with the Grand Maester's left eye. "You tortured us. For cycles. You were the nightmare that haunted my dreams, even long after we'd escaped this hells of a place. You are the only monster in this room. The worst in the world. You are the one that needs to be eradicated."

Roska grabbed the man roughly by the few strands of hair that still remained on his wrinkled, sun-splotched head. He brought the ice dagger down slowly across Grand Maester Auron's face, dragging a long, bloody line across his heartless face.

If the Grand Maester cried out, Roska was oblivious to it. He was so fixated on his own rage and revenge that he couldn't hear anything else.

Which was probably why he didn't hear the guards burst into the room.

All he felt was a sharp blow to the back of his head before darkness enveloped him.

Chapter 28

B RIGIT KEPT BUSY WHILE Roska was away. Miguel took her to the gardens, where she helped him harvest various fruits and vegetables for the castle's meals. He showed her around the kitchens and took her out to the stables once to check on a mare who was due to give birth any day.

He did a decent job of distracting them both from Roska's absence, but he had work to do in the castle and couldn't keep her company all the time.

On the third day after Roska had left, Brigit began wandering the castle on her own. She wouldn't have called herself *lost* exactly, but she wasn't entirely sure where she was or how to get back to her rooms. After a few mindless turns, she started opening doors at random. A storage closet. A study. A library. The scent of leather-bound pages and aged parchment drew her in, like a moth to a flame.

The room itself was massive and at least two stories tall. Huge, crystal-clear windows lined the far wall, filling the room with bright sunshine and illuminating even the darkest shadows. She imagined it was a pain in the ass to light the chandeliers that hung overhead each night, but the space was stunning. Thick, highly polished tables sat strategically between bookcases that had been filled to the brim but were clearly loved and well taken care of.

There wasn't a single speck of dust on any of the shelves as she wandered. Lush rugs carpeted the room, muffling the sounds of her steps and absorbing any ambient noises, making the expansive room nearly completely silent. The silence, however, wasn't oppressive as one might expect. It was cozy. Like the room itself wrapped around her, cuddling her in a soft blanket and welcoming her into the space.

As a child, Brigit had never learned to read. Her mother had said it wasn't something they'd need, so she prioritized teaching them their numbers, sewing, and cooking. Still, Brigit had always loved the idea of books. The escape that they could provide in a dreary world.

Brigit pulled a book at random off the shelf and curled up in one of the plush, over-stuffed chairs by a window overlooking the courtyard. She traced her fingers over the gold filigree that decorated the edge of the cover, spiraling into elaborate vines that wrapped around the spine and back of the book. Reverently, she lifted the tome to her nose and took a deep inhale.

"Um, what are you doing?" The quiet voice startled Brigit so much that she nearly dropped the book.

She looked up to see a young girl trying—and mostly failing—to hide her amusement. Heat flushed Brigit's face as she tried to act as though she hadn't just been sniffing a book.

"It's all right," the girl added with a smile. "The books do smell lovely. I love to come here in the afternoons. No one is around, and I can read whatever I want without being interrupted."

The girl turned on her heel. Her short blonde hair bounced around her shoulders as she sauntered over to a shelf and plucked a thick, navy blue book from it. Then she waltzed back over and took a seat in the armchair opposite Brigit.

"Do you know this one?" She held up the book to show Brigit the cover. Silver letters were etched into the blue leather, but Brigit couldn't have read it if her life depended on it.

Too embarrassed to admit such a failing, Brigit shook her head. The blood was slowly easing from her face, but she knew if she stayed much longer, the girl would realize that Brigit couldn't read. She needed to leave. Now.

"I'm Delilah, by the way. What's your name?" Delilah sat with her feet tucked under her, the book wrapped in her arms, tight against her chest, as though she were protecting something precious.

"Erm, I'm Brigit," she said finally. "But I was jus' leavin'. I'd hate to ruin yer quiet time." She stood to leave, but Delilah quickly jumped up and offered her the blue book she'd been holding so lovingly.

"You don't have to go. You can read this one, if you like. It's my favorite. About a witch who fights off the violent men in her world, saving the world from their tyranny." She covered her mouth quickly. "Shyt, I'm sorry. I didn't mean to spoil the ending. Loads of exciting stuff happens in the middle, though! And the witch is amazing. I wish I had powers like that." Delilah looked fondly at the book in her arms. Then she thrust it back at Brigit. "I think you would like it."

Brigit caught Delilah's stare pausing a hair longer than was polite on her damaged hand. Ah, so she'd heard about Brigit's time with the Brothers, then.

"Gods, I'm so sorry." Delilah blanched at having been caught.

Brigit watched the blush creep over the girl's face. "How old are ye, lass?" Brigit asked gently.

"Thirteen cycles this past frost season, ma'am." She gave Brigit a deep bow, keeping her eyes fixed on her shoes and avoiding looking Brigit in the eye.

"Ach, lass, none o' tha." Brigit placed her good hand on Delilah's shoulder, encouraging her to stand tall again. "Ye dinna hurt my feelin's, child. The man who did this to me will pay in due time. Nothin' ye can do about it now."

"I didn't mean to stare. I'm just..." Her voice trailed off for a moment, as she seemed to be choosing her next words carefully. "My sisters and I suffered some dreadful things before King Niko and Mistress Elena took power. This book was the first one I read on my own after Mistress Elena taught my sisters and me to read. It made me feel good, reading a story about a powerful woman who put down the men who hurt her and the people she loved." Delilah swallowed hard, then raised her chin proudly. "I think you would enjoy it, too."

She handed Brigit the book again, and took a step back, giving Brigit space to walk away. Brigit ran a finger along the letters etched in the leather. Weighing her options, she decided that if this young woman could own her past and persevere over her own trauma, then Brigit should at least be able to admit her shortcomings.

"Actually"—she sat back down in the plush armchair with a bit of a dramatic thump—"I canna read."

Delilah's face lit up like the sun breaking through the clouds after a growing season storm. "You can't read?" There was no judgment in her voice, only what sounded alarmingly like excitement.

Brigit smiled as Delilah sat back in her own chair. "Aye. My mum never had the time to teach us." It wasn't entirely the truth, but Brigit didn't feel the need to spoil this girl's view of the world by informing her that Brigit's own mother didn't think reading was a valuable skill for a girl. She much preferred to see Delilah thrive and grow in ways Brigit never would have dreamed of at her age.

"Can I teach you? I promise I'm a good teacher. I helped teach both of my sisters." The pride in her voice was enough to banish any self-doubt Brigit might have felt. Delilah reminded her so much of her sister. Evalyn had been thirteen when Brigit left them to find work in Nexton. She'd been headstrong, confident, and compassionate, even back then.

Brigit wiped a sly tear from her cheek and smiled at the bouncy young woman before her. "Aye, I would like that very much."

Chapter 29

R OSKA STRUGGLED TO OPEN his eyes. The pain in his head came in waves, making him nauseous. Slowly, he forced himself into an upright position, leaning back against the cold, damp stone wall. Squinting, he tried to determine where they were.

It was nearly pitch black in the small room, hard, packed earth beneath him with stone walls all around. The only light came from a tiny, barred window in the door across from him.

Gods. They were back in their old room.

Roska's breath came in short bursts. He couldn't seem to slow his heart rate or steady his lungs. Without warning, the dinner he'd eaten the night before made a reappearance as it forced its way back up his throat. The taste of it burned his tongue like acid. All he could hear was his own gagging and the pounding of his pulse in his ears.

Closing his eyes tightly against another wave of nausea, Roska pressed his back to the cold stone wall. He focused on his breath. In through his nose. Slowly out through his mouth. Over and over until the pain in his head began to subside.

I think they gave you a concussion. Demoni exhaled a cool breath across his clammy brow.

Wouldn't be the first time, he replied dryly. *We need to get out of here.*

He braced himself against the wall, trying to push up to stand, but instantly lost his balance, nearly falling to the ground and smacking his head again.

We can't go anywhere with you like this.

Well we can't just sit around here, can we? He didn't mean to snap at her, but the feeling of being trapped at the mercy of the Brotherhood again was debilitating. They needed to escape. They'd die if they stayed here. It was surprising that they hadn't killed him already. He pulled his legs to his chest, wrapping his arms protectively around them as he tried to steady his breathing once more.

Can you use your magic? Demoni climbed up his leg to sit atop his knee.

Raising one hand, Roska called on his powers. It was slow, but the ice came when he summoned it. Demoni hopped from his knee to his arm, coiling around his wrist and blowing her power to mingle with his.

Make a cane. Something to help you walk out of here. She spoke calmly in his mind as she poured more and more of her power into his hand.

Roska watched her wings as she shared her magic with them. They shimmered in the faint torchlight that leaked in through the small window. They extended off her body nearly as long as Roska's forearm, effectively doubling her size. Structured similarly to a bat, they had a single claw at the joint of each wing and thin bones that extended to the edge of the webbing, enabling her to curl and control them as she flew. He casually wondered if she had tried to fly since they'd been brought into this cell. He was mesmerized by the color of them—iridescent teal. The webbing was translucent, but he knew it would be strong. He could recall—faintly—memories of them when her wings had first unfurled.

They'd been around six cycles old. Roska had been so confused at first, not understanding what was happening to her. One day, they'd woken up to find lumps on either side of her spine. He'd been terrified that she was sick or even dying. Young Roska had scooped her into his arms and raced to the gardens in search of the only Brother who didn't look down his nose at him: Brother Liam.

Brother Liam had studied her back for several moments before silently leading Roska to the library where he pulled out a book about dragons. The book was filled with images of dragons from all over the world. Supposedly, all were extinct, but Demoni's lumps were very similar to some of the drawings of young dragons in the book. Brother Liam assured him that she wasn't sick or dying, merely growing her wings. It had been blown young Roska's mind. The day they'd finally burst through, Roska had cried. Demoni had spent the next two days learning to control her wings. She never flew far—they weren't sure how far she truly could go, without damaging their tether—but it had been exhilarating to see her take to the sky.

Her tiny claws dug into the thin skin at his wrist, forcing his mind back to the present.

A cane. He was supposed to be forming their ice into a cane.

It took longer than he liked, but they were able to craft a sturdy cane from their combined magics. With it, Roska pulled himself up off the floor and gingerly made his way across the small room. His head was still throbbing, but it had lessened to a dull ache, rather than a raging storm.

Demoni crawled up his arm to his shoulder and launched herself into the air. It was a bit like watching a bird take flight after having recovered from a broken wing: clumsy, but ultimately effective. She made it to the window at the top of the door easily enough, pulling her wings tight to her back as she squeezed between the narrow bars.

There's no one out here, she told him. *Can you pick the lock, or should we just freeze it and smash it open?*

I'd prefer to pick the lock, if I can. Quieter.

Relying heavily on the cane, Roska knelt before the keyhole in the thick wooden door. He reached into his pocket, only to realize the Brothers had removed everything he'd brought with him. Including his iron daggers and lock picks. *Mux.* It was pure luck that they hadn't taken the enchanted cloak as well.

Taking several deep breaths, Roska focused all of his magic on the tip of his right index finger. He watched in bemused fascination as his ice began to climb off the tip of his finger, taking the shape of a key. Shifting his weight, he rose and braced himself on the cane, then inserted his ice-key into the keyhole. He couldn't form the shape of the right key without knowing what it looked like, but if he could feel around enough... *click.* The lock turned freely, and the door opened without a sound.

How the hells did you do that? Demoni asked, awe thick in her voice.

I'm not sure, exactly. I just imagined the ice filling the space, matching the tumblers, and turned the key. I didn't really think it would work though.

He snapped the ice-key off in the lock, knowing it would likely melt before the Brothers even knew they were gone.

Let's get out of here.

Hobbling as quickly and quietly as he could, Roska followed Demoni as she flew ahead, leading the way and warning him of impending guards. They only encountered one on their way back to the garden in the courtyard, but Roska was able to knock the man out—much like they had done to him—with a quick strike to the back of his head with his cane. It didn't even chip the ice.

Roska was surprised to find the sun hadn't risen yet. Either he hadn't been unconscious for as long as he thought, or he'd actually been out for a full day. Based on the clouds covering the moon, however, Roska was inclined to believe it was still the same night.

As much as he wanted to seek out Grand Maester Auron and finish what he started, he knew he wasn't in a position to fight anyone. As if to remind him of his current weakened state, another wave of nausea rolled through him. Tightening his grip on the cane, Roska shuffled through the shadows of the garden, out of the iron gate, and into the night, in search of his horse and a safe place to rest.

✳ ✳ ✳ ✳ ✳ ✳

"Thank the gods," Roska muttered as he stumbled into the clearing to find the horse still perfectly content, munching on the grass where he'd been tethered.

The cane had nearly melted to the point of uselessness as he collapsed on the soft forest floor beside the remains of their fire. Demoni circled overhead, testing her wings and enjoying the freedom they afforded her. Roska sighed heavily. His breath had become ragged again; the strain of escaping and walking through the untamed woods had taken a heavy toll.

Rest, but don't sleep. Elena said sleeping with a concussion can cause you to never wake up. A death sleep, she'd called it. Demoni pulled a blanket from one of the saddle bags that lay on the forest floor and dropped it—rather gracelessly—onto his lap.

You're welcome, she thought ruefully.

I wasn't passing judgment, he thought in return but realized a moment too late that he might have been. *Well, I didn't mean to. I have a head injury. I'm not responsible for my thoughts.*

Is that how you're going to play this? She flicked her tongue out at him, a few flecks of snow falling from her mouth as well.

Roska smiled sheepishly, a shiver racking his body, causing his teeth to chatter involuntarily. Clumsily, Roska grabbed the cloak and wrapped his body as well as he could. He needed a fire. He wasn't *exactly* cold-blooded, like Demoni, but he always felt a little colder than most, and he'd expelled a great deal of energy escaping the compound. Demoni dragged the saddle blanket over to him, covering his legs as best she could, before diving into one of the cloak's unending pockets and retrieving a flint.

You'll have to spark the flame, but I think I can do the rest. Taking to the air once more, Demoni made quick work of collecting small twigs and dry leaves to start their fire. She brought over a few heavier limbs, snapping them into more reasonably sized pieces with her vicious teeth. She laid them over the twigs until she'd built a small pyre in the middle of the stone circle that served as their hearth.

Roska struggled to sit upright, knuckles white as he gripped the flint and sparked it against a stone. It took several attempts, but a spark finally ignited and landed perfectly in the small bundle of tinder Demoni had made for him. He collapsed against a tree trunk as Demoni nosed the smoking tinder into the heart of the pyre she'd built. Blowing on it slowly, keeping her frost from her breath, she breathed life into the fire. Within minutes, the smoke faded as the flames burned off the leaves and focused its energy on the wood.

Thank the gods. Roska exhaled as the warmth from the fire began to cut the chill from his bones. *And thank you.* A tired smile crossed his face as his eyes found his newly-winged companion. *I would be lost without you.*

Aye, you'd be dead without me.

* * * * * *

Roska drifted in and out of sleep over the next several hours. Demoni had agreed to let him rest but insisted on waking him every half hour to ensure he didn't slip into Elena's death sleep. Needless to say, it was not very restful.

Still, he felt markedly better as the sun rose high overhead. He had a meal of travel biscuits, black tea, and fresh berries Demoni had collected from a bush along the river. Garnet emberberries weren't native to this part of Waverly, but they were Roska's favorite and he was grateful that Demoni had collected so many.

As the sweet flavor of the berries exploded on his tongue, Roska let his mind wander back to the night he'd left. In the stables with Miguel. The sweetness of the berries was almost as delicious as the taste of that man's lips.

They'll be expecting us back soon. Demoni interjected.

We're going to be late. Roska frowned. He didn't want them to be worried, but there was no way he'd make it back before the deadline Miguel had given him. It was far more likely that they would run into Miguel and Brigit and whatever "rescue crew" they'd cobbled together as he and Demoni made their way back home. He chuckled at the thought, only to wince and grab his head at the throbbing his laughter had drawn out of him.

Are you sure these are what Aiden meant for us to retrieve? Demoni flapped her wings, stretching the newly-reattached bones and sinew, flexing the muscles that controlled her beautiful wings.

I don't feel the magic pulling me to the compound anymore. I have to assume this was what the vision had wanted us to find. Roska frowned again, remembering all the strange things he'd seen in Grand Maester Auron's office. So many creatures had been killed, just for his grotesque collection.

I think I saw a selkie's fur in one of the shadowboxes. Demoni flapped her wings, breathing fresh air into the embers of their fire, then dropped a few more limbs to encourage the flames.

Roska shuddered at the memories. *I knew he was evil, but this was so much worse than I expected. He deserves all the fires and tortures hells has to offer.*

They spent the rest of the day soaking in the heat of the sun and feeding their fire. As the sun began to disappear beyond the trees, Roska rose and tested his strength. He still felt off, but the massive pain in his head had faded to a dull ache, and he felt fit enough to travel.

He offered the stallion a carrot before loading the animal down once more. They'd travel slowly, but Roska knew they needed to get moving. The Brothers would have noticed his absence in the early morning hours. It was a gift from the Mother that they hadn't been hunted and discovered already. The sooner they could put distance between themselves and those self-righteous, villainous monsters, the better.

Chapter 30

"IT'S BEEN NEARLY FOUR weeks," Brigit grumbled. "Shouldn't he be back by now?"

"He said he'd be back in three, didn't he?" Elena turned to Miguel, who nodded.

"Yeah, but that wasn't a realistic timeline. I think he was just trying to pacify us by saying that." Miguel looked thoughtful for a moment. "Or maybe he simply misjudged the distance?"

"I can send a scout to find him, if you'd like, Firefly." The King popped a grape in his mouth, clearly unconcerned. Brigit wasn't sure if she found his nonchalance comforting or disturbing. Surely he would care about the well-being of his future brother-in-law? He wasn't being glib, she told herself. He was confident in Roska and Demoni's ability to take care of themselves, and she should be too.

Elena twisted her napkin at the breakfast table. She was anxious. Brigit understood that feeling well. King Niko took Elena's nervous hands in his, thumb stroking across the back of her hands. "He's all right, love. Roska is a strong, clever man. He'll be home soon. Would you like me to send a scout out to search for him?"

Elena's eyes flicked to Brigit's and then Miguel's before she shook her head. "No, no. You're both right. He's probably fine. It's just a longer journey than he had expected." She held Brigit's gaze for a moment longer, lightning dancing in the depths of her resolute brown eyes, then added, "But if he's not home by week's end, I'm going out to search for him myself."

* * * * * *

By the end of the week, Brigit was on edge. She spent the better part of her days on the balcony of her rooms, looking out to the east in the hopes of catching a glimpse of Roska through the trees. It was a pointless endeavor—the trees were so thick, it would have been impossible for her to see him even if he was standing there waving his arms like a lunatic.

"What's going on?" Quinn startled her out of her thoughts, causing her to nearly drop her cup of tea over the balcony. "Shyt, sorry. I didn't mean to scare you. I knocked, but no one answered."

"Which he should have taken as a sign to leave you alone, but here we are," Lyra huffed as she jumped into one of the wicker chairs that encircled a small bistro table.

It had taken a while, but Brigit was finally starting to get comfortable with the idea of talking animals. It was still odd to her, hearing words come out of the mouths of such creatures, but it didn't scare her anymore. That felt like progress.

Brigit smiled at the firefox and turned away from the balcony. "Gods, I'm sorry." She placed her now-cold tea on the table and sat hard in the chair across from Lyra. "I shouldna be so jumpy. I'm just worried. He's been gone for longer than he'd planned. Wha if somethin's wrong?"

"Roska has been through hells. He'll be back soon, you'll see." Quinn sat in the last empty chair and tossed her a wink. "You can even yell at him for being late when he gets home." He leaned forward, picking up her tea and wrapping both hands around the porcelain. Brigit watched in amazement as his hands took on an orangish hue and steam began to rise from the cup. He handed it back to her with a comforting grin. "He's stronger than he looks, I promise."

Brigit took the proffered tea, cautiously taking a sip. It was the perfect temperature again. "Thank ye, sir."

Quinn flopped back dramatically into his chair. "Gods, woman. When are you gonna stop that shyt? I'm not a sir, milord, or anything else. I'm just Quinn. Or Q, if you'd like. Next time, I'll leave your tea cold." He flashed her a teasing grin.

She chuckled as she took another sip of the black tea. "Aye, all right, *Quinn*. I'll try to drop the formalities."

Quinn rolled his eyes like he knew she wouldn't really try that hard, but he sat up and poured himself a cuppa and snatched a couple of biscuits off the tray. Tossing one to Lyra, he leaned back in his chair and gazed off in the direction of the Brotherhood's compound. "He'll be back soon," he said again, more to himself, as he took a slow sip of his tea.

They sat in companionable silence for several long moments, soaking in the morning sun and simply being. It was nice to have someone she didn't have to put on a show for. Brigit knew Elena and King Niko didn't expect her to be so formal with them—in fact, Elena had also asked her to stop calling her "milady" and "Mistress"—but titles and formalities were very important amongst the commonfolk. It wasn't something she could unlearn so easily. She'd seen one too many children get caught by a lord's whip for being informal in the streets of Nexton and Shadowvale.

✳ ✳ ✳ ✳ ✳ ✳

Some time later, a knock at the door was quickly followed by Delilah poking her head in the doorway and asking, "Is now a good time, Mistress?"

Brigit flinched at the title. It wasn't a formal title, of course, but she'd always only ever been Brigit. Having someone—even a young woman—refer to her as anything else felt wrong. Backward.

Q raised an incredulous eyebrow at her, pointing out the hypocrisy in her reaction to being formally addressed. "Time?" Quinn looked at Brigit questioningly.

Brigit fumbled for a moment, but Delilah caught on quickly and answered for her. "Apologies, sir," she offered Quinn a quick bow. "I've been giving Miss Brigit tours of the castle. Helping her to find her way around more easily."

Brigit exhaled a breath she hadn't realized she'd been holding. "Aye," she added. "I wanted to get a feel for the palace. I felt bad relyin' on Miguel all the time, especially when he's got his own work to do. Young Miss Delilah offered to help me get settled."

It wasn't entirely a lie; Delilah had been giving Brigit a tour of the palace as they made their way to the library. The young woman had insisted on taking different routes throughout the castle each time they met up for Brigit's reading lessons. She was quite unwavering in her goals to teach Brigit to read as well as to navigate the many halls and passageways that created a labyrinth within the castle's walls.

Quinn eyed them both suspiciously, but Lyra quickly leapt down from the chair she'd been napping in and sauntered over to Delilah. She twined her way around the girl's legs—not unlike a house cat—demanding affection. Delilah was more than willing to accommodate, kneeling and scratching the firefox between the ears and under her chin at once. Brigit was certain if Lyra had been capable, she would have been purring at that very moment.

"All right, you." Quinn crossed the room and held the door open for Lyra. "Let's leave these two to their tours. Delilah," he added with a bow of his own, "always a pleasure. Are your sisters in the kitchens today?"

Delilah looked up from her kneeling position, never slowing her affections toward Lyra. "Yes, sir. Ivy is learning to make jam today. Lilly has volunteered herself to be the official taste tester." She smiled up at Quinn with a look bordering on adoration.

Lyra licked her lips, pressed her head once more into Delilah's hands, and bound out the door. Brigit thought she heard the firefox say something about free samples as she disappeared down the hall.

Quinn laughed. "I guess that's where we'll be if anyone needs us." He offered a hand to Delilah, helping her to her feet, and gave them both a quick bow and a cocky grin before slipping out the door after his familiar.

Delilah smiled after him for a moment. Brigit studied her expression. She'd expected to find a hint of a young woman's misguided affections, but all she saw was pure, platonic love.

She turned back to face Brigit, the smile never leaving her face. "I hope that was ok. You didn't seem ready to tell him what we're really doing, and I thought this would be all right since it's not really a lie."

"Aye, it was perfect, lass. Thank ye." She paused for a moment, debating whether or not to ask the next question, but decided there would be no harm in it. If Delilah didn't want to say, she wouldn't push. "You and Quinn seem rather close. How do ye know each other?"

She looked back over her shoulder as though he were still standing in the doorway, warmth brightening her face. "He's the one who found us, you know," she added with a casual shrug.

"Found who? What do you mean?"

"You don't know our story? I guess that shouldn't be surprising. The triplets are very considerate of our privacy. I don't know why I'd assumed otherwise." Delilah opened the door, gesturing for Brigit to follow her as they headed to the library. "A few cycles ago, when my sisters and I were serving as the chambermaids for the castle, Quinn found us. We'd been locked in a cabinet by one of the Queen's handmaids. My youngest sister, Lilly, had accidentally tracked mud on a rug, and the Queen had lost her head over it. It wasn't the first time we'd been locked in the cabinet, you see." She waved her hand like it was common practice. "Truthfully, it was the most preferable of punishments that had been visited upon us over the cycles."

Brigit tried to keep her emotions in check, not wanting to scare Delilah off finishing her story. The idea of children being locked in anything made her blood boil.

"Anyway," she continued, turning to the left and guiding them down a hall decorated with paintings of the river through the seasons. "Quinn found us and brought us to King Niko where we served as witnesses to the murder of the former King by the Queen. The handmaids who'd administered the bulk of our punishments—and enjoyed it, those bitches—" She gasped, clamping a hand over her mouth at the curse. "I'm sorry, Mistress. I shouldn't have—"

"Hush now. It sounds like those vile women deserve all the harsh words you have an' then some." Brigit squeezed Delilah's shoulder with her good hand. "Ne'er apologize for speakin' the truth, lass."

Pink flushed Delilah's cheeks, but she nodded and continued. "Well, King Niko had them demoted to chambermaids." Glee filled her voice at the memory. "My sisters and I were given new positions as Mistress Elena's guides. She'd never been to the castle before either, and we are very knowledgeable about the castle's layout. They gave us our own suite, with real beds," she smiled wistfully. "The softest beds we'd ever seen. Fresh clothes and *shoes*. It was a dramatic change for us, and it took many moons for us to feel comfortable even looking Mistress Elena in the eye. She's been so good to us. They all have." Tears brimmed along the girl's lashes as she spoke. "I don't think we would have survived much longer if Quinn hadn't found us."

There was adoration in her eyes as she spoke about Quinn. He'd saved Delilah and her sisters from a life of torment and pain.

"Here we are!" Delilah pushed open the side door of the library, leading Brigit to what had become their regular table. Waiting for them was a stack of fairytales and children's books.

Brigit sighed. She appreciated Delilah's willingness to teach her, but it was rather discouraging to still not even be able to read the titles of the books without help.

"Come on," Delilah said with a smile. "You've made a lot of progress already! Let's practice sounding out two-syllable words today."

She took a seat at the table, pulled a book in front of her, and motioned from Brigit to join her.

Mux it all. Here we go again.

Chapter 31

*B*RIGIT AND *M*IGUEL ARE *going to be pissed*, Roska thought as they made their way through the forest.

They'll understand. Demoni was soaring ahead of him, dipping and flying through the air as though she'd been doing it her whole life. She looked completely natural and at ease in her wings. Roska couldn't help staring as the sun glinted off her iridescent scales.

Then he registered what she'd said. *Understand? Ha. I imagine Miguel is organizing a rescue party as we speak.*

Maybe, Demoni said with a casual shrug. *But they'll understand once they see us and we explain what happened.*

She was probably right, but it didn't stop Roska from feeling guilty as they rode along the river's edge. The horse was surprisingly calm about the dragon flying around his head. Roska imagined the King's stables had learned to adjust quickly once Quinn, Elena, and Roska had shown up with their magical familiars. They would have had to.

Can you see the castle yet? Roska and Demoni had been testing the bounds of their magical tether. It was interesting to see just how far she could venture from him. It had been much farther than they'd anticipated.

Flapping hard, Demoni disappeared into the tree branches, rising higher and higher until she flew well above the treetops. A tightness formed in Roska's chest, the only indication that she was stretching the edges of their bond.

We should arrive by sunset. With that, Demoni pulled her wings in tight against her body and dove back toward him. She spiraled quickly, free-falling straight toward the ground. At the last second, she threw her wings wide, catching the wind and soaring back above him, making slow, lazy circles over his head.

Having fun? he asked, a proud grin splitting his face.

Gods, yes. More than I've ever had in our life. She pulled her wings in tight, performing a barrel roll as she flew away from them.

Roska chuckled, enjoying her happiness as he led the horse onward. His head still ached, but Demoni seemed confident that the threat of Elena's death sleep had passed. She'd still insisted on waking him regularly, so he didn't sleep too deeply. By nightfall, he would be back in the safety of the castle walls. A true healer would be able to assess his injury, and he'd be sleeping in his own bed after a proper meal.

They were almost home.

✳ ✳ ✳ ✳ ✳ ✳

Roska was starting to suspect that his injury had caused Demoni more pain than she was letting on. They were connected, of course, and they shared each other's pain, but he'd always assumed that the one who experienced the injury directly suffered more for it. He was beginning to wonder if that was true.

Demoni's flying had become more erratic. Roska imagined the only other time a flying creature had performed these unpredictable dives and twists was when Castor had a little too much celebratory wine at their mothers' mating ceremony last harvest season. The moonbird had nearly flown into several windows that night.

I'm not drunk, Demoni snapped, but her words were slightly slurred.

I didn't say you were. Only that you look intoxicated. Perhaps you should take a break and ride with me for a while?

Demoni had barely stopped flying since they woke up that morning. Clearly, she'd been thoroughly enjoying the freedom her wings provided her. As hesitant as she was to let that freedom go—even for a few moments to rest—Roska knew if she kept on like this, she'd end up hurting herself.

Realizing the truth of his thoughts, Demoni glided back down and coiled herself around the saddle horn.

Fine, she thought tiredly, *but only for a few moments.*

Her mouth stretched into a large yawn, showcasing her rows of viciously sharp teeth. Flicking her tongue out once more, she rested her head on the stallion's neck and was asleep in a matter of heartbeats.

Roska chuckled to himself. Gods, she really was the most stubborn creature on this earth. They rode the rest of the day in silence. He snacked as the hours passed, not wanting to waste time stopping for a full meal, or risk waking Demoni.

The sky had faded from bright blue to a soft lavender as they approached the main road that would lead them to the castle. Roska led the horse to the line of people returning to their homes within the castle walls. He watched patiently as the guards greeted the citizens, asking after their business for the day, making friendly small talk, and subtly questioning the citizens about any distressing news or gossip they'd heard during the day. Roska didn't know much about running a country—thank the gods he didn't have to—but he assumed these little conversations were a very effective way to learn the goings on in and around the city.

When it was their turn to approach the guards, Roska was prepared to remind the men of his relationship with the future Queen and his connection with the King. Much to his surprise, Roska didn't have to say a thing.

"He's returned!" The guard on the left ran into the watch tower and pulled a thick cord that hung just inside the doorway, sounding a bell that echoed throughout the city streets. Just as the first tolls of the bell began to fade, another bell sounded, farther within the city walls. Then another and another.

The guard to Roska's right bowed deeply, then rose, averting his eyes, as he guided Roska's horse through the gates. The guard led Roska all the way to the stables near the entrance, tethering the horse and finally raising his eyes to meet Roska's.

"Welcome home, milord. The King and Mistress Elena have been eagerly awaiting your return. If you'll follow me, sir, we have a carriage waiting with a fresh horse to take you directly to them."

Roska uncoiled Demoni from the saddle and dismounted, desperately hoping that his confusion didn't show on his face. This level of fanfare was reserved for visiting royals. He was barely a Lord, and only because Niko had insisted on granting him and Quinn titles.

Without a word, Roska turned to begin unpacking his horse, but the guard quickly stepped up, taking the saddle pack from Roska's hands.

"Please, milord. We have people who can do this for you." He looked deeply distressed that Roska was attempting to do any manual labor. "The King is waiting," he added quickly, to cover his chastisement of Roska's un-lord-like actions.

"Yes, of course." Roska nodded awkwardly. Patting the horse on his neck, he thanked the animal for his time and energy, then followed the guard to the carriage on the far side of the stable.

A coachman was already waiting for him, as the guard opened the door and Roska climbed into the elegant carriage. The door closed with a firm *click*, the coachman flicked the reins, and they were off.

This is excessive, Demoni observed. She'd woken when he had taken her from the saddle and now lay stretched out across the back of the bench opposite him.

Roska agreed, it was excessive, but it also screamed of Elena. She always liked to make a big production of her brothers' return to the castle. As the future Queen, she rarely left the castle or the capital for any length of time, but Quinn and Roska had the freedom to travel as much as they pleased. Roska knew this carriage and the accompanying fanfare was Elena's doing. She wanted to be made aware of his arrival the second he approached the gate, and she wanted to ensure that he came straight to the castle. No distractions.

Excessive as it might have been, Roska didn't bother fighting the broad grin that plastered itself across his face as soon as the carriage had begun moving. They were home. They were going to see Brigit and Miguel again shortly—because there was no possible chance that they had missed the announcement of his return. He could almost ignore the throbbing in the back of his head as they rode through the city streets, making their way—rather quickly—to the castle.

If he thought the bell ringing and carriage ride were excessive, Roska didn't have words for the extravagant greeting that awaited them at the front steps of the castle. Banners hung from the lampposts that lined the entry to the Great Hall. Navy blue cloth bearing snowflakes embroidered with teal and silver thread. They were the banners typically reserved for the Frost Solstice celebration, but clearly Elena had repurposed them to celebrate his return. He laughed, unable to contain his glee at having arrived safely home. Standing at the top of the stairs, waiting with a mixture of excitement, pride, and love, stood Elena, Niko, Quinn, Miguel, and Brigit. Agon and Lyra were tumbling around on the ground but immediately hopped up and bounded down the stairs as Roska stepped out of the carriage.

Demoni, wrapped around his neck and partially hidden under his cloak, thought, *Watch this*, and launched herself into the air, spreading her wings wide and flying high above them.

The look of awe and confusion on the faces of the people they loved was utterly priceless. They stood in stunned silence for a few heartbeats, and then Q's guffaw of surprised amusement echoed down the stone stairs. Tears seemed to be flowing freely down Elena's face as she raced down the stairs. Niko stared in open-mouthed awe as Demoni performed a barrel roll, diving down at Agon and Lyra only to pull up at the last second and glide gracefully above them in a slow, lazy circle.

Roska looked at Brigit and Miguel, trying to read their faces despite the distance that still separated them, but before he could pinpoint the emotions on their faces, he was tackled—nearly to the ground—by Elena. Laughing through her tears, she wrapped her arms so tightly around his neck that Roska struggled to contain his own tears. He didn't mind in the slightest as he wrapped his arms around her middle and lifted her up into a welcome embrace.

"Welcome home, brother," she choked out through gleeful tears. "I see you found what you were looking for." She pulled back enough to see his face, placing her hands on his cheeks and studying his eyes for a moment. "Gods, I was so worried. Don't tell Niko," she added conspiratorially, "but I've been planning a full-scale invasion with Jamieson for the past few nights. We were supposed to leave in the morning."

"You aren't that stealthy, Firefly." Niko joined them at the foot of the stairs, raising an incredulous eyebrow at his intended. "Do you really think the captain of *my* guard wouldn't tell me if my bride was planning to start a war?"

"Mux you both then," Elena quipped, shamelessly wiping tears from her face.

"No worries, El," Quinn said, wrapping an arm around Roska and Elena's shoulders. "I would have happily invaded that muxing compound with you, with or without His Royal Haughtiness's approval."

"Hey, now." Niko raised his hands in defense—or perhaps offense. "I didn't say I was against it. I was simply saying that my armies don't go to war without my expressed consent." His eyes found Roska's then. "And I would have consented. There's no way I'd have let those bastards have you. Not if there was something I could do to help."

Demoni glided down and landed confidently on Roska's shoulder.

"So that's what you were after, then?" Niko asked, eyeing Demoni's beautiful wings as she showed them off from her perch.

"I think so," Roska replied. He still wanted to talk with Father and determine if Demoni's wings were all that they were meant to retrieve. For now, though, he was thrilled to be home. Thrilled to be back with his people.

He looked back up the steps to see Miguel with his arm wrapped around Brigit, pulling her into his chest as it looked like she was wiping tears from her cheeks.

Tears? Gods, he hoped they were happy tears.

Following his gaze, Elena saw what had stolen Roska's attention and quickly stepped in. "We're having a feast in honor of your safe return. Dinner is set inside. We'll be waiting when you're ready." She added a wink, then grabbed Niko and Q, pulling them away and back up the stairs. They disappeared beyond the wooden doors of the Great Hall, leaving Roska alone with Miguel and Brigit.

Slowly, without taking his eyes off them, he climbed the stone steps and came to stand before them. Hit by a sudden wave of anxiety, Roska worried that they had bonded while he'd been gone and neither of them needed him anymore. He looked away, studying his boots as he debated what to say.

"Yer late." Brigit interrupted his internal struggle.

"I... uh, yes, I am. I'm sorry." He didn't look up from his boots.

A warm finger lifted his chin, forcing his eyes to meet theirs. "You're not allowed to go off alone again." Miguel's voice was firm, but the sparkle in his eyes told Roska that he was fighting back tears.

"I promise." Roska's voice caught on the words. Before he could utter another sound, Brigit and Miguel pulled him into them, embracing him so tightly Roska wasn't sure he'd ever be able to take a deep breath again. He hoped they'd never let go.

✳✳ ✳✳ ✳✳

While Roska could have stayed wrapped in their arms for the rest of his life, his stomach voiced its own opinion rather loudly mere moments later.

Brigit's throaty chuckle vibrated Roska's chest as she pulled back a bit, smiling up at him as she asked, "Hungry, eh?"

Roska pulled her back into him for a heartbeat, nodding into her hair, not quite ready to release her.

"Come on, loves," she whispered to them both. "Let's go see what that sister of yers has planned for dinner."

Brigit and Miguel unwound themselves, each taking one of Roska's hands as they led him through the courtyard and into the Great Hall. Elena had really leaned into the frost season decorations. Snowflake banners hung from the tapestry hooks along the walls. There were also snowflakes crafted from paper hanging from the chandeliers that illuminated the room.

A wide smile spread across Roska's face as he took in the space. The scents of all his favorite dishes wafted in from the kitchens. The table was set for the six of them, along with a short table beside the fire, laden with meats and fruits for their familiars. The kitchen staff knew that, as creatures of magic, the familiars didn't *need* to eat, but it was also common knowledge—because Lyra complained loudly for weeks when they first moved into the castle—that they *liked* to eat.

Demoni launched herself from Roska's shoulder and soared across the room to join her animal siblings at their low table.

"So... Should we just dive into the whole 'Demoni has wings' thing now or wait until after we've had some food?" Quinn pulled out a chair, his back to the fireplace as he faced the grand doors of the hall.

Elena sat beside him, Niko to her left. Traditionally, the King was meant to be the center of everything, and if this had been a formal affair, he would have been seated at the head of the table, but this wasn't a formal meal. This was a family dinner.

"Aye, I'm quite curious about that one myself." Niko offered the basket of warm rolls to Elena before taking one for himself.

Miguel led Roska and Brigit to the table, pulling the chair out for Brigit, and then Roska. He seated himself directly across from the King. Roska appreciated the small act of kindness. Miguel and Roska both knew that Niko was nothing like his father and that he was an amazingly compassionate king. Brigit, however, needed more time to learn to trust the man, so Miguel had placed her across from Q instead. A man she already knew well enough to feel comfortable. Roska smiled inwardly at Miguel's thoughtfulness.

They loaded their plates and feasted while Roska regaled them with his adventures. He tried to keep the story as light and carefree as he could, highlighting their wins and glossing over the part where he was imprisoned again and nearly killed. No need to add to their worries. He was fine now, that was all that mattered.

He took a long sip of wine after he finished the story. He rarely spoke that much; he was parched. Not to mention, all that story-telling had meant he still hadn't eaten much.

Brigit, seeming to notice his largely untouched plate, caught his eye and looked pointedly at his food. A small smile slipped across his face as he took a large bite of his mashed potatoes. He held her stare as he ate three more bites before she nodded approvingly and turned back to her own food.

"I have so many questions!" Elena exclaimed.

"Literally no one is surprised by that, Firefly," Niko chuckled behind his goblet.

She swatted his arm but turned quickly back to Roska. "You made ice creatures? That's amazing. Can you make one now?"

"That was your takeaway from all that shyt?"

"Gods, Q, you're in a castle. Can you at least *try* to use more polite language? And no, that wasn't my *only* takeaway, but it does seem incredibly intriguing. You make giant flaming soldiers. Now

Ros is making ice animals that he can manipulate and see through. It's astounding."

"And you're jealous," Quinn quipped.

Elena's face turned bright red as she stared open-mouthed at their brother for a moment. "I am not!"

Niko's boisterous laugh was met by a glowing blue glare as Elena turned on him. "Sorry, Firefly, but come on. I don't have any magic at all, and I'm jealous as hells. It's completely fine and understandable that you're a little envious of your brother's newfound skills."

"Darling," Elena said, her voice was so sweet it made Roska's teeth hurt. She reached a hand out to gently rest on Niko's forearm where it sat on the table. "Shut up." With that, a small, brilliant blue bolt of lightning danced from her fingertip to singe the cloth of his sleeve.

Niko gave a very un-king-like yelp as he rubbed the spot where she shocked him. "I'll get you back for that. Later." He gave her a sly wink and the red in Elena's cheeks deepened.

Before, this sort of exchange would have made Roska feel awkward and out of place, but as he sat there, sandwiched between the two people he loved, he just smiled. Lowering his hands from the table, he reached out to either side and placed a hand on Brigit and Miguel's respective legs. He was so damned happy to be home.

Quinn roughed his knuckles on his chin, scratching the coarse hair that seemed to have taken up permanent residence there. "Right, well now that things have gotten considerably more awkward, wanna show us your new trick, Ros?"

Roska nodded as Demoni flew over and joined him at the table. He lifted his hand from Brigit's lap and the frost dragon coiled herself around his forearm, her head coming to the base of his wrist.

What should we make? Demoni asked silently.

How about a rabbit? Closing his eyes, Roska imagined the small rabbit they'd seen in the woods on their journey home. He called on his power, drawing it to his upturned palm as he felt the weight of the ice began to take shape. In seconds, he heard Elena's gasp and Brigit's coo of adoration.

Opening his eyes, Roska placed the ice-rabbit on the table. The instant its paws touched solid wood, the rabbit began to hop about, jumping over dishes and maneuvering around the expanse. Elena reached out to touch it, so Roska directed the creature to hop over and sit before her.

Her eyes flew to his. "Did you...?"

He nodded. "Yes. I can control where it goes, see what it sees, hear what it hears."

Elena held his gaze as she leaned forward, her lips nearly touching the rabbit's icy ears. She spoke with a voice so soft, Roska was sure no one else could hear it, directly into the rabbit's ear. "I stole the last bite of Niko's birthday cake."

"I knew it was you!" Roska laughed. Elena's eyes sparkled at his reaction to her confession.

"What?" Quinn looked confused.

"What did you say?" Niko asked curiously.

Elena smirked but didn't answer. Roska just chuckled.

"Ok, my turn." Quinn put his hand under the table. "How many fingers am I holding up?"

Roska closed his eyes once more, directed the ice-rabbit to hop down from the table, and announced, "Three. No, five. Now four. Three, again. Well, now, that's just rude."

An impish grin tugged at Quinn's lips as he put his single finger away, laughing at his own childish prank and taking a long drag from his wine. "Gods, Ros, that's muxing amazing. You have your own fleet of spies."

"Well, I don't know if I have a fleet of anything. I've only made one or two at a time. And only small things. Field mice and a couple of moths. I also tried making a horse, but it melted pretty quickly."

"What happens if it melts while you're using its senses?" Elena asked.

"I get thrown back into my body. And I end up with a headache. Although, now that I think about it, the headache might have been caused by the blow to the head more than the magics." Roska hadn't thought much about it, but the two things had happened pretty quickly. It was possible that the headache had nothing to do with his powers at all.

"Aye, Gods, ye likely need to see a healer. Tha blow sounded pretty strong. Ye might've suffered some serious damage." Brigit leaned closer, trying to examine the back of his head, despite the room only being lit by candles and the fireplace along the wall.

"I feel fine now," Roska argued, but Brigit wouldn't hear it.

"I dinna care how ye think ye feel. Yer seein' a healer." She glared at him, daring him to continue to argue.

Roska smiled and nodded. He'd do whatever she said if it meant she'd keep that fiery tone. The passion that flared in her eyes was enough to drive him to do whatever she said, without question.

"Good," she added with a nod of finality. The matter had been settled. She relaxed into her chair again, although Roska noticed she leaned closer to him. If their chairs had allowed it, he was sure she would have curled right into him at that moment. He desperately wished they were alone.

Seeming to pick up on his desires, Elena rose from the table. "It's getting late, and I'm sure you're tired." She motioned for Niko and Quinn to rise as well. "Get some sleep, Ros. We'll talk more in the morning. I'd like to hear more about that Grand Maester's office. It sounds absolutely horrific, but I wonder if there's anything in there that we could use to justify military action and shut him down for good."

With that, the three of them left, Agon and Lyra bounding after their respective humans as they all headed off to bed.

"Right then." Miguel rose from his chair. "Time for a healer, and then off to bed with you both."

Chapter 32

T HE HEALER'S SURGERY WAS located in a building beside one of the herb gardens. This garden was tended entirely by the healers, filled with plants used exclusively for medicinal purposes.

Roska half-heartedly attempted to discourage or delay a visit to the healer, claiming it was too dark for the healer to be able to see the back of his head properly anyway, but Brigit and Miguel remained unmoved. They led him straight to the healer's door, and—much to Roska's disappointment—they found the healer wide awake in a room lit so brightly that it seemed as though the sun itself was alight in the space.

Miguel knocked firmly on the door. Seconds later, a short, wizened old woman opened the door. Her wiry white hair tied tightly in a knot on the top of her head was a stark contrast to her ebony skin. The knot itself barely reached Roska's chest. She looked up at them with clear blue eyes that hinted at the brilliant mind behind them.

"Can I help you?" Her voice was smooth as silk, despite her wrinkled and leathery visage.

"Aye, ma'am. Our..." Brigit paused for a moment, as though searching for the right word. "Our friend here took a nasty blow to the head, and we wanna ensure there wasna any lastin' damage."

"Of course, *ma cherie*." The old woman stepped aside, holding the door wide for them. "Come on in. We'll see what we can see."

Miguel led the way, then Roska, with Brigit closing the door behind her as she followed them into the healer's space. The surgery was nothing like Roska had expected. It was brightly lit by some sort of magical orb that hovered just below the ceiling, providing the space with so much light that Roska might have believed it was the middle of the day.

"It was a gift from a dwarf," the healer said, following his gaze. "I saved the poor man's husband from a nasty bit of goring from a wild hog. He was so grateful that he made me this device. It absorbs the sun's light during the day and allows me to continue my work at all hours of the night."

Roska stared at it, the bright light burning his eyes, but he couldn't look away. He was fascinated by such magic.

"Come, *monseigneur*. Take a seat here and let me examine you." She gently took Roska by the arm and led him to a stool beneath the orb. Roska blinked, seeing a large black spot in his vision from staring at the light. He tried to take in the rest of her room, but the spot made it hard to see anything clearly. "Look up, *monseigneur*, let me see the back of your head." She tilted his head back and Roska winced as she brushed his hair aside. "*Ventre-saint-gris*, you weren't exaggerating, *cherie*. This is quite the bump."

She moved around to stand before Roska, tilting his head back down and studying his eyes intently. "Headaches? Nausea? Trouble sleeping?"

Roska tried to reply without moving his head too much. "Uh, yes. Headaches and I was a little nauseous when it first happened."

"And when was that?"

"About two weeks ago." His gaze flicked to Miguel, who was trying to hide his irritation. Roska knew the man was more irritated with himself than anything. Miguel would be internally berating himself for allowing Roska to go alone. He'd blame himself for Roska's injury for a long while, despite Roska's protestations to the contrary.

"Two weeks. Have you been sleeping?" She pulled his face back to meet hers and brought the orb down, closer to his face, practically blinding him. He squeezed his eyes shut against the light. The healer clucked her tongue, muttered something in a strange, guttural language, and the light dimmed. "Open," she demanded.

Roska complied, remembering to answer her question as well. "The first couple of nights, Demoni woke me every half-hour or so. She was worried I might go into a death sleep."

The healer nodded, a hint of a smile tugging at her thin lips. "Good, good. This Demoni of yours sounds like a clever friend."

"Thank you, Mistress," Demoni hissed from her position around his neck.

The healer startled ever-so-slightly. "I didn't notice you there, *mon petit dragon*." Her smile quickly warmed and her eyes flashed with emotion, but it was gone before Roska could pinpoint it. "It was good of you to keep him awake. It looks like you have a mild concussion."

"Oh, gods. Is that bad? Will he be all right?" Brigit's voice was tense with worry, her knuckles white from where she clasped her own hands so tightly.

"Nothing to fear, *cherie*. It could have been much worse. Immediately after such a violent blow, he could have fallen into—what did you call it? A death sleep? But his quick-thinking little friend here kept him safe. You will likely have a wicked headache for a few more days, but the worst is over. Get some rest." She spoke directly to Demoni as she added, "Don't let him sleep too deeply for a few more nights." She turned away from them both, bringing the orb with her and rummaging through several jars of herbs and tonics on the shelves that lined her walls. "Take this." She handed a small, dark glass vial to Roska. "Add three drops to your tea, morning, noon, and night, for the next three days. Then come back to see me."

"What's in the vial?" Miguel asked protectively. Roska got the feeling that he didn't distrust the healer, but he was acting with an abundance of caution.

The healer waved her hand dismissively. "It's an oil for the headaches. Made exclusively from the herbs in my garden. Have some yourself if you're worried I'm going to poison him." She raised an eyebrow in challenge as she faced Miguel. "I'm a healer, *monsieur.* I would never intentionally inflict pain."

Miguel paled at her harsh words. "Apologies, Mistress." He bowed deeply. "I didn't mean to imply otherwise."

The healer clucked her tongue again and turned back to the shelves. "All is forgiven. I can see you're only worried about your *friend.*" She said the word as though it were some sort of code, clearly intended to mean something else.

Roska felt the heat rush to his face. He wasn't embarrassed or ashamed of his relationship with Miguel, but he wasn't sure he was ready to have his relationship with Miguel *and* Brigit become public knowledge. Hells, the three of them hadn't even spoken about what was going on between them yet. The healer wasn't judging them for it, though. Roska got the sense that she was simply pointing out the ridiculousness of referring to themselves as mere friends.

"Thank you, Mistress." Roska tucked the vial into his pocket and rose to leave.

"One last thing, *monseigneur.*" The healer turned back to face him, studying his eyes one last time before saying, "I can see you've been through quite the ordeal, and I'm glad you've made yourself whole again." Roska blinked, unsure if the woman was speaking of his head injury, or if she somehow knew about Demoni's wings. "You aren't done with that place yet. I'm sorry."

Ice flooded Roska's veins. Metaphorically, but also literally as ice daggers formed—unbidden—in his hands. Miguel stepped forward, placing a firm hand on Roska's forearm, as Brigit came to stand at his other side, the warmth of her body a stark contrast to the frost filling his.

"What do you mean by that?" Roska couldn't keep the threat from his voice.

"I don't mean to frighten you, *monseigneur*. I'm only sharing the message that has been sent to me."

"What message?"

"Who sent you a message?"

Brigit and Miguel's questions were spoken over each other. Roska didn't have any words. His brain, much like his hands, was filled with ice. He couldn't have formulated a coherent thought at that moment if his life depended on it.

The healer took a single step back, not in fear, but in an effort to give the three of them some space to breathe.

"I'm sorry, *monseigneur*. That is all I know."

She motioned for them to take a seat at a round dining table. She turned and walked to the potbellied stove that sat in the corner of the room, knelt before it and filled its belly with dry wood, then whispered "*Allumer.*" Roska blinked in surprise as the wood caught fire instantly. The healer closed the grilled door of the stove and pushed up from her kneeling position. "*Nom d'un chien*, these old knees aren't made for that anymore."

No one spoke as the healer filled her teakettle and set it on the stove to boil. She tutted around the surgery, collecting herbs and grinding them, then once the kettle began to whistle, she pulled the water from the stove and began to steep the fresh herbs in four porcelain cups. She set the cups around the long table, grabbed a small plate of sweet-smelling bread, and joined them at the table.

"I can't tell you much, because I don't know how it happens or who sends me these images, but I can tell you that you aren't finished with that man. The one who pompously calls himself *Grand Maester*, as though giving himself such an auspicious title would somehow make him more educated and prestigious than he actually is. The bigoted *maroufle*." Using a small spoon, she stirred honey into her tea, then offered the sweet nectar to the others. Roska accepted her offer, but the others seemed too distracted by her words to care about their tea.

By all rights, Roska should have lost his appetite as well, but he felt oddly numb by the whole situation. Once his ice daggers had been recalled, it felt like his powers had spread throughout his body, covering his heart and mind with a thick layer of ice. A magical shield from the world. Hardening him from the truths he knew this woman would speak.

"You have visions?" Demoni slithered down his body and came to sit between his forearms, blowing a cool breath on his tea before he took a sip. It was sweet and soothing. Roska tasted hints of lavender, peppermint, and chamomile. Inhaling deeply, he took another sip, awaiting the healer's answer.

"Yes, *mon petit dragon*, I do. Nothing like your father," she added quickly to Roska. He wanted to ask her how she knew about Aiden and his visions, but he assumed the answer would be simple: She saw it in one of her own visions. "I see small glimpses of what could be. Pictures of future events. Some of them are inconsequential. Some of them foretell potential world-changing events. I first saw you"—she held Roska's gaze—"when you were just a child. I watched what that monster did to you both." Her eyes fell to Demoni. Specifically, her wings. "I didn't know if I was seeing something that had already happened or something yet to come. I was still a young girl myself, at the time. I wanted to help you, but I didn't know who you were, or where. Or when, for that matter." Tears lined her eyes as she spoke. "I've thought about that vision every night since it first came to me. I wanted so desperately to find you." She reached across the table. Roska thought she might grasp his hand, but she pulled back at the last second, seeming to think better of it. "I'm sorry I couldn't protect you, *monseigneur.*"

Roska didn't know what to say. She'd seen the torture that would befall him, but she hadn't been able to stop it. She'd seen it before he'd even been born. He couldn't think of any words, so he offered her his hand instead.

Her arthritic fingers gripped his hand tightly as a silent tear slid down her wrinkled cheek. The heartbreak and kindness shining in her eyes nearly broke him. She'd cared for him, worried about him, long before he'd even been conceived.

"What did ye see this time?" Brigit asked, breaking the spell that had settled between Roska and the healer.

She blinked several times, shaking her head as though to clear the old visions from her mind. Releasing his hand, she wrapped hers around her delicate teacup and raised it to her lips. "I only saw flashes of images." She took a sip of her tea. "A strange room filled with violence. Grotesque jars of magical body parts on display like hunting trophies. Magical and mythical items locked away in a huge, metal chest. And that man. That vile man, gloating and manipulating the world from his self-righteous throne made of the bones of his victims."

Grand Maester Auron plagued him, even in the comfort of the capital. Gods, would he ever truly be free of that man?

There's only one way to rid ourselves of his type of evil. Demoni eyed him, conveying the weight of her meaning through her shrewd, black eyes.

Roska had never wanted to kill anyone, but since being free of the Brotherhood's compound and finding his way in the world, he'd been forced to take a life more than once. He never relished it and often tried to find any other solution, but sometimes there was no other way.

Chapter 33

MIGUEL AND BRIGIT BOTH insisted on keeping an eye on him overnight. Brigit added the medicine to Roska's tea while Miguel stoked the fire. Roska had tried to explain that it wasn't necessary and that he was perfectly capable of taking care of himself, but he might as well have been talking to a wall. They weren't budging.

Resigning himself to be cared for, Roska allowed himself to be banished to the bathroom, slipped into the tub with warm water, and took the longest bath of his life. He hadn't realized his head had bled so much until he began working all the dried blood out of his hair, then he scrubbed all the dust and grime from travel off his worn body.

The water was chilled by the time he climbed out of the tub. He threw on a pair of linen trousers and a loose shirt, then joined Miguel and Brigit on the balcony.

"Well it's about time," Miguel sighed dramatically. "I thought we were going to have to come fish you out of there."

Roska smiled and accepted the teacup Brigit offered him, sitting between them and looking out at the stars that winked in and out through the night's clouds.

"How are ye feelin'?" Brigit tried to keep her tone neutral, but Roska could hear the anxiety in her voice.

"I'm all right." He leaned forward and took her hand, giving her his full attention. "I swear to the Mother, I'm ok. A little headache, but the healer's tonic will help with that."

Brigit squeezed his hand, not quite seeming to believe his words, but accepting them just the same.

Roska didn't want to dwell on his health anymore. Returning her squeeze, he released her hand and made a show of taking a deep sip of the medicated tea. Leaning back in his chair, he asked, "What have you two been doing while we were gone?"

He wasn't certain, as the moon was only a quarter tonight and the clouds kept her hidden, but Roska thought he saw a hint of blush creep across Brigit's cheeks. Miguel smiled warmly, nodding encouragingly at her but didn't speak to her. Instead, Miguel answered Roska's query.

"Well, I've spent the last week trying not to go out looking for you by planning our next attack on the compound. I've been working with Balor and Asha to put an end to the Brotherhood once and for all."

Roska was surprised. That wasn't what he'd expected, although honestly, he didn't really know what he'd expected. Definitely not battle plans.

"What have you come up with?" Roska leaned forward, bracing his arms on the table to try and keep himself steady.

"We can go over it tomorrow," Miguel said, waving the topic off.

His dismissive attitude irked Roska, but he also knew the man well enough to know that he wasn't brushing off the topic to be rude. He was prioritizing Roska's needs, including—despite Roska's objections—protecting his space. Roska's rooms weren't a place for battle plans and strategy. Miguel had been very clear about that when they'd first started spending time alone together. The suite was meant to be a sanctuary from the rest of the world, which meant all things to do with violence or plans against the Brotherhood would be kept out of that space.

Roska had loved that idea in the beginning. He thoroughly despised it now.

"Brigit," Miguel said, effectively changing the subject entirely. "Would you like to tell Roska what you've been doing these last few weeks?"

Roska was a little thrown by the way Miguel was addressing Brigit. It seemed like an odd question. Almost like he was asking her permission to tell Roska something? Or giving her permission to tell him?

Brigit's eyes flicked between the two of them, clearly unsure of what to say. Miguel reached for her, giving her forearm a comforting squeeze. "It's ok, love. I know he'll be happy to hear anything you want to tell him."

She held Miguel's gaze a moment longer, then took a deep, steadying breath and said, "I've bin learnin' to read."

※ ※ ※ ※ ※ ※

Brigit held her breath as she waited for Roska's reaction. When Miguel had found out last week, she'd been mortified. He was so clever and accomplished—hells, he was one of the King's top strategists, despite spending nearly all of his time in the gardens or kitchens. Brigit had been sure he would laugh at her and mock her for not being able to do something as simple as read a children's book of fairytales.

She'd been floored when he'd expressed such enthusiasm for her progress. He'd even started reading with her most nights. He'd read a story to her, and she'd follow along. Then, last night, she'd read a story to him. It had been quite an exhilarating experience.

Brigit's skin heated as she recalled how she'd nearly kissed Miguel after finishing the story on her own. She'd been so caught up in the moment, she'd thrown her arms around his neck and been seconds away from pressing her lips to his before she caught herself and quickly pulled back. She cared for Miguel, of course, but she didn't know if he was even attracted to women. Needless to say, it had been a bit awkward, and she'd quickly excused herself to go to bed shortly thereafter.

Watching Roska now, his slow blink as her words sank in, she was sure he would think less of her. How could he not? She was a ruined girl with no skills outside of being a tavern wench. And now, with only one functioning hand, she wasn't sure she'd even be able to do that anymore. Add to it that she was illiterate? Gods, she was the worst possible match for him.

Brigit couldn't bear it any longer; she closed her eyes and moved to press up from the table when Roska said, "You're learning to read? That's amazing! Who's teaching you? Not Quinn, I hope. He's an excellent teacher when it comes to fire, but I wouldn't trust him in a library."

Brigit's eyes flew open at his words. He was beaming at her. Pride and admiration shone through his sky-blue eyes. He wasn't judging her or looking down on her. He was praising her.

Brigit blinked back tears as she took in the pride on the faces of both men before her. She'd been so worried they wouldn't accept her. She'd never been happier to be wrong in her life.

"Ah, yes," she swallowed, clearing her throat. "I mean, no. Quinn isna teachin' me. I'm no even sure he knows where the library is. Delilah has bin helpin' me, and Miguel." A blush spread across her freckled face again at the memory of their almost-kiss. Her eyes flicked to Miguel to see him watching her intently. Something almost fiery danced in his eyes. Brigit wasn't sure what to make of that, so she turned back to Roska. "Delilah started teachin' me right after ye left. I've bin readin' children's fairytales for a few nights now. Last night, I read one without any help." His smile was so wide, she couldn't help but return it.

Mother Goddess, I dinna kin wha I did to deserve such men, but thank ye from the bottom of my heart.

"Will you read to me?" The optimism in his voice was intoxicating.

Then her mind registered what he'd asked. Gods, *could* she read to him? Brigit valued his opinion so much, she wasn't sure she could willingly embarrass herself by reading to him now.

"I, uh, I dinna kin... I'm no tha good yet." She looked nervously from Roska to Miguel. He'd been reading with her for a few nights. He knew how often she stumbled over the words. He was proud of her progress, but he wouldn't let her make a fool of herself in front of Roska, would he?

Miguel gave her an encouraging nod.

Brigit took a deep, cleansing breath. "Ok." She rose from the table on the balcony and crossed the living space into the bedroom she'd been sleeping in since Roska left. She knew she probably shouldn't have taken over his bedroom, but she felt safer in his space. The bed smelled like him, and it helped her to sleep so much better than when she tossed and turned in the guest room Elena had given her.

Brigit retrieved the fairytale book from the bedside table and returned to find the boys had relocated. They were sitting on the large couch before the fireplace, candles lit around the room giving it a warm, soft glow. Miguel and Roska were sitting on opposite ends of the couch, waiting patiently for her. Roska smiled up at her as Miguel patted the empty space between them.

Clutching the book to her chest, Brigit crossed the room and settled onto the couch.

"What tale would ye like?" Brigit offered the book to Roska, giving him the option to pick from the table of contents.

"Surprise me." He leaned back, resting his head on the back of the couch, eyes half-lidded.

"Are ye tired? I can read to ye in the mornin', if ye'd rather." Brigit didn't want to be the reason Roska didn't get enough rest. He'd been through so much already.

"No, no. I just want to focus on your words and your voice." He shifted so that his thigh was pressed against hers and his head was nearly laying on her shoulder. She could feel the warmth of his breath on her neck. "Besides," he added with a wry grin. "The healer said I can't sleep too deeply anyway."

Miguel chuckled, reaching his arm across the back of the couch to flick Roska's ear.

"Hey, that's not necessary," Roska grumbled, but he adjusted himself again, bringing his head to her shoulder as Miguel began to toy with his white blonde hair.

Brigit was surrounded by the warmth of them. Miguel pressed along her left side, his arm draped across her shoulders as he reached for Roska. Roska was nearly flush against her entire right side. It should have felt confining or restrictive to be so thoroughly surrounded by these men. Instead, it gave her a sense of peace and protection. They were hers.

Swallowing hard, Brigit opened the book to a random story and began to read. She started out a bit rough, stumbling more than normal, but as the boys settled in around her, she began to read with ease.

It was the story of a young girl seduced by a mesmerizing serpent. The girl had traipsed into the marshlands, ignoring her mother's warning not to wander off, looking for her lost pet rabbit. Instead, she found herself face to face with a Lamia. The creature first appeared as an anaconda. It rose to the girl's height and began swaying before her, holding her in its hypnotizing stare. The young girl became frozen in its gaze. At once, the Lamia revealed its true form. The face of the snake transformed into that of a woman. Scales shifted to display a female torso with scaled arms and claw-like hands. The Lamia snatched the child up and cooked her in a stew with her rabbit.

"Wait. That's it?" Roska sat up a bit, although he stayed close to her, his eyes studying the story, eyebrow raised incredulously. "The monster eats the kid? What the hells kind of children's story is this?"

Miguel snorted as he tried to hold back his laughter. "It's a fable." He gently took the book from Brigit's lap, closing it so Roska could see the cover. *Fables From Across The Sea.* "It's supposed to teach a lesson. A moral. The little girl should have listened to her mother. Then she wouldn't have become dinner."

"Gods, that's terrible." Roska lifted the book from her lap. Brigit tried to ignore the spark that shot through her body as his fingers grazed her thigh. She tried to convince herself it was just static from his contact with the fabric of her dress.

"All o' the stories are depressin', honestly, but it was the only children's book in the library." Brigit shrugged. She'd read quite a few stories lately about kids not listening to the adults in their lives and getting killed or eaten because of it. She knew the stories were meant to teach children to be obedient, but she thought they were awful. "The moral of all of them is 'obey or die.' It's terrible."

Roska flipped through the pages, looking at all the pictures of violent deaths inflicted on children who didn't obey their adults.

He shook his head in astonishment or annoyance a few times. When he turned to the image of the Lamia, he froze.

The temperature of the room dropped as Roska stared—almost entranced—at the artist's rendering of the monster.

Demoni flew up from her pillow by the hearth and landed on the back of the couch, studying the book.

Brigit knew that the two of them could communicate telepathically, but it was still a little unnerving to witness. Roska's grip on the book became dangerous as his ice began to freeze his fingers to the pages. Brigit caught Miguel's eye before cautiously shifting on the couch and placing her hands over Roska's. The cold of his ice bit into her flesh, but she didn't pull back. Her ruined hand sat awkwardly atop his as she tried to break his concentration.

"Roska," she said gently. He didn't seem to hear her.

"Ros." Miguel rose and knelt before him, placing his hands on Roska's knees.

Roska seemed utterly oblivious to their presence.

"Look out," Miguel warned her as he took a pillow from the couch. Brigit wasn't sure what he intended to do until he lifted the pillow over his head and motioned for her to scoot back a little.

The *whoosh* of the pillow arcing through the air was brought to an abrupt end when it met the side of Roska's face.

To Brigit's great relief, Roska released his hold on the book. As he blinked several times, the cold in the room began to dissipate as Roska regained control of his power.

"What the hells?" he cried out, clutching the pillow and glaring at Miguel.

"Hey." Miguel shrugged casually. "We tried talking to you first. You were too focused on your secret conversation and staring at that half-naked woman to hear us."

Brigit flinched at his bluntness, although she did appreciate knowing that he felt left out of Roska and Demoni's telepathic communication as well.

"I wasn't—" Roska looked down at the open book again. "All right, well, I guess I was, but it's not what you're implying."

Miguel spread his arms wide. "Enlighten us then."

He sat on the low table, directly in front of Roska. Brigit tucked her legs beneath her on the couch, suddenly feeling anxious and out of her depth. She didn't like the idea of Roska so enraptured by another woman's form. Even if she was the monster in a child's fable.

Roska glared pointedly at Miguel for a moment, then looked at her. He must have seen the frayed nerves in her eyes because he sighed and nodded. "I've seen this thing before." He lifted the book, pointing to the Lamia.

"No shyt. It's a very common fable." Miguel seemed more irritated than Brigit thought was warranted.

Roska rolled his eyes at him. "Not like that. I mean I've seen *these* before. In person." He pointed to the Lamia's glowing, cat-like, bright green eyes.

"What are ye talkin'?" It was just a children's story. The Lamia wasn't a real creature. Maybe Roska had hit his head harder than they thought. Perhaps they needed to go back to the healer.

"I saw them embedded in a staff on one of Grand Maester Auron's shelves."

A gentle breeze could have knocked Brigit over. Grand Maester Auron—that vile monster of a man—had magical items. Including magical body parts? She was going to be sick.

"Why would he have Lamia eyes?" Miguel asked, stunned by Roska's announcement.

"What do Lamia do?" Roska countered.

Brigit took the book and flipped to the glossary in the back. She hadn't been able to read all the words of it yet, but she recalled seeing more information about the creatures in the fables listed in the back of the book. She found the section of the Lamia and began to read aloud. "'The Lamia are said to have ca...cap-tiv-a-ting eyes.'" She looked up to see both Roska and Miguel watching her intently. Miguel nodded for her to continue. "'They can enchant or control those who look into them.' Oh, gods." Brigit's eyes flew up to meet Roska's. "Ye don't think he's usin' them to...?"

"Control people? Absolutely." Roska's eyes glowed a stunning teal blue, a sure sign of his growing rage.

"But why? He's already the leader of the most violent organization in the entire continent. Why does he need mind control?" Miguel reached for the book, and Brigit handed it over. He continued reading aloud. "'While they can also use their hypnotic songs to lure children to their death, the Lamia's eyes are the true source of their power. It is said that whoever possesses the eyes of a Lamia can rule the world.' Mux. That's terrifying and depressing."

Roska took the book from Miguel, running a frustrated hand through his hair and studying the glossary.

Brigit exhaled harshly. How could they defeat a man who controlled minds? Was that even possible?

What the hells were they going to do?

Throwing the book on the low table beside Miguel, Roska rose quickly as though he intended to race off to stop the Grand Maester right then. Brigit stood beside him, catching him as he swayed, clearly made dizzy by the sudden movement.

Miguel jumped to their aid, placing his hands on Roska's shoulders to steady him. "What the hells are you doing?" Miguel chastised him, trying to guide Roska back down to the couch.

Roska widened his stance, closing his eyes against his obvious dizziness. "I'm going to the library." He spoke as if this was the most logical thing he could do. "We need to learn more about the Lamia so we can stop him."

Brigit wrapped her good arm around Roska's shoulders and helped Miguel direct Roska to the bedroom. "Ye canna read or learn anythin' new with yer brain like this. Ye need rest. We all do."

Roska tried to shake them off, but either he wasn't trying that hard or—more likely—his body was too weak and tired to fight them. He let them lead him to the bed. Roska sat on the edge of the large mattress, sighing in defeat. "Fine, but only for a couple of hours."

Brigit tutted, not bothering to respond to his foolish demands. Laying him back in the bed, she pulled off his boots and placed them by the door. Miguel helped Roska pull himself into the middle of the bed, laying his head on several down-feather pillows. Brigit and Miguel worked together to pull the blankets out from under Roska—he'd climbed into bed without bothering to pull them back. Once he was settled in the middle, she and Miguel tucked him in and began to creep out of the room.

"You're leaving?" Roska asked, his eyes nearly completely closed as his words broke the gentle silence that had filled the room.

"Ye need sleep, love." Brigit smiled at him as she and Miguel backed out of the room.

"Please, stay with me?" He sounded so weak and tired. But there was a hint of fear in his voice. Brigit couldn't deny him.

She locked eyes with Miguel for a moment, sharing their own silent conversation. While they couldn't communicate telepathically like Roska and Demoni, she imagined their conversation going something like this:

Do you think this is a good idea?

Aye, I dinna kin if he'll sleep wit'out us here. He's too wound up to properly relax.

Are you ok with this? Sharing a bed with both of us? Miguel's eyebrows rose in question

It's no like this is the first time I've had a man in my bed. She smirked at him, a sly wink making him chuckle quietly.

She hooked her arm around Miguel's and escorted him over to the bed. He pulled back the quilt for her, and she climbed in beside Roska, curling into his side and resting her head on his chest.

Miguel rounded the bed, kicked off his own boots, and crawled under the quilt on Roska's other side. He propped himself up on a couple of pillows just as Roska turned and laid his own head on Miguel's chest. Miguel wrapped an arm around Roska's shoulders, his hand coming to rest lightly on the back of Brigit's head. She shifted slightly, holding his gaze for a moment. He flexed his fingers in her hair, sending a rush of shivers down her spine. Involuntarily, she closed her eyes and pushed back against his hand, like a cat demanding affection. Miguel exhaled a silent laugh, flexing his fingers and massaging her scalp.

Roska's breathing deepened and slowed, telling her he'd already fallen asleep. She adjusted her position, not wanting to lay on top of him too much for fear of making him feel trapped by their bodies. As she started to pull her lower body away—not quite ready to release the connection of Miguel's hand in her hair or the sound of Roska's steady heartbeat under her cheek—Roska unconsciously wrapped an arm around her, pulling her flush against him. He sighed in his sleep, the most heartwarming sound she'd ever heard.

Brigit drifted off the to sound of Roska's steady heartbeat under her head and Miguel's soft snoring. She'd never felt more at peace than she did at that moment.

Chapter 34

T HE SUN SHONE BRIGHTLY through the window, the glare
of it bouncing off the highly polished stone floor and
reflecting aggressively in Roska's eyes. He squinted against the
onslaught, praying to the Mother that she might banish the sun,
just for a couple of hours more. When She didn't immediately
grant his request, Roska grumbled under his breath and shifted
to turn away from the blinding light.

Much to his surprise, there was little room in the bed for him
to move. Brigit lay curled up against him to his right, her long,
red hair twisted around his arm, with her leg thrown over his.
Her face was half covered by her fiery mane, but he could hear
her steady breaths through a curtain of hair that shielded her
from the sun's devastating light.

Miguel was on his left, propped up on so many pillows
he was practically sitting upright. His eyes were closed, but
Roska could tell by the shallowness of his breath that he was
awake—or nearly.

Blinking against the rudeness of the sun, Roska's eyes quickly adjusted to the well-lit room, trying to recall how they'd all
ended up in his bed.

You invited them, Demoni supplied from her spot, coiled at
the foot of the bed.

I did? Roska could barely remember getting to the bed, much less inviting them to join him. *Did anything... happen?* He hated to think that he'd done something foolish or stupid.

You were asleep before they even made the decision to join you. I don't think they noticed though.

Roska tightened his grip around Brigit, pressing a soft kiss into her hair. He looked up to see Miguel watching him through half-lidded eyes like he was trying to spy on their interaction without letting on that he was awake.

"I hope you're stealthier than that when you spy for Niko," Roska whispered teasingly.

"I have no need to spy on you," Miguel replied plainly. He stretched his left arm overhead, twisting his spine until it cracked. He reached over Roska and massaged Brigit's head a moment. She reacted instantly, a quiet moan escaping her parted lips as she moved closer to them both, unconsciously encouraging Miguel's affections.

Roska smiled at her, turning back to Miguel with a single eyebrow raised in question.

Miguel offered a subtle shrug and carefully climbed out of the bed, motioning for Roska to join him.

I'll stay with her, Demoni offered, moving from her makeshift nest of blankets at the foot of the bed. Roska scooted out from under Brigit just as Demoni shimmied under her, resting her cool head on Brigit's collarbone.

Roska placed another gentle kiss on Brigit's head, scratched Demoni under the chin, and crept quietly from the room with Miguel.

He pulled the door mostly closed, and joined Miguel at the small dining table across the room. The kitchen staff had already sent up a breakfast of fresh fruit, biscuits, jams, bacon, and eggs. A steaming carafe of coffee sat in the middle of the table, with three empty mugs encircling it. Roska made a plate and mug of coffee for Miguel before making one for himself.

They ate in silence for a few moments before Roska finally gave up on Miguel freely offering insight into the events of last night. If he wanted answers, he was going to have to ask the questions buzzing around in his head.

"You and Brigit seem to be getting along well," he began. Roska didn't want to push if this was something Miguel wasn't ready to talk about yet, but he loved the idea of the two people he loved finding comfort in each other as well.

"Yeah, that surprised me, too." Miguel popped a grape into his mouth, chewing thoughtfully. "I've never really had much interest in women. I mean, sure I've slept with a few, but it was never anything emotional. Just a physical need being addressed. With Brigit, though..." He trailed off, that thoughtful expression intensifying. "I don't know, honestly. There's just something about her that calls to me. She feels like coming home after months lost at sea."

Roska nodded. He understood that sentiment completely. Hells, he felt the same way about both Miguel and Brigit. There was something so natural and *right* about being with them.

Miguel blinked, seeming to come back to himself, and added, "I think we almost kissed the other night." Roska wasn't sure, but he thought he saw a hint of blush creep under Miguel's tan skin.

"You think?" he asked, trying and failing to keep the incredulity from his tone.

"Shut up." Miguel tossed a small piece of bacon at him. "It seemed like she wanted to, but then she pulled away at the last second. Maybe I misread things. Maybe she doesn't see me that way."

Roska thought Miguel sounded hurt, or maybe just anxious, by the idea that Brigit wouldn't be interested in him. He placed a firm hand on Miguel's thigh. "I'm sure she wants to. Only an idiot wouldn't want to kiss you." He looked pointedly at Miguel's mouth, licking his own as he remembered the last time he'd had the privilege of tasting those plush lips.

Miguel was definitely blushing now.

Roska leaned forward, gently tightening his grip on Miguel's leg, desire burning in his eyes as he tore his gaze from Miguel's lips to his eyes.

Miguel met him in the middle, placing both hands on Roska's cheeks and pressing the gentlest of kisses on his lips. Pulling back, while still keeping Roska's face in his hands, Miguel pressed his forehead to Roska's and spoke barely above a whisper. "Thank the Mother you're home. I don't know what I would have done if you hadn't come back to us."

A soft cough drew them out of the moment. Miguel didn't remove his hands as he looked over Roska's shoulder to see Brigit drifting into the room.

"I dinna mean to interrupt." She sounded shy, her voice a little rough. She wasn't fully awake yet, but she'd come to find them anyway.

I tried to get her to sleep longer, but she insisted she was fine.

Roska squeezed Miguel's leg, pressed a kiss to the man's cheek, and rose to greet Brigit.

"Please, join us." Roska pulled out the third chair, pouring coffee into a mug for her and then piling an obscene amount of food on her plate.

"I can leave ye two—" she began, but Miguel cut in.

"Nonsense. You didn't interrupt anything. I was just thanking the Mother Goddess for bringing our boy home safely."

Brigit's face warmed at the reference to "our boy." It seemed that even if she and Miguel were unsure of what they meant to each other, they were both set on what Roska meant to them.

Heat bloomed up his neck and warmed his cheeks at the thought.

Gods, you're all so dramatic. Just think what's going to happen when you finally stop acting like hormonal teenagers and vocalize how you feel to each other.

❄ ❄ ❄ ❄ ❄ ❄

Breakfast was brief. They agreed to meet in the library once they had all changed into clean clothes.

On his way to the library, Roska ran into Delilah. The girl had grown so much since they'd first met. She was considerably taller, although Roska wasn't sure how much of that was physical growth and how much was simply a result of her standing tall and not trying to make herself invisible anymore. She smiled up at him—despite her growth, he was still a head taller than her—and offered to accompany him to the library.

"I actually wanted to talk to you," Roska said as she pivoted and matched her steps to his.

"Oh?"

"I wanted to thank you. Brigit said you've been teaching her to read. She said you're an excellent teacher." Delilah glowed at his praise. He bumped her with his elbow. "Thanks for taking care of her and being so kind."

Delilah's laugh surprised him. He looked down to see her quickly cover her mouth, trying to capture the sound that had escaped her. "Gods, I'm sorry, milord. I didn't mean to laugh. I just think it's funny that you and your family keep thanking *me* for *my* kindness. If it weren't for the three of you, my sisters and I would likely be dead. Or wishing we were."

Roska stopped in the middle of the hall, catching her arm gently. She turned back to face him, an inquisitive look on her face. "Delilah, you don't owe us anything." She was already shaking her head to argue, but he held up a hand to silence her. "No, you and your sisters don't owe us *anything*. You should never have been treated the way that you were. We were only putting to right what had been so violently done wrong to you three."

Delilah looked away, her hair falling from behind her ears to hide her face a bit. Gods, she looked so young then. She was so strong-willed and mature that Roska sometimes forgot she was only thirteen. He leaned forward, looking into her eyes behind her curtain of hair. "You didn't deserve what was done to you. None of you did. My siblings and I are grateful for you each and every day. You went through hells and you came out the other side strong, brave, and compassionate. It takes a special kind of person to endure what you went through and come out the other side with empathy and patience, rather than hate."

He reached out slowly, allowing her a chance to pull away if she didn't want his touch. When she didn't move, he lightly thumbed the tears from her cheeks and held his arms wide. She wrapped her arms tightly around his waist, and a sob escaped her lips, muffled by his tunic where she'd buried her face in his chest. He rubbed his hand up and down her spine, allowing her this moment without saying a word. Delilah was a strong kid, but she rarely let anyone see her as anything other than humorous, witty, or sarcastic. Roska could count on one hand the number of times he'd seen tears in the girl's eyes, and three of those were in the first moon after Elena had promoted the sisters to her royal guides.

Roska wasn't sure how long they stood in the hallway, but when Delilah's breathing had returned to normal, his tunic was rather damp.

"Gods," Delilah muttered, trying to wipe the tears from his clothing. "I'm sorry, milord. I didn't mean to ruin your tunic."

Roska shooed her hands away. "Firstly, you have to stop calling me that. I'm Roska. Just Roska. Secondly, it's fine. The cloth will dry. I'm more concerned about you." He held her gaze, still studying her face. "Are you ok?"

Delilah flashed a shy smile but nodded. "Yes, mi-Roska." She corrected herself, although it looked like saying his name left a strange taste in her mouth. "I'm fine. I'm just not used to people being so nice to me. I love reading with Brigit. I'm glad she's enjoying it too. She's a very quick learner! Mistress Elena would be very proud of her progress. Well, she would be if she knew. Brigit asked me not to tell anyone, so I haven't mentioned it." She added the last part quickly, seemingly nervous that he might get upset with her for telling Brigit's secrets.

Roska's eyes crinkled as he smiled at her. Delilah truly was an amazing young woman. He couldn't wait to see what she did with the rest of her life.

❄ ❄ ❄ ❄ ❄ ❄ ❄

They were the last to reach the library, finding Miguel and Brigit already pulling large tomes from the shelves and laying them out on one of the tables in the center of the room.

"Took you long enough," Miguel teased, greeting them at the door and placing a chaste kiss on Roska's cheek before planting one on Delilah's head. "We've been pulling every book that has any reference to snake-woman creatures."

Delilah looked at the growing pile of books on the table. "What exactly are we researching...?"

"Ye dinna tell her what we're lookin' fer?" Brigit stood beside the table, hand on her hip as she teasingly scolded Roska.

"I was going to—" Roska started to defend himself, but Delilah jumped in.

"We started talking about me instead. I am the most interesting conversation topic, as you both well know." Delilah smiled broadly, rubbing her hand over imaginary facial hair and stalking into the room like she owned the place. Roska couldn't help but laugh at her obvious impersonation of Quinn.

Miguel practically rolled over in uncontainable laughter. Brigit's faux-stern face cracked as she too began to laugh.

Demoni soared overhead, entering the room through an open window. Circling above them, she showered them with tiny ice particles. "We have work to do," she chided as she landed beside a massive pile of books.

"Buzz kill," Delilah teased, walking over and scratching Demoni under her chin. "Your wings are absolutely beautiful, by the way." Demoni flapped them with a flourish, showing off the shimmering teal scales and near-translucent webbing that allowed her to fly once again. With Demoni appeased, Delilah turned back to Brigit. "So, what are we researching?"

"We're lookin' for anythin' about the Lamia."

"Specifically, how one might use their eyes to control someone else," Miguel added, pulling another book from the shelves.

"Gruesome." A wicked smile spread across the young woman's face. "I like it!"

"Has anyone told you you've got a dark side?" Roska asked, walking over to a shelf labeled *Mythical Creatures* and glancing over the spines for a promising title.

"Oh, yeah. Your sister tells me that all the time." Delilah cackled behind him, pulling a book from the pile on the table and flipping to the back. "Are we looking to do some mind-controlling? Because I have a few people I'd like to test it out on, if that's the plan." Her face had turned deadly serious as she thumbed through the glossary.

Roska briefly wondered who she'd want to control, but decided against asking. It was probably safer to not know. He didn't want to become an accomplice to her future—albeit likely entirely justified—crimes.

"We're not trying to control anyone," Miguel said. "We're trying to stop someone else who is using the Lamia eyes to control a lot of people."

"Oh, well, all right," Delilah smirked at him, the darkness that had clouded her face vanishing as she found what she was looking for and flipped to the page she needed.

The rest of the day was spent scouring books, learning everything they could about the Lamia: where they came from, how to kill them, and how one might use the Lamia's eyes to control others. Everything they'd found was purely theoretical, unfortunately, because according to every book in the castle, it had never been done before.

Despite the expansive library at their disposal, there was little to be learned about defeating a Lamia, much less stopping someone who was already using the creature's eyes. Their biggest challenge was finding a way to stop the Grand Maester and destroy the eyes without causing permanent damage to anyone who was currently under his control.

"I still think our best bet is to smash the eyes." Miguel stretched his arms over his head, twisting slightly and releasing several unsettling pops from his spine. He grinned unapologetically as Delilah made a gagging sound at him.

"Aye, but what if that wrecks the minds he's controllin'?"

This had been the ongoing discussion for the better part of the day. How to avoid collateral damage—as Miguel had called it—while destroying the Grand Maester's control.

Roska took a sip of the summer cider a maid had brought for them along with lunch hours before. The cool, crisp taste of watermelon with a hint of mint kept him alert as they poured over book after book, trying to find a fool-proof solution.

"I think that may be a risk we have to take," Roska finally admitted. It wasn't ideal, but stopping the Grand Maester had to be their top priority.

Brigit's jaw dropped as she stared at him. Clearly, she'd been expecting him to be on her side. "Ye canna truly be all right with potentially killin' all those men. I kin they've been hurtin' folks and causing tragedy wherever they go, but killin' them makes us just as bad, does it no? There must be another way."

He hated being at odds with her, but he also couldn't let Grand Maester Auron continue his shady machinations.

"I don't *want* to hurt them. I don't want to hurt anyone, but if it's our only option, then we have to." Roska ran a hand through his hair, trying to will another idea to come to mind. When nothing came, he looked sadly up at her.

She held his gaze a moment longer, then slammed the book she'd been reading down onto the table and stormed from the library.

Roska rose to follow her, but Miguel held up a hand. "Give her time," he insisted. "She'll come around. It's just hard for her to accept that this is the only way. Sometimes you have to sacrifice a few to save the many. It's unfortunate, but it's a fact of life. "

Roska sat down hard, elbows on the table and his head in his hands. He wished there was another way, but he couldn't see it. The man needed to be stopped, no matter the cost.

Chapter 35

"**Y**OU'RE LEAVING TOMORROW, THEN?" Niko asked over dinner a few nights later.

Roska nodded, his mouth too full of stuffed chicken to vocalize his response.

"And you're sure you don't want me to come?" Quinn asked.

Quinn was back from Andover, having gone for a visit to check on Amelia and bring some presents to Hannah, Elena's friend's daughter. The little girl would be celebrating the completion of her fourth cycle soon, and Elena had insisted that Q bring her gifts, as the future Queen wasn't able to leave the capital for an extended time yet. Planning a wedding while learning to be a ruler was taking up a great deal of her time. While Q had been away, Roska and Miguel had been working closely with Commander Jamieson to plan the ruination of the Grand Maester.

"I'm sure we don't want to burn the entire place to the ground." Roska tossed a roll at Quinn. "Besides, we're hoping to be a bit more surgical about this. If Grand Maester Auron truly is control-ling minds, then it's very likely that the majority of the Brothers aren't as violent and hateful as he is. We need to break his control over them, not destroy the entire compound. Not yet, anyway."

Quinn sighed dramatically. "Fine. I never get to burn shyt down anymore."

"Don't you teach an entire class about burning things?" Elena leaned forward in her seat to see Quinn around Niko.

"Yeah, but it's not the same." Quinn sighed mournfully, raising his hand and lighting the tip of his index finger on fire. "When I'm the teacher, I have to be all responsible and shyt. I can't just play with fire and burn things for the hells of it."

"Thank the Mother for that." Niko chuckled. "I don't think our training field could handle much more of your so-called fun."

Lyra muttered something across the room where she ate with Agon and Demoni. Roska couldn't hear what she said, but Quinn said, "Not yet, girl. We'll get him back when El's not here to defend him." Roska couldn't help the grin that tugged on his lips, nor the snort that escaped before he could stop it.

Elena raised an eyebrow in a challenge at both her brothers, lifting her hands, bright blue lightning dancing across her fingertips.

"All right, you two," Niko leaned forward, placing himself between his future bride and her fiery brother. "We have important things to discuss. My impending immolation isn't on the itinerary for tonight."

Q recalled his flame, tossing a cocky grin at Elena and stabbing his chicken with unnecessary zeal. Roska wondered if bringing Q along might actually be a good idea, if for no other reason than to give their brother an outlet for his pent-up energy.

"Don't worry, Ros," Elena spoke, seeming to read his mind. "I have a very special job for our dear brother. He won't be bored here for too long."

"Oh, yeah?" Quinn sat straighter, attempting to see their sister around Niko's thick, curly hair.

"Yes, but it will have to wait until tomorrow," she replied. "We need to get the last things sorted with Roska before he leaves. You and I can talk about it over lunch."

Roska's interest was piqued, but he didn't pester Elena with questions. She was right, they had things that needed to be settled tonight before he left in the morning.

"You're taking the same crew?" Niko asked, moving the conversation back on track.

"Yes, if that's all right with you, Your Majesty." Miguel's tone held a hint of mockery as he addressed the King with such formalities.

Niko rolled his eyes at Miguel but kept the smirk on his face. "Of course, Captain. Take whatever you need."

Miguel's eyes crinkled as a small smile flitted across his face. It was gone just as quickly as it appeared, but Roska knew he was enjoying teasing Niko.

"I think I should come wit ye." Brigit worried the napkin in her lap. She'd been trying to convince them to let her come along all week, but Miguel pointed out that she wasn't fully healed. Brigit countered that Roska had only just finished his tonics from the healer, but he'd been cleared by the wizened old woman as well. Brigit was still walking with a hint of a limp, not to mention she'd only just begun working with the healers to try and repair her hand. The whole limb looked like a massive purple bruise.

Roska took both of her hands in his, careful not to press too hard on her injuries. "I want you to come with us; you know that. You deserve to see that monster fall as much as I do, but I can't risk losing you. Not again. Not when I'm in a position to keep you safe."

Brigit glared at him. He knew she felt like he was patronizing her, and he hated it. He hated what had been done to her simply because of her proximity to him, but more than that, he was concerned that if she were there with them, he might be too worried about her well-being to do what needed to be done.

It was going to be hard enough with Miguel by his side, and he was a highly trained Shadowcloak. It would take all of Roska's energy to focus on the job and not worry about him. Roska didn't think he could take worrying about her, too.

"Yer a damn fool, Roska. Both of ye," she added, turning her ire on Miguel. "I *deserve* to be there. More than anyone else yer botherin' to bring along. I went through hells in that godsforsaken place. I should be there when it all comes fallin' down."

Brigit ripped her hands from his grasp, pushed up from the table, and strode angrily from the room.

"She'll be all right, Ros," Q said. "It's hard being left behind, even if it's for a good reason."

Roska nodded. He appreciated his brother's insights and attempts at comfort, even though it only added to the guilt weighing him down. Elena said nothing, but her silence seemed to carry the heavy weight of an unspoken opinion she was trying to keep to herself.

The remainder of the meal was spent discussing their plans, contingencies, and backup plans for their contingencies, until Roska's brain was a muddled mess and he was ready to fall asleep at the table.

"Get some sleep," Niko said, pushing up from the table and offering Elena his hand. "We'll see you off in the morning. You should be back by the next black moon."

They bid each other good night and headed off to their various rooms.

Miguel and Roska strolled down the quiet halls to their room. It had become *their* room, rather than Roska's. Brigit had apparently moved in while he'd been gone. Roska hadn't even noticed until the second morning when he went to get dressed and found a pair of female leggings in with his wool socks. She'd been embarrassed about it at first, but Roska had been thrilled. Since then, Miguel had brought in his own clothes, and they'd found a way to fit all of their belongings comfortably in their shared space.

"How pissed do you think she is?"

"Gods, I'm praying she's asleep. I can't stand to see that disappointment in her eyes." Roska never liked being the reason someone was unhappy, but the hurt in Brigit's eyes was unbearable.

"I know, Ros." Miguel wrapped an arm around Roska's shoulders. "But we're not doing this to be mean to her. She needs more time to heal. She'll see that."

Roska wasn't so sure.

He was even less convinced when they walked into their living space to find the room had been turned upside down. Pillows had been strewn about. Dishes were smashed after clearly being thrown into the stone walls. Roska and Miguel's clothes were thrown all over the room.

"Maybe I was wrong..." Miguel gazed around the room, a mixture of shock and pride on his face. "She's livid."

✳ ✳ ✳ ✳ ✳ ✳

Brigit hadn't meant to destroy their room, but she hadn't fought the urge either. It felt good to vent her rage, even if it was dramatic and destructive. When the boys came back, their awe and the pride in Miguel's voice inflamed her rage once more.

"How dare ye think I canna handle those muxin' bastards?" She stalked angrily into the room, throwing anything she could get her hands on. Pillows. Shoes. The last remaining undamaged teacup.

She picked up a heavy, leather item, raised it over her head, and froze as her mind registered what her hands had grasped. Pulling the book into her chest, angry tears began to stream down her face, unbidden and unwanted. Just like she was.

Brigit glared at them both, trying to ignore the tears, and spoke around the tightness in her throat. "I've bin through too much to be left behind. Abandoned here while ye two go off to fight for my honor? Mux that. I'm a fighter, injured or no. I fought every second of every day in that damned cell, despite the endless hours of torture that muxin' Brother put me through. I have as much of a right to be there as Roska, and a hells of a lot more than anyone else in yer damned crew." She flexed her hands around the leather cover of the book, trying to rein in her tears and project the anger and injustice she felt. She *refused* to be coddled.

Roska lowered his hands from where they had been shielding his face and quickly closed the distance between them. "Brigit, I'm sorry. We didn't mean to hurt your feelings or imply that you aren't strong and capable. We all know you are." He eyed her cautiously before gently wrapping his arms around her and pulling her—and her book—into his strong embrace. "I'm so sorry," he whispered into her hair, placing a kiss on the crown of her head.

As much as she resented being treated like a child, Brigit felt the fight drain from her as she melted into him. He was warm and safe and everything she ever wanted to find in another human. He was her person—well, one of them—despite his pigheaded behavior.

Miguel joined them, placing a hand on the back of her mess of curls and drawing her attention to him. "I'm sorry, too. I never meant to make you feel less than you are. You two are the strongest people I've ever known. I can't stop him from kicking this muxing hornet's nest, but I was hoping to protect you by keeping you from the fight. I see now how stupid and thoughtless I was being. Please, forgive me."

"Ye canna keep me from this fight. I can protect myself." The Brotherhood had caught her off-guard before; it was the only reason they'd been able to capture her. Well, that and there had been four of them, so she'd been heavily outnumbered. But Brigit would *never* let herself be taken by those monsters again. She'd die first.

Which was likely why her men didn't want her to come.

Her men? When had she started thinking about them like that? Still, she stood, wrapped in their arms, studying their beautiful faces and feeling the beats of their hearts against her skin.

Aye, they were hers. They had been ever since that first night they shared a tent. She'd been plagued with nightmares for moons. Even after she'd been rescued and was sharing a tent with Asha, the nightmares still reigned supreme. Until that night in the tent with Miguel and Roska. Brigit hadn't slept that well in solar cycles. Possibly ever, if she was being completely honest. These two men, with all their stubborn arrogance and misguided attempts at protection, were her men. She knew then that she loved them more than anything and would fight to protect them with everything she had.

But that didn't mean she had to forgive them just yet.

"Ye canna leave me behind." She held Miguel's gaze for a moment, then flicked her eyes to Roska. "I will steal a horse an' follow ye. Ye canna stop me."

A hint of a smile tugged at Miguel's lips, although he tried to hide it. Pride flashed in Roska's clear blue eye.

For a moment, neither of them said a word. Brigit mentally began preparing a second argument, making a list of all the ways she would be beneficial on such a trip: her cooking skills, and her needlework was excellent when it came to patching Asha's leg. They'd likely need that again.

Roska tore his eyes from hers, looking over her head at Miguel. Some unspoken conversation took place in a matter of seconds, then Miguel said, "Brigit, please come with us and help us put an end to that monster of a man."

Brigit stared at him for a moment, sure she'd misheard him. Her gaze flicked to Roska, but his broad smile told her he was thoroughly supportive of the idea. Brigit understood their desire to protect her; she felt the same way about the two of them. That was the real reason she wanted to go with them. Of course, seeing the Grand Maester's world fall apart around him would be exhilarating, but she was more concerned with making sure her men came home safely. Brigit wasn't sure she'd be much help in combat, but she knew she'd fight tooth and nail to keep them safe. That was all she needed to know.

"Aye," she whispered, wrapping an arm around Roska's waist and leaning her head into Miguel's hand. "I forgive ye. Yer both damned fools, but I lo—forgive ye."

Roska beamed down at her as Miguel tightened his grip in her hair. His gaze turned molten as he brought his face closer to hers. His eyes flitted to her lips for a moment, then back to her eyes.

Was he asking permission to kiss her?

Her tongue darted out, moistening her lips as her mouth went dry with anticipation. She tilted her head in his hand, giving him access and permission with that simple movement.

Miguel didn't hesitate. His lips crashed into hers as Roska's hands tightened around her.

Miguel's kiss was feverish and demanding. As though he'd been craving her for a lifetime and was finally able to get his fill. Roska's hands were cool on her back, even as Miguel's tongue slipped past her lips and began to burn her from the inside.

As a quiet moan escaped her lips, she leaned into Roska, dropped the book, and grabbed a fistful of Miguel's dark curls.

"Gods," Roska whispered, pressing his own kiss to Miguel's neck. Brigit felt Miguel's groan in her mouth.

Panting, Brigit broke their kiss, resting her forehead against Miguel's while leaning heavily on Roska.

"Should we...?" Miguel asked, glancing towards their bedroom.

Roska took a deep breath, his heart racing against her ear. "Are we sure this is a good idea?"

A laugh bubbled out of her mouth, and Brigit pulled back a little to face them both properly. "Gods, yer both bloody fools. Stop tiptoein' around an' take me to bed."

Chapter 36

T HE MORNING SUN FOUND them in a tangle of limbs and sheets, sated and more content than Roska had ever thought possible.

"Shyt, we're late!" Miguel shot out of the bed as though it were on fire, shoving his legs into his trousers and pulling a loose-fitting shirt over his head.

Brigit groaned and rolled to face him, resting her chin on Roska's chest as amusement danced across her face. "Careful, love, yer gonna tri—"

She spoke too late, and Miguel tumbled to the ground, feet tangled in Roska's pants from the night before.

Miguel grumbled as he righted himself, sitting up to glare at them. "You're late too, you know." Miguel thumbed over his shoulder, where the sun shone brightly through the crystal clear glass.

"Mux," Roska muttered, shifting gently out from under Brigit. "You're right. We were supposed to leave at dawn."

"We're never going to hear the end of this." Miguel tossed Roska's pants at him as he pressed up from the floor. "You need to get dressed, too," he added to Brigit. "Unless you've changed your mind about coming with us?"

There was a hint of hope in his voice. Hope that Brigit would decide to stay in the capital, within the castle walls, where there was an army surrounding her to keep her safe.

She threw off the blanket, huffing something about arrogant men, and walked into the closet. Roska watched her walk away, naked and unashamed. He loved that about her. Gods, he really was the luckiest man in the world.

Miguel threw an arm around Roska's shoulder, leaning his head against Roska's. "She's muxing amazing." He sighed as she disappeared beyond the bathroom door, carrying her clothes with her.

"She really is," Roska agreed.

Brigit yelled at them through the partially closed door. "Stop talkin' about me an' get dressed. We're late, remember?"

Huffing a laugh, Miguel released Roska and finished getting dressed, as directed. Roska pulled on the pants Miguel had thrown at him and grabbed a linen shirt from their closet.

✳✳ ✳✳✳ ✳✳

Elena, Niko, and Quinn were waiting for them with a quick breakfast when they finally made it out of their room.

"Someone's moving a bit slow this morning," Quinn teased with an exaggerated wink.

Brigit's face instantly turned a violent red. Roska threw a snowball directly into his brother's face. Miguel just smiled.

Yes, fine, everyone knew something had happened. Did they really have to talk about it over breakfast though? Roska wasn't even sure what this meant for the three of them. He knew he loved them both, and their night together had been magical but they hadn't had a chance to talk about it or establish what—if anything—it meant in the long run.

"Q, that's none of our business," Elena admonished him, although there was a glint of amusement in her eyes. She seemed to be happy about whatever had transpired and was eager to know more. Roska gave her a sheepish grin but didn't respond. He'd need to figure things out with Brigit and Miguel before talking to his sister about anything.

"Have you heard from Commander Jamieson?" Miguel addressed Niko, ignoring Q's comments altogether.

Niko nodded and swallowed his bite of bacon. "They should be waiting for you by the eastern gate. He said they had everything packed for the mission, you just needed to retrieve your horses from the stables and meet them as soon as you're able."

Niko's last words were delivered with a knowing smile, but he didn't say anything else on the topic.

"We'll need a third horse." Roska reached for Brigit's hand.

"Oh thank the Mother!" Elena exclaimed, clapping and beaming at Brigit. "You convinced them they were stupid to leave you here. I'm so happy for you! All that 'stay home and stay safe' bullshyt was so glaringly misogynistic and stupid." Niko grabbed Elena's hand a little too late, as she blushed and closed her lips tight in embarrassment. Whether she believed what she'd said or not, she hadn't meant to blurt it out like that.

"What? Ye wanted me to go wit 'em?" Brigit's shock was palpable.

Truthfully, Roska was just as surprised at Elena's outburst as Brigit seemed to be.

"Well, of course." Elena shrugged, seeming to accept that she couldn't take back what she said, so she leaned into it completely. "You are a strong, capable woman. They would be complete idiots not to take you with them." She locked eyes with Roska as she spoke, driving home her point.

A smile slipped across Roska's lips. His sister was right, of course, but he wasn't going to give her the satisfaction of voicing that. Not yet, anyway.

"Why did ye no say somethin' last night?" Thankfully, Brigit didn't seem upset by Elena's pronouncement. Curious, maybe, but not hurt or angry.

Elena broke her stare with Roska, eyes flitting nervously to Niko. She seemed to be debating what to say next, but Agon had no such tact.

"She didn't want to get in the middle of your relationship," the *raju* called out from across the dining hall, his little voice echoing off the stone walls.

A blush spread across Elena's cheeks at his words. She didn't argue them, though.

"I appreciate that, El," Roska began. He reached across the table and offered her his hand. She took it, although the heat didn't fade from her face. "You could have just told me, though. I think we all know by now that the men in our family can be a bit thick at times."

Roska's gaze shifted to Quinn, who nodded solemnly in agreement while still opening his mouth and adding, "Yeah, you and Aiden are stubborn dumbasses. I'm just lucky I missed that family trait."

The entire table erupted in laughter. Q's hand flew to his chest, clutching imaginary pearls in mock offense.

When the laughter died down, Brigit spoke again to Elena. "Thank ye for havin' faith in me. Next time, feel free to jump in an' tell yer brother he's bein' a damn fool."

"Gladly."

* * * * * * *

Three horses were saddled and waiting for them when they reached the stables. Roska offered to boost Brigit up, but she quickly waved him off with her bruised—but no longer broken—hand, smiling down at him as she got herself settled on the back of the chestnut horse she'd chosen.

Pride swelled in Roska's chest as he watched her turn to lead the beast from the stable and out onto the road.

"Looks like that healer is working some more of her magic," Miguel observed, mounting his own horse.

"I never thought she'd be able to use that hand again," Roska agreed. The healer was impressive, but she'd been very clear that she wasn't a miracle worker. She could repair Brigit's hand some, but it would never be the same as it was. Brigit had been thrilled to have any mobility and functionality back in the limb.

Roska hooked one foot in the stirrup and threw his other leg over. Grabbing the reins, he followed Miguel and Brigit as they navigated the busy morning streets and out the eastern gate.

Balor, Asha, and Zara were waiting for them, playing cards and cursing each other.

"You cheated!" Balor cried out, pointing accusingly at Zara.

Zara smirked, scraping together her winnings and tucking them away in a leather pouch tied to her belt. She leaned back, and Roska could see why Balor had cried foul. Zara's breasts were nearly completely exposed. Her tunic had been deliberately untied, leaving very little to the imagination.

"It's not my fault you're so easily distracted," she claimed as she rose from the stump she'd been using as a chair and began to fix her top, tying the laces back to conceal her exposed flesh.

"Perhaps if you thought with the head atop your neck rather than the one betwixt your fat legs, you'd be the one taking home all the coppers."

Balor roared with laughter, slapping his thigh and nodding his agreement. Asha just smiled, shaking her head in amusement.

"You three ready to head out?" Miguel asked.

"Been ready since sun up, Cap." Balor grinned, rising to his feet and untying the horses they had tethered loosely to a nearby tree.

"Let's get moving then. We've got a long way to go and a lot to discuss before we get there."

* * * * * *

Demoni soared lazily overhead, swooping and gliding as though she hadn't a care in the world. Roska knew that wasn't the reality of the situation, but it was soothing to watch her fly nonetheless.

Roska tuned out most of the conversation on their journey. Miguel laid out the plan for the others, explaining Roska's new-found skills so succinctly that Roska only had to create one small mouse to demonstrate but didn't actually have to speak or explain anything. It left his mind plenty of space to wander, although that was likely not a good thing.

He was grateful to not be making this trip alone. However, he couldn't stop his mind from calling up images of the worst-case scenarios over and over. Gruesome images of Miguel or Brigit's torture and death. Violent, bloody pictures of finding them in underground cells, flayed and broken.

"Ye all right, love?" Brigit spoke softly to avoid being overheard. The others were too wrapped up in their conversations to notice, though. Something about Balor being cheated at dice by a topless young pirate.

Roska nodded, but he could tell she didn't believe him, so he added, "I'm just nervous. There are so many ways this can go wrong. I don't want to lose you. Either of you."

"I dinna want to lose ye either." She reached over, gripping his hand with her bruised hand.

Roska looked at the injured appendage. "Looks like you're healing quickly," he commented, desperate to change the topic.

Smiling broadly, Brigit pulled her hand back and flexed her fingers. "Aye, that healer is a gift from the Gods."

Maybe we should have brought her with us, Demoni whispered in his mind as she dove under a low-hanging branch.

That would have been a good idea. We'll just have to pray the Mother keeps us safe and that we get through this relatively unharmed.

Roska wasn't a very religious man. Why would he put his faith in a deity or deities who left him to suffer at the hands of the Brothers for so many cycles? But he had faith in their abilities as a group to get into the compound once more, destroy the eyes, take down Grand Maester Auron, and hopefully free the world of the Brotherhood's influence.

We're really putting a lot on destroying those eyes. What if he's not even using them to control people?

Roska was taken aback. Demoni had never voiced this concern before. Honestly, they hadn't really considered it was possible that the Brothers all *willingly* followed Grand Maester Auron. They'd learned about the potential for mind control and immediately latched on to the idea. It made more sense to Roska that the Brothers weren't in control of their actions than to think they were all as violent and bigoted as their leader.

What if they really believed in his cause?

They'd be muxed.

Chapter 37

THEY ARRIVED AT THE edge of the forest, looking out at the Brotherhood's compound, just after sunset six days later. They'd made good time, but Roska couldn't help feeling like they were late.

Candles flickered in the lanterns along the top of the wall that surrounded the compound. By the looks of things, Grand Maester Auron had increased security.

"Looks like your last visit made quite the impression," Zara observed, kneeling beside Roska as he watched the guards pace back and forth atop the wall.

"Aye, they'll make things a tad more complicated." Brigit was on his other side, her hand resting on his shoulder. "No impossible, though."

Roska admired her confidence. He gestured behind them with his head, then silently rose and crept back into the woods where the rest of their crew was waiting.

"He's tripled the guards along the wall," Zara announced to no one in particular.

"Well, considering their security was laughable before, that's really just upping their game to a reasonable level." Asha lounged against a thick tree trunk, the horses grazing behind her.

"What's the plan, Cap?" Balor asked Miguel.

"The plan stays the same. We sneak in and either destroy the Lamia eyes and Auron's method of controlling these men, or we find undeniable proof of his antics and bring it to the King so he can justify a full-scale attack."

Roska huffed. He thought the entire idea of finding any proof of wrongdoing was ridiculous. Grand Maester Auron had been at this for as long as Roska had been alive, and likely many cycles before that. He wouldn't be careless enough to leave proof of his deeds for them to find. Assuming such proof even existed outside the minds of the Brothers he controlled.

"That is the plan," Miguel added, glaring pointedly at Roska.

"Yes, of course. That's the plan. Destroy the eyes. That's the only way to break that vile monster's hold on the compound." Roska raked his hand roughly through the white blonde hairs that tickled his brow. He just wanted to get this done. He didn't care about the politics of it all. He wanted to bring Grand Maester Auron to his knees and watch the arrogant, abusive man crumble to the magic he openly hated but secretly used to manipulate everyone around him.

Ice cracked along Roska's fingertips as he subconsciously flexed his hands into fists. Blinking, he realized everyone was staring at him and there was a thin layer of frost covering the ground around him.

"Shyt," he muttered. Opening his hands and stretching his fingers, Roska recalled his power and tried to ignore the weight of their stares. "I'm going to take a walk."

Turning on his heels, he disappeared into the woods, ignoring Brigit and Miguel as they quietly called after him. He needed some time to think, regain control of his magic, and calm down before he froze them all to death.

* * * * * *

Roska stalked through the thick underbrush. He'd lost control of his powers, again. He'd been doing that a lot lately, accidentally unleashing little bouts of frost and ice when he was overly stressed. Granted, he'd gotten some pretty decent control over the last few solar cycles. Every time things got a little too intense, he still ended up dropping the temperature by several degrees.

You're being a little hard on yourself, don't you think? Demoni swooped down low, landing flawlessly across his shoulders.

No, I don't, he sniped, but he sounded petulant even to his own ears.

Everyone loses control a little when they're upset or stressed.

Roska grunted, stepping over a large branch in their path. *Maybe, but not everyone turns things to ice when they're having big feelings.*

No, some people burn down buildings or reduce people to ash, Demoni said, giving him a pointed stare.

Yes, his siblings had also lost control of their powers on occasion, leading to the untimely deaths of a few violent criminals. Roska didn't blame Quinn or Elena for how they handled those situations. They were simply trying to protect themselves and others.

That's not the same thing, and you know it.

Maybe not, but the point is that no one is perfect and running away doesn't actually solve anything.

Roska ignored her, but he felt the truth of her words sink into his bones. Roska had spent so much of his life denying who he was and trying to bottle up his feelings, it was hard to let go of that instinct. He was about to respond when Demoni froze. Her tiny claws dug into the flesh of his shoulders, causing him to freeze and sink down to a crouching position behind a thick tree.

What is it? he asked her silently.

I'm not sure. I smell something. Wood smoke, roasting meat, and coffee.

Roska kept low to the forest floor, slipping around the tree and making his way closer to the source of the smells. He noticed them now, as they moved farther from their own campsite. He heard the shuffle of feet and caught a glimpse of a hunched figure moving around an outdoor fire.

Roska hid behind a cluster of saplings, watching the old man as he putted around the fire. He seemed familiar.

What is he doing out here? Demoni flexed her claws, adjusting her position to see better through the branches of the young trees.

Roska was more interested in who the man was than why he was living in a small hut in the middle of the forest.

"I can hear your heart pounding from here. Just come out, friend. I'm no threat to you."

That voice. That *voice.* A wave of warmth spread through Roska as his memories caught up with his mind.

Brother Liam.

✳ ✳ ✳ ✳ ✳ ✳ ✳

Brigit paced anxiously between the horses and the crew, constantly looking through the trees in the direction Roska had gone in the hopes of catching a glimpse of him as he returned.

"Should we no've gone after him?" she asked nervously for the fourteenth time.

"He's fine, darlin'. Come have a seat," Miguel patted the ground beside him. "He just needs to cool down."

"More like warm up, am I right?" Balor winked wryly at Brigit. His playfulness drew a smile from her, despite her concerns.

"I dinna like when he's upset like that." She sighed heavily, then walked over and sat on the forest floor beside Miguel. He pulled her into a one-armed embrace, planting a soft kiss on her temple.

"He'll be back soon. And you know he won't have gone far. He's too worried about us to leave us alone for long." Brigit felt his smile against her skin, sending a warmth tingling through her and relaxing the growing tension in her shoulders.

Leaning into him, Brigit inhaled his scent deeply, letting the notes of leather, fresh baked bread, and something else that was uniquely *Miguel* wash over her.

"So, what's going on with you three anyway?" Balor asked, gesturing to Brigit and Miguel with his water canteen.

"Balor!" Asha chastised, slapping him on the back of the head. "That isn't appropriate to ask. And it's *none* of our business."

Balor rubbed his bald head, looking more confused than anything. "I didn't mean to cross a line, Asha. I was just making conversation. Those three have been thick as thieves since we left the castle. Not to mention, they were *all* late to leave. It's a harmless question."

Brigit looked at Miguel, studying his profile as he seemed to ponder the best way to address the question. She waited to feel some level of embarrassment or worry about their judgment, but no such feelings arose.

She reached up and cupped Miguel's cheek with her now-considerably-less-damaged hand, bringing his full attention to her. Leaning in slowly, she pressed a gentle kiss on his warm, slightly salty lips. She pulled back to see affection—maybe even love?—glowing in his eyes.

"We're together," Miguel said simply, never taking his eyes off hers. He leaned in, planting a much more passionate kiss on her lips, leaving her breathless and heated. Resting her forehead against his, she inhaled his intoxicating scent, closing her eyes and immersing herself in him completely.

"Great. I'm glad for you. All three of you." Zara didn't quite sound glad, but Brigit didn't push. She didn't know the woman that well. Maybe she was a reserved person. Maybe Fae didn't openly express emotions like humans.

Brigit caught her eye for a moment and thought she saw a hint of something.

She wasn't certain, but it almost looked like jealousy.

✳ ✳ ✳ ✳ ✳ ✳

"Brother Liam?" Roska practically stumbled into the clearing the man had made before his tiny hut.

The old man turned; his eyes were clouded over, and strange scars marred his eyelids. The rest of his familiar face was much the same, although with considerably more wrinkles than when Roska had last seen the man.

"Roska? Is that really you? Praise the Mother!" Brother Liam shuffled over, raising his hands before him and nearly knocking Roska over when he finally made contact.

The old man's arthritic hands gripped Roska's tunic with more force than Roska would have thought possible. His hands slowly loosened and felt their way up his chest, shoulders, neck, and ultimately to his face. Gently, Brother Liam cupped Roska's cheeks, wiping away tears Roska hadn't even noticed were falling from his eyes.

"Hush now, dear boy." Brother Liam's soothing voice nearly shattered what little self-control Roska had managed to muster.

He collapsed on the forest floor, kneeling before the old man and wrapping his arms tightly around the man's soft middle. Brother Liam, to his credit, didn't shy away from Roska's unexpected outpouring of affection. Instead, he rested his hands on Roska's head, smoothing his hair and letting him cry like he always had when Roska was a child.

When he finally regained control of himself, Roska sniffled, wiping the last of his tears away with the bottom of his tunic. Brushing his hair from his face, he rose to stand before the man who'd been the closest thing to a father Roska had ever had.

"I apologize, Brother Liam. I didn't mean to..." Roska trailed off, unsure how to put into words his dramatic outburst.

"None of that, boy. I have always told you to embrace all of your feelings. Not just the pleasant ones. All of your feelings are valid and burying the unpleasant ones isn't helpful or healthy." He took Roska's arm, escorting him to a stump that seemed to serve as a chair beside the cooking pit. "And it's just Liam. I'm no Brother."

There was a bitterness in his voice.

"What happened to you?" Roska asked, barely above a whisper.

"It's a long story."

"I've got time." Roska shifted on the stump, reaching out to take the former Brother's hand and giving it a reassuring squeeze.

Brother Liam's blind eyes searched the forest around them, tilting his head this way and that for a moment before exhaling slowly and nodding. "All right," he said, "but you don't have as much time as you think. The Brothers will find your friends soon if they don't quiet down."

Roska strained to pick up on whatever Brother Liam had heard, but all he could hear was the sing-song chirp of a mother bird and the rustle of a small creature racing through the branches.

Demoni shrugged against his ear, clearly not hearing whatever Brother Liam had either.

"Just after you were sent on your mission to free the *turmio*, I confronted Auron. I'd been noticing a change in the Brothers: less compassion and more anger. Even the new members, those who came to us with hope and love in their hearts, quickly turned to rage and aggression toward the magical creatures of the world. I had a feeling he was up to something when I saw a hunter creep into Auron's office in the middle of the night. Auron met with the man, handing him a sack of coins in exchange for several grotesque jars. Once I saw the hunter leave, I burst into his office, hells-bent on addressing his behavior and discovering what he'd done to the Brothers." Liam took a deep breath, glaring off into the distance. "Auron turned on me. He'd been using the hunter for moons, collecting magical artifacts and using them to influence the Brothers. He held a staff with two large, cat-like eyes embedded in the top up to my face and began ranting about the evils of magic. I felt rage like I'd never known start to build within me. I didn't know how he was doing it, but I couldn't stand there and let him turn me into another of his violent, hate-filled puppets. I grabbed a vial labeled 'giant hogweed tincture'. I thought it was odd that he'd have such a dangerous plant made into a tincture, but I was grateful for it. I took the vial and poured the entire contents on my eyes. It burned like the Lord of Hells himself had come to claim my soul."

Roska stared, mouth agape, as the old man screwed his eyes shut at the memory.

"I woke up three days later in the infirmary, vision completely gone, my arms tied to the cot they'd laid me out on. Auron told the Brothers he'd bound me for my own good, but I knew it was to prevent me from escaping. I didn't understand how those eyes were manipulating the men, but I knew then that I couldn't stay there. It took a few more weeks, but I finally convinced Brother Marcus to unbind me. Do you remember him? Nice young man, very adept at herbalism. The second he left me alone, I fled. It wasn't easy, mind you. I'd spent the majority of my life in that compound, but I still managed to get turned around a few times. I hadn't gotten used to being without my sight yet." Brother Liam carefully lifted the coffee pot from the grate it sat on over the flames and poured them both a mug of the simmering beverage. "I made it as far as the woods before stumbling and falling hard. It took some time, but I got far enough away to feel safe and spent the next several moons building this place." He lifted his mug to gesture to the hut behind Roska. It wasn't large, but it was thick and sturdy. Roska knew it would keep the old man safe in the frost seasons.

"And you've been living here ever since?" Demoni's voice startled Brother Liam, causing the old man to spill a bit of his coffee as he jumped.

"Gods, I'm sorry, Brother Liam." Demoni launched herself from Roska's shoulder, blowing her cool breath onto Liam's hand where the coffee had splashed his skin. She flapped her wings, creating quite a flurry of dry leaves, tiny snowflakes, and smoke from the irritated fire.

"My darling girl." The Brother sat down on a log beside Roska. He raised his hands up to touch her, and she flew down to rest on his lap. "My gods, you are absolutely stunning, aren't you?"

Demoni pressed her head into his open hand, rubbing against him like a stray cat begging for a spare morsel.

She turned and snapped at Roska. *I'm no stray cat.*

Roska chuckled despite himself.

"I'm glad the two of you are well." Liam stroked Demoni's back, fingers slowly caressing the lines of her leathery wings. "Looks like you're finally back in one piece again, too. I'm so happy for you." His blind eyes looked up, seeming to lock his gaze with Roska even though that couldn't be possible. "Both of you seem quite happy."

"Yes, sir. We're doing well. Thanks to you and your kindness. I don't think we would have survived that place without you."

Brother Liam shrugged, rolling off Roska's gratitude with a look that said he didn't feel like he deserved it. "I should have done more for you. Gotten you out of that place. I'm sorry I failed you."

Roska blinked back tears, staring openly at the man who'd cared for him more than anyone in that godsforsaken compound. "Brother Liam, you took great care of us. We learned so much from you. You protected us as best you could. That's more than anyone else in that awful place ever did."

He moved from the stump, grasping the Brother's hands and placing them on Roska's cheeks. "Feel my face, hear my words, and trust their meaning. You were a kind man in a place that regarded kindness as weakness. You are the reason we are still alive today."

Brother Liam's rough fingers rubbed Roska's cheeks, wiping away the tears as they silently slipped down his cool skin.

"Thank you for caring about us." Roska's words were a rough whisper, emotion clogging his throat as the old man beamed down at him.

"Hush now, dear boy. You are a strong, brave young man because of what's in here." He poked a knobby finger into Roska's chest. "You are exactly who the Mother created you to be, regardless of my input."

Roska didn't respond. There was no point in arguing with the old man. He was too stubborn to accept that he was the reason Roska was brave and strong. The Mother Goddess had abandoned him to hells. Just like his own biological mother and father. He'd forgiven them—mostly—for their careless actions, but that didn't mean he was on good terms with the Mother Goddess.

Liam cleared his throat, rising from the log and shuffling back to the cooking pit to stir his stew. "What are you doing out here with me when your friends are clearly worried about you?"

Roska sat back on his heels. His friends were right to worry. He was barely in control of his powers. He could easily cause the next ice age if he didn't get a handle on things.

Instead of addressing the question, he asked, "How did you know they're worried?"

Brother Liam gestured to his eyes. "It's true what they say. Once one sense goes, the others pick up the slack. I might be as blind as a bat, but my hearing is just as good as one as well. I can hear your friends pacing. The light-footed one keeps wandering the same path over and over. A lot of nervous energy, that one." Brother Liam smiled as he tilted his head toward Miguel and Brigit's encampment.

Roska looked off in the distance. He was sure he'd traveled a good way from their camp. He couldn't see or hear any hint of them.

"Don't worry, Roska. They'll be fine. Sounds like the big, stompy one is getting them into a card game." Brother Liam retrieved a bowl from under his prep area beside the cooking pit. He scooped a large portion of stew into the bowl and handed it to Roska, as well as a dented spoon and a thick slice of bread. "Eat up. Tell me what's going on and why you're hiding from your friends."

Roska spent the next hour eating and telling Brother Liam everything that had happened to him since he left the compound. From releasing the *turmio* to finding and reconnecting with his blood family. Losing Elena. Fighting to get her back. Everything with the Queen. His search for Brigit. Rescuing her from the Brothers—Liam was especially livid about that part. He was enraged that Grand Maester Auron would kidnap and torture a young woman for cycles merely because of her assumed relationship with Roska. He relayed the tale of finding Demoni's wings and the evolution of his powers to create and control frost creatures. And finally, the discovery of the Lamia and Auron's use of the creature's eyes to manipulate the entire Brotherhood to do his bidding.

"Gods, it makes sense now." Brother Liam shook his head in disappointment. "So many of the Brothers I'd grown up with had changed so much. By the time I fled, I barely recognized them anymore. They came to the Brotherhood so optimistic and loving. Excited to dedicate their lives to the service of the Gods and their fellow citizens. Auron has infected them with his hate. We have to help them, Roska. Those men don't deserve to be used as pawns in Auron's sick and misguided war."

Mux. Roska hadn't even considered how the Brothers might feel. He'd been so fixated on stopping the Grand Maester that it hadn't really occurred to him that the Brothers might not *want* to follow him. He'd started to convince himself that the entire Brotherhood was the problem, but maybe Brother Liam was right. Maybe they just needed to remove Auron's influence and the rest of the Brothers would be free to return to their normal, congenial selves.

Not all of them were so kind, Demoni interjected. *Many of the men who "took care" of us enjoyed the torment they wrought.*

Roska nodded in silent agreement. Auron clearly attracted some like-minded men, but Brother Liam had a point, too. Not all the men in the Brotherhood were exclusively good or bad. Nothing was black and white—as much as Roska wished it was. There was nothing but grey before him.

Mux. Mux everything.

Chapter 38

"**M**AYBE WE SHOULD GO look for him?" Brigit looked anxiously over her shoulder in the direction Roska had stormed off over an hour ago.

Miguel desperately wanted to follow her lead and hunt down that stubborn man, but he knew it wouldn't solve the problem. Roska needed to address his own struggles, internally, and stop denying his full range of emotions.

Gods damn him and his attraction to damaged men. Why couldn't Miguel find himself interested in emotionally stable people who'd already processed and dealt with their traumatic pasts?

Because the damaged ones are the sexiest, he reminded himself. He loved Roska, but damn it all. That man was the most stubborn person he'd ever met. And frustratingly good at compartmentalizing and refusing to deal with the root of his problems.

He was even more skilled with his tongue…

Miguel shook that thought away. He needed to stay focused, for Brigit's sake. He scooted closer to her on the log he'd claimed as a chair.

"He'll be back soon, love. Just give him time. He's got a lot of shyt to process that he's been avoiding for cycles."

Brigit sighed heavily and leaned into him. She was resting on the forest floor in front of him, leaning her back against him where she sat between his legs. Her arms were wrapped around one of his legs as she laid her head to rest on his thigh. He stroked a hand through her wild red hair, working the tangles out with deft fingers. Brigit sighed again at his touch, more an exhale of release and relaxation this time.

Miguel continued his work with her hair as she drifted off to sleep on his lap. He marveled at himself and the stunning woman between his legs.

He'd never been attracted to women before. Sure, he'd tested that theory as a younger man, sleeping with a handful of the maids and kitchen girls, but he'd never really cared much for them either way. They were just... there. It sounded cruel and heartless, but he just wasn't interested in them.

Miguel had grown up in the castle, watching the last King rut anyone who caught his eye—regardless of their willingness—and Miguel had thought that look of disdain or disinterest in a lover was normal.

Until he'd met a valet serving a lord who'd come to Riverayn on a trade mission for Maehelm. The lad was a cycle or two older than Miguel and had been near god-like in his beauty. He was the first to stir true feelings in Miguel's jaded heart and it had been the most magical and thrilling three nights of his life. From then on, Miguel had exclusively slept with men. They were the only ones who stirred him in such a way.

Then came Brigit. He didn't know what it was about her, but she pulled at something in him that he'd thought was long dead. She made him want to explore the female form with a fiery passion that was almost painful.

Their night together—the three of them in a tangle of limbs, hair, moans, and cries of pleasure—had been utterly intoxicating, and he couldn't wait for the next time the three of them were alone together.

Miguel got lost in the vivid images replaying in his thoughts as he absentmindedly worked the last of the knots from her thick hair. He was barely aware of their surroundings when Zara shifted, pressing her leg against his, as she twisted to face something just beyond the light of their small fire.

They'd intentionally kept the flames low, to avoid detection, but it was still enough to cause a bit of fire blindness in them all. Thankfully Zara's pointed ears were more adept at picking up distant sounds than his human ones.

"What is it?" Miguel whispered practically directly into her ear.

"Someone's coming," she replied, slowly pulling the dagger from her thigh sheath. The only sound echoing in Miguel's ears—aside from the pounding of his pulse—was the subtle scrape of the metal as she poised to strike the intruder.

❄ ❄ ❄ ❄ ❄ ❄

Roska wasn't sure how the group would feel about him bringing Brother Liam into their camp, but the man had insights that they'd need to execute their plans. Demoni flew ahead, to let the others know he was bringing a friend. He hoped that would lessen the shock and avoid any unnecessary violence.

You're not going to believe this. Demoni's voice was cool and smooth in his mind.

What's wrong?

Nothing is wrong, but you two should hurry up.

Mux everything. What could possibly have happened while they were away? They weren't even gone that long! Gods, could nothing just go right for once?

I told you, everything is fine. We have company. He could hear Demoni's smile through her thoughts.

Company?

Roska hurried Brother Liam as much as he dared. He didn't want the old man to fall or get injured hiking through unfamiliar woods without his sight, but Roska couldn't ignore the ominous feeling that settled in his chest.

Anyone who knew about the location of their campsite was a potential threat. They couldn't trust anyone, not this close to Grand Maester Auron's mind-controlling influence.

As they approached the clearing, Brother Liam seemed to perk up, a small smile growing on his face as if he'd just thought of something amusing. Quiet laughter filtered in through the trees ahead of them.

"That man," Brother Liam whispered, chuckling and shaking his head.

"What man?" Roska asked, feeling utterly out of the loop.

Pulling the low branches aside, Roska let Brother Liam into the clearing and discovered exactly which man the Brother had been referring to.

Pierre Louis Thibodeaux Beauchamps.

"Ach! There ye are! We've bin worried sick." Brigit leapt up from where she'd been seated on the forest floor between Miguel's legs. She raced over to him and pulled him into a tight embrace.

Roska was shocked by the open display of affection, but instinctively wrapped his arms around her, pulling her closer and burying his face in her wild red mane. Gods, even out in the woods for days, she still smelled like lavender and serenity.

Balor cleared his throat loudly, catching Roska's attention and nodding to Brother Liam.

"Oh, apologies, Brother." Roska pulled back from Brigit a bit, shifting her to his side while keeping one arm firmly wrapped around her. "Everyone, this is Brother Liam, the kindest man you'll ever meet."

Brother Liam smiled but waved off Roska's introduction. "Please, it's just Liam. I'm not a Brother anymore. Haven't been for several cycles now."

"Aye, young Master Liam is quite the adept forest chef, though," Lou interjected, rising from his seat before their small fire to embrace the Brother as though they were old friends.

Roska studied their interaction, the way Brother Liam clasped Lou's forearm, pulling him into a firm, one-armed hug. Perhaps they really were old friends after all.

"It's a pleasure to see you again. All in one piece this time, I hope?" Brother Liam grinned at their private joke as Lou snorted a barely contained laugh.

"Of course! I'm the human equivalent of a cock roach. I'm damn near impossible to kill."

"Doesn't seem to stop people from trying though, does it?" Brother Liam let Lou lead him to a stump, helping the old man get settled and handing him a warm mug of what smelled like mint and citrus tea.

Roska blanched at their interaction, completely floored by how comfortable the former Brother seemed to be with Lou, a master spy for the King.

Brigit's hand on the small of his back drove Roska to the empty space beside Miguel, who was looking thoroughly bemused but not entirely surprised by the interaction between Lou and Liam.

"And how do you two know each other?" Asha asked, a slightly strained smile seeming to be permanently affixed to her face.

Everyone seemed to be intrigued by this unexpected connection between the spy and the old man.

Refilling his own tea, Lou turned to Brother Liam. "Would you like to tell them how we met? I have to be honest, dear friend, I don't actually remember our first encounter."

"Of course you don't," Brother Liam said, sipping his tea. "You were cold as ice and bleeding rather profusely from a deep gash in your shoulder. I'm surprised you made it through the night, in all honesty."

"Well, I had a brave soul tending to my every need. Who wouldn't want to stay alive for that?" Lou grinned broadly, clearly reveling in the story.

"How were you injured?" Zara asked.

"Oh, you know, a mission for the King, most likely." Lou waved off her question as though it was silly to ask.

"That's not how I recall it," Liam replied. "If I remember correctly—and since I wasn't the one with a head wound, I think we can take my word for it—you'd been caught in bed with someone's betrothed. From what you told me, his fiance was none too pleased to find you with her soon-to-be husband and used the fire poker to express her displeasure."

Laughter exploded around their small camp, startling the birds in the trees above them and causing the horses to stomp their hooves in annoyance.

Lou beamed at them with unashamed amusement, pulling the collar of his shirt aside to show the large scar that spanned from the middle of his left pectoral, across his chest, and ending under his left arm. The scar itself was thick and jagged. Roska imagined it must have bled a great deal. He was pretty confident such an injury could easily kill.

Balor bumped Lou with his shoulder—likely with more force than he intended as the old spy nearly fell off his stump at the contact. "You old dog! A mission from the King, eh? Unless 'The King' is what you call that thing in your pants, sounds like you were on a mission you assigned yourself there, buddy."

Lou cackled, nodding vehemently and nearly choking on his tea. "It was a hells of a good night before the *fille* showed up."

"I imagine she wasn't too happy about how the night ended either," Zara deadpanned.

Roska looked down at Brigit where she sat on the forest floor between himself and Miguel. He worried that this sort of crude humor would upset her. He shouldn't have been. Brigit's cheeks were flushed and her eyes were sparkling with unshed tears of laughter.

You forget, Demoni put in, *she worked in a tavern for Goddess only knows how long before we met her. This sort of conversation is nothing new for her.*

Roska didn't like thinking about Brigit's time in the tavern. He'd heard Elena's stories about her time at Amelia's inn and tavern. Even with Quinn by her side at nearly every turn, she was still assaulted twice and forced to take the lives of her would-be rapists. Roska hated to think of Brigit in similar circumstances.

"So you stitched him up, Brother?" Miguel prompted once the majority of the laughter had died down.

"Aye, I did. And please, I'm just Liam."

"All due respect, sir," Brigit spoke up. "We've all heard wonderful stories about ye from Roska. Yer everythin' the Brotherhood should be. If it's all right wit ye, I think we"—she paused and glanced around the circle, looking for any objections and finding none—"would prefer that ye keep the title, as a representation of what other Brothers should aspire to be."

Roska watched as Brother Liam's face reddened and tears danced along his pale eyelashes. "Aye, lass. If you're sure, who am I to object?" His voice was rough, tight with emotion, but he looked genuinely honored by her words.

As he should. Brigit was right. Brother Liam was everything a Brother should be. Kind, caring, thoughtful, honest, and compassionate. If only the rest of the Brotherhood were more like him. They wouldn't be in this position at all.

Clearing his throat, Brother Liam finished the story, his voice gaining strength as he brought the tale to a close. "I stitched him up, fed him soup and teas for near ten days, and kept his bandages clean. It was tedious work, and the fool was easily the worst patient I've ever had. He kept trying to get up and leave. I think I had to restitch you what? Two? Three times?"

"Aye, something like that." Lou grinned.

"Anyway, once he was healthy enough to leave, he vanished in the night. I woke one morning to find myself alone in my hut again. I thought I'd never see him again."

"Wait," Asha grabbed Lou by the collar like an ill-behaved child. "You disappeared in the night? You abandoned the man who bent over backward to save your dumb ass without so much as a 'Bye, thanks for keeping me alive'? What the hells is wrong with you?"

Lou gently pried his shirt from her grip. "If you'll release me, I'll tell you what happened."

Asha grunted but relented. Roska had never seen this side of her. It was unexpected and seemed a bit over-the-top, but she wasn't wrong for calling him out on his bad behavior.

"Like the kind Brother said." Lou straightened his shirt, fixing the collar where Asha's tight grip had twisted the fabric. "I did leave in the night, but only because I was actually on a mission for the King and I needed to report back. I came back to check in on the old man a few days later. I brought him fresh supplies, including medicines and linens to replace the ones he'd used caring for me." Lou pointedly glared at Asha as he added, "I've been coming to visit at least once a moon since then."

Asha bristled under his glare but didn't say anything for several tense moments. Roska thought the matter had ended until she quietly said, "Well, at least your mother raised you to be kind. If only she'd taught you to stay out of other people's beds."

"I didn't know she was your sister." Lou sighed, dejectedly.

"But you knew *he* was betrothed," Asha shot back.

Mouths dropped all around. The woman who'd scarred and nearly killed Lou was Asha's *sister?* Roska hadn't even known the woman *had* a sister. Based on the looks on everyone else's faces, they hadn't known either.

"I've said I was sorry. What more can I do?" Lou looked pleadingly at Asha, begging for her forgiveness for a crime that—based on the healing of the scar—had happened cycles ago.

"There's nothing." Asha sighed, rolling her neck and drawing several loud cracks from the vertebrae. "She's mated to another man. A faithful one. They have three beautiful—if a little spoiled—children together."

Lou's eyes brightened at this news. "So... you're saying that I really did her a favor. Sparing her from a loveless marriage to a sexy idiot." Asha slapped his arm, but there was no anger in the gesture. "If anything, you should be *thanking* me," Lou added with a confident gleam in his eyes. "She could have been tethered to that man for the rest of her life. And, I might add, he wasn't all that impressive of a lover. She's better off, really."

That got everyone laughing again. Asha swatted Lou's arm once more, and that was the end of it. Unfortunately, that wasn't the end of their night. Roska still hadn't told them all why he'd brought Brother Liam to their camp in the first place.

* * * * * *

"Brother Liam, you were telling me about how you became blind," Roska prompted the old man after everyone had calmed down and had some dinner. "Why you blinded yourself rather than look into the eyes Grand Maester Auron tried to use on you, right?"

A tense hush fell over the group. They'd suspected that the Lamia eyes were how the Grand Maester was controlling everyone, but it was entirely different when their suspicions were confirmed by an outside source.

"Yes, I chose to give up my sight rather than my free will. It was a choice I would happily make again." The group watched Brother Liam as he shifted his robes, getting comfortable before he retold his experience with Grand Maester Auron's abuse of magical creatures. The silence that reigned after he'd finished his tale was no longer merely tense. It had evolved to a heavy level of barely contained violence that Roska had only ever experienced once before: when he and his family had confronted the Queen. That heavy tension had ultimately exploded into a violent magic battle that had nearly torn the roof off the Great Hall. It had taken several moons to get the room repaired after the Queen had been deposed and relocated to Harbor Ridge to serve out her life sentence.

The tension weighing down their campsite now wouldn't be so easily released. They didn't have a villain before them, not yet anyway.

"Thank you for sharing your story with us, Brother." Miguel placed a strong hand on the old man's shoulder. "It confirms what we suspected. Do you know any way into the compound that won't be guarded? Any suggestions on how to infiltrate with minimum attention?"

"Aye, Captain-no-fun over there nixed my plan to blow the whole place up." Asha looked genuinely disappointed as she picked at her fingernails. Roska had listened to this argument for the better part of the last week. Asha *was* the explosives expert, but it seemed a bit extreme to blow the entire place up if it was only Grand Maester Auron who was the real problem.

"I appreciate your compassion, Miguel." Brother Liam smiled sadly. "The Brothers aren't all bad; they've had their free will stolen from them. They can't be held responsible for Auron's actions."

Brigit seemed to flinch at Brother Liam's words. Roska couldn't help but agree with her. She'd been held and tortured for cycles. Even if the Grand Maester had been controlling everyone's minds, it would be hard to forgive the actions of her tormentors. Those were still the faces of the men who haunted her nightmares and caused her to wake in a cold sweat more often than not. Roska reached out and offered her his hand, which she eagerly grasped, gripping tightly as she began to take slow, deep breaths.

"So we destroy the eyes and free the Brothers. Simple enough, eh?" Balor asked, lounging against a large oak across the small fire from Roska. He unsheathed the battleaxe from his hip and made a dramatic show of twirling it and hacking off imaginary heads.

"Hopefully." Roska nodded. "Brother Liam, do you know anything about the Lamia? My biggest concern is that we destroy the eyes and shatter the minds of those who'd been under its control. We want to free these men, not devastate them."

"I'm sorry, son. I didn't even know the creature's name until you told me. But if the choices are being under Auron's control or being released unto the Fade, I think most—if not all—of the Brothers would choose eternal freedom."

Roska hoped Brother Liam was right. Either way, it would all be settled by morning.

Chapter 39

MIGUEL WOKE FIRST, AS he often did. They'd agreed to a short rest, just a few hours to recoup some of their energy from the near-week's worth of traveling. He crept into the woods, leaving the others to enjoy a bit more sleep before he roused them all for their pre-dawn "attack" on the compound.

He didn't approve of the word "attack" in this context. They weren't invading or launching any sort of outright violence, but they were going to enter the compound without consent. Brigit pointed out that that would inherently be an attack under any circumstances. Gods, she was quick and clever. He loved her and her brilliant mind.

He was refilling the waterskins when he heard light footsteps shuffling up behind him. Dropping low, he slipped the dagger from his boot and crept behind a bush to see who was watching him.

"It's just me, boy. You wouldn't attack a blind old man, would you?"

Miguel instantly sheathed the weapon and rose from his hiding place. "Apologies, Brother. I didn't know who was sneaking up on me. Better safe than sorry, right?" He offered Brother Liam his arm as he led the man to the creek side.

"Aye, of course, lad. I didn't mean to startle you. I don't sleep as well as I used to. I heard you walking off so I thought I'd take this time to get to know the man who's stolen my dear boy's heart."

Miguel blushed, suddenly very self-conscious as he adjusted his tunic and tried—but failed—to fix his unruly hair.

"I don't care what you look like, son." Brother Liam smiled, gesturing to his clouded eyes.

Feeling like an idiot, Miguel clenched his teeth several times before speaking. "I'm sorry, Brother Liam. That was thoughtless of me."

"Nothing to worry about. I've been blind for cycles. This is all new for you." Brother Liam chuckled at his own joke. Kneeling slowly beside the creek, he dipped his hands into the water and took a drink from the cool stream.

"How could you tell it was me walking to the creek and not one of the others?"

Roska had mentioned that the Brother's hearing had strengthened to balance out his loss of sight, but being able to identify someone by their steps in the woods—without ever having met that person before—was beyond the pale.

"Balor snores. Zara grinds her teeth in her sleep. Asha is a very heavy sleeper—ought not let her out on a mission overnight alone. Brigit and Roska were quite entwined, with Demoni awake but silently resting on the stump above them. To be honest, lad, I was surprised you didn't want to stay wrapped up with them."

Gods, the man was painfully observant.

"You don't take issue with our relationship? The three of us being together and such. I understand that the Brothers are more... traditional in their preferences about matings."

"Aye, some are. But when you spend the majority of your life in a compound of only men, finding physical comfort in the arms of one another doesn't seem so unreasonable. And the three of you seem quite happy. I just wanted to make sure that the relationship was well-balanced. I'd hate for one of you to feel left out."

It was a leading comment. Brother Liam was giving Miguel an opportunity to vent any frustrations or misgivings he might be feeling, without fear of judgment. He really was a remarkably kind man. How the hells he'd come out of that vile Grand Maester's organization was beyond Miguel.

Offering Brother Liam his hand, Miguel pulled the old man to standing and began leading him back to their camp.

"I appreciate your concern, Brother. We are well suited, though." Miguel pondered for a moment, lifting a tree limb from their path, and added, "Do you know of the triskelion?"

Brother Liam nodded. "Aye. Three interlocking spirals. It's said to represent the unity of mind, body, and spirit."

"Roska, Brigit, and I are tied together, like the triskelion. We are tethered to each other, strengthening and supporting one another. We are perfectly balanced because we complete each other."

They reached the camp just as Demoni was rousing the group.

"Ach, little monster!" Balor shouted, shaking the ice off his face from where Roska's familiar had doused him with snow.

"Isn't there a nicer way to wake people?" Asha asked as she brushed snow from her shoulders.

"Probably," the little dragon replied, flicking her tongue out and catching a snowflake as it fell from Zara's hair. "But nothing quite as effective."

Miguel smiled, unable to think of a counterargument. He tossed waterskins to the group as they rose and stretched. One by one, they disappeared into the woods, relieved themselves, and returned looking considerably more alert.

"Are you ready for this?" Miguel asked Roska as he handed him the last waterskin.

"No. But it doesn't matter if I'm ready. It's time."

* * * * * *

Brother Liam took their horses back to his hut, promising to keep them safe and well-fed until they returned. The crew crept to the edge of the forest, watching as the first blush of dawn began to lighten the sky from a dark navy to deep purple.

Roska, with Demoni coiled around his wrist, crafted two small ice bats and turned them loose on the compound. Closing his eyes, Roska rode a bat into the depths of the compound, soaring over the walls and dipping into the garden unnoticed. The bat's vision was nearly useless, but their hearing more than made up for it. Roska had specifically chosen bats after his conversation with Brother Liam. The bat's eyes weren't how they hunted, and with Auron most likely having locked himself away in his study, Roska wouldn't have been able to see anything anyway. But he could hear.

"Brothers, it's time. We cannot sit idly by any longer. Magic and its vile creations are ruining our great country. We must not stand by and let those monsters destroy everything that is good and sacred in this land."

Quiet murmurs of agreement emanated through the stone walls. Roska guided his ice bat to find the source. The Brothers were congregated in the dining hall. Odd, considering it wasn't yet dawn. When Roska had lived there, most of the Brothers met for breakfast an hour after dawn, having spent the first light of day praying and offering penance.

This doesn't feel right, Demoni's worried voice slipped into his mind.

We need to figure out what's going on. Can you get inside?

I think my bat is melting. I'm having trouble hearing things clearly anymore.

Roska had hoped that their ice bats would last a bit longer, but the growing season nights were getting steadily warmer. Roska imagined soon enough, his ice creatures wouldn't last more than a few moments in the heat of the day.

Releasing his hold on the magic, Roska and Demoni returned to their bodies. Brigit was watching them intently while Miguel and the others kept watch on the compound.

"Did ye see anythin'?" Brigit offered him her hand as he rose to stand.

Roska gratefully took her hand, squeezing gently and embracing the warmth of her touch on his chilled fingers. "Something is happening. Grand Maester Auron sounds like he's rallying them for some sort of offensive."

"That doesna sound good."

"It sounds like we need to move. Now." Miguel spoke with finality. If they'd had any reservations about their plans, Miguel dismissed them now. If the Brotherhood was going to be *more* open, actively taking more steps to hurt or kill those with magic, simply for existing? They needed to act now. "We'll block all the exits but one. Balor, bar the south gate. Asha, go with him. Set a small bomb in the locking mechanism so it can't be opened. Zara, take Lou and barricade the western gate. Roska, Brigit, and I will meet you all at the east gate."

Roska didn't like the idea of splitting up, but he was grateful that the Brothers didn't have a fourth point of ingress. The south and west gates were more like servants' entrances than proper entries. They were small, single-door entryways that were rarely used. The main gate, the eastern gate, consisted of two large, wood and iron doors that could be barred from the inside. It was the main point of entry and egress for those visiting the compound, and therefore it was the most ornate and secure.

"When we get inside, use only nonlethal attacks. We don't know who is under Auron's control and who is truly hateful. We'll knock them out, tie them up, and destroy that damned mind-control staff of his. Once we've removed that obstacle, we'll be able to tell who our true enemies are. Understood?" Miguel held everyone's gaze for a moment, ensuring that they understood the plan. Each nodded in turn.

Balor seemed most disappointed as he sheathed his battle axe but grunted his agreement, picking up a thick branch from the forest floor and testing its strength. Seeming pleased with its flexibility, he nodded to Asha, and they slipped off toward their assigned gate. Zara and Lou took off toward the western gate, not saying a word and with such light footsteps that Roska would never have known they'd left if he hadn't seen them disappear into the tall grass.

Miguel, Brigit, and Roska held hands for a moment, the three of them intertwined together once more, sharing their warmth and attempting to impart confidence to each other. Roska could see the worry lines marring Miguel's face, even in the faint light of the near-dawn sun. This wasn't like any of the missions Miguel had told Roska about. It wasn't a stealth recon mission. It wasn't even an assassination—although Miguel had assured Roska he'd never actually participated in an assassination. He'd only planned a couple, but they'd never been put into action.

This was a full frontal attack. Granted, a *mostly* nonlethal attack. It was a direct assault nonetheless. Miguel had once stated that he wasn't comfortable on the front lines. He preferred to stick to the shadows. In this fight, however, there were no shadows. Or perhaps the entire thing was shrouded. It wasn't a perfect metaphor.

Roska locked eyes with Brigit for a moment, assessing her mental state as best he could. Her hand still continued to improve—her grip on his hand now was quite impressive—but he wasn't sure she was ready for combat. Seeing the steely look in her eyes, though, he knew she'd fight tooth and nail to put an end to the people who'd tortured her for so long. Despite Miguel's insistence that this be a nonlethal assault, Roska had given Brigit his blade. He could form weapons from ice, so he didn't need the steel, and he refused to let her go into that hells without a proper, deadly weapon in her hands. Miguel had agreed wholeheartedly.

Flicking his eyes back to Miguel, Roska could practically see the iron will solidifying within the man's bones.

They were ready.

As ready as they could be, anyway.

Demoni launched herself from his shoulder, flying as high as she could within the confines of their magical bond, so as to avoid being noticed by the small retinue of guards keeping watch along the wall. Roska, Brigit, and Miguel crept through the meadow, following the road while staying out of sight, right up to the front gate.

Demoni, serving as lookout, alerted them to the rest of their crew's progress. *Looks like Balor and Asha finished their door. They're on the way to you now. Zara and Lou are reaching their door now.*

As Brigit gripped the dagger in her good hand, Roska silently thanked the Mother that the Brothers hadn't broken her dominant hand. Pride swelled in his heart as he watched her crouch into a proper fighting stance, prepared to attack any unwelcome soul who came upon them.

Miguel, despite his reservations about direct combat, was cool and confident, sheathed sword in one hand and a thick tree branch serving as a makeshift club in the other. Roska admired his commitment to the nonlethal, while still being thoroughly prepared to end lives if need be.

Balor and Asha joined them, lining themselves up in the shadow of the wall behind Brigit. Zara and Lou joined moments later.

Once their crew was reunited, Miguel led them to the gate, keeping as close to the wall as humanly possible. He and Roska slipped into the alcove that held the massive doors and studied the lock.

"I'm not going to be able to pick this," Miguel whispered dejectedly. He roughed a hand over the day-old scruff on his chin, debating their options.

"I can freeze the hinges and we can smash through. It won't be quiet or stealthy, but it will be effective." Roska knew from experience that his ice could freeze and break iron hinges. The door on the tower his mother had locked him and his siblings in that frost season three cycles back was proof of that.

"Asha could blow the lock as well, but I'd rather find a more subtle way to break in if we can."

"What do you have in mind?"

Miguel studied the lock once more. "Can you freeze the internal mechanism of the lock? Then maybe we could just break the inside of the lock and slip in."

Roska studied the lock. He couldn't see well in such dim light, but he thought it was worth it to try, so he nodded and began pulling his ice to the tip of his right index finger. This lock was far more intense than the one on his old cell door. He had hoped he'd be able to mimic the key like he'd done when he and Demoni had escaped a few weeks ago, but he wasn't confident.

A long, frail-looking shard of ice grew from the tip of his finger, and he slid it into the lock. Closing his eyes, he tried to imagine the inner workings of the locks he'd seen while learning to pick locks with Q. He felt around for the tumblers, finding what he hoped were the pins and letting his ice envelop them. He withdrew his ice, recalling his power and admiring his handiwork. From the outside, it looked as though nothing had happened, but if he looked closely, he could see the cool mist seeping out of the keyhole.

Miguel stepped up, placing the tip of Brigit's dagger into the hole and quickly hammered it with the hilt of his sword. A small crack echoed through the alcove, causing Roska to glance over his shoulder, for fear that they'd been overheard and the might of the Brotherhood would come crashing down on them at any moment.

Brigit shook her head, indicating that nothing was amiss, and Roska exhaled.

After returning the blade to Brigit, Miguel cautiously tried the door. Pulling ever-so-slowly, Roska held his breath once more, watching as the door gave way and opened without a sound. Thank the Mother for well-oiled hinges.

Miguel pulled the door open just wide enough for them to slip through, one at a time.

Roska debated crafting more ice creatures and sending them forth to investigate but decided against it. If they could just get to the Grand Maester's office, they could destroy the Lamia eyes without being noticed and avoid confrontation with the mind-controlled Brothers. Then they'd only be fighting the truly vile humans who claimed divine superiority as justification for mass murder. In theory, that would be a considerably smaller force to contend with. Roska hoped, anyway.

Unfortunately, the second they stepped into the courtyard, Roska knew nothing would be that easy.

Chapter 40

G RAND MAESTER AURON STOOD on a dais in the middle of
the courtyard, surrounded by Brothers armed with shovels,
canes, frying pans, and garden hoes. The pale light of dawn provided little illumination, but Roska could see the glow of hate in
the Grand Maester's eyes.

"The prodigal son returns once more. This time with his army
of heathens and magic sympathizers." His words were cold, filled
with vitriol and disdain. He leaned on the large staff he had
clutched in his arthritic grip.

Roska stepped forward, placing himself between the Brothers
and his loved ones. "It doesn't have to be like this, Brothers." He
addressed the crowd surrounding the Grand Maester, not bothering to try reasoning with the willfully ignorant and hate-filled man.
"You aren't in control of your actions. He's been controlling your
minds, using the magic he claims to hate so much to manipulate
you into doing his bidding."

A couple of the Brothers seemed to react to this proclamation,
blinking and shaking their heads as though Roska's words might
have broken something loose in their minds.

"He lies!" Auron shouted, rage filling his voice as he thrust the
staff into the air. "He is a creature of magic, one of the many
that have been wreaking havoc on this world for eons. It's time

to free the world of their ilk and let the magept rule as the Mother intended!"

Several of the Brothers closest to Auron cheered, raising their weapons and shouting for an end to the magical creatures.

Balor and Miguel stepped up beside Roska, nonlethal weapons in hand.

"Remember." Miguel's voice was barely audible over the angry cries of the Brothers. "We aren't here to kill anyone if we can avoid it. Roska, get that damned staff. We'll handle these idiots."

Before Roska had a chance to respond, the Brothers attacked. They may have been predominately older men, and their weapons were more kitchen and garden tools than tools of war, but the Brothers were driven by blind hate. Hacking, slashing, and swinging their makeshift weapons with reckless abandon. At least thirty Brothers rushed them, splitting their group as they fought to avoid brutal injury or death without causing the same to the mind-controlled Brothers.

Roska called forth his magic, crafted two thick, icy clubs in his hands, and began swinging. Blocking a garden hoe with one club, he knocked the Brother wielding it in the back of the head with his other. The sickening crack of bone against ice caused a shudder to race up his arm and down his spine. Roska flinched at the feeling as the Brother collapsed. He didn't have time to dwell on it, though, as the sharp crack of a cane struck across his shoulders. Roska cried out in pain as the impact reverberated through his body. Even through the layers of clothing, the sensation was sharp and jarring, momentarily taking his breath away as pain flared from the point of impact. The fabric provided little protection against the stinging force of the strike, leaving a lingering ache that pulsed beneath the skin. Anger flowed through him as he turned on the man who struck him. Brother Jeremy.

The Inquisitor. The Torturer. The man who got off—sometimes quite literally—on inflicting pain and punishment.

The man who had assisted Grand Maester Auron in cutting Demoni's wings from her spine. The man who had tortured and tormented Brigit for moons.

The man who haunted her dreams.

A roar of unfiltered rage tore through Roska's throat as he charged the man. Swinging wildly with his clubs, he managed to knock the cane from the abuser's grasp, but Brother Jeremy always came prepared. He pulled two small blades from behind his back, stabbing quickly and cutting deeply into Roska's forearm. Warm blood raced down his hand, causing Roska to lose his grip on one of the clubs. It slipped from his hand, but he couldn't let that slow him down.

They began to circle each other as the fighting raged on around them, a dance of death as they tested each other's boundaries, looking for any weakness.

"You were foolish to come back here. It was pure luck that you managed to escape before. You won't be so fortunate today," Brother Jeremy taunted, an arrogant smile on his face.

Can you back him into the herb garden? Demoni asked. *I have a plan.*

Roska chanced a glance toward the herbs, seeing Brigit's back to him as she battled against a younger Brother that Roska didn't recognize.

"Checking on your girl, eh?" Brother Jeremy asked, following Roska's gaze. "She was quite the sweet treat. I hope you haven't been playing with my toys."

Rage filled Roska's senses as he lunged. Brother Jeremy's reflexes were quick as he brought his daggers up to shield himself from the blow. He laughed in Roska's face; his breath stank of rotten meat and stale ale. "So predictable. I thought we'd beaten all this naive sentimentality from you ages ago, but it seems you require another session with me." Excitement gleamed in the man's eyes at the prospect.

Roska spat in his face, an ice dagger forming instantly in his injured hand. He stabbed the Brother in the thigh.

Brother Jeremy roared in anger, dropping one of his daggers as he grabbed his now bleeding thigh, the ice dagger protruding from the meat of his exposed leg. Roska took the opportunity to shove the man backward, toward the herbs and the black ice Demoni had laid out on the stone path between the garden beds.

Brother Jeremy stumbled, unable to put weight on his leg, slipped on the ice, and fell on his back. His head hit the bricks surrounding the mint garden, splitting his temple. Blood poured from the injury and Brother Jeremy looked slightly dazed. He struggled, trying to stand again, but was unable to get this footing thanks to Demoni's ice and the dagger slowly melting away in his thigh.

Brigit appeared at Roska's side. He hadn't even realized she'd seen him, much less knocked the man she'd been fighting unconscious, but he was grateful for her strong presence. Blood leaked from a small cut on her cheek, but rage burned in her eyes as she looked down at the bloody man before her.

Roska wanted to end this man. Remove him from the world so he could never hurt another living creature, but—more importantly—so he could never be a threat to Brigit again.

*＊ ＊＊ ＊＊ ＊

Brigit stepped forward, closing the distance between her and her torturer, and knelt beside him in the ice and blood.

"Ye deserve all the fires an' tortures the hells have to offer. Ye heartless, soulless monster." She hissed the words with venomous hate, unlike anything she'd ever felt before. But, if anyone could bring that side out of her, it would be Brother Jeremy.

"Come now, darling," he practically purred at her, despite the violence in her eyes and the blood leaking into his. "I was just trying to get to know you. We had some good times, you and I." The loathsome man had the audacity to wink at her.

"Ye tortured, abused, an' *raped* me." Without warning, Brigit stabbed him in the stomach.

Brother Jeremy lurched forward, likely trying to grab her blade, but she was far too quick for him.

"Ye cut me." She stabbed him again. "Beat me." Stab. "Burned me." Stab. "And enjoyed every bloody second of it." Stab. Stab. Stab.

Brother Jeremy wasn't holding his head up anymore, unable to support its weight as blood poured from all the new holes in his chest and stomach.

"Ye took what wasna yers an' made me beg for forgiveness I didna need. Gods take ye." Brigit leaned in close, her mouth a mere breath from his ear. "I'll see ye in hells, ye sick mux." Pulling back, she stabbed him once more. Right in his crotch.

※ ※ ※ ※ ※ ※

The fighting raged on around them—a cacophony of shouts, cries, and the clash of weapons—but Roska couldn't hear it. All he heard were Brigit's words as she put an end to the man who'd taken so much from her.

She left her dagger, hilt-deep, in Brother Jeremy's lifeless body and turned to face Roska.

Roska hadn't known about the rape. He'd suspected, as that seemed to be a favored torture technique when it came to female victims, but he hadn't known for sure.

Now that he knew, he wanted to burn the compound to the ground and salt the ashes.

Brigit dusted the mud and ice from her skirts as best she could, avoiding Roska's eyes.

"Gods, you are truly amazing." Roska exhaled a tense breath he hadn't been aware he'd been holding.

Brigit's eyes flew to his. "What?"

Roska stepped forward, holding out his arms but giving her plenty of space to decline if she wasn't interested in his touch. To his great relief, she collapsed into his arms. He placed a hard kiss on her temple. "You astound me."

They stood like that for several breaths, ignoring the world around them as the weight of Brother Jeremy's abuse and torment lifted and flew away on the morning breeze.

The sounds of the fighting around them eased, and Roska opened his eyes, taking in the scene around them. Demoni had frozen many of the Brothers' feet to the stone pavers of the courtyard, making it quick and easy work for Asha and Lou to come up behind them all and knock them out, one by one. Zara, Miguel, and Balor had Grand Maester Auron surrounded, blades pointed directly at him, while all of their gazes were averted. They all seemed to be staring at his feet.

"Oi, you two!" Balor shouted from across the courtyard. "If you'd like to join us, we could use a little of that ice magic right about now."

Demoni swooped in, blasting Auron's boots with the last of her magic. Roska could feel just how tired and drained she'd gotten in the battle. She landed roughly on his shoulder and practically collapsed around his neck.

Roska pulled Brigit into a one-armed hug and led her over to face Auron. They kept their eyes downcast, unsure what the range was on the Lamia eyes and not wanting to give the Grand Maester any opportunity to manipulate them.

The eyes are set into the top of the staff he's grasping in his right hand, Demoni offered.

Roska released his hold on Brigit and stepped up on the dais directly in front of Grand Maester Auron. Keeping his eyes down, he grabbed the staff from the old bigot, ripping it from his hands and covering the eyes with both hands. Ice flooded from his palms to encase the eyes.

Jumping down from the dais, Roska raised the staff over his head and prepared to smash it onto the unforgiving stones.

"No!" Auron shouted, but he was met by three sharp blades pressing into his chest and neck.

Roska brought the ice-covered staff down hard, putting all of his weight into demolishing the tool of violence and hate. The head of the staff shattered against the stones, exploding in a glorious wave of magic, wood, and ice shards.

He tossed the remainder of the staff aside and turned to Auron.

"You are a selfish, bigoted, old fool. You preach blind hatred for magic, then use it to control the minds of those who don't share in your ignorant beliefs." Roska strode toward the man, calling forth his ice daggers once more. He stepped up on the dais as the others withdrew their blades. "You are the evil in this world, not magic. You chose to do harm every chance you got. You will pay for your crimes."

"Who are you to condemn me?" Auron spat at him. "I have been trying to save you from yourself since the day you showed up on my doorstep. You are wicked. I have been trying to purify you and give your life purpose."

Roska leveled the man with an icy stare. Based on the fear now emanating from Auron's wrinkled face, Roska assumed his eyes must be glowing teal with his barely contained power. "I didn't need you to save me. I saved myself *from* you."

Roska broke the ice encasing Auron's feet, grabbed him roughly by the collar of his robes, and turned him around. Taking the rope Zara offered him, Roska bound the disgraced Grand Maester's hands behind his back and led him down from the dais.

Chapter 41

OVER THE NEXT FEW days, Miguel interrogated each of the Brothers, determining which had been willful participants and which had been under Auron's control. It was easy enough to find the bigots once Demoni volunteered in the interrogations. Her mere presence in the room was enough to set most of the bigots off. A few tried to hide their true intentions, acting as though they couldn't remember what had happened, but the second Demoni blew a single snowflake or flew around the room, they'd crack. Pleading with the Mother to save them from her evil magics.

It was pathetic, truthfully.

The bigots were quickly locked away, in a separate storage cellar from Auron. Roska had placed that monster in his old room. He thought it was a poetic end to the man's reign of terror, making him spend his last few nights in the compound locked away in the room he'd used to torture and abuse Roska throughout his childhood.

The truly innocent Brothers had been left dazed and confused. It had taken a full day after the eyes had been destroyed for them to even comprehend what had been done to them and what they'd been forced to do as a result.

Miguel had sent Zara and Lou into the woods to fetch Brother Liam and their horses. Brother Liam had been most helpful in calming the victimized Brothers and bringing some semblance of order to the compound.

He'd even gotten the Brothers back into their routine enough for them all to have dinner in the dining hall as the sun disappeared beyond the compound walls by the end of the week.

Their crew sat together at a table along the wall closest to the kitchens. Brother Liam directed the cooks to serve each table in turn, starting with theirs. He claimed that the "liberators of the Brotherhood" should be thanked and treated with the utmost grace and respect.

Roska had tried to convince the kind man that it was unnecessary, but he'd received a firm—but mostly gentle—rap on the back of his head for his objections.

"Now what?" Balor asked around a mouthful of rosemary glazed ham.

Miguel gave him a chiding glare for his lack of table manners but answered the question. "We will take the traitors and abusers back to Riverayn with us to stand trial for their heinous actions and receive just punishment."

"Right..." Balor said after swallowing a large swig of ale. "But how? There are at least a dozen of them. Are we just supposed to march them halfway across the country? That could take weeks."

It was a valid concern. The six of them had made good time because they traveled light and had plenty of horses between them. Escorting fourteen prisoners—several of whom were elderly—would take at least twice that, likely longer.

"Which is why I've already sent a message back to the King requesting wagons and guards to escort the prisoners." Miguel scooped a fresh serving of cheesy potatoes onto his plate, then offered to do the same for Brigit, who nodded appreciatively.

"Oh, thank the gods," Balor cheered. "I didn't want to try and drag all those muxers through the woods."

"Balor!" Asha chastised him, swatting his arm. "Watch your mouth! We're in a... sacred? Religious place?" Asha turned to Roska, eyebrow raised in question.

"Mux that," he said. "This place has a long way to go before I'd call it anything other than hells on earth."

Balor's laughter reverberated off the stone walls of the dining hall, drawing raised eyebrows and confused looks from the tables around them.

They couldn't have cared less.

Chapter 42

I T HAD TAKEN NEARLY a full moon cycle for Niko's soldiers to arrive and escort them all back to Riverayn. Miguel had offered for Roska and Brigit to take two of their horses and head back early, but Roska refused. He needed to see this through to the end. He wanted to personally escort Auron to face his long-overdue justice.

When they did finally make it back to the castle, prisoners in tow, Elena organized a massive, week-long festival to welcome them home and celebrate their victory.

Quinn even brought in some of his best students from Harbor Ridge to put on a fire show on the last night. It had been quite impressive. Roska especially liked the snowflakes made of fire that fell to ash just as they landed on the lake in the center of the capital.

Roska was exhausted as he crawled into bed with Brigit and Miguel, all freshly bathed and feeling both drained and utterly free.

"I canna believe it's really over." Brigit sighed, snuggling into Roska's side and resting her head on his chest.

Miguel stretched out beside her. "It's surreal, but it's done. King Niko will sentence them tomorrow. Likely, Auron will get a quick death, which—if you ask me—is better than that wretched man deserves. But with all the evidence and testimony we collected at the compound, no one can claim it isn't warranted."

Roska reached beyond Brigit, slipping his hand around the back of Miguel's neck to massage the tight muscles there. "It's been a long time coming. I'm just glad we can finally put all this shyt behind us."

Roska hadn't realized until it had faded, but the trauma he'd been carrying his whole life had been slowly healing and lifting since he'd escaped the Brotherhood's clutches when they'd sent him to release the *turmio*.

No, not "they." That mission, along with the majority of Roska's childhood abuse and trauma, had been inflicted by—either directly or indirectly—Grand Maester Auron.

Or, inmate 5248, as he was now known. Soon to be executed inmate 5248.

The execution would be swift. Auron and his most ardent supporters would meet the executioner's blade at dawn. Those who Niko hoped could be rehabilitated would be serving their time in the King's prison with daily labor in the gardens or digging a new sewer line for the capital. They would also be subjected to what Elena referred to as "exposure therapy." Every day, she or another enchantress would sit and interact with the disgraced Brothers. Exposing them to magic and allowing them to witness the beauty it brought to the world, in the hopes of changing their minds on the subject.

Niko hadn't been thrilled by this treatment, but Elena hadn't been willing to budge. Niko loved her enough to trust her judgment and give it a chance. Roska didn't have high hopes that it would make a dramatic impact, but he prayed to the Mother he was wrong.

Brigit was softly snoring in minutes, while Roska still worked at the knots in Miguel's neck.

"What should we do after the executions tomorrow?" Miguel asked, his voice sleepy and barely above a whisper.

"Whatever you like, love." Roska closed his eyes, letting the thrill of freedom wash over him. "We've got nothing but time."

Acknowledgments

THIS IS MY FOURTH book, and I honestly don't know what to say here at this point. I'm so grateful to you, the reader, for taking a chance on me and my slightly damaged but thoroughly loveable characters.

This particular book served as a nice bit of therapy for me, working through some of my issues with organized religion, hypocrites, and abusers. Being able to brutally kill Brother Jeremy was very cathartic. I highly recommend naming characters after the villains in your life and giving them the justice they deserve that they might otherwise evade in real life.

If you have experienced even one-tenth of the hells these characters went through, please know that none of it is your fault. You didn't deserve what was done to you. You are an amazing human, and you deserve only good things in life. I love you, you magical badass.

About the Author

Mallory lives in Texas with her husband and their two young boys. She spends her days homeschooling and full-time parenting. Her nights, and any free time she manages to carve out during the day, are devoted to reading and writing.

If you enjoy this story, please be sure to leave a review on your favorite sites. Thank you so much!